The Good Mother

Born in 1943, Sue Miller left school in Chicago at sixteen and went to study at Harvard University. She married immediately after graduation from college and her son Ben was born when she was twenty-five. After her divorce a few years later, she worked as a day care teacher and administrator until she won a writing fellowship at Boston University. She has been teaching writing in the Boston area ever since.

SUE MILLER

The Good Mother

Pan Books
London and Sydney

First published 1986 by Harper & Row, Publishers, Inc., New York
First published in Great Britain 1986 by Victor Gollancz Ltd
This edition published 1987 by Pan Books Ltd
Cavaye Place, London SW10 9PG
9 8 7 6 5 4 3 2 1
© Sue Miller 1986
ISBN 0 330 29814 3

Photoset by Rowland Phototypesetting Ltd
Bury St Edmunds, Suffolk
Printed in Great Britain by
Richard Clay Ltd, Bungay, Suffolk

ONE

The post office in East Shelton reminded me of the one in the little town near my grandparents' summer home in Maine. In the days of that vanished post office, when I was small, my grandfather was usually the one to drive in and pick up the mail each day; but he almost always took one of us cousins along to row him across the lake, the first leg of the trip – even though at that stage he was still a strong man, a better rower than any of us. We vied for the privilege, the treat of a town visit. Now, as I watched my daughter mount the wooden steps in East Shelton and cross the long narrow front porch – her sandals slapping the boards noisily, her small legs flashing as she ran ahead of me, eager to be first through the door – I remembered the deep pleasure of entering that other post office of long ago; the same array of brass-trimmed letter boxes, the same worn wooden floors, nicked counters; the same grille across the opening where, when you rang the bell, the postmistress would appear from the similarly mysterious bowels of her house. If memory served me, and wasn't being distorted by the push of the present, the postmistress here even looked like that other one. She was seventyish, skinny and stern, with gray hair and glasses and skin so white, so floury, you half expected her touch would leave powdery prints on the envelopes she slid towards you under the grille.

Here my daughter would ask for the mail, because there was just our name to remember. In that other post office of my memory, after allowing me to ring the bell, my grandfather would greet the postmistress and then pronounce the three or four family names for whose members mail might

5

be waiting. It was the cousin's job, though, to distribute the mail after the long trip back to camp down the dirt road, across the lake.

It would be lunchtime, the family gathered on the wide screened porch around several tables laden with dishes, food. The lucky mail carrier of the day made the rounds, reading aloud the names on the envelopes; and people with letters were expected to open them then and there and read relevant bits of their correspondence to the assembled group. It amazes me now to think of that strange innocent intimacy. Did none of those aunts or uncles or cousins have an illicit lover, a shady business partner, a possible secret? Apparently not. The letters, mostly to the women, were full of news of invitations, dinners, luncheons, marriages, deaths, births, gifts.

When I pushed open the wooden screen door, the bell attached to its frame jingled faintly. Inside, the postmistress stood leaning forward behind her grille, listening to Molly. In her hands my daughter held a white envelope, but she didn't turn to me with it yet. She was telling the postmistress about the movie we were going to see. Though the old woman was unsmiling, Molly liked her. Her attention was absolute, and she'd given Molly several presents – once a piece of hard candy, and another time a stack of change-of-address cards. She nodded to me as I approached the grille, and gestured to Molly to hand me my letter. Without interrupting her flow of conversation, Molly did. As soon as I really looked at the envelope, I knew it was about the divorce. There was something antiseptically formal about it, something which smacked of officialdom. I checked the return address quickly before I tucked the letter into my purse. Lloyd, Fine and Eagleston. Yes indeed.

I was in no rush to open it. It couldn't be anything urgent, since our court date hadn't even been set yet. Molly and I talked with the postmistress for a while, and then set out on what was by now a routine series of adventures for the afternoon. I forgot all about the letter. We explored the playground on the town green and went to a grainy, light-

6

struck version of *Peter Pan*, which Molly seemed to like, but slept through half of. It wasn't until I reached into my purse to put my keys away at the Tip Top Café that I remembered the letter. I got it out and set it on the table, thinking I might read it while Molly ate. But she was in a talkative mood, it turned out, and all through dinner the envelope lay next to my silverware, rectangular and white, like an extra napkin; and I listened to my daughter.

She was kneeling on the patched maroon vinyl booth opposite me – the crisscrosses of duct tape nearly matched its color – playing with the little jukebox attached to the wall above us. When she turned the red plastic wheel on its top, the cards advertising the selections flipped around noisily, so many small revolving doors. She liked this, and was taking a long time to finish what was left of her meal. I didn't mind. Someone else in the Tip Top, someone with a penchant for country music, was feeding the jukebox, and I was enjoying its cheap emotionality. It reminded me of the music I had listened to in my teens – full of the disasters of love and marriage, full of longing, of heartbreak and betrayal, accidental death. That's the way popular music had been in the late Fifties, early Sixties, before it got serious or political, or was allowed to be cynical about sex. And I had believed in that early cheap music, knowing nothing else about life. I had expected that these would be the consequences of love.

'What's this song?' Molly asked, pointing to a title behind the bulging plastic case. I leaned over and looked past her small finger. Her hands and breath smelled of the French fries she was eating.

'It's called "In the Mood,"' I answered.

'Why?' she asked. I noticed that when she removed her finger from the case she left a tiny streak of grease. I wiped at it with my napkin.

'Because when someone wrote that song he was in the mood to call it "In the Mood."'

'Why?' she asked again. She moved back over to her plate and drank some milk. It left a mustache across her top lip.

7

Napkin still in my hand, I resisted the temptation to dab at it too. It would only offend her keen, recently developed sense of independence.

I shrugged. 'Who can explain moods?'

'Who can?' she asked. She scuttled on her knees over to the jukebox again and flipped several of the cards around. Whack whack. Then she looked at me, impatient. 'Who *can*, Mommy?'

'I don't know, baby,' I said.

'Mommy,' she protested. A tiny crease appeared in the smooth skin between her eyes. '*I'm* not a baby.'

'That's true, honey,' I said. 'I'm wrong again.'

'*Ethan* is a baby,' she said, naming an infamously immature friend from day care. 'But I'm not.'

'Right,' I said, and had another swallow of beer. 'You're much bigger than Ethan.'

The song playing on the jukebox stopped and there was a sense of suspended time in its wake, an absence of tone. Voices in the Tip Top dropped, until from the speakers studding the tiled ceiling a female voice started an *a capella* lyric. Tammy Wynette. The bass joined in, then violins again.

The Tip Top was full tonight, but we were distinctly the early shift – families with kids, couples on their way to the movies or shopping. No one working very hard at getting drunk, although the Tip Top had a promisingly seedy atmosphere and a little area of bare floor cleared for dancing in front of the upright jukebox at the end of the room.

'What's this song, Mom?' she asked. I looked again.

'It's called "Love Is a Rose,"' I said.

'Why?' she said.

I had some more beer. 'Well,' I said. 'I suppose that someone thought you could compare love to a rose: that love is nice, like a rose, and love smells good, like a rose, and love can grow, and love can die.'

She looked at me soberly and long to see whether I was making a joke. Her eyes, like her father's, were opaque and

8

milky blue, unreadable. 'That's silly. Isn't it, Mom?' She didn't really know; she wanted me to tell her.

'If you think it's silly, then it is,' I said.

She sat back for a moment. I could see only her head and shoulders over the scarred formica between us. She was blond, paler blond than I. Even though she'd turned three a few months before, her hair was still really nothing but wisps clinging to the shape of her skull. But her body was sturdy, and she had delicate, completely regular features. Except for her nose, which was unusually long – strong, I liked to call it – for a child her age. We had called her the Schnozz when she was an infant, in order to mask our fears that she'd grow up to be ugly. Now I couldn't tell anymore if she was ugly or not. I never tired of looking at her. Sometimes she'd find it annoying, as though I were taking something from her by loving her so greedily with my eyes. 'Don't *look* at me, Mommy,' she'd say, and cover her eyes with her hands as though then I couldn't see her anymore.

'You know what?' she asked.

'No,' I said. 'Who's what?'

She was blank for a moment, then got it. '*Mom*,' she protested. 'That's not what I was talking about.' Her voice was prim, disgusted.

'Okay,' I said. 'What were you talking about?' The waitress walked by, looked over to see if she could take our plates, and Molly defensively rose to her knees and grabbed another French fry.

'That I can make love all by myself.'

This interested me, even though, or maybe because, I doubted she could mean what I at first thought she meant. 'Fantastic,' I said. 'Incredible. Tell me how you do it.'

She solemnly ate another French fry, allowing me a full view of her small grayish teeth at work. '*L*,' she said slowly with her mouth full. '*O*,' she chewed. '*V*, and *E*.'

'That's great,' I said. 'That's just how I do it too, but I leave out the *and*.'

'Sometimes,' she said grandly, 'I leave out the *and*.'

For a few minutes she munched silently. I thought again

about opening the letter. But then she stood up to look at the young couple in the booth behind her. They had, for a while, pretended to think she was cute. They'd used a game of peekaboo with her over the top of the booth to charm each other with their playfulness. Now they'd forgotten her, though, and they seemed impatient when she'd pop up to say hello again from time to time, unaware that her usefulness to their relationship was over.

'Molly,' I said, before she could start.

'What?' She didn't turn around.

'I want you to sit down and finish supper now.'

She looked at me, not sure yet whether she'd choose to be cooperative. Her eyes were flat and cold. We might have been enemies.

'Would you like a swig of this here beer, dear?' I asked quickly.

She grinned and nodded and knelt again. I held the mug out across the table. Her hands cupped around it and tilted it into her mouth. She took barely a sip. As she swallowed and released the mug, her eyes filled with tears. Beer, which she loved, always made her eyes water, and this surprising taste for something obviously painful and difficult for her touched me.

'And then after we're done,' I said, 'I thought we'd go and get some ice cream.'

'Ice cream,' she said, and smiled a dreamy smile.

This wasn't as much a bribe as it would have been normally. We had ice cream nearly every day during those weeks. There was nothing to do but exactly what she and I wanted to do; there was no one to be with but each other. And though I occasionally got tired of being a character in her games, of answering her endless questions, I was, for the most part, happy. The previous four or five months had been ones of real strain for me and her father, though we'd managed to be kind to one another; and this was a reprieve, a retreat, before life began again.

We were staying for three weeks in a rented cottage about ten miles outside the town of East Shelton in New

Hampshire. Even the town seemed a part of our suspended reality. It was tiny, unfashionable, unchanged for several decades. When we sat down with our cones on the wooden steps in front of the ice cream store, also the town's only drugstore, we could have been models for some bucolic calendar scene out of the Forties. I felt a sense of deep nostalgia sweep me as we sat there, Molly with strawberry, I with chocolate, a nostalgia which was absurd: I'd grown up in a large town and a city as unlike East Shelton as they could be. Where did this yearning for a past I'd never had come from?

We finished the cones and rinsed our hands at the granite drinking fountain on the corner. Molly was alert even during the ride home. Her nap in the movie seemed to have fueled her for a long evening. The sky was still light, a bright, even, pale blue above us as we turned down the steep dirt driveway to the cottage. But in the shade of the pines which surrounded the house, it seemed dusky. We went inside, and while the water thundered steamily into the deep tub, I squatted in the house's twilight and took off Molly's clothes. Her body seemed insubstantial, gleamed white as a dream as she jumped around naked. When I switched on the yellowing light in the bathroom and she returned, herself, her skin rough and gray on her knees and sunburned pink on her shoulders, I was startled by her solidity. Dust from the worn earth under the swings in the playground was imbedded between her small, wormlike toes.

She played a long time in the bath I'd run for her, while I put away the groceries we'd bought earlier and washed the dishes left from our lunch. The bathroom was just off the kitchen, and her monologue, her tuneless singing floated in to me on the humid air, seemed, like the air itself, the clear medium through which I moved. My face and shoulders were reflected in the window just over the sink, bending, turning, reaching in the shadows under the shaded bulb on the wall, bringing order to the tiny world in which Molly and I were living. I stood motionless for a moment, looking at my warped reflection in the crazed panes of glass.

Molly was singing a song her father had taught her about a bullfrog teasing a bulldog. I wanted to freeze the moment, to make myself remember everything about it. It seemed one of those momentary revelations of the harmony and beauty that underlie domestic life, a gift.

I left the dishes to dry and went to wash Molly. The tub was the old freestanding kind with claw feet. Kneeling on the floor next to it, I reached in and rubbed her body with the soapy washcloth. She was quiet. getting sleepy at last, I thought, probably a little drugged by the warm water. She turned her body lazily this way and that when I asked her to, or sometimes just in response to the motion of my hands. But just as I reached down to wash between her legs, she asked abruptly, 'When will I see my daddy the next time?'

I stopped, and sat back on my heels. In the low light of the room her pupils were enormous, her eyes dark with the swelling black. I understood. Brian had always been the one to bathe her. Sometimes if he was late getting home from work, I would fill the tub and undress her, help her in; but almost always he was home in time to wash her. They had special songs, special rituals they'd worked up together. She was missing him.

'Do you remember what I told you?' I asked.

She nodded.

'Can you tell me?'

'That Dad'll come to see me right when we get to the new house in Cambridge. Right the day when.'

'That's right, honey,' I said. I leaned forward and began to splash water gently on her soap-slicked body.

'But Mom,' she said. I stopped.

'But Mom, how will he find us in the new house?' The little worry line creased her forehead.

I leaned forward and pulled her to a standing position in the tub. As I got a towel and bent to pick her up, I said, 'Daddy always knows where to find you, honey. Daddy knows right where the new house is. I don't want you to worry about it.'

I carried her wrapped in a towel down the long hallway to our bedrooms, and dressed her for the night. Mosquitoes and moths danced outside the screens on Molly's bedroom windows, tapping them lightly over and over as I read her a story. She leaned against my breast while I read, and her head moved slightly with my every breath, as though she were still part of my body. With one tiny forefinger she rhythmically flicked at the button eye of her stuffed bear, and from time to time she removed her thumb from her mouth long enough to ask about something in the story. When it was finished, I kissed her good night and gave her her pacifier. I turned the lights off and lay beside her in the dark. Outside it seemed to grow lighter and lighter as she fell easily into sleep. Stars, the shapes of trees, the occasional erratic flight of a bat emerged in what had been the blackness behind the screen. When her breathing was completely regular, I got up and walked down the long wood-smelling hallway to the living room.

As I was picking up, I remembered the letter I'd been carrying since early afternoon. I went into the kitchen and fished the gallon jug of white wine out of the refrigerator. The only wine glasses in the house were little jelly jars. I filled one and carried it into the living room. I got the letter out of my purse and sat on the lumpy couch, the pale glass of wine set on its fat arm, to open the envelope.

It contained a short note from Brian's lawyer and two copies of some last-minute changes we'd agreed to in the divorce settlement. The letter said that the court date had been set, unexpectedly, for the following Tuesday. I needed to sign the copies the lawyer had sent me in front of a notary public, and get them back in the mail special delivery in order to have them incorporated into the agreement.

It would mean a trip back into town early the next morning, that was all, to find a notary public before the post office's Saturday closing time of noon. Even so, I was aware of a dragging sense of reluctance to confront the chore. But there was, of course, no question of not doing it. I reminded myself of how much of the burden of getting us divorced

Brian had taken on himself. It was he who would have to appear in court on Tuesday to see it through.

Throughout the process of filing, my contact with lawyers had been absolutely minimal, at my request. And Brian and I, both impatient for the whole thing to be over, and guilty over our separate reasons for impatience, had worked out with almost no difficulty the details of pulling apart forever: I would have custody of Molly. Brian would send me a monthly check to pay for her upkeep, and, since he had so much more money than I – would always, we assumed, have so much more money than I – he would be responsible for all her major expenses as she grew up – schools, medical care and the like.

But for the first time in my life, I would support myself. I had insisted on it. I had to see a lawyer only once. He went over the terms with me to be sure I understood them. Everything had seemed as reasonable to me as the end of our marriage. The only thing not reasonable, not right, was that we had Molly, and now were tearing her world in two.

We had started thinking of divorce about a year earlier. Typically, it wasn't any emotional crisis that precipitated the talk. Brian's office was opening another branch in Washington and he wanted to go there. As he began to discuss the change, I realized I didn't want to go with him. At first, I spoke of my work, but when we began to argue about it more seriously, and I confronted the reality of my work situation – I was a piano teacher, but I'd never had more than ten pupils at a time – I realized that that really wasn't it at all. I just didn't want to go with *him*. He seemed in every way peripheral to my life. I mentioned a separation, tentatively. He didn't protest, said he'd think about it. I began to speak about feeling remote from him, feeling unhappy. We held hands and talked about trying harder. And for a period of time, we did try to force ourselves back into being married. But it seemed more and more artificial. And once we began also to talk about divorce, about the possibilities of a divorce, that talk, that arranging, seemed more liberating, more real than the talk about how often to

14

make love, about who we might have over for dinner, about when we might have time for a family picnic. Each tentative confession of a feeling of distance by one of us brought a relieved parallel confession from the other. It began to seem exciting, as though at last we were going *towards* something in our marriage.

The careful friendly balance tilted abruptly just after we'd filed, around Christmas. At this time, Brian and I hadn't even figured out how to live apart, except that I would take Molly. We'd been at a party for Brian's firm and had both drunk a lot of eggnog. He volunteered to drive the babysitter home and I got undressed. I was happy, I remember. A light dry snow had been falling on the way home, transforming the world. The divorce seemed to me a fine, brave thing to do. I had a sense, a drunken irresponsible sense, of being about to begin my life, of moving beyond the claims of my own family, of Brian, into a passionate experiment, a claim on myself. Somehow, in this vision, I romanticized Molly into a sidekick, a companion, Robin to my Batman.

I wandered in my nightgown into the bathroom and washed my face and brushed my teeth. The bathroom was dark, and in the slanted light falling in from the bedroom, my face, to my own drunk eyes, seemed newly pretty, interesting, a stranger's. I turned it this way and that, put a bright smile on it, pleased with myself. I began to brush my hair, and heard Brian coming in. I meandered back into the bedroom and sat crosslegged on the bed. After what seemed like an inordinately long stop in the kitchen, Brian walked slowly into the bedroom, a stricken look on his face. I was frightened suddenly. *Molly*, I thought, though I knew she was safe in her crib. I'd gone into her talcum-smelling room and listened to her even breathing when I'd come in from the party.

'What is it?' I said. I wanted to say '*Don't.*'

Standing in the doorway, he began to cry. It was horrible, embarrassing, that raw unexpected sound in our tiny neat bedroom. Somehow, too, though I could see his tears, it seemed false to me.

15

'Oh, Jesus, Anna,' he said.

'What is it?' I asked again, more coldly this time. My moment of panic was gone.

He gained control of himself, wiped at his eyes. 'I've wanted to tell you.' His face threatened to crumble again. He tilted it up towards the ceiling and bit his lip. 'Oh God.'

'What?'

He looked at me, lifted his hands to me. 'I'm going to get married again. When the divorce is final. I'm going to marry Brenda.'

I didn't say anything. I thought of Brenda, her tidy asexuality. She was a partner at Brian's firm and she had been at the party we'd just come from. When I'd asked her if she was going to Washington too, she'd blushed and said she supposed she might. She seemed suddenly shy to me, and I'd found that touching in her otherwise crisp, businesslike manner.

'It didn't start. I want you to know, it didn't start until after we'd agreed to split up. It's important to me that you know that. Believe that.'

I started to brush my hair again.

'Do you believe me?'

I nodded.

He began to cry again.

'Please don't do that,' I said. He looked at me, surprised at my tone. 'You look so stupid,' I said. He turned away and went to stand by the window. Beyond him, the snow fell. I brushed my hair over and over, ferociously. 'Brian and Brenda,' I said, finally, 'It's very cute.'

He turned toward me. 'Don't,' he whispered hoarsely.

I threw the hairbrush at him. It caught him in the forehead, just above the eyebrow, and his hands rose quickly, covered his painstruck face. I thought, unexpectedly, of how his face looked when we made love, the same sudden wrench of agony at the end. I stood up and walked across the bed. Standing above him, I hit him several more times before he turned to me and pulled me down. He held me gently, sitting on the edge of the bed, as though I were a child. He was crying again. I understood that he thought I was angry because he'd hurt me, and I tried to cry too, but I couldn't. I felt miles away from my body, from his sorrow. I was thinking all the wrong thoughts, I knew. I was thinking that now everyone would believe that this was why we were getting divorced. That our kind, careful separation would be public property, would be explained by this ugly twist. That I would seem what I wasn't – an enraged, abandoned wife. I let Brian hold me and comfort me because of the pain he thought he was causing me, and felt nothing, felt like a woman I didn't like. But it made palpable for me, finally, the unbridgeable distance between us, and I understood, as I hadn't understood before, the real emotional necessity for the divorce.

We lay down together after a while, and when he stopped crying we started to talk in a loving way. I let him think I was nobler, more generous and forgiving than I was, because the alternative was to tell him how little it all mattered. I did feel a kind of jealousy of Brenda though. She had taken something I thought was securely mine, even though I wasn't aware of wanting him anymore, and I envied them both their feelings for each other, their passion. I asked him questions: how it had started, what he felt towards her, what they did together. In the dark, his whispery voice swelled with pleasure to be talking about her, to be telling me things she would have hated for me to know. But it was really not a betrayal. I was his oldest friend; he was glad to be able at last to share his happiness with me. And I was glad for him, in the end. 'I'm not surprised, really,' I said, just before I fell asleep. 'I mean, it seems only right that you should have wanted someone else.'

'Why?' he whispered.

'Well, the sex between us was always so . . . nothing. So terrible.' I didn't think of this at the moment as a cruel remark. It seemed so self-evident, so true, that I was certain it would bring, like so many other confessions of the past months, pained agreement. This must be what he had felt all along too.

'I never thought so,' he said.

I was very sleepy, but not so much so that I couldn't hear the pinched quality in his voice. I remember reaching out to touch his face in silent apology. Later I would wonder if he was not making me pay, in his unconscious way, for my unconscious cruelty then. And after this, we didn't talk anymore; we were just waiting for the moment which would end it.

I sat with the wine and finished the glass. I'd been drinking a lot in these evenings alone after Molly went to bed. The owners of the cottage had a collection of 78 records that required constant monitoring and changing, and this and the wine had filled my evenings with mindless but true pleasure. I drank and listened to Eartha Kitt singing 'Santa Baby'; to Nelson Eddy singing 'When I Grow Too Old to Dream'; to Danny Kaye singing 'I've Got a Lovely Bunch of Coconuts.' Who knew what tomorrow would bring, today having brought something as unlikely as this.

When I woke in the morning, the algal smell of Greely's Pond and the light lapping of the water beginning to stir confused me momentarily; I couldn't think where I was. But then I heard Molly moving around in her room across the hall, the plastic pads of her pajama feet sliding sibilantly on the wood, the low steady murmur of her voice as she talked to herself, sometimes taking on roles – 'I *told* you not to do that, you dummy' – sometimes just commenting to herself about what she was doing. We had collected pine cones and needles, rocks and acorns to substitute for the toys left in packing boxes in the basement of the apartment in Cambridge, and she had built a whole variety of games around them. She was, then and later, the kind of child whose imagination transforms everything, who sometimes has trouble coming back to the reality of a situation, an object. As I lay there listening to her private play, I felt I was hearing the expression of her independence, the potential for her existence without me. Sometimes in those weeks alone with her, I had felt overwhelmed by her need to use me as playmate (though it was I who had structured it this way,

18

who had romanticized our month together alone in the country). Hearing her that morning, so competent at imagining her own world, made me believe she would be all right, she would heal and recover from what Brian and I were doing to her.

After about half an hour, she came and got into bed with me. For a while she lay still next to me, believing me asleep. Occasionally I opened my eyes and sneaked a look at her. She was sucking her pacifier rhythmically and twisting a strand of thin hair around her finger again and again. Her eyes were steady and blank as she looked up at the ceiling. Finally she sighed, as though called by duty, and turned to me. I opened my eyes again. 'I think it's late enough for you now, Mumma,' she lisped through the thick nipple between her teeth. Her breath smelled sweet and rubbery.

'Then I'm pulling the plug,' I said. I hooked my finger through the ring on the pacifier. She tried to shut her mouth, to hold on, as she always did in this game, but she was smiling and couldn't maintain the suction. I pulled against her mouth's weak pull; the pacifier popped out.

Most mornings in the cottage, we had wandered around until late in our night clothes, sometimes even going for short walks on the soft bed of yellowish pine needles around the house before changing into bathing suits and drifting down to the edge of the pond for the morning's play. Today, though, I hurried us through our routines. Breakfast at the speckled white table in the kitchen, bright orange juice in the little jelly jars, and Cheerios swimming in bluish milk. While Molly laboriously spooned them one by one into her mouth, I had a second cup of coffee. Then we went to her room to get her clothes. On the floor by her bed sat her sandals. Both were full of acorns, and they were surrounded by a ring of pine cones. Boats, she told me. People sailing in boats across the sea. I fetched plastic bowls from the kitchen, and we moved the acorns carefully into them, and got her dressed. She was glad to be going back into town so early. She had her own agenda: she wanted to do exactly what we'd done the day before. I promised her lunch at the

Tip Top, and another trip to the park, but told her that first we had to do a special errand for me.

The postmistress named two notaries, Mr Healey in town, and Mr Franklin, on a road about ten miles out of East Shelton in the opposite direction from our cottage. We tried Healey first. His house was a large gray frame structure whose wide porch was littered with dried-out rockers. A wooden sign announcing rooms to let hung from an iron post in the front yard. Molly ran down the porch, setting each chair swinging stiffly, wildly back and forth. I tried the bell three or four times. It chimed loudly within, but the house was empty and dark. I gave up and sat next to Molly for a few minutes in the rockers, imagining we looked like two old ladies on the country porches of my youth. Then we got back into the Valiant and drove out to Mr Franklin's. It was a trailer, silver and pale green, propped up on cinder blocks. A fat woman with oiled-looking skin answered the door and told me she wasn't sure when to expect Mr Franklin. He'd left that morning before she was awake to go fishing. She was still wearing a bathrobe, elaborately ruffled around her neck, and she looked like some overblown but pretty flower. Her toenails, under the long skirt, were painted pink. Canned laughter from a television swelled out merrily behind her.

'You tried Healey, in town,' she said, frowning sympathetically.

'Yes.'

'What, he's out too?'

'Yes, and I desperately need someone. I've got something that has to get in the mail by noon.' In the car Molly jumped up and down in the front seat. She was chanting something, and occasionally a note reached us on the stoop. Mrs Franklin shook her head. 'I don't know what to tell you, dearie,' she said. 'Of course you could try Brower.'

'Brower? Is he another notary?'

'That's right. No one likes to use him, but that's what he is.'

'Where is he?' I asked.

She gave me directions which would take us back through town and miles past the turnoff to our rented cottage. I thanked her and walked over to the car. Before I got in, I called back, 'How come people don't like to use him?'

'Cats,' she yelled ambiguously, and went inside.

Molly was getting bored. 'This is too much errands,' she said as I strapped her into her car seat. We stopped in town for an ice cream cone for her. It was ten by the clock in the drugstore. I began to worry about time, so I made her finish the cone in the car while I drove. She wasn't able to eat it fast enough, though, and thick drops of ice cream rolled down over her clenched fingers and onto her legs. She began to whine. I pulled the car over onto the shoulder once and wiped her fingers and legs with the paper napkins I'd brought with us, but bits of them clung in cottony tufts to her still-sticky hands. When I swung out onto the road again, she began a fussy crying that seemed forced, deliberate to me. For a while I drove along, feeling a familiar hateful anger rise in me, the anger which occasionally tempted me to shake her, to hit her. Stop it, I willed. 'Stop it, Molly,' I said.

'I can't help it, Momma,' she said. 'This is too sticky. I *hate* this sticky stuff,' and she went on with her hoked-up fussing.

When we came to the dirt driveway to our cottage, I turned sharply and we bounced down it. At the bottom, without a word to her, I pulled the keys from the ignition and ran into the cottage. On her bed I found the pacifier. I picked it up and ran back down the long hall, through the steady hum of the kitchen appliances, into the sun-flecked stillness around the car. I opened the door on her side. When she spotted the pacifier, her fussing intensified momentarily. She sounded, really, like a baby. I inserted it. Her noise stopped. Her sticky hand reached up to start twirling her hair. I unbuckled the belt to her car seat.

'Now Miss Whiner,' I said. 'Why don't you climb over into the back seat and lie down while we finish this stupid errand?'

Wordlessly, with a boost from me, she clambered out and over to the back. She rolled down to the crack of the back seat and curled up, her cheeks pulling steadily on the pacifier, her eyes already glazed. I turned the car around and headed noisily up the drive again.

Brower's place was easy to spot, as Mrs Franklin had said it would be. It was a tiny white peeling farmhouse with a police cruiser parked prominently in the front yard. A hand-painted sign by his mailbox said *Notary Public*. When I shut off the engine and turned back to Molly, she was sound asleep. Dirty, sticky, her hair knotted where she had twisted it with ice-cream-coated fingers, she lay heaped on the back seat. I thought of waking her, carrying her in with me half-asleep and fussing, but decided not to. Instead I took my jacket and laid it over her body and bare legs. When I got out of the car, I shut my door quietly in order not to wake her.

There was an enormous brass knocker on Brower's front door. I lifted it and struck it twice. After a minute, he opened the door. The pungent odor of cat wafted out from the house behind him. Several of the animals had followed me from the car to the house, meowing loudly, and they darted in when the door swung open.

'Help you?' he asked.

He was a skinny man, and he hadn't shaved yet. His beard prickled white on his chin and cheeks. He must have been around fifty. He was short, shorter than I was, and he seemed to be wearing three or four heavy shirts, underneath which I could see, grimy at his neck, a whitish T-shirt.

'You're Mr Brower?' I asked.

'I'd be a liar if I told you no,' he said and smiled.

I smiled back, politely. 'I wonder if I could come in for a few minutes,' I said. 'I think I have some business with you.'

'Yes, yes, of course. Of course,' he said, and stepped back to let me pass into the almost total darkness of his hall. The cat odor was overwhelming as he shut the front door.

'Come on this way,' he said, passing in front of me. He

22

walked to the back of the dark hall and pushed aside a blanket hanging over a doorway. He held the blanket back for me until I caught it, and then we moved into the room. We were in the kitchen, and I had to squint against the sunlight which flooded the room from a series of grimy windows. They faced out on an overgrown meadow where several rotted-out wheelless cars hunkered down in the tall grass. It was cold in the room. He moved over to a small table.

'Sit down here,' he commanded, pointing to the chair opposite his. A cup sat at his place, with a tea bag and spoon resting in the saucer. A spotted white tin canister sat next to it. Obediently I sat opposite him and looked around the room. It was hard not to stare. It was filthy. The walls were decorated with dozens and dozens of out-of-date calendars featuring country scenes, antique cars, pouty women of the Thirties and Forties in one-piece bathing suits. Five or six cats were in motion over the flecked and littered linoleum floor, and half a dozen others snoozed in the bright patches of sunlight. What seemed to be trash was heaped in the corners of the room. Against the wall twenty deep were cat-food cans, some empty, some with food in them. Several of the animals were picking their way among the cans, eating in that gingerly dainty way cats have.

Brower stood at his place. 'You want some tea?' he asked. The rotten fishy smell of the cat food mingled with the odor of cat piss and something else in the kitchen. 'No,' I said. 'Thanks.'

He sat down and raised his cup. 'Well,' he said. 'What can I do for you?'

'You are a notary public, Mr Brower?' I asked.

'Well, there are several of us, of course,' he said. 'But I'm one of them. Plus,' he set his cup down, 'deputy police and now fire marshal too. So you see.'

'You must be very busy,' I said, and reached into my purse for the letter.

'Oh, I just got the fire marshal thingy. I had to pass quite

23

a test up at East Shelton for that, I'll say. Quite a test.' He eyed me expectantly.

'Oh?' I said. A mistake.

'Yes indeed, I'll tell you. They used the entire basement of the Elks Hall for this test. Fire station wasn't big enough. This test was a national test.'

'Well, it's wonderful you passed.' I set the envelope on the scarred and greasy-looking table. Brower drank some tea. His lips seemed to reach for the edge of the cup and he made a sucking noise as he drank. He set his cup back in its saucer.

'Well, it wasn't easy, I tell you,' he said. 'Point number one, you're blindfolded. Point number two, they fill the room with this smoke. And you've got to wear one of those *breather* masks, you know.'

I nodded. A cat sprang into my lap. I patted it carefully while Brower talked. It turned around several times to get comfortable, and I had to arch my head back and away from its uplifted tail, its wrinkled pink anus. I stopped patting it when I noticed clumps of loose hair flying off into the dusty sunlight with each stroke, but the cat nestled on my lap anyway and shut its eyes.

'Then you've got to crawl around this obstacle course,' he was saying. Where were those famous taciturn New Englanders when you needed them? 'Pulling a two-hundred-pound sack of sand – to be like a body – while they drop bricks and wood all around you, even a couple of buckets of water.' He looked at me, his graying eyebrows raised, and waited for a response.

'It sounds awful,' I murmured.

'Wearing your *hat*, of course,' he added.

I nodded again, as though this had been my assumption all along.

'The point being, as you can no doubt tell, that it's got to be like what you might one day go through. They don't want people who don't know what they're doing, what they might be up against, fooling around in a real fire.' His expression was stern.

'No.'

'I tell you, that was a rough one.' He shook his head, then slurped some more tea. 'Makes that police test look easy.'

'What I came about, Mr Brower,' I said quickly.

'Oh, you can call me Sammy,' he interrupted. 'The people around here generally do. You're not from around here,' he said, narrowing his eyes.

'No, I'm from Chicago.' In the distance I could hear the yowl of a cat starting a fight.

'I thought so. Somewhere out west, I thought to myself. I'm a good one with accents.'

'What I came about,' I began again, 'was getting something notarized.'

'Well, you came to the right place. I can surely do that for you.'

I felt a little wave of relief.

'As long as I can find my *seal*,' he said. He looked around the kitchen with a befuddled air. My eyes followed his. Then, 'These are the documents?' he asked. He was pointing to the envelope I'd laid on the table.

'Yes. I'm supposed to sign them in front of you.'

'That's right,' he said. 'That's the way you do. Now I assume you've got some proof of identification?'

'Oh, yes,' I said. I got out my wallet and found my license. As he took it I noticed that his fingernails were untrimmed, there were black crescents under them. He frowned and stared at the picture on the license.

'Seems like you might have a different color *hair* in this picture.'

In the distance the yowling intensified, like the crying of a baby. 'Yes. Well, no. Not really. I had a permanent then, and it makes my hair look lighter. *Made* my hair look . . .'

'Now look here,' he grinned suddenly. 'Don't explain. I was just teasing you.' I saw that his teeth and gums were utterly false, front to back, some dentist's dream of the perfect mouth.

He set down the license and reached over to pick up the envelope. He opened it, spread out the documents over his legs and began to read. I looked down at the cat sleeping on my lap. A flea emerged from the hair around one eye and sat on its eyelid. I remembered reading somewhere that fleas travel daily to their host's eye for water. I lifted the cat from my lap and set it down on the floor. It looked startled for only a moment, then shook its head vigorously and sat down to lick itself. I realized abruptly that I was breathing unevenly, trying to avoid the smells in the room.

Brower looked up. 'These are *divorce* papers,' he said.

'Yes,' I confessed. In spite of myself, I felt oddly ashamed.

'I don't hold with that,' he said sternly.

I shrugged. 'Well, these things happen, though,' I said. 'Do you want me to sign them now?'

'There's too much of that nowadays, to my way of thinking,' he said. He looked into his teacup. He sloshed its contents around and tilted it down again. He went back to reading the papers.

I found a pen in my purse. 'I'm just going to sign them now,' I said, and held out my hand to take them from him.

'Don't be in such a hurry,' he said. He turned quickly in his chair, as though to deny my claim on the papers. A ripple passed among the cats, five or six of them shifting position suddenly in response to his motion.

For a moment I sat silently watching him. A cat eating out of one of the cans scraped it gently across the floor. Brower's eyes moved slowly back and forth across the lines of print. 'Well, the fact is I am in a hurry . . . ,' I said. I had been planning to say *Sammy*, to strike a note of camaraderie, but at the last moment I couldn't bring myself to do it, and there was an embarrassing sense of blankness where his name should have been. 'I've got my little girl waiting for me in the car.'

He nodded, tightening his lips, as though this were something he might have expected of me. 'People these days,' he said, 'think that the minute things get a little bit rough, they can just walk out. Just leave.' He wouldn't meet my eye. 'Children and all,' he said. 'It makes no difference to them.'

'I really need to get going, Mr Brower,' I said. 'I have to get these things in the mail by noon.'

'There's a fee for this service, you know.' He stared at me suddenly with cold eyes.

'Well, I guess I assumed there might be,' I said. I was struggling for control. *Make nice*, I thought. The tip of my stomach pinched with tension and nausea at the mingled smells. I got out my wallet again. 'How much will it be?'

'The set fee is five dollars.'

His eyes followed every move of my hands. I had a five-dollar bill; I laid it down on the table. He set the papers down and picked up the bill.

I reached out and set my hand on the papers. I slid them over the sticky table to me. He watched. 'I'd like to sign these now,' I said.

'It won't do you no good to sign them unless I can find my *seal*,' he said.

'Perhaps I can help you look,' I said, desperate. I stood up, as though ready to begin poking through the heaped-up trash, the finger-smeared cabinet drawers. Several cats recoiled in waves from me, arched, frozen in fear.

'You'll just scare these animals,' he said, looking up at me. There was some threat in the way he said it. 'You'd best sit down and let me do it.'

Obediently I sat. To my relief, the skinny man actually got up, went over to the cabinets, pulled out the top drawer. It seemed to be full of jumbled utensils and crumpled papers, old letters, cat-food cans. As he pawed through the debris, he talked to me. I understood that I was to sit and listen. There was no possible response. His back was to me, and the seat of his pants was slick with wear. 'In my day,' he said, 'we married for better or for worse, and that's what we meant. Came illness; came poverty; none of it mattered. We stayed. That's what marriage meant, in those times. Why you people even bother to make those vows is beyond me, when you've no intention in the world, none whatsoever as far as I can see, of keeping them. Just so many *words* to mouth.' He shook his head. The contents of the drawer

27

rustled and clattered as he pushed them around. 'Just mouth service. Lip service,' he corrected himself.

It wasn't in the first drawer. He pulled out the second one and continued his monologue. His voice went on and on. I felt fury rising in me as I listened, and slowly I realized that it had to do not just with how long it was taking to get him to notarize the papers, but with exactly what he was saying, and a rush of defiance I felt against the sense of shame it triggered in me. Everyone in my world had been understanding about the divorce, sympathetic, politically correct. But this man was talking to me as my parents or grandparents might have, and I felt the rebellious, self-righteous fury that an adolescent feels when she's caught in an act which she knows to be morally doubtful. This was the opinion of the world I'd emerged from, the world I thought I was shaking off. The more he made me feel ashamed, the angrier I got. Twice he turned to me and asked if I had no sense of duty. I'm not sure what I answered. A cat rubbed purring against my legs; the muted yowling continued in the distance. I watched Brower's trembling dirty hands rifle one drawer after another and tried not to listen to his words, his stupid words. Finally he extracted an immaculate nickel device from the flotsam in the fourth drawer down. For a moment, it looked oddly like a speculum to me, but that was a connection, I later realized, that my sense of shame, of exposure, made for me. He turned and walked slowly back to the table and sat opposite me. He stared at me for a moment, and then his eyes narrowed. 'I see you're still wearing your rings,' he said.

I wasn't sure I wouldn't start to cry. 'Mr Brower,' I burst out. 'If it'll make you any happier, I'll take them off.' I began to pull at the rings. He watched me steadily, his eyes as flat as Molly's when she was angry. They wouldn't slide over my knuckle and I finally had to lick my finger and ease them slowly over the slick joint. His eyes took it all in. 'There,' I said, putting the rings into my purse. 'There. Now I'm going to sign the papers.'

His grizzled face was blank. He would give me no permission.

'I'm signing them now,' I repeated, as though speaking to an idiot, a child. I wrote my name on each one where the lawyer had left a blank for me. Brower pretended not to watch. For another moment we sat in silence. Then I slid the papers and pen over to him.

Slowly, as though aware that this was his last moment of any power over me, Brower picked up his seal and the papers. One at a time, elaborately, he signed and sealed the papers and handed them back to me. The minute I had the second one in my hand, I got up to go. 'Thank you,' I said reflexively, in spite of my rage. My mother would have been proud. I tried to think of something more, something cruel and conclusive, but couldn't. I lifted the blanket and passed through to the hallway.

It was black and close after the bright cold light of the kitchen. I sensed cats moving around my feet. I shuffled slowly through the dark stink, feeling along the walls until I came to the front door. I ran my hands down to the knob, turned it. The door wouldn't open. I turned the knob again, pulled. Nothing. A cat rubbed against my ankles. I thought I felt the multiple light caress of fleas jumping on my shins. I rattled the door, near desperation.

Suddenly, a dim light entered the hall from behind me. I turned. Brower stood in the kitchen doorway holding the blanket partway back. His shape was outlined against the light from the kitchen windows. 'Turn that latch right,' he said curtly.

I found the latch in the dim light and turned it right. The door still wouldn't open.

'Too far,' he said, and the hall darkened again as he dropped the blanket and walked towards me. I stepped aside and let him work the latch. Light and air rushed in as he swung the door open. I walked past him, saying nothing. Just before he closed the door behind me, he whispered, 'You should be ashamed.' I turned, but the door was already shut. Four or five cats had dashed out with me, and I stood

29

on the porch a moment, watching them disperse over the flattened dirt of the yard. Then I started back to the car.

I think that even before I really looked at it, I knew something was wrong. But what I saw as I began to run towards it was that the door to the back seat was hanging open, that my jacket, the one I'd used to cover Molly, was lying on the ground just outside it. I nearly tripped across a cat in my haste; it shrieked and fled off into some bushes.

Incredibly, she still lay in the car. Or not still, I realized, but again. Again. She had been out, and had climbed back in. Now, even dirtier than before, her grimy face striped white with the wash of tears, she lay, sucking in air on each breath with a shuddering sound that told me she'd exhausted herself crying. Looking for me. I thought of the distant yowling I'd heard as I sat in Brower's kitchen. How long had it gone on? Five minutes? Ten minutes? Her pacifier curled in her hand near her mouth. Her eyelashes were gummed into points, as though she were wearing mascara. Her soft flesh swelled slightly over a long bloody scratch on one cheek.

'Molly,' I whispered, and pulled her to me as I clambered in. Her body began to shape itself to mine, to cling to me, even before she really woke up. 'Molly,' I said. 'Molly.' And then suddenly, with consciousness, her grip tightened and she started to cry, screaming in sharp pain like a child who's just fallen, who's bitten her tongue, who's put her hand on a hot kettle, who's lost.

'Mommy!' she screamed, she cried, and held me tighter even than I held her. 'Mommy! Mommy!' she shrieked as she would over and over in my memory of this moment. And I sat hunched in the back seat with her in my arms until she was still, feeling only that I could not do this alone, I was not strong enough, good enough to do this alone, I could not do this.

Some things worked out the way I had told Molly they would. Nearly as soon as we got back to Cambridge, her father arrived and found us in the new apartment. It was still full of unpacked boxes, awkwardly placed furniture, stacks of books and kitchen utensils, but I left him and Molly in it, as we'd arranged ahead of time, and went to stay at a friend's house for the weekend. Brian drove me there in my car. I sat in back with my suitcase. Molly was in front, next to Brian in her car seat. This rearrangement – when we were married, the car seat was always in the back, and Brian and I sat together in front – seemed a reminder, lest we forget, of the deeper disturbances going on in our lives. I wished I'd thought to put the car seat in back before the trip.

It must have made Molly uncomfortable too, because she kept trying to turn her head to see me, and then she'd stare soberly over at Brian. He sat silent at the wheel. The water sparkled deep blue in the river. In our other life he or I would have been pointing out to her the stiff white wings of sailboats, the brightly bobbing ascent of a kite. Instead, from time to time, I'd lean forward and tell Brian about some quirk in the new apartment – you needed matches to light the stove, the toilet handle sometimes needed jiggling. 'Okay,' he'd say without turning his head. 'Thanks.'

The road swung out of sight of the river; we drove past Mass. General and up onto the highway. Molly stared down at the piers and miniature buildings sprawling far below her. Then abruptly she turned to Brian. She had a brave coquettish smile on her face, and she said, 'I really hate my mom, don't you? We *hate* her, right?'

My heart seemed to squeeze tight with pain, though I knew it was out of her own hurt and confusion that she spoke: she didn't know quite what was being asked of her with this changing of the guard. And if she had to choose between us, she'd pick Brian, the one she didn't see enough of, the one she yearned after. I was just the medium she lived in, as familiar to her, as taken for granted, as air and food.

I wasn't looking at Brian when he spoke. I'd turned my head towards my window so Molly couldn't see the quick tears which stung my eyes. But his voice was gentle and loving, just right. 'No,' he said. 'I can still love Mom even though she and I don't want to live together anymore. And you can still love her, even though you're being with me for a few days. You can always love us both.'

Molly didn't answer, and I didn't dare look at her. After a moment, I touched Brian's shoulder to thank him, and he nodded and began to talk to her about the bridge we were going over: what river ran under it, how they'd built it. She responded brightly, as though she too were relieved for the moment to have passed. Through the rest of the drive up, she chattered happily with Brian, and when I leaned into her window to kiss her good-bye, she made loud smacking noises with her mouth against my cheeks and lips. I walked quickly into the house so I wouldn't have to watch the car pull away, the familiar shape of Brian's head and shoulders on the driver's side, and the squared-off top of the car seat standing for Molly in all her vulnerability and confusion.

The house I was staying in, an odd vertical warren of rooms on a twisting street in Marblehead, belonged to a couple who'd been friends of both Brian's and mine. John was a lawyer too, had been in law school with Brian, actually; and Charlene owned and ran an expensive little shop in Marblehead, a shop full of tasteful handcrafted goods. Brian and I had often driven together up to their house for dinner, sometimes bringing Molly and putting her to sleep on their big bed. Steadily swimming in her dreams, she would slowly work her way across it, so we had to check on her frequently.

John and Charlene were away for the weekend – they rented a share in a country place – and the little house was intimidating in its silence, its sense of abandonment. It wasn't the same sensation at all that I'd felt walking into the rented cottage in East Shelton. There, almost all clues to the owners' personalities had been carefully removed. A few odd hints remained – the records for example – but for the most part what they'd left behind were the bare necessities. Here, John and Charlene were everywhere present, but *not*, and I felt more constrained in their absence

32

than I would have if they'd been there, taking up real space, moving among their possessions. The next morning I noticed that I woke up in almost exactly the same position I'd fallen asleep in, and that I was perched on the very edge of the king-sized bed, as though they were both also in it.

Slowly over the weekend, though, I began to explore their life. Shamelessly I opened bureau drawers and medicine cabinets. I picked up and examined the photographs which sat everywhere. I pawed through the little heaps of objects set around carelessly in saucers and baskets – odd coins, stubs, pills, jewelry, notes, lists. I looked through books, noting which ones were his, which hers, reading the marginal comments. I stopped short of reading their mail, though it seemed like hair-splitting at that point.

Part of it was boredom, part prurience. But in addition, Brian and I had decided that it would be easiest on Molly for me to abandon the apartment to him each time he came up to visit her; and I had the sense of his being able to look at me in my absence as I was looking at Charlene and John. Though I'd barely unpacked at that point, I knew I would slowly begin to claim the ugly apartment with the objects I chose, with possessions which also possessed me. What would I tell him, what secrets would I give away that I hardly knew I had?

I discovered, for instance, that Charlene had both a diaphragm and a stack of cheerful yellow birth control pills on discs. What did it mean? That she had an irrational terror of pregnancy and used both? That she had used one but switched to the other? And what was she using this weekend, having left all this behind? Or were they not making love? Or were they madly making love, but using nothing, trying to get pregnant?

It wasn't until midday on Sunday that I finally steeled myself to call my parents. I'm not sure why I hadn't told them earlier. Part of it was certainly the distance I kept from them generally, but part was something more, some specific reluctance and shame which had to do with the meaning of my family to me. Listening to Sammy Brower's diatribe had

33

given me at least a partial sense of what I'd been avoiding, but it wasn't until I heard the willed cheerfulness of my mother's voice on the phone that I understood how difficult it was going to be. It was as if some part of her knew that I'd called with bad news, and she felt that if she just made enough noise, stayed buoyant enough, she could float through, perhaps even prevent me from announcing it.

While she waited for my father to get on the extension, she began to tell me about redecorating their bedroom. She described in careful detail the choices among papers, and what was right and wrong about each. In the midst of this discussion, I heard the click on the line which meant that my father was listening now too, but he didn't interrupt her and she didn't acknowledge him until she'd finished her presentation. Then she announced, as though I wouldn't have known it otherwise, 'I think Daddy's here now, too.'

'Hello, Anna,' he said, on cue.

'Hi, Dad,' I said.

'Well, darling,' my mother said. 'What's up?'

I had rehearsed the lines, and alternate lines too, over and over in front of the mirror. Even so, I was surprised at how stark, how bald they sounded.

'Well, I'm afraid that my news is bad,' I said. A brief pause, but not long enough for them to start imagining anyone's death. 'Brian and I have decided to get a divorce.'

'Oh, don't tell me that!' my mother cried, and burst into tears. My father said nothing, but after a moment I could hear him clearing his throat. He was always incapacitated by my mother's tears. I waited for a minute or so, until my mother had calmed herself slightly, and then began to present them with the details. Brian had, in fact, already transferred to Washington. Molly would be with me, and see him several times a month, and for holidays and summer vacations. She seemed to be managing all right. I had a new, less expensive apartment.

Slowly my mother began to be drawn in. Details were what she liked, were what made her comfortable. She asked questions about the new apartment – how much space, what

34

furniture I had for it. I kept comforting her, assuring her that everything would be all right, *was* all right; and meanwhile, some part of me was standing at a distance and noting how ass-backwards it all seemed. Shouldn't she be comforting me?

In the middle of a discussion of how the movers had hoisted the piano in, my father interrupted. 'I hope he's going to do the right thing by you and Molly,' he said.

For a moment I didn't understand what he was talking about.

'You mean Brian,' I said.

'Yes,' he said.

'You mean money?' I asked.

'Yes,' he said. 'He'll have a bundle one of these days, and you ought to see some of it.'

'I think we have a fair agreement,' I said.

There was a brief silence. Then he said, 'You know best,' as if wiping his hands of the whole affair. I felt stung, and yet regretful. His tone was hurt, and I realized that he had been offering love in the only way he knew. I felt a yearning towards him, a momentary impulse to lie, to say there were things I didn't understand, needed his help with. But my mother pushed in again to smooth things over.

'Daddy's just worried about you, darling,' she said.

'I know,' I said. 'I'm sorry.'

'Oh, Anna, it's not your fault,' she said. But I couldn't help feeling it was. Not just the divorce, but the thousand small misunderstandings out of which my relations with them were made.

'I know,' I said again. I was remembering a visit I'd made to them when I was about six months pregnant with Molly. There was no special reason for it except that I hadn't seen them in nearly a year. Most of my students were on summer vacation, and Brian was going to be away on business for a week, so I flew to Chicago for a long weekend.

I slept in my old bedroom. On the last day of the visit, I woke early, needing to pee. When I slid back into bed, I lay looking around at the pretty, figured wallpaper, the pale pink curtains, and felt gratefully how much had changed in my life since I would wake in high school feeling trapped by my body, my circumstances, by what my parents seemed to want to make of me. The baby, who I was sure then was a boy, swam and flopped freely inside me, and I lay still and made resolutions about how differently I would raise him from the way I'd been raised. Then I fell asleep again and didn't wake until late in the morning.

I went down to breakfast at around eleven-thirty or so, wearing my summer nightgown and an old bathrobe that wouldn't shut over my belly. On my way across the dining room, I stopped in front of the picture window to watch my father in a corner of the yard. He held enormous pruning clippers in his hand and was slowly and carefully decimating the lilac bushes which separated my parents' property from their neighbors'. Suddenly there was a flash of motion above me and a loud bang. I started, and then looked outside. On the patio lay a bird, stunned. A grackle. I went to the door and stepped outside. The slate patio was cold and damp under my feet. I bent over the bird. Its wings beat the ground at my approach, and then it stilled. One wing was hanging limply off its body. It fluttered its good wing again, moving about a foot over the ground; then collapsed, its small bright eyes seeming to watch me. I stood up. I remembered feeling a sense of vulnerability and fragility because of the pregnancy. Normally I wasn't squeamish in the least, but I wanted someone else to manage this. I wanted my father. 'Daddy,' I called. 'Daddy.'

He crossed the yard to me, carrying the clippers. I pointed to the bird, flopping again across the slate. Wordlessly he disappeared into the shed and came back carrying a snow shovel. He raised it over his head and brought it down onto the bird. I turned away quickly, but I could hear the dull thumps, and under them, the repeated click of the bird's bill against the metal. Three, four times he raised the shovel and brought it down. When he stopped, I turned to him. He looked quickly down at my belly and then away, a flicker of disgust having momentarily touched his face. I looked

36

down too as I tried to pull the bathrobe shut. My belly protruded in the diaphanous nightgown, the extroverted navel like an obscene gesture. It was the only time during my pregnancy that I felt grotesque or unattractive.

Now my mother's voice interrupted the long silence on the phone. It was edging towards tears again. She said, 'I just don't know how I can write about this to anyone.'

Here was where we'd been heading all along, I thought. 'I think I can manage that, Mother,' I said. I could hear the coldness in my tone, the way you can on the telephone.

'Oh, if you would, darling,' she said. 'I'd appreciate it so much. If you could just write to everyone.'

'No, that's fine,' I said.

For a few minutes more, we made the smallest of talk, and then we said good-bye.

'We love you, darling,' she said brightly.

'I know,' I said. 'Me too,' and then I heard one click, another, and the phone began to buzz quietly in my hand.

TWO

My family history is neatly bisected by geography. When I was fourteen, we moved to Chicago, and after that nothing was the same. For all of us – my father, my mother, and me – the world was made new. But only for my father was the change unambiguously positive.

Up until then, we had lived our lives clamped in the grip of my mother's family. We saw them frequently; we spent summers at my grandparents' camp in Maine, and we often traveled to their Connecticut house at Christmas or Easter or for someone's birthday. My mother talked to her sisters or her mother on the telephone several times a week. Even as a young child, I could tell when one of them was on the other end of the line. My mother's voice was different; it thickened with pleasure.

They were a handsome, high-strung group, my mother's family, full of nicknames and even elaborations on nicknames. The only son, my uncle, had been christened Frank Junior. But because of his lugubrious personality, as a boy he was called Eeyore. That eventually became Or, which grew back again into Orrie. Uncle Orrie. The youngest aunt was Edith, but she was 'the baby' while she grew up, and this shortened easily to Babe. My mother was Bunny, and the two middle sisters were Rain and Weezie, for Lorraine and Louise.

They were all dominated by my grandfather. He was, in my earliest memory, tall and muscular with abundant white hair and black eyebrows curling wildly in all directions, the same combination then as later of expansiveness and pure authority. His parents had been immigrants from Scotland.

They had wanted, expected, the world for him. As a young man, he had patented a wear-resisting heel for shoes. He sold the patent to B. F. Goodrich when he was twenty-seven, and after that his work consisted solely of learning to make money from money. Each of his daughters had, in turn, married a man of great business promise, but somehow each one, my father included, got stuck as a middle-level executive, none so gloriously successful as my grandfather.

My grandmother seemed overwhelmed in their company. In the few remaining family pictures of her alone, before the children were born, she is a radiant debutante, a smiling, confident bride. But as I recall her she is mostly just a silent presence: a cool hand on my forehead through a feverish night, or someone to make intercession with Grandfather over a minor infraction of the rules; but of herself, inexpressive. She was the one I loved the most as a child, though; the only one, in fact, I was aware of feeling love for, though at the time I would have asserted, automatically, that I loved them all. But even then, loving her pulled at me in some way I was only barely conscious of. It made me feel uncomfortable, guilty.

As a group, my mother's family held a kind of invisible standard up to all its members' lives and ambitions. All the family bonds translated, finally, into appraisal, a push for achievement. For me, this centered on the piano. I took lessons for years, starting when I was five – my mother thought I might have it in me to be a professional musician – and I remember that I used to associate even the names of the composers with my grandfather.

'Who are you working on now?' he'd ask, and then nod and repeat the names I told him. 'Ah, good, Chopin. Mozart, Schumann, excellent, excellent.' As a young child I thought that he might be old enough to know those people. And though now it seems clear that he was just glad to have me playing the works of artists whose names he recognized, when I was eleven and twelve I assumed there was some scale in his mind, some order of importance among their works, their names, which was inaccessible to me, but which

39

he understood and was measuring my ability against.

After we moved to Chicago and I began to listen to rock and roll, I had a sense, at first guilty, then exhilarated, of moving across some barrier, beyond the pale. The names from this world – the Danleers, the Solitaires, the Delfonics – these names had no connections with my past. These were names I could purely claim.

I had a stack of records that I used to play in my room some evenings before I began my homework. There was a special record player just for the tiny 45s, with a thick phallus for a spindle, a technology entirely separate from the one which existed for the classical music my parents listened to on 78s or 33s. I would pile the spindle with the music of white boys imitating black boys, black boys imitating white boys. As the records dropped, as I segued from Elvis to Chuck Berry to the Miracles, I would stand in front of the mirror and lip-sync the lyrics. Sometimes I danced.

Once my mother stopped in my open doorway to watch me dancing. I knew she was there and I wanted to stop, or to close the door. But to do either would have been to acknowledge my self-consciousness, to acknowledge the power she had over me, over my life. Even though I didn't look directly at her, I knew how she appeared as she watched me: frowning slightly over whatever chore she was performing, in her arms a stack of laundry or sewing or fresh towels – one of her responsibilities which, unlike me, made her happy. We'd abandoned the dream of the piano at that time, and I think we were both confused about what would take its place in my life and between us. For years everything had been shaped around the discipline of practice imposed by her, accepted by me. While I danced that night, I felt I was announcing some change in myself connected with all that, although I couldn't have said what it was. I danced more wildly than I ever would have with a boy. The record was something by Jerry Lee Lewis. It went on and on, and I gyrated and whirled to its beat. Finally it ended. I stood panting in the pretty room my mother had decorated for me. The arm of the record player lifted noisily, ground over to its resting pad, clicked off. We looked at each other. She was holding a stack of my father's shirts. My breath rang in my ears. I licked my dry lips. 'I hate to see you move like that,' my mother said, and left.

Before the move to Chicago, I spent every childhood summer with my mother's family at my grandparents' summer home – really what used to be called a camp – which consisted of several buildings on the far shore of an inland lake in Maine. The road ended on the near side, so the first people to arrive at camp in June had to bushwhack their way around the lake, open the shed, and lower the leaky rowboats into the water; then return for the boxes and trunks and whining, disheveled children. Subsequent arrivals would park and honk their horns, one long, three short. There was always some eager cousin waiting to row across and fetch them.

My grandparents' summer home had no electricity, no running water, no telephone. We used only canoes or rowboats for transportation. There was an unspoken contempt for those weekend families across the lake, whose clusters of electric lights twinkled merrily at us after dark while we huddled around kerosene lamps; who polluted the lake with motorboats, and had names on their cabins like Bide-A-Wee or Cee-the-Vue. In the last decade or so, because they are old now and made more uncomfortable by the camp's inconvenience, my grandparents have paid to have electric wires run around and bought a small power boat. But then it was pristine, Edenic.

The buildings were all painted white, with dark green trim. Just after Molly and I moved into our Cambridge apartment, I used those colors to paint her bedroom, and it was only as I recognized their source in the finished job that I realized how frightened and homesick I was for something familiar and safe.

My mother always sent me to my grandparents as soon as school was out. Sometimes, in fact, it would be my grandfather and I who made our buggy way around the

41

lake to get the first rowboat. I would sit in the stern and bail all the way over to get my grandmother and back, while the water seeped steadily through the dried-out boat in dozens of spots that would swell shut within a week. My mother came up in midsummer for a month or more, leaving my father alone in Schenectady. GE allowed him only two weeks, and he didn't usually appear until August. Then he seemed uncomfortable, as did the other brothers-in-law. They spent their time growing beards and fishing. The walls of the main house were dotted with birchbark reproductions of record catches, traced by the men in an unspoken competition that had developed over the years. When they were all up at camp at the same time, the brothers-in-law and my Uncle Orrie tended to cluster awkwardly together, apart from their wives and children, like a group of oversized boy cousins. It seemed as though they felt, in that setting, that it wasn't appropriate to assert any kind of sexual or paternal claim.

One childhood night, late in August, the fathers were talking about business. They had the choice seats, a semi-circle of wicker chairs around the big stone fireplace. My grandfather sat off to the edge of the group, but he was reading. He never talked much to his sons-in-law, those only moderately successful men who had compromised his daughters' lives. I wasn't really listening to them either. I can't remember what I was doing. I might have been reading, or stirring fudge, or just watching the fire. No matter what, the fathers, the uncles, didn't interest me. It was the aunts whose talk I cared about. Their conversations seemed to be about things that mattered – love, death, mutilation. This was the stuff that seemed important to me, although later I was to learn that it wasn't. It didn't count. And the preoccupation with it was what kept women from doing anything of consequence in the world. Tonight my Aunt Weezie was telling my mother about a friend of hers who had had her whole insides removed. 'All of it,' Weezie said portentously. I sat trying to imagine this, trying to imagine how the woman survived, hollowed out this way.

My mother and Weezie were both knitting, pushing and counting their stitches as they pursed their lips and said what a tragedy this was. Fat Weezie leaned into the lamplight and said emphatically to my mother, 'You can't tell me they had to do that to a girl that age, twenty-four. They love their knives, those surgeons.'

When my own father began to speak, though, I turned to listen. He was so silent at home that I yearned to know him better, if only to justify somehow the passionate love I felt for him. I was just over twelve at the time. I moved closer to the men and watched my father's face.

He seemed like a stranger. His nose and cheeks looked flushed in the orange light. He hadn't shaved since he'd arrived, two days before, and his whiskers were like a film of grime over his lower face. He was wearing a plaid woollen shirt. He'd taken off his waders outside, and his pants were crumpled. His feet rested on the floor in thick wool socks. At home even on Saturdays he was impeccably dressed. His workclothes came in paired sets of khaki and olive green, the shirt and pants always carefully pressed; his work shoes were polished a dull orange, and their thick soles rippled under his feet like two ruffled, gummed skirts.

He was telling the other fathers about some copper mines in South America that he'd persuaded his immediate superior to buy up. The older man had felt that the mines were exhausted, but my father insisted that they only seemed so because South American technology was so backward. In the end my father had won the argument: GE had taken over the mines and brought in new personnel, new technologies. 'And now,' my father said, 'that mine is turning out copper like there's no tomorrow.'

There was a little moment of silence while the uncles contemplated the story or the fire.

'And I have to credit Reynolds,' my father added abruptly. 'He admitted to me that he'd been wrong. "Dave," he said, "I have to admit it: on my own I wouldn't have taken the risk." I give him credit for that.' My father bent forward and uselessly stirred the fire with the poker, the

43

same way various of my cousins did from time to time. But when we did it, one of the aunts or uncles always spoke sharply: 'Please, will you leave that fire *alone*.' Now pink and white embers rustled down from the grate into the ashes.

'And it probably wasn't easy for him to admit it, either,' my father was saying. 'Him being a big wheel in the company like that, and me just a self-made man.' There was a tone of deep self-satisfaction in my father's voice which embarrassed me a little, and I looked to see if any of the uncles were sharing his pleasure.

'Excuse me, David,' my grandfather broke in. My mother, sitting across the room, looked up to hear what her father had to say to her husband. The quick motion of her head caught my eye, but her face was in the shadow of the bright kerosene lamp, and I couldn't see it. Weezie went right on talking, her head bent over the needles and the yellow yarn.

'I couldn't help hearing you refer to yourself as a self-made man, and I just want to correct you on that.' My grandfather's pronunciation was carefully precise, with not a trace of the Scotch brogue that his parents had spoken all their lives. 'I don't mean to take away from your achievement in the least. You must know I respect and admire you for how far you've come. But *self-made*!' My grandfather smiled at my father, the kind, condescending smile of a teacher to a particularly backward child. 'I'm a self-made man, David. Let me tell you what that means. That means no . . . pension plan, for example. No company ladder to climb, to protect you every step of the way. No *company*. That's what self-made means.' He paused. Then: 'You. You're a company man, David. A company man.' He tilted his book back up on his abdomen again, as if to begin to read it once more. He smiled again. 'I just thought you ought to be aware of that distinction.'

I didn't really understand the distinction my grandfather was making, but I knew I shouldn't look at my father. After a moment I could hear the *chunk chunk* of the poker striking the wood. My grandfather had gone back to his book and seemed totally involved. I looked at my mother. Her head was bowed again over her knitting, her face carefully averted from the group by the fire, and she seemed to be listening intently to Weezie. I wanted her to do something, to say something. I wanted her to defend my father, to *cleave only unto him, forsaking all others*, as she and I both knew she should do. But she sat, and Weezie's bright loud voice encircled her as the lamplight did. By her silence, I felt, she contributed to my father's shame, and I hated her.

In a few minutes, when one of the uncles had started talking again, I went and sat on the arm of my father's chair. I put my arm along his shoulders and leaned my head towards him. But he didn't want me around. His head moved away from contact with mine. After a moment he asked me irritably why I didn't play with one of my cousins. 'Grownups are trying to *talk* here,' he whispered sharply to me.

My father had *married up* as they used to say, though I didn't understand that phrase until later in my teens. All I understood at the time I'm speaking of was that somehow my father was vulnerable to my mother's family and I was the only one who seemed likely to try to protect him. On my father's account I was especially afraid of my grandfather, that stern, seemingly generous man whose every gesture, every gift, was a kind of rebuke to the parsimony of the normal lives around him. We were all, somehow, victims of his largesse, and no one ever stood up to him or defied him. Except Babe.

Babe was my mother's youngest sister, my grandparents' youngest child. She was tall and slender, with pale brown skin and wild full brown hair. She was beautiful in a way none of the other sisters were. They were all large, blond, Wagnerian, like my mother. Babe was like a wood sprite, a nymph compared to them.

She had been an afterthought of one sort or another; everyone had always known it. But no one ever dared to ask, and so no one knew, whether she was a mistake, or one last yearning look back at a stage already well past for my grandparents. My mother was twenty-two years older than

45

her sister. She told me once that she had at first thought her mother was joking when she said she was going to have another child; and then was ashamed and embarrassed by it. She said it ruined her senior year of college.

I was the oldest grandchild, five years younger than my Aunt Babe. In her isolation, Babe befriended me. Reciprocally, I adored her. I had no siblings. I was dominated completely by my mother, and Babe seemed the ideal older sister, glamorous, strong, and defiant. Through those long family summers of my childhood, Babe and I were, in a certain, initially enforced sense, inseparable.

There were four cottages at camp, but most of us cousins slept together on the sleeping porch of the large main house, the only one with a kitchen. Each child had an iron hospital bed, and we were grouped by families. Since I was an only child, and Babe an aberration, we slept together. Babe had rigged up a curtain to separate our corner of the porch from the rest. She didn't mind my hanging around watching her paint her toenails or curl her hair. But if one of the younger cousins poked a head under the curtain, she was harsh. 'No brats!' she'd snap.

In the early morning the sunlight reflected off the lake onto the whitewashed ceiling of the sleeping porch. As the air began to stir, the motion of the ripples increased until the ceiling shimmered with golden lights. I lay still and watched them; watched my beautiful aunt sleep, until my grandmother arrived from her cottage to the kitchen. With the smell of coffee and bacon, the squeak of the pump by the kitchen sink, I'd get up, easing my weight slowly off the steel mesh which supported my mattress in order not to disturb Babe, and go to help Grandmother make breakfast for the fifteen or twenty cousins and aunts and uncles who would rise when she rang the bell.

Babe was always quite distinct in my mind from the rest of them. I felt, even then, a strong bond with her, a sense of shared possibilities. In fact, I think we were two sore thumbs, Babe even sorer, I'm sure, than I. The other sisters grew more expansive and thick as thieves as summer wore on, seeming to pull away from us children. They told secrets, laughed at private things, often made fun of Uncle Orrie's wife, who clearly was never to be one of them. In general they seemed transformed into people we had never known, could never know. Into girls, in a sense, but girls whose club was private and exclusive and cruel. Babe was, of course, not a part of the club. But she was also clearly not one of us cousins. Her singular status was a constant irritant to my aunts and my mother. They wanted someone to be in charge of Babe, her appearance, her language, her behavior towards the nieces and nephews. They turned in vain to my grandmother. She was, in her silent way, almost proud of Babe's eccentricities. She'd say, 'Oh, that's just Babe's way' or 'But you know, dearest, I can't do a thing with her.' Neither could they, so she existed in a no man's land, nobody's child, nobody's mother.

She was sometimes a leader of the cousins, and sometimes tormented them. I was honored to be her ally in whichever direction she went. I felt I had no choice, and didn't want any. To be more than just myself, to be like her, that was the opportunity she offered me. Even now I feel I would have been a fool to say no. And when I occasionally tried, she made me ashamed of myself. 'But Babe,' I'd say, 'Aunt Rain *said* . . .'

'You want to grow up to be a creep like Rain?' she interrupted. 'The most exciting thing she's done in the last ten years, she finished that thousand-piece jigsaw puzzle last week.'

Babe was a born teacher, and she bound us all to her through crime and her own special insights into the adult world. She swiped food regularly, and kept a supply in the icehouse which she sometimes shared. She pilfered cigarettes and taught us all to smoke. We had a meeting place, a dappled clearing far back in the woods; and I can see her now sitting on a rock, puffing a Pall Mall, her fuchsia toenails glimmering on her dirty bare feet, and pronouncing all the aunts and uncles, our parents, a bunch of fucking assholes.

47

Another time she pulled down her pants and showed us where the hair was going to grow when we were as old as she was. We thought it was disgusting, ugly. We hoped she was wrong, that it wouldn't happen that way to us. But we adored her for doing it.

The few years after this Babe grew more remote from me. Her adolescence fell like a shadow between us. She was simply gone a good deal of the time, off with young men in power boats from the other side of the lake where the houses clustered close to the shoreline. They would come swooping into our inlet to get her, shearing off endless cotter pins on the unmarked rocks which studded it, and then hover helplessly fifteen feet from shore. We had only rowboats, so no need of docks. Sometimes I or a cousin would row her out the little distance, but often she waded out, holding a bundle of dry clothes above the water with one hand, swimming the last few feet awkwardly. She often came back after dark, and occasionally so late that she swam in quite a distance, theoretically so that the noise of the boat wouldn't wake the family. The lake was so still at night, though, that I'm sure my grandparents lay in their beds listening, as I did, to the dying whine of the motor's approach, the murmur of voices, laughter, carrying over the still water, and the splash as she dived in. Her teeth sometimes chattered a long time after she slid under the layers of covers on the cold sleeping porch.

My grandfather was always angry at her now, but his methods of punishment had no effect on Babe. He was stony with her. I heard him talk more than once of her 'betraying his trust.' He withdrew his charm and warmth, of which he had a considerable supply, from her. She simply didn't care. Occasionally he would force her to stay home in the evening. She would pace around the sitting room of the main house, where we all passed evenings together, occasionally stopping to try and fit a piece into whatever the ongoing puzzle was, sighing, picking up and putting down whatever book she was reading. She made everyone nervous, and we were all just as happy, in truth, to have her gone.

48

The two summers after this, my mother enrolled me in music camp, so I saw Babe only for a week or so at the ends. When I again spent all summer at my grandparents', she was nineteen, in college, and I was fourteen. From the start of the summer she was preoccupied and dreamy. She wrote long letters daily, and usually made the trip into town herself to get the mail in my grandparents' old Packard. Sometimes I accompanied her, as she seemed to be at a stage again where she didn't mind my presence. Once or twice we sat in the car for a long time listening to popular songs on the radio while the battery ran down. There was no radio allowed at camp.

She seemed plumper, softer, tamed. Yet, mysteriously to me, she still seemed to create a furor in the family. There was constant tension between her and my grandfather and aunts. Sudden silences would fall when I or the cousins came around. Yet her behavior by contrast with previous summers seemed impeccable.

I was myself preoccupied because of the music camp. Somehow, it was clear to me, the decision had been made that I was not, as my mother had hoped, musically gifted. My teacher's attitude had shifted during the previous year, from that of rigorous demand to a kind of empty approval. I knew she and Mother had talked. I would not go to the camp again. Mother said it seemed a waste of money, when I could have such a good time at my grandparents'. I don't remember that the decision about music had ever been mine, but I had accepted it and wanted to be good. Now I felt that my life as a serious person was over.

Near the end of August, Babe and I went on a picnic together at Blueberry Island. I swam briefly, feeling my usual anxiety about brushing against unfamiliar rocks or trees in the strange water. Babe lay in shorts and a man's shirt, with sleeves rolled up, and sunbathed.

I came out of the water and dried off. Babe sat up. We chatted briefly, about my mother, about how disappointed she was in me. Babe offered the theory that she probably lost interest in my musical career when she discovered you didn't wear little white gloves to play in concerts. I went down to the rowboat we'd pulled up onto the shoreline and brought back a sweatshirt for myself, and two blueberry pails. We walked into the center of the small island, screened from the lake by trees and brush, and knelt down to pick the berries. After a while, I asked Babe why everyone seemed so angry at her, why all the doors kept slamming shut on family conferences. Babe's lips and teeth were stained blue and she leaned back on her heels and said, 'You might as well know now, I guess. I'm going to have a baby. I'm almost three months pregnant. They're all in a twit. They *hate* my boyfriend, he's not respectable enough. They think I'm too young. Daddy brought me up here this summer to get me away, to bring me to my senses he said. They want me to go to Europe next year.' Tears began to slide down her face. 'All I want is just to be with Richard.'

I was stunned and appalled and thrilled, just as I had been when she had shown us the secrets of her adolescent body. I remember I asked her why she and Richard didn't run away, and she said he had no money. He needed to finish college. He was ambitious and poor, and besides, he didn't know she was pregnant.

I asked her how she knew, and, eternally the teacher, she wiped her nose on her sleeve and carefully explained to me the way. Then she said she also knew almost right away by her body, how it looked and felt, and that was how Aunt Weezie had found out about it – by seeing Babe naked and guessing.

'How does it feel, Babe?' I asked, knowing she would tell me.

She smiled. 'Oh, wonderful. Kind of ripe and full. Like this.' She held up a fat berry. Then she put it between her teeth and popped it and we both laughed. A sudden shy silence fell between us. Then she said, 'Do you want to see?'

'Sure,' I said, trying to sound casual.

Babe stood up and stepped out of her shorts and underpants. The big shirt covered her to mid-thigh. She unbuttoned it ceremoniously, top to bottom, and took it off. Then undid her bra and let it drop. I was silent, embarrassed and aroused. Babe was beautiful. She had been beautiful even at my age, but now she looked like a woman to me. If her waist had thickened at all, it was just slightly, but a kind of heaviness seemed to pull her belly lower so it had a curve downward, and her thick fleecy hair seemed tucked underneath it. But her breasts were what most stirred me. They were still smallish, but they seemed fat, and the nipples were flat and wide as poker chips. She looked down at herself with satisfaction, and began, unself-consciously, to explain the sequence of changes she was going through. I remember she held one breast fondly and set two fingers gently across the pale disc in the center as she talked. If Norman Rockwell had ever gone in for the mildly erotic, he might have found a subject in us: Babe, beautiful anyway, and now lush, standing in a pool of discarded clothing, representing a womanhood I felt was impossible for me; and me, all acute angles, caught on the edge of pubescence, gaping at her in amazement. She smiled at me.

'Do you want to feel?'

I nodded, though I wasn't sure what I wanted. She stepped towards me, reaching for my paralyzed hands, and raised them to her breasts. Her skin was softer even than it looked. My skinny brown hands, laced with tiny white scratches from the blueberry bushes, the nails clipped short out of habit for piano practice, seemed hard, male, by contrast with her silken perfection. Her voice was excited, telling me – what? I can't remember. She moved my hands down her waist, then to her abdomen. I felt her fur brush against my fingertips, dry, and yet soft. As soon as she loosened her grip on me, I pulled my hands back.

When we returned, my grandmother uncharacteristically kissed Babe to thank her for the berries. She cooked them in pancakes for everyone the next morning, and suddenly the whole family, with their blue teeth, seemed part of Babe's secret to me. Except my grandfather. His breakfast was invariable, grapefruit and poached egg on whole-wheat toast, and his smile stayed impeccably his own.

Less than a week later, Babe left, abruptly and tearfully, for Europe, accompanied by Aunt Rain. I rowed them across, facing my grandfather in the stern of the boat. He was to drive them to the train station in town. They each had only a small suitcase, but my grandmother was going to ship Babe's things to her later. As we walked up the path to the road where the car was parked, my grandfather pointed out places where it was growing over and suggested I bring the scythe with me when I rowed back to pick him up again.

Babe hugged me hard, and kissed me once, on the mouth, as though it were Richard she was saying good-bye to, not her niece. I noticed I was taller than she, and the taste of her tears stayed in my mouth until I swallowed. I waved to the retreating car until all I could see was the dust settling behind it.

That fall we moved to Chicago; and through the months of getting used to a new place, a new world, I waited for news of Babe's baby. From the family came reports of her adventures in Europe. She was doing well in school in Switzerland. She had enjoyed learning to ski in the Alps. She stayed with friends of the family in Paris at Christmas. She sent me a card from Paris. It showed the Madonna and child on the front – the child a fat, real, mischievous boy, penis and all. Inside it said 'Noel.' She had written on the back: 'Life goes on, Europe isn't quite all it's cracked up to be, but the wine is wonderful, and I go through the days here agreeably, as I'm supposed to, a Jack o' Lantern's grin carved on my face. Keep up the good fight. Love, Babe.'

In the spring, striving to sound casual, I finally asked, 'Mother, was Aunt Babe ever going to have a baby?' She was sewing, and she looked up for a minute over the edge of her glasses. Her mouth pulled tight, and then she smiled.

'Of course not, dear. Aunt Babe's never even been *married*. You knew that.'

I recall that I blushed uncomfortably. My mother looked at me sharply, but then turned back to her sewing, and nothing more was ever said.

My life went on also. My body changed in some of the ways Babe had promised, though it took me a long time to grow as comfortable in it as she would have had me be. But Babe and her life began to seem less a model to me than a cautionary tale. She seemed to shun most family gatherings for a while. On those infrequent occasions through my teens and the early years of my marriage when I did see her, she was usually fortified by a fair amount of booze and a new man. For a while after college she had a job in an art gallery in New York, and later at the Whitney Museum. Over the years, as I drifted away more from the family, Babe had apparently gradually effected a gingerly reconciliation. In fact her death occurred at a family party celebrating my grandparents' fifty-fifth wedding anniversary.

She drowned. She was drunk, which wasn't unusual for her, and she and Uncle Orrie were rowing home together in the dark from the family picnic. She objected to the way he rowed. 'My God, Orrie, look at you, batting at the water in that half-assed way,' she had said. 'Jesus, put a little life into it. I could swim home faster than this.'

Orrie told me that she sat still for a minute after this, and the only sound was of the oars slipping in and out of the black water. Then she stood up, kicked off her shoes, and dove in.

The boat rocked violently after she sprang off. Orrie thought he might have jerked his hand off the oar to pull back from her splash; or maybe the rocking itself bounced the oar out of the oarlock and his hand. It slid off into the water at any rate, and he spent several minutes retrieving it. My aunt floated on her back near the boat briefly, and he said he spoke sharply to her, told her she was 'a damn fool or some such thing.' She laughed at him and blew an arc of water up into the moonlight, 'a great jet' he called it, then rolled over and swam off. By the time he got the oar back into the oarlock, he could barely hear her in the distance. He tried to row in her direction. He said he would row for a few strokes, pulling hard for speed, then coast and listen for her. By the third or fourth interval he knew he'd lost her. All he could hear was the gentle rush of water against the bow of the coasting boat. He rowed around in wide circles in the moonlight for a while, and then he had to row home and tell my grandparents. They found her two days later.

The rowboat wasn't used until three days after that, Orrie said, when my grandparents headed into town to retrieve her ashes. As my grandfather carefully handed my grandmother in, she spotted Babe's Papagallo shoes in the stern of the boat where she'd kicked them off before her dive. At this my grandmother – who'd taken it all 'like a brick, a real brick' in my uncle's words – became hysterical. She began to scream rhythmically, steady bursts of sound. When my grandfather tried to loosen her hands from the edge of the boat, she hit him several times. She broke his glasses. Dr Burns had to be summoned from his cottage across the lake to administer a sedative. 'My baby, my baby,' she whimpered, until she fell into her chemical sleep.

Orrie told me all this, compulsively told everyone who would listen all this, at the memorial service a week later. I hadn't been at the family picnic, but I had made it a point to come to the service.

We had lined up by generations in the church, my mother and aunts in the row in front of me and the other cousins. I could watch my grandparents sharing a hymnal in the front row, the one ahead of my mother. It seemed a reminder of our mortality, this arrangement; the blond and jet black of my row giving way to the gray of our parents, and then to the yellowish white of Grandmother and Grandfather and the two extant great-aunts. My grandfather's voice sang out bravely and joyously the words to the hymn. My grandmother, I noticed, did not sing at all. The eulogy was short and somewhat impersonal, focusing on the untimely nature of Babe's passing instead of saying anything about who she was.

My mother and her sisters seemed to be crying occasionally in the church, but in the car on the way to the family luncheon, Mother expressed what seemed like resentment over my grandmother's grief for Babe. 'After all,' she said, 'it isn't as though Babe were the one who did anything for her or Daddy all these years.'

For a little while, there was a kind of deliberate sobriety to the luncheon, but shortly after the fruit cup the aunts began to chatter, and my cousins to compare house purchases, pregnancies, and recipes. Only Orrie, sitting on my right, who couldn't stop telling his awful story over and over; and Grandmother, stony at the end of the table, seemed affected.

I was the first to leave; I had to catch the afternoon plane home. I went around the table, whispering good-byes to those who might be hurt if I didn't – my mother, grandfather, and the aunts; then I stopped at my grandmother's chair, and knelt next to her. She swung her head slowly towards me like someone hearing a distant call. I realized she was still strongly sedated.

'Gram?' I said. 'It's Anna. I came to say good-bye to you. I have to go.' I spoke clearly and slowly.

She reached out and touched my face in a kind of recognition. 'Say good-bye,' she repeated.

'Yes, I have to go. I'm sorry I can't stay longer. But I wanted just to come, to remember Babe today.' She kept nodding her assent.

'Edith,' she said mournfully.

'Yes, Edith. I was so sorry, Gram.' She nodded.

'I'm going now, Gram. Good-bye.' She stopped nodding as I leaned forward to kiss her. Her hand clutched at mine. Her grip was bony and tight.

'Don't go,' she whispered.

'I'd like to stay, Gram, but my plane . . .'

'Don't leave me.' I looked at her face. It stayed inexpressive, but tears sat waiting in her eyes. Impulsively I put my free arm around her and held her. 'I can stay just a minute, Gram,' I said, patting her back.

She whispered in my ear, 'Don't leave me alone.'

Her body felt empty but for the frame of bones. I held her until her hand loosened its grip on mine. When I leaned back away from her, her face was completely blank again. I kissed her cheek. 'Good-bye, Gram.'

I sat alone on the plane. I ordered a drink but even before it arrived I had begun to cry. The stewardess was concerned, asked me if I was all right. I assured her I would be, I had just been to a funeral. As I sipped the drink and stared out into the blank sky, I realized that I had never before heard anyone in the family call Babe by her christened name.

It was the fall after Babe's abrupt departure from camp, the fall she spent in Europe, that we moved to Chicago; and because the balance of power between my parents shifted, I noticed its existence for the first time. My father had taken a job as vice president of a can manufacturing company. It was a step up for him, and much more money for us. The moving men swarmed through the stucco Schenectady house, their loud voices echoing in rooms where I'd never heard anyone speak above a polite conversational level. They carted away all the visible signs of our life there from the large, sunny rooms. I remember standing in the room that had been mine. Where pictures from my childhood had hung on the wall – a Degas print, the cow jumping over the moon – the green striped wallpaper was lighter, unmuted by age and the soot the coal furnace had blown gently over us all those winters. The room seemed enormous. In the driveway, my mother directed my father with the suitcases: which would go near the top so she could get at it on the trip, which could be buried deeply. From my window I could see her foreshortened figure moving in and out of the garage, the part on her blond head as sharply defined as if someone had taken a ruler and pencil and drawn it.

I looked once more at the barren space I'd lived in. For three or four years I hadn't had anyone over to play, despite my mother's frequent inquiries about whether there wasn't some nice girl I'd like to invite. Now, standing in my empty room, I made promises to myself about how it would be in Chicago. I would be popular, I would be outgoing. I would never let anyone know that I had played the piano, how hard I had studied. I would have a record player in my room, and my friends would come over and we would lie on my bed and talk about records and boys. I would paint my toenails pink. I would tease my hair. Over the murmur of my mother's voice, my father's occasional response outside, I pressed my hands against my nearly flat chest and promised myself transformation. 'I will, I will,' I whispered, I swore. My voice hissed surprisingly loud in the hollow space.

The ride to Chicago took just over two days. As the landscape grew flatter, stretched itself lazily out, my father seemed to expand. I had never heard him talk so much. He didn't address me. I was, I think, never very real to him, and certainly not at that time. But to my mother he talked endlessly, continuously. He explained the new job to her. He reminisced about his boyhood, further west than we were now. And as he talked and she sat, silent, massive, and blond, I could see, finally, why he'd wanted her. He cared so intensely about her smallest response. The withholding cool quality which I hated her for on his behalf was the very thing he played to, the thing which spurred him on. I sat in a corner of the back seat and felt like an intruder while my father wooed my mother. She was quieter than usual, and I recognized in her silence my own fear of what was coming, my own steeling myself to make it work as I wanted it to. I remember thinking abruptly as I looked at her profile – which was examining the Indiana cornfields as though she could master the very terrain by will power – I remember thinking that I was like her, more like her than I was like him.

The episode which is clearest to me from the trip happened in a little town in Ohio, a town of surprising beauty, of wide lawns and big frame houses painted white. Blackish elms, all of which must be dead by now, arched over the town, dappling it. We were driving slowly, more than conscientious about the speed limit, and an older, dented green sedan pulled out beside us to pass. From the window on the passenger side leaned a dark, beautiful woman, laughing. Her hair was black and full and blew back across her face and open mouth. She held a baby out over the road, a tiny boy. The woman's hands tightly circled his waist. He was naked except for an undershirt, his legs curled up to his fat belly as though he were squatting. His eyes squinted shut against the wind. He was urinating, and the drops danced horizontally out behind him like glistening jewels suspended in the air. Just as the car swung in front of us, she pulled him in.

My father's laugh was loud, a bright bark. He sounded boyish and carefree. He had to hit the wheel several times to gain control of himself. My mother's lips tightened as she looked over at him, as though seeing a side of him she hadn't known about before.

We spent both nights in motels, and I shared a room with my parents. I had never done this before, and I loved everything about it: the tiny perfumed bars of soap, the immaculate strip of white paper across the toilet. I got to stay up as late as my parents and watch television, although the reception both nights was snowy and irregular. When the only station we could get played 'The Star-Spangled Banner' – a vague, distant flag flapping and flapping in the white-speckled box – my mother would get up and turn the set off, and then the lights. We all said good night to each other, making a joke of it by repeating it several times over. I had never felt so strongly the sense that we were a family.

The third day, in the afternoon, we drove through the stinking smoky mills of Gary, and up over the skyway bridge into Chicago. Through the brownish haze, the city loomed over the lake far to the right. I had the sense of arriving somewhere rough and exciting and turbulent. I'd read Sherwood Anderson then, a little Willa Cather. I knew what Chicago was to them, and I swore again it would be such an escape, such a way out of my life's prairie for me.

The house on Woodlawn wasn't as distinctive architecturally as the house in Schenectady had been. From the outside, in fact, the dark bricks made it look gloomy, boxy. But inside, it was larger and far more elegant. My mother set about decorating it with a passion which finally seemed to obliterate me from her consciousness. My room was done first, and with the least planning. Basically she tried to reproduce as closely as possible the room I'd had before. When she was finished, I found an empty packing box in one of the unused rooms, and I shoved into it all the things – my dolls, my piggy banks, even several of the pictures from the walls – which might remind me of my other life. When I asked if I could store the box in the attic, she stared at me a moment. She bent over the box and slowly explored its contents, her hands lingering especially on the dolls. Then she turned her head away from me and said yes. It was like a kind of giving up.

She was under strain too, and probably grateful to turn over the running of my life to me. I had, after all, failed her at being extraordinary; probably I could manage being a perfectly ordinary teenager on my own. She, in the meantime, was having to learn a new set of rules for her life. I remember feeling unfamiliar moments of sympathy for her during this period. Once or twice I came home from school and found her sitting in the enormous kitchen, writing to one of her sisters or her mother, and I could tell she'd been crying. She'd jump up to fix me the after-school snack, but with apologetic haste instead of the self-satisfied certitude in her correct mothering that usually made me unable to eat more than a few bites. Now I'd want to eat and eat, to show her there were things which she did as well in this new world as she'd done in the old.

As for me, although things weren't evolving exactly as I'd planned them, they were much better than they'd been in New York. I was, at any rate, accepted. I dressed right. I did just well enough in class to seem smart, but I resisted the impulses I had to satisfy the teachers, to please them. I had made the mistake in my other life of thinking that the grownups' satisfaction with me could help me in any fundamental way. Here that would not happen. And though I still didn't know what to say around the others, I found myself oddly comfortable not trying very hard.

And then changes in my body transformed my relations

with the world. My breasts grew, suddenly and thoroughly, between October and about February. In the bathroom, if I stood on the toilet and leaned to the right, I could bring my chest in front of the mirror on the medicine cabinet. While the tub filled with water and the steam floated in the room, I would hang out in the air and survey my lopsided breasts – lopsided because of the angle I had to lean at to see them at all. It was like watching balloons slowly fill with water, watching them first assume a shape, then a weight. By day, I strapped them into a viselike bra which utterly distorted their shape and kept them from moving in any way independently of my body. Any girl who had breasts in that era had these same regimented, improbably high little icons on her chest. It was as though we all shared that gene.

And a gene for popularity. Suddenly I began to be asked to parties because, certain girls told me, certain boys wanted me there. The parties were all the same. We would dance in somebody's rec room, the linoleum floor gleaming, the lights too bright, the record player nasally spewing out 'In the Still of the Night,' or 'Tears on My Pillow.' After the first awkward and tentative approaches by the boys, we paired off and stood in grappling couples. The trick in dancing, I discovered, was to let the boy grind into you without responding, to seem utterly innocent of what was going on. In corners, in the bathrooms at school, the girls would giggle about how hot you could get the boys, about *hard-ons*, *blue balls*, *wet dreams*. But with the boys, they maintained an air of stupefying naïveté. This was easy for me, this willed passivity. I felt finally that something was being asked of me socially for which I had a gift. Their hands slid down towards my ass, slid forward towards the sides of my breasts; they breathed irregularly in my ears and pushed their still slightly miniature erections against my thighs. I chattered about other things or sang along obliviously with the music. I was careful never to arch my back, never to push my body forward against theirs – that would be cheap, like being a make-out – and when the dance ended, I, like the other girls, broke brightly away from their humid embraces.

But when the rules changed, I wasn't ready. We were at Karen Needleman's house – her parents were somewhere upstairs – and we had the living room. It was harder to dance in than the basement rooms we were used to because there was thick carpeting on the floor; and slowly the milling, nervous group dissolved into couples sitting on the sofas, or on the floor with the walls as a backrest. Someone turned out all the lights except the one by the record player. When one record stopped and before the next one dropped, the room was full of the multiple rhythms of heavy breathing and an occasional, almost always female, laugh.

I was with Bill Nestor. He was a diver on the swim team. His eyes were chronically bloodshot, and he always smelled damp and slightly chlorinated when we danced. I didn't like him because I remembered too clearly the bulge in his trunks when he stood balanced on the end of the diving board waiting for the impulse to spring. He chewed gum and cracked it. Occasionally he would offer a piece to someone he was dancing with, which panicked the other girls. 'Smell,' they'd say, and breathe into a friend's face, something I could never have done. 'Do I have bad breath? Bill Nestor offered me *chewing* gum.'

We were leaned against the wall, our legs out in front of us. Bill's upper body and hips were turned towards me, and I could feel the steady pressure of his knotted sex against my left hip. His big hands were making the usual rounds, from the waist up to the sides of the breasts, back to the waist. His jaw rocked steadily in time to the music, even when his breathing grew irregular. I was almost relaxed. Though this was a variation, the theme was familiar. '*Sho do, sho be do,*' sang the Five Satins over and over.

His hand moved in on my breast, cupped it. He seemed to wait a moment for me to protest, and then his hand began a possessive massage. I was frozen. If I didn't want this, I had to say no. I had to say *no* out loud. I had to acknowledge what he was doing, and tell him to stop, or move his hand, or laugh and slap him as I had heard several other girls do around the room.

I did nothing. His hand kneaded my breast over and over. His breathing speeded up and he stopped chewing gum. The knob of his erection pushed against me again and again. I felt caught in a vise, but a living, pulsing one. I stared straight ahead of me. Bill's rhythm changed, he moaned slightly in my ear and pushed against me in a slower, twisting way; and then was still. After a few moments, his hand loosened on my breast, and I heard his gum crack damply again in my ear. 'Hey, Anna,' he said. 'You're all right.' Then he began to croon along with the Fleetwoods. In a few minutes, he excused himself and disappeared.

Word got around quickly, though not so quickly to the girls, I think. The boys would only dance once or twice with me before they wanted to push me into darkened corners, into other rooms, even into closets. Making out grew more popular generally as an activity, but I knew from what the other girls said that they felt as *in charge* of it all as they did when they danced; whereas I didn't know what to do, and so did nothing while a whole series of boys ground groaning against me, their eyes shut against seeing me, their hands on my breasts, and finally in my blouse, up my skirt.

I felt nothing, less than nothing. I'd thank the parents who appeared at the door at the end of the party, and slide into the front seat with my mother, who waited outside in the row of cars as she had waited outside at grammar school; and who had almost the same questions to ask me as then: Did you have a nice time? Who else was there? What did you do?

I answered her almost too eagerly because I was afraid she might guess something like the truth; and I could see as she responded to my seeming openness that she thought we'd reached some new stage of intimacy in our lives. Her gratitude, her softness to me, bruised my guilty spirit, and I came to hate her even more.

Now there was nowhere in my life I felt at home. I felt completely false to myself, that there wasn't any center to me, that there was no situation in which I told the truth or acted on the truth with anyone. Sometimes when I saw the stacks of music sitting on the unused piano in the living room, I felt a yearning for the time they represented; for the purity of my old life of practice and loneliness. I remember leaning towards my mirror in my bedroom and staring deeply into my own blank, false face. It seemed grotesque to me, the hideous freckled eyelids with their strawlike lashes. I blinked and thought of a frog. Then I raised my hand to my cheek, fitted the palm along its slight curve and rested it there. Tears began to cluster above the rim of my lower lids. Suddenly they too disgusted me, seemed melodramatic and false. I quickly lifted my hand from my face and slapped myself as hard as I could. Then the other cheek. 'Liar,' I whispered. 'Liar.'

Spring came reluctantly to Chicago. The grimy ice melted and froze again and again on the foot-pocked dirt outside the high school. The skies stayed leaden, a heavy, portentous sullen gray which seemed to derive energy from the lake. The air, even on days when the temperature rose into the fifties, was rimmed with the chill of winter. Still there were the parties, the moaning, oblivious boys, the gummy hands, the embarrassed abrupt abandonment. When my mother picked me up from parties or appointments, the heater gently blew on my chapped legs. 'This weather!' she'd say. 'Here it is April. Back home the lilacs would be starting.'

Timidly, I began to experiment with self-mortification. After one party where two different boys had pushed me into the darkest corner of the room to rub up against me, I swallowed twelve aspirin. I held lighted matches to the skin of my forearm. Nothing was sufficient to restore to me my forgotten sense of self. And I knew, even as I went through these motions, that I wasn't doing any real damage. My lack of courage disgusted me further. I began to yearn for the end of the school year, for summer, although the thought of going to my grandparents', where I had been innocent and ambitious, disturbed me. It was at about this time, too, that I asked my mother about Babe's pregnancy. Her reply

63

confused me. I was too naïve to understand what had happened to Babe. In fact, I didn't understand it fully until years later when, drunk after a family party, she told me about her lonely labor in a Geneva hospital, about the one glimpse she'd had of the baby before the nurse carried him out of the room. All I knew as an adolescent was that somehow whatever had happened to Babe made me feel a sharp sense of distaste and distance from the world my mother's family occupied.

So when my father, in what seemed the first clear assertion of the change that had taken place between him and my mother since the move, announced that he thought it was time I spend part of the summer with his parents, I was ready.

'But what will she *do* there?' my mother asked.

'What do you mean?' We were still at the dinner table, my parents drinking coffee – Sanka actually – and I waiting to be excused to do my homework. I played with the few grains of rice left in my pudding dish. They often talked of me this way, as though I weren't there.

'Well, they're so *isolated* there,' my mother said. We'd been to visit my father's parents several times for short periods, when I was much younger. Not even my father saw them very much anymore. They lived in Colorado. My grandfather had been a farmer, and my father had grown up helping him. But at about the time my father went away to college, my grandfather had the first of a series of heart attacks. During his recuperation, my grandmother started teaching school part-time, and after his second attack, he sold off most of the land, and she supported them.

They *were* isolated. The nearest town was Alamosa, about thirty miles away. But what isolated them most was their silence. My other grandmother (to me, my *real* grandmother) was silent also, but the swelling energy of her children and my cousins around her, the stern, articulate precision of my grandfather, made up for that. My father's parents were both uncommunicative, and my father was an only child. At lunch or dinner at their house, my mother had chattered helplessly about recipes, clothing, the weather; and everyone else silently ate the large bland meals my grandmother prepared. The only spiced dishes were the three or four kinds of pickles piled in plastic bowls on the table.

The last time we drove away from their house, my mother began to weep in frustration. My father pulled the car off the road in a swirl of dust, and tried to console her, while I stared relentlessly at the prairie dogs popping up and down in their complicated world a few feet away, and wished I were anywhere else.

'I just never know what to *say*,' my mother had blubbered.

'They don't expect you to say anything,' my father reassured her. He rubbed her bare freckled shoulder where it stuck out from her pink sundress. I could see his fingers slip under the fabric of the dress.

'But that's just it!' she wailed. 'How can you talk to someone who doesn't care?'

There was a long silence. Then he said, 'They care, honey. They just have a different way of expressing it from your folks.'

'I'll never understand them,' she had said, with a vehemence that sounded angry. 'Never.'

Now it was my father's turn to be angry. He set his coffee cup down noisily in his saucer. 'They're just as isolated at *your* parents' place,' he said. I could feel the tension in the air. My mother's clothes rustled as she pulled herself up straight. She didn't look at my father, but her voice was tight, offended. Clearly she was shocked that he didn't understand there was no comparison to be made between her parents and his.

'But in Maine she has cousins at any rate. Other young people. Plus my sisters.' Orrie, as usual, was left out.

He looked at her a moment. His voice, when he spoke, was conciliatory. 'Look, Bunny, all this is beside the point. This doesn't have to be an either/or arrangement. She can do both, after all. All I'm saying is maybe it's time she visited my parents, after all these years of just visiting yours.'

I said, 'I'd like to go.'

65

Startled, they both stared at me. My father grinned abruptly. 'Well, that's that,' he said, and pushed his chair back from the table. 'I'll drop them a line sometime soon and see what they've got to say about it.' His relief, his need to retreat from the tension with my mother was palpable. He went into the living room where he usually sat in the evenings to read the paper and watch TV. We could hear the bright music of a commercial start up.

My mother sipped at her coffee and avoided looking at me. When she finally did, her eyes were full of fury. My gaze slid back quickly to my own hands on the tablecloth. 'Really,' she said coldly, 'I had no idea you were so fascinated by Daddy's parents. When did all this happen?'

I shrugged.

'You might have mentioned earlier that you wanted to visit them. Then I wouldn't have wasted my breath – and risked offending Daddy – trying to argue against it.'

'I didn't think of it until Daddy mentioned it.'

I met her eyes again. She looked slightly mollified. 'Well, I hope you see what an awkward position you put me in.'

'I'm sorry,' I said. 'May I be excused?'

'Certainly.' Her voice was cool, efficient as ever. As I went up to my room, I could hear the clink of dishes, her footsteps as she carried the first load to the kitchen.

My Gray grandparents had never sent me a birthday or a Christmas present, had never made the long-distance calls on holidays my mother's parents had; had never noticed or even known about the milestones in my life – recitals, graduation, school awards – that my mother's family had fussed over so thoroughly. They received me into their lives in Colorado with the same lack of ceremony. Grandma Dora had two more weeks of school to teach when I arrived in early June, something she hadn't mentioned to my parents. Every morning I lay in the bright guestroom off the kitchen and listened to her getting ready to go. She had told me just to sleep in as late as I wanted, and I pretended to take her up on it, although I woke early each morning. But I didn't

66

want to have to talk to my grandfather at breakfast – to sit in silence with him really. So I lay motionless and hot in the room. The only furniture was a maple bureau and the bed, whose mattress was thin and pitted in the center. The maple was of a kind that I knew my mother would have considered cheap. Café curtains hung uselessly at the windows, since the sun poured through the bleached-out print, and there were no neighbors for miles around anyway. There wasn't a clock in the room, so I could never tell ahead of time how long I lay sweating, propped up in bed. Sometimes I read one of the three or four books I'd brought with me for the train journey, but often I just lay there, listening as my grandmother began her day with the solitary clanking of the few dented pots and pans she used to make breakfast. The sun in my room smelled of dust and the fading dye in the curtains. There was no breeze. My grandmother left a pot of coffee on the stove each day, and, in the top of the double boiler, turning brown and dry around the edges, hot cereal, in spite of the fact that it was already in the high 70s when she got up. After a while, she'd go out of the house, and then I could hear the car starting and driving out of the yard. I could hear the car, actually, for several miles, and I would lie very still and try to discern the moment when I couldn't hear it anymore, when its dying mutter became silence, became the noises I didn't hear the rest of the day.

Some time after this, my grandfather would come downstairs, moving more slowly than my grandmother had, and talking softly and steadily to himself. He rarely spoke to anyone else, perhaps only once or twice to me the entire month I spent there, but he kept up a continuous stream of comments to himself. They were mysterious, truncated, elliptical, mere punctuation to whatever was going on in his head. Once as I was walking away from him, he said, 'Dave's girl. Nice enough, I suppose.' To himself he said things like, 'So you say, so you say,' or, abruptly, 'Not likely!'

It was only after he'd left too, sometimes in the old pickup, sometimes walking towards the creek with fishing rod and creel, sometimes just to the shed where I could hear him hammering and banging as he repaired things, that I'd get up. After the first week I wore dirty clothes because my grandmother didn't inquire about my laundry and I was afraid to ask. The kitchen clock read eleven-thirty, twelve, occasionally later when I emerged, and often I was dizzy and headachy from lying in bed so long, thinking aimlessly or reading. I'd have my overcooked solitary breakfast and do the dishes. Usually after this I'd sit on the front porch for a while or go for a walk, staying close to the creek so I wouldn't get lost. By the time I got back, my grandmother was usually home, in the kitchen, starting one of her elaborate, bland suppers.

The isolation was absolute, but after the first three or four panicky horrible days, I began to feed on it. It seemed to me just the kind of purification I'd been seeking with my timid attempts to wound myself. Sometimes, walking through the dry air, wearing the jeans and shirt I'd worn five or six days in a row, I thought I could feel the moisture being sucked from my lungs. I felt cleaned, like the little dried skeletons of turtles I found along the stream bed. I could sit for hours tracing the flight of the cliff swallows in and out of their nests above the creek, and watching the light shift in the green and gold cottonwood trees.

Even the conversations seemed clear and pure to me, uncomplicated, unhurtful. 'Here she is,' my grandmother would say, without looking up as I came in. 'Now take the dishrag off that dough and see if it's time to punch it down.' Or, 'Supper's in half an hour. Roast chicken, mashed potatoes, green beans and bread pudding for dessert.' No one ever asked what I'd done that day, no one ever knocked on my door, no one ever suggested any more productive or useful or ambitious way of spending my time. I was expected to take care of myself, but how I did that was entirely my business.

All three Saturdays I was there we drove into Alamosa for the day and the evening. Each time my grandmother would call me into the kitchen beforehand. She'd open her worn white plastic purse and pull out a man's billfold.

Ceremoniously she'd extract a five-dollar bill. 'Now you don't want to hang around with us,' she'd say. 'You go off and have a good time, and we'll meet you at Pete Rock's for supper.'

There was a five-and-dime in Alamosa, a J. C. Penney's, a Sears Roebuck. I'd make the rounds, buying cheap doodads and makeup in one or the other store, but mostly I bought candy. Baby Ruths, Butterfingers, sacks of malted milk balls, Three Musketeers. I gorged on them all afternoon, ate until I felt sick, stuffing the paper wrappers into my pockets. Sometimes I went for walks in the residential streets, staring at the tiny bungalows and careful yards, sprinklers arcing rainbows over the trimmed green. The second Saturday I found the town library, an imposing granite building with wide stairs leading in. I spent the afternoon in its cool reading room, listening to the ticking of the fluorescent bulbs overhead and reading back issues of *Saturday Evening Post*, *Photoplay*, *Modern Screen*.

At five-thirty, I'd go to meet my grandparents at Pete Rock's café. I tried to be a little late, because I didn't want to get there first and have to take a booth by myself. I was surprised each time when I saw them sitting there, at how like each other they looked. Both were small and trim, with iron-gray hair. Both had sharp noses; both wore glasses. But my grandmother wore a gold chain attached to the stems of her glasses. Gold, studded with fake pearls at regular intervals. It was like the announcement of some ambition he didn't share.

Our dinners at Pete Rock's were the only times my grandmother seemed to feel any pressure to keep a real conversation going. She'd begin by assuming my curiosity about something in their lives. The second Saturday she told me about how my father had run away one winter. He'd headed east, and got as far as Pennsylvania before pangs of conscience about how my grandfather would manage in the planting season overtook him, and he boarded a train back home. 'Sat at that kitchen table and bawled like a baby,' she said. I tried to imagine my slightly balding, paunchy and dignified father bawling. It was impossible. 'I couldn't figure out a way to tell him it was all right. I never saw a kid work as hard as he did that season, like he had to make it all up to us. It was the year after that that your granddad had his first attack.' She sighed. 'Of course, one good thing to come out of it all: once he stopped farming it cleared the way for your own daddy to leave again. For good.' Her eyes behind their bifocals looked watery and distant. 'And I guess that's just what he needed to do to grow up to be rich like he is.'

One night my grandmother shooed me out of the kitchen after the dishes were done. She said she had things to do, but I suspected she just wanted to be alone, not to have to try even the sporadic attempts at conversation which marked off pieces of the silence we occupied together. I was going to go sit on the front porch, but I could hear the slow squeak of the swing and I knew my grandfather was out there. Instead, I wandered into the parlor. I had been in this room two or three times since my arrival. My grandparents sometimes sat in it in the afternoon or evening to listen to the radio, but that seemed to be its only function.

There was a small upright piano set in front of the fireplace. A Methodist hymnal and a thick book titled *Beloved American Songs* sat on top of it. I flipped up the keyboard cover and idly struck a chord or two. The piano was badly out of tune. I found that somehow reassuring. I sat down and picked up the Methodist hymnal. Using lots of loud pedal to cover any mistakes, I played 'A Mighty Fortress Is Our God.' It had been more than a year since I'd played anything. Next I turned to 'Nearer My God to Thee,' and played it through slowly, melodramatically, three times. The last time, I could hear my grandmother's high-pitched, fretful voice join in from the kitchen. '*Still all my song shay-ull be,*' she sang in the same flat accent which I barely noticed now in her speech, but which seemed almost comical to me as she sang the hymn.

When I stopped, there was silence in the house. Not even the swing on the porch sounded.

I flipped through the book hurriedly, and began 'Love Divine All Loves Excelling.' My grandmother knew all the verses almost perfectly, slipping only briefly here and there into '*da da, dee dah*.' I did an *amen* at the end of this one, and when I looked up, she was standing in the doorway.

'You know your granddaddy's favorite,' she said, nearly whispering. 'It's "Onward Christian Soldiers."' I found it quickly. As I began playing the tune, she disappeared back into the kitchen. From the front porch came a loud groaning noise which I realized was my grandfather's singing.

I played for over an hour, dipping into *Beloved American Songs* at the end for 'Aura Lee' and 'Whistle a Happy Tune.'

I hadn't played since the move to Chicago, when, by tacit agreement with my mother, we hadn't looked for a new teacher. When I'd practiced in Schenectady before we left, the painful concentration was visible on my mother's face as she passed in and out of the room. She was listening for, but unable to hear, I knew, the quality in my playing that made it deficient, that had made my teacher suggest I not go to music camp again. My playing, competent as it was, could give her no pleasure.

When I got up from the piano and went back to the kitchen, my grandmother was sitting at the table with a glass of iced tea in front of her. The ice cubes had already shriveled in the heat into pellets that resembled mothballs. She smiled at me. 'That was awfully pretty, hon,' she said. 'I surely enjoyed it.'

'Thanks, Gram,' I said.

'You should always keep up with your playing,' she told me. 'It'll be a gift to your children.'

'Yes, ma'm,' I said.

'I used to play a few tunes myself, but I let it go, and now I've just forgotten it all. But *you*, now. Don't you let that happen to you.'

'No, ma'm,' I said, and went to the bathroom to get ready for bed.

I had trouble falling asleep. It seemed to me that in their responses to my music lay some mysterious and profound difference between my mother's and my father's families. It was more complicated than the tension in one family about achievement, and the lack of it in the other. And it wasn't just that my mother and her family knew what was fine and that my Grandmother Dora didn't; although that too seemed true to me. But as I lay in my lumpy narrow bed, the same sweaty sheets on it that had been on it the first night of my visit, I realized I was dreading leaving my grandparents' farm to go home, to go East, where I was surrounded by love, by protestations of love; but love conditional on so much: on being good, whatever that meant; on doing well; on making the family proud. The demands themselves, I realized, were often the clearest expression of the love.

Here the love had been harder to feel, because of my experience with my mother's family, but now I thought I understood where it resided. I had played a hymn that evening whose words my grandmother had quaveringly sung in the kitchen – 'O, Love, That Will Not Let Me Go' – and that phrase ran over and over in my mind. *That* was the trouble with my mother's family. I thought of how my father's parents *did* let go, of my grandmother saying what a good thing it was my father could get away from the farm. This *letting go* seemed exciting to me suddenly, where before a part of my mind had connected it to the dirty sheets I slept on, to the boring, slightly nauseous long afternoons reading *Modern Screen* and eating candy in the public library, to what had seemed the unnatural, inhuman silence between my grandparents. Now I saw it as a sign of love, a freer love than I had thought possible, a love I decided that night that I chose for myself.

Every night for the remainder of the visit, I played the piano for my grandparents. By day I huddled in my hot room, I wandered the empty countryside or sat reading and drinking lemonade on the front porch swing; and by night I filled the air with the tinny thump thump of bad music, my freely given, unjudged gift of love to them.

It changed nothing. The next year I spent again sitting in darkened rooms while boys who didn't care for me, whom

72

I didn't care about, rubbed me and rubbed against me because I couldn't find a way to tell them no. And sometimes I thought of hurting myself again. But then I'd think of Colorado, of my silent grandparents, the dry, pure air, the sunlight rippling off the creek onto the cottonwoods; and I'd feel that there was a way out for me, a reprieve.

But when my father wrote his parents the next spring to say I'd like to come again, my grandmother responded with a letter written in pencil on onionskin paper. I remember the faint rustle it made as my mother spread it out on the kitchen table. She read it aloud with bitter satisfaction – she hadn't gotten over the state of my clothes on my return from the visit there. They surely had enjoyed their time with me, my grandmother wrote. 'But we're not as young as we used to be, and it was hard for us to put ourselves out that much for the girl. Perhaps when she's a bit older and can take better care of herself we can have her again, but til then Grandaddy and I both feel it would be a mistake for us.' The letter went on for a while, and my mother read it all, slowly, but I didn't hear any more of it. When she was done, she pushed it towards me across the table. I had no impulse even to look at it. It wasn't just that the summer itself had been cancelled, or that my grandparents seemed to be rejecting me; but that some larger, nameless escape, an escape from myself, was being cut off.

Looking at me, my mother seemed suddenly to realize that she'd caused me unnecessary pain by reading the letter aloud. She stood up, embarrassed, and began to move around the kitchen uselessly, chattering about alternative plans.

That spring I let three different boys go all the way. The first time we were standing up in someone's back hallway, amid plastic buckets and oversized boxes of Tide and Spic 'n Span. Leaning against the wall next to me like an overblown dandelion was a mildew-smelling, dried-out mophead. The two other times we were in cars parked a block or two from the parties we were still technically attending. That summer, alone among the younger cousins at camp, I decided and convinced my parents, through long logical letters, and ardent pleading once my mother had arrived, that I wanted to go to a different school, a girl's school, when I got back to Chicago. By fall, miraculously, my father had arranged it.

When I got home, I took my record player and my stack of 45s up to the attic and set them down next to the box with the stuffed animals, the piggy banks, the music boxes, the dolls.

THREE

It took me more than a month to get the apartment unpacked and comfortable for me and Molly, but sometime in late September or early October I sat down, as my mother had requested me to, and wrote everyone.

'Writing everyone' had a special meaning in my mother's family. Straight through the misery of the divorce with Brian, of watching him move buoyantly forward into his new life while I made arrangements for our more marginal existence, straight through all the monitoring and correcting of Molly's confusion about what was going to happen to her, I'd continued to receive triumphant news of my mother's family – news of my countless cousins and the fruition of their lives – on the family grapevine. Catherine was in France on a Fulbright, loving it. Douggie had had his first poem published in *The New Yorker* and was teaching expository writing at the University of Arizona. Lettie's husband Al had the number one epidemiological position with the Ford Foundation in Pakistan. It was basically the parents, my mother's siblings, strutting their kids' stuff. And knowing that anything I claimed or did would become part of this epistolary competition had made me pull away slowly over the years from all of them, but especially from my mother.

Although perhaps this is a little suspect. For if I'd had news, if my life had been the trajectory to success some of my cousins' lives seemed at that time to be, might I not have stayed in closer touch? Perhaps some of what I claimed as independence had to do with a sense of comparative failure. After all, the last real feather in my mother's cap had been Molly's birth. After that there was silence, and before that, for some years, there was just the marriage, only Brian's achievement.

But what I was aware of in not communicating was a growing sense of freedom, a sense of actively extracting myself from what I thought of as their sticky grip, their insistence that whatever else we might be, we were first of all members of the tribe. Now, with a kind of rageful pity for my mother, who could not abandon them, for whom their judgments would always rank more permanent and scarring and important than anything the world or God could mete out, I wrote to her sisters and brothers, to the aunts and uncles and grandparents and cousins, claiming my failure as my own, and thereby, I suppose, helping my mother dissociate herself slightly from it.

In the last two or three years, a few younger cousins have divorced also, some more messily than I. I confess to having taken a certain pleasure in this. Several others have failed at work or relationships in ways that their earlier successes made impossible to imagine. One, Agatha, was picked up in New York recently for prostitution and possession of a controlled substance. My clearest memories of her were as a young child in Maine having her diapers changed. She was late to be toilet-trained, early to talk. 'PU,' she'd say, as her mother, my Aunt Rain, unpinned her. '*Big* stinky.' Once my grandfather, birdwatching through binoculars on the front porch at a little distance from the daybed she was being changed on, turned to Rain and suggested quietly that any child old enough to comment on the size and odor of her stools was old enough to be out of diapers. After that Aunt Rain took her away when she needed changing.

At any rate, if any of my letters are extant now, they are like shards from another culture, relics of a time when a failure as banal as divorce could still seem important to the family. Or maybe all they say is that my mother was the oldest child in a large family, and I her only offspring and hope for worldly achievement in their eyes; and that I failed her.

Dear Aunt Weezie and Uncle Hal, I wrote. I'm sorry to have been out of touch for so long and now to be writing you bad news.

Dear Grandfather and Grandmother, I wrote, It's hard for me to have to tell you this, but Brian and I have decided to get divorced.

Dear Aunt Rain and Uncle Tom, I wrote.

Dear Uncle Orrie and Aunt Cass.

There was a way, I have to admit it, in which I didn't mind writing them all. In which I felt that some ritual of freeing myself – literally writing them off – was being enacted as I sat at the dining room table with the box of thick white stationery I'd bought to do the job. I had regrets about a few of them – especially my silent, loving grandmother. But for the most part, it seemed the final liberating act in the drama of disentanglement I felt I'd been playing out with them all my life. It took me nearly a week of evenings to finish.

The dining room, where I sat to work – and my bedroom as well – looked out over the train tracks headed for suburbia from Porter Square. When the commuter cars or occasional freight train lumbered past below us, the whole building shook gently. Liquid tilted back and forth in containers, pictures and mirrors swung slightly on their hooks, as though we were feeling the aftershock of a distant earthquake. We had gotten used to it quickly enough, though Molly had sometimes waked at night in the first week or two. Our conversation would stop and then pick up again half a minute later as though the noisy interval hadn't existed. It made the apartment cheap, so I couldn't afford to mind.

Above me as I wrote the letters, the crystal chandelier suspended over the table, legacy from the ancient sisters who'd lived in the apartment before us, tinkled gently with the trains too, like the sound of ice in a tall clear summer's drink. I'd met one of these women when I'd come with the real estate man to look at the apartment. She was plump with yellow-white hair and a low, looping bosom which hung down over her belt in front. 'Oh, a piano teacher!' she

77

said. 'How lovely. How I wish I could stay and be a little fly on the wall. I've always adored music.' They were moving into 'retirement homes,' the dealer told me when we left.

From them too we'd inherited the elaborate dark wallpaper in each room. I'd painted Molly's room and my own right away, but partly because of my own laziness and partly because Molly liked what she called the *pictures on the wall*, I got no further. For months that fall and winter, the cans of paint, the roller and stiffened brushes sat on a square of newspaper in a corner of the hall, while over our lives presided the repeated figures in the paper: in the dining room, a curtseying woman sinking into her ballooning skirt while again and again a man in riding clothes presented her with a bouquet of bright flowers, now all faded to pastels. The living room had little Oriental figures in a vast stylized landscape, and the dark hall was thick with tropical palms and bamboo.

Those letter-writing evenings were the first ones in which I simply occupied the apartment, instead of unpacking or stripping wallpaper or painting – the first evenings it seemed fully mine. As the intervals between the commuter trains grew longer and longer, and my pen drew out my sad story on the fine white paper, I was sometimes able to feel a quiet kind of joy and pleasure even in the shabbiness which surrounded me. Brian and I had begun the upward purchasing spiral together. We'd spent whole weekends, a tiny Molly whimpering in a backpack, comparison shopping for a tastefully neutral Haitian cotton couch, for stereo components, for china. This time around, I'd made my purchases hastily at yard sales and junk stores. I had a rickety Windsor chair with a stained floral pattern on its cushions, a secondhand couch with Victorian aspirations. The dining room table itself, where I sat to work, was enormous, with ornately carved legs. It was painted bright red, but had chipped and peeled through here and there to show previous coats of white and brilliant blue. Sometimes this multitude of colors cheered me.

At other times, though, the opposite feeling would overwhelm me. A turn of phrase in one of the letters and the sense of absolute solitude once Molly was asleep would trigger in me, very much against my will, tears of purest, crystalline self-pity. Over that week or so I felt the way people traveling alone for the first time are said to feel, so absolute was the swing between the sense of joyous competence and bitterest loneliness.

But then the letters were gone and my life seemed slowly to begin again. There were the piano students, and then a new job, a change to full-time day care for Molly. After an interval of several weeks, a month, I began to get responses. Only a few – I'd purposely constructed the letters so no one would feel he had to answer. Most were short, conventional expressions of regret, substantially lifted in style from the condolence letter. My Uncle Orrie, an awkward, kind man, asked me to let him know if I needed a loan at any time. It wasn't until late in October that I heard from my grandparents – from my grandfather actually. He invited us to join them for Thanksgiving. There was something in the proprietary condescension of his letter that rankled me and I decided I would go. I would go as a divorcée, to defiantly represent failure in that nest of accomplishment. What he actually said was, 'Your grandmother and I admire the way you are dealing with the new set of limitations the life you have chosen imposes on you. How your Molly will deal with them, remains, of course, to be seen, but we will hope for the best for her. We would welcome you both at our table at Thanksgiving this year.'

It was overcast and silent Thanksgiving morning as we drove out of Cambridge. There wasn't much traffic – most people had gone where they were going the night before – and once we got out of the city, the landscape seemed purified by the sudden absence of leaves. Only a week or so earlier they had still been clinging to the trees in a garish, desperate last display. As we drove south through the even gray day, I talked intermittently to Molly about the old grandparents she was about to meet, much older even than

79

my parents or her father's. 'Do they like girls like me?' she asked, and I assured her they did before it occurred to me, and was too late to ask – she'd moved on to something else – what she meant by that.

There was a steep circular drive up to the house. At the top, the frame structure loomed dark and oppressive. It was painted deep green with yellowish shutters. Four or five other cars were parked at the edge of the drive near the front steps, indicating the presence of other cousins or aunts or uncles, including, I was sure, Uncle Orrie, who lived near my grandparents and, in the family words, 'looked after them.'

As soon as the front door opened and the familiar smells enveloped us – the elaborate cooking odors, lemon furniture polish, old leather books, dampness, odors which were as familiar to me, I discovered, as my heartbeat, my breathing – I felt it was a mistake to have come. In spite of myself, I cared too much about this world. And I'd forgotten my grandmother, as it was too easy to do. She shuffled slowly forward to embrace me, her face revealing nothing. She murmured something I couldn't make out over my grand-father's louder greeting, my cousins' hellos. And then she was kissing Molly. The small hands reached up to touch the old woman's lined face as it descended towards her, and my grandmother stayed bent down an extra moment or two, murmuring, talking, while I was distracted by the business of shedding my coat, greeting and being introduced to those I knew and didn't know. Then my grandmother disappeared, back to the kitchen. I'd had no sign, really, whether she'd registered me at all. And through the rest of the morning and early afternoon, she hovered in the background, vanishing frequently, often taking Molly with her for short periods. Sometimes I would look at her as she moved around slowly, but then feel my eyes skittering away, the way they might have from a scar or a missing limb. When our eyes did meet, there was no answering spark of life behind the thick glasses, no real acknowledgment of me. I hadn't seen her in two and a half years, not since Molly was a baby, and I wondered whether in that time she'd begun to let go of her world, her connection with people. Did she know, even, who I was? *Bunny's girl*, I wanted to say, though it was the very thing I'd come to her house to deny.

Once, I made a motion to follow her out to the kitchen, but my grandfather checked me. 'Oh, stay here, Anna,' he said. 'My darling has all the help she can use out there, and we haven't seen you in too long for you to hide your light under *that* bushel.'

And so I stayed, a part of his captive audience. The living room was cavernous and dark. There was an enormous fireplace at one end under a stone mantel. A fire blazed in it throughout the day, but it didn't warm the room perceptibly. The huge windows made that virtually impossible. One after another they paraded around two long walls of the room, framed by darkly carved wood. Threadbare Oriental rugs covered the floor, and the furniture was old and comfortable.

The group in the living room shifted some over the first hours I was there. There were new arrivals; the younger cousins and their friends went outside for a while to play football; various family members were successful in extracting themselves and going to help Grandmother. At different times I talked to my Uncle Orrie and his wife Cass, my cousin Bob and his wife Marie, Garrett and Catherine, and a much younger cousin, Michael, his girlfriend, and some members of a rock band he played in. My grandfather ran the conversation. The hostages were still being held in Iran, and he seemed personally offended by it. Something should have been done the minute they invaded our foreign space, he said. They had committed no less than an act of war, and we should have responded immediately. I recognized it as a set piece, like so many I'd heard throughout my childhood; but Michael got into a long argument with him. Uncle Orrie would gently try to divert them both. But Michael seemed to be enjoying goading the old man, and my grandfather was too committed to be distracted. Around the edges of this conversation, the usual family information, the real substance of the gathering, was being exchanged: who was pregnant, who was planning on getting married, who was Phi Beta Kappa, or had had stitches out or had ended an engagement.

No one asked me about the divorce, and I volunteered nothing. At the point when my grandfather seemed most lost in his argument, as intent as a Jehovah's Witness at the door about pursuing his own line of thinking ('Young man, do you understand what it means to have an embassy in another country? Do you understand the sort of relationship that implies with another government? That was the equivalent of US soil, it is as though they'd invaded a town on the US mainland . . .') I made my exit, crossed the enormous front hall, and circled back through the pantry to the kitchen. Molly was there, standing at the kitchen table with an apron on, stirring powdered chocolate into a glass of milk. Drops of the grayish liquid, granules of the chocolate were scattered across the tabletop. Orrie's wife, Cass, smaller and homelier than her sisters-in-law, was at the stove making gravy, and Garrett was gathering implements to set the table. I kissed Molly and moved to help Garrett. My grandmother and Marie were filling serving dishes.

There was a white cloth on the table. A floral arrangement sat in the center, and around it were scattered salt and pepper shakers, serving pieces, plates of butter and cranberry sauce and pickles and celery and olives. Cream-colored china plates and heavy white napkins had been set at each place. Garrett and I arranged the silverware around them. Then he began to push in the extra chairs. There was a wooden high chair for Molly, and he set it in the middle of one long side of the table. My grandmother came to the kitchen door to check on us. He turned to her. 'Does this meet with your approval, Gram, my sweet?' he asked. The younger cousins, particularly the boys, spoke to her with an easy, familiar affection that made me slightly nervous. She was silent for a moment while we both looked expectantly at her. Her thin hair was frizzed around her head, and the mortal curve of her skull gleamed dully beneath it. She looked at me quickly, then away.

'If Anna doesn't mind,' she said, 'I'll have the baby up by my place.'

Instantly I remembered how, in all the long summers I'd spent with my grandparents in Maine, she'd always surrounded herself with the babies, the littlest of the family. At meals, she'd be cutting meat, spooning cereal for two or three of her youngest grandchildren; and while all the other cousins and aunts and uncles talked volubly, garrulously, Gram's sentences were three or four words long. If you leaned closely you could hear her gentle voice as she spoke softly to Agatha or Freddie or Garrett. 'More?' she'd ask. 'More what? Can you say it? Cookie? Cookie! More cookie! *Good* for you!' Whatever else shaped us as a family, I think we all must have been marked by the diminishment of love with time and age because of that pure lost bond we had all shared with Gram. And I felt now, as I said, *oh no*, it was fine with me for Molly to sit by her, the sense we sometimes have as adults of living things again through our children, of restoring to ourselves those things we've lost, of giving ourselves those things we never had. 'I'm sure she'd love it,' I said, and meant it.

My grandfather carved. It was his moment as the official center of attention, and he prolonged it. He had a whetstone next to his place, and he took several minutes before he began, ceremonially whisking the long knife back and forth across it. I thought of all the families across the United States listening to the dull whirr of electric carvers, and yearned for a Thanksgiving like theirs, unweighted by personality. My grandfather was wearing a three-piece, herringbone tweed suit with a gold watch chain draped across his belly. When he leaned forward to attack the turkey, the chain curved away from his body and clicked against his water glass. He stopped for a moment and removed the watch and chain from his pocket and set it on the table.

He always dressed like old money, although the chances were the watch and chain were purchased at an antique

83

store or perhaps made especially for him. At any rate, they were hardly the old family pieces they looked like. His parents had worked in a textile mill when they'd first come to this country, and then his father had a small coal and ice business in Boston. My grandfather was wealthy, had been wealthy for most of his adult life; but his carriage, his clothing, his manner of speaking, all were intended to suggest a wealth which reached back deep into the nineteenth century, which had its root perhaps in oil or railroads or the invention of some industrial process, not in his own skill as an inventor and hustler, which was the case.

Oddly, it was my grandmother, still wearing a voluminous flowered apron as she served vegetables at the foot of the table, her head tilted up at an awkward supplicatory angle to see the creamed onions, the mashed potatoes, in front of her through the lower lens of her bifocals, who came from old money. But she had long ago passed down to her daughters – my mother and her sisters – the jewelry, the household treasures from her family, which would have publicly announced that connection. The garish engagement ring, which, along with her wedding band, was the only jewelry she still wore, was, of course, a gift from a younger, less confident version of my grandfather, his guess as to what elegance might be.

She didn't speak much of her family, but her sisters had often visited us in the summers at camp. I'd heard one of them suggest once that it was my grandfather who was to blame for her servantless imprisonment with all those mouths to feed. My instant recognition of this as the grossest misconception possible of my grandparents' relations marked it as one of the few times I had a sense at all of what their relations might be, of the choices she had exercised in marrying him, an immigrant nobody, and was still exercising in somehow silently insisting on her own austere version of the proper attitude towards her wealth. She had repudiated a whole way of life in marrying him; and then, I think, found herself locked in an endless struggle with him, who had at least in part been trying to embrace that life in marrying

84

her. And so there were these peculiar inconsistencies in their use and display of money. But more and more, now that they were old, he seemed like the aging scion of a great and powerful family, and she like a dowdy country cousin who couldn't stop helping out in the kitchen.

The plates were passed up and down the table, and we began to eat. Garrett, sitting next to me, was talking about film school and I was trying to avoid Molly's glance. She had looked scared when she first sat down, miles away from me across a sea of damask and silver and china, and I thought a sympathetic glance from me might be enough to send her into a full-scale rebellion against all that was being asked of her. For my own sake more than hers, I wanted her to enjoy being next to my grandmother, and so I hid my head behind Garrett's. I drank my wine and stared intently into his eyes as I asked him questions about his projected career.

At the head of the table, my grandfather talked through the first course with the younger cousins placed all around him. His mild condescending voice dominated, but they all seemed to respond politely enough. When I had finished eating, I sat back and listened to him. He was at that point arguing with Michael's girlfriend, Ivy. She was defending the lyrics to rock music as her generation's poetry. Suddenly my grandfather began to recite 'Crossing the Bar.' Conversation stopped momentarily as everyone at our end of the table turned to listen. I leaned forward and saw my grandmother's head bent towards Molly, Molly's face lifted and open with expectation as she took in whatever Gram was telling her privately.

In the break between courses, all the younger people stood and cleared the table. We could hear them in the kitchen, released from the politeness of the dining room, laughing over the clatter of dishes. Molly climbed down from her highchair and sat in my lap for a while, but when Michael and his friends came back from the kitchen carrying four kinds of pie and big silver bowls of whipped cream and ice cream she wanted to go back and sit by her great-grandmother again. She slid off my lap without looking back at me. When I looked at her after a few minutes, I saw that the entire plate in front of her was covered with pillowy white – she didn't like pie – and my grandmother was watching her lift a gooey spoonful into her mouth.

Suddenly, someone across the table from me, Michael, asked me what I was doing now. The *now* implied that he knew all about the divorce – I didn't need to go into *that* – so I began to talk about a part-time job I'd just gotten in the clinical psychology department at BU, testing rats for memory retention. I was doing a comic turn on it, describing it more as an animal training job, which it in fact also was, than an experimental one. It seemed to me the first moment my dubious status in the family might be scrutinized. I'd lost track of how much wine I'd drunk; my voice was a little too loud. I tried to control it.

Suddenly my grandfather interrupted me.

'Of course,' he said to the table at large, 'Anna is really a pianist.'

There was a little silence. My grandfather went on eating, as though he didn't anticipate any argument, any response to his assertion. I smiled. I tried on his smile, a gracious, condescending one. 'Well, I've never made any money at that, Grandfather. I thought we were talking here of how I made my *living*.'

He looked at me as he chewed. Then slowly he drank some coffee. Only after he carefully set the cup back in its saucer did he respond.

'You make your living at least in part from teaching the piano, isn't that so?'

'Yes,' I answered. I felt a sheepish blush rising.

'In that sense, anyway, surely you can call yourself a pianist,' he said. He looked around our end of the table with his smile, as though to get all those listening to agree that I was being silly, perverse, cute.

'Perhaps I could,' I said, my voice audibly edgy. 'Though I think piano *teacher* would be more accurate then.' He took a breath, as though to answer me, and I hurtled ahead. 'But rat trainer is at least a substantial part of it right now too.'

'Anna, Anna,' he said, shaking his head. 'Why this *nostalgie de la boue*? It's tiresome in a woman your age.' And he turned away and began to talk to Ivy again. I looked around me quickly. Everyone was engaged with eating or talking. No one seemed to have noticed or cared about the exchange. I was breathless, a little stunned, but I tried to cover for it. I focused my energies on Garrett again – he must have thought by now that I was quite in love with him – and chatted for a while to him and Michael about background music in films. After the meal, I went into the kitchen to help clean up. I stood at the sink, rinsing plates and scraping food into the disposal. Molly had pushed her stool over next to me, and was running her finger over the whipped cream left on the dessert plates. My grandfather came in. He spoke to several different people, then came to where I stood and asked me if he could talk to me in his study for a minute. I nodded, and after I'd finished what I was doing, followed him out of the kitchen.

His study was a large, square room tucked under the stairs. On their slanted underside, a carved walnut panel angled into the room, and his desk sat under this panel, its own walnut gleaming darkly. It faced towards a picture window. Outside, the ground fell steeply away from the house. The slate of a neighbor's roof was just visible below, then woods. He was sitting behind the desk when I entered. He gestured to the chair opposite it, but I shook my head and continued to stand. He turned away for a moment. Then, without preamble, he said, 'Your grandmother and I are worried about Molly.' His face was utterly grave, gave no hint of a smile.

'You don't need to worry about her,' I said. 'I can take care of Molly.' I thought of her, suddenly, lying scratched and dirty on the back seat of the open car.

'Please,' he said, raising a hand. 'I'm not trying to discuss whether or not you can take care of her. In some sense, finally, that issue lies between you and Molly.'

I felt the anger rise in me. Yet what was not true about

87

what he was saying? I turned away and began to examine a collection of paperweights on the shelves along one wall. Once, I remembered, Babe and a few of us cousins had stolen several of these during a holiday visit, and put them in the basement near the back of the coal bin. The idea, as I recalled it, was that we would return them in a day or two. We simply wanted to see whether he'd notice they were gone. But what were we trying to get at with the theft? Were we curious about the meaning of material possessions to him? Were we just being bad? I couldn't remember. The next day at breakfast he had announced to the group that 'certain things' were missing from his study. He had leaned forward then, and pierced the yolk of his poached egg. We all breathlessly watched the slow seep of intense yellow over his toast, onto his white plate.

'Now,' he had said, 'as soon as all of you have finished eating, I want you to disappear from my sight' – he said it genially enough, but it had the power of an imprecation for us – 'and if those paperweights are not in my study by the time *I* have finished eating, I shall begin to think of what an appropriate punishment might be.'

Babe, the oldest of us and our leader, acted as though none of this could have anything to do with her. She actually reached forward and poured herself a cup of coffee – she didn't even drink coffee! – to signal her innocence. The rest of us, though, slunk quietly away to confer, to decide who would have the dangerous assignment of returning the paperweights to their shelf. I couldn't remember who had done it, though I knew I hadn't. I was always only an accomplice in other people's daring schemes.

'It's simply that we may have it in our power,' my grandfather was saying now, 'to help you – her, really – at this difficult stage in her life, and yours. We'd be remiss not to offer out of some artificially heightened sense of delicacy, as I'm sure you see.'

I turned back to him, and though I had an answer ready, in my shrinking soul I felt like a twelve-year-old, a ten-year-old, a seven-year-old again. 'What I'm not sure I see, Grandfather, is why you think Molly needs help, just what kind of help it is you think she needs.'

He looked startled, as if the answer to this should have been self-evident and he wasn't prepared to have to make an explanation. Then his face fell back into its familiar deep lines of self-composure. 'Well, for an example,' he said. 'Day care. That she should have to be in day care. She's not, after all, the child of factory workers.'

'Neither are most of the other kids she's in day care with,' I answered. And then I was furious with myself. This was hardly the defense to offer. But one of my grandfather's strong suits was making arguments take place on the terms he constructed.

He raised his hand. 'But you see my point,' he said calmly. 'There's no reason why *she* should suffer because of the decisions you've made about your life. Because of your . . . perspective, let us say, on suffering.'

'Grandfather, she's not suffering. *I'm* not suffering.'

He was silent a moment, looking out the window at the darkening day. Then, as though he hadn't heard me at all, he said, 'Let me tell you what you learn through suffering. You learn to be an animal, a brute, a . . . *pig*. You learn cruelty. You learn how to take what you need from anyone weaker. That's all. That's all. There's nothing grand about suffering.' He shook his head.

'I'm not suffering,' I said again, loudly. 'I haven't *ever* really suffered. I doubt if I even have the capacity, so well have you all raised me.'

He looked at me sharply. 'If that's true, which I doubt, then I'm glad for you. Glad.' There was anger in his voice.

'And Molly's not suffering either,' I said.

'She's not suffering,' he repeated, a tiny ironic smile touching the corners of his mouth.

'Well, of course she *has* suffered,' I began, near exasperation. 'There's been a lot of pain for her and I'm not sure she's understood all the time what was going on, but . . .'

He interrupted. 'Then why add the strain of day care to her burden? Your grandmother and I would like to make, perhaps, a monthly contribution to your income, the money to be set aside for someone to come into your home and care for Molly there.'

'She'd be bored stiff,' I said flatly. And then, again feeling sidetracked, I shook my head. 'No,' I said. 'No. I really have enough money, and that's not the way I want to care for her, anyway. And I just don't want it.' My voice was rising, and I took a moment to get it under control. 'Thank you,' I said. 'I really don't feel that would be helpful.'

He stared at me for a moment under his curling eyebrows. As a child I had been frightened of those eyebrows. They were like the devil's eyebrows, I thought. They seemed to me to reveal some deep truth about him that belied the courtliness of his manner.

'It seems to me,' he said slowly, 'that you suffer from romantic ideas about poverty. There's no romance in poverty. None whatsoever. And even if you must insist on it for yourself, it's nothing short of criminal for you to inflict it on your daughter.'

'It's not poverty I care about, Grandfather. And Brian's helping us anyway. We're hardly poor. It's independence. It's being my own person.'

'Being your own person,' he repeated, the famous smile slightly lifting the lower part of his face.

'Yes,' I said.

'And in order to do this, you give up everything you've been good at, everything you've shown promise in, to take care of mice . . .'

'Rats,' I corrected.

'Whatever,' he said. He shook his head, smiling, at me. 'Rats, then,' he said, and his smile broadened and he continued to shake his head.

I felt shaken with rage, with the impulse to throw something, a paperweight, at him.

'I think we've finished this conversation,' I said. I started to turn towards the door.

'Anna.' His voice was sharp. I turned back. He had his sternest face on. 'I won't make this offer again,' he said.

'But it will stand, and I want you to think about it, about everything I've said to you.'

I looked at him a moment, and then left the room. My entire rib cage shook with every heartbeat.

As I came out into the huge central hallway, I stepped into a noisy game of Nerf football. Michael, Ivy and Pete, the bass player in the band, were playing with Molly. Two other of Michael's friends sat on the stairs watching. Faintly I smelled marijuana.

Molly was wild, shrieking, trying to grab the ball from first one, then another of the kids. They would pass it low, at her level, and scoop it away from her just as she was about to reach it. 'Mine, mine,' she was yelling as she danced around. I tried to watch for a moment to be sure she was genuinely enjoying herself, but then I heard my grandfather's study door open behind me and I went into the living room.

Some of the aunts and uncles were sitting around in the chairs near the fireplace. The noise from the game made real conversation impossible, but there was clearly a post-prandial, desultory quality to this gathering anyway. Someone would offer a comment, on the weather or the current activities of an absent member of the family; one or two others would add information or answer ('Yes, but just thank your lucky stars you're not in Utah right now. Did you read about that snow?' 'I wouldn't mind being in Utah if I had my skis.' 'The eternal jock.'); and then another easy silence would fall. Through it all we could hear Michael's running commentary on the game, Molly's wild cries for punctuation: 'He passes to Ivy, Ivy has it, she's got it. But *Molly* tries to grab it. She may have it folks, she may have it now; but Ivy hands off to Pete! He drops back to pass. And here comes Molly again, you can't keep her down, she just will *not* quit . . .'

My grandfather had poured himself a glass of brandy or liqueur and had sat down on the opposite side of the room from me, next to my Uncle Orrie. They began to talk, seriously and intensely, probably about money. I was sitting next to Bob's wife, Marie, who was telling me about the trip to China she and Bob were planning. My grandfather fastidiously avoided looking in my direction. This was the treatment for intransigent children and grandchildren; it would last until he had his way. For years it had dominated his children's lives and the grandchildren's summers. After a while, a silence fell between me and Marie, and I stared across the room at the old man, feeling the anger I'd felt in his study rise again. *Fuck him*, I thought furiously. *Just fuck him.*

Abruptly, as if echoing my thoughts, Molly's strained voice cried out clearly in the hallway, 'Fuck *out*, fuck out, you crocodile!' and she burst into loud tears.

There was a moment of silence among the group in the living room before I gathered my wits to go out to her. As I was rising, Orrie broke it by leaning forward and saying, 'Someone should tell her, Anna, it's fuck *off*.' Everyone laughed nervously; I smiled at Orrie and went out to the hall. Michael was squatting next to Molly, touching her shoulder, but she turned her back to him and stood resolutely solitary in her sorrow, wailing. He looked up at me guiltily. 'Jeez, I'm sorry Anna. I didn't know . . .'

'It's OK,' I said, squatting and taking her in my arms. 'She's just had a long day, and no nap. Don't worry about it.' I picked Molly up and sat with her on the wide staircase until she had calmed down. She looked awful. Her wispy hair stuck up here and there in a food-stiffened spike; she'd spilled something on her dress. Her nose was running from crying, and hectic red dotted her cheeks. My grubby grubby Molly. When she'd stopped crying, I took her into the bathroom and washed her face and hands with warm water. Then we went to get our coats and say good-bye. I found my grandmother in the kitchen, and kissed her. She followed us back out to the front hallway; but my grandfather wouldn't look at me when I spoke to the group in the living room, and he didn't get up from his chair when we left.

In the car, Molly and I talked quietly until I got on the Wilbur Cross Parkway. Then, with the steady highway rhythm, she fell soundly asleep. Before that, though, she told me she liked her grandmother – 'She gave me only whip cream that I like' – but not that big dummy Michael.

'I don't know,' I said. 'I think you liked Michael for a while. That game he played with you looked like fun to me. But he was just too wild for you.'

She was perched in her tilted car seat like a queen in her litter, completely relaxed and swaying gently with the car's motion. After a minute she said, 'He *was* too wild for me. *And* he was a big dummy that I don't like.'

I shrugged. 'Well, *c'est la vie,*' I said.

'*La vie,*' she responded obediently.

I looked over at her and smiled. 'You're my funny bunny,' I said. Then, after a minute, I asked her, 'Does Jeremy say "fuck out"? Who says "fuck out" at day care?' Instantly I was ashamed of myself. It seemed to me my assumptions about day care were just like my grandfather's, really. I wondered if he'd felt confirmed in his opinions by her outburst. Or perhaps he thought she was merely echoing the way I talked at home.

'Alex does,' she told me. Alex, another wild man. Whenever I'd seen him, he was wearing a Superman cape and moving fast. His mother told me he wore it even in bed.

'He says bad words, and the teachers don't like it and he has to take time outs. He says "fucking shit" to the teachers and they say, "I don't like that, Alex." And once he put his egg that he had from his lunchbox in the bathroom in the hole for the water and turned it on and it made a big flood everywhere. But then *Jackie* said "shit" too.' Jackie was the teacher.

'I'll bet,' I said.

'I say "shit" sometimes,' she said, in a dreamy voice. Headlights flicked by, though there was still pinkish light in the western sky behind us.

'Me too,' I said. 'It's not such an awful thing to say. But if it bothers your teachers, it's probably better not to say it around them.'

'I don't say it,' she said. 'I *hate* time outs.'

'Did you have to take time out one time?' I asked after a minute.

'Only when I bit Tanya,' she said. 'I didn't say "*shit*."'

'I didn't know you bit Tanya,' I said.

'I didn't,' she said. 'But I was very very very very angry and I forgot.' And then she fell asleep.

I drove along for a while, listening to her breathing. When I started to feel sleepy, I turned on the radio. It was AM, and all I could find were talk shows, weirdos using talk-show jargon to express predigested views on sex, bond issues, the hostage crisis. Finally I found one I could bear, on automotive repair. You called in your car's symptoms and the host told you what was probably wrong, whether you could fix it yourself or needed a pro. I didn't mind so much listening to the pathology of automobiles, so I left it on. Besides, I thought maybe I could learn something. All the car's noises made me uneasy since I didn't know what caused them, whether they were normal or not. And I liked the mechanic's cheerful voice. Happy man! to know that what he offered was something the world needed to have. After a while though, the talk about carburetors, emissions tests, became mere background too, blank comfort, like the little lights twinkling on the dash or the steady pulse of warm air from the heater. I thought about the long afternoon. In the end it seemed to me that I'd used Molly, both to hold myself away from what was going on and to feel myself part of it. Her pleasure sitting next to my grandmother, her rage at the end, seemed to be things she'd done for me; and I worried that I was too bound up with her. But then I reminded myself of the feeling I got when I forgot her for twenty minutes or an hour or an afternoon – the feeling that I was too separate from her. How could I love her without damaging her, I wondered. Not too much, not too little. Is there such a love?

I couldn't wake her when we got home, so I carried her in. Our building was a brown triple-decker tucked behind a slightly more elegant gray one. A long asphalt sidewalk led back to it. Molly's dead weight felt heavier than it really was, and I had to stop to catch my breath and rest my legs on each landing of the stair. When I swung our door open and the light sweet chemical smell of paint greeted me faintly, I had a sudden rush of familiarity with the apartment. For the first time since we moved in, I felt, as I carried her across the palm-studded hall to her room, that we were coming home.

FOUR

Now began a period of real ease for us, of finally moving into our new life in Cambridge with some sense of ownership. It was the ugliest time of year for the part of town we lived in – winter. The few lindens on our street stood black and hopeless once their leaves had fallen, their brutally pruned limbs exposed in awkward V shapes around the looping telephone wires. The snow fell and stayed and turned black with car exhaust, carbuncled with dog shit. The vast pot-holed parking lot at the Porter Square shopping center grew dirty mountains of plowed snow at its periphery, down which the tough kids of the neighborhood slid on stolen garbage can lids or plastic trashbags. On our weekends together, Molly and I took long walks punctuated by stops in the various stores up and down Mass. Ave. I was struck with the ugliness of the low storefronts, the yellow brick, the peeling wood, the granite grown dirty. By contrast with the Back Bay, where Brian and I had lived, it was antiarchi-tectural, completely without beauty. But its very lack of distinction appealed to me, comforted me, just as my shabby furniture did. And more specifically, the terrain reminded me of Chicago, the bunched-up groups of small stores which studded Chicago neighborhoods, the boxlike frame houses – triple-deckers here – the lack of beauty which promised an opening, invited the imagination in a way polished red-brick Boston didn't. It seemed both new and familiar, and I was excited by both aspects of it as we poked around the hard-ware stores, the laundromats, the five-and-dime, Sears.

Life during the week was hectic and full of chores. I had the piano students, the rats to run, meals, laundry, constant worries about money. But I also had long ritualized evenings with Molly. She painted or played with play dough while I did the dishes. Then there was a bath and a story, or sometimes we'd just sit in the rocking chair and listen to music. Once or twice a week, when I was too tired or she was too hungry to wait for me to fix dinner, I'd prepare popcorn and fruit and we'd eat curled up on the couch in the living room or on her bed instead of at the table. I usually went to bed only an hour or two after she did, but the time alone began to feel less like a burden. I began to think of myself, ironically, happily, as a divorcée.

I had thought frequently of Brian, I had missed him during the long fall. Sometimes I had an impulse to call him, to share some small event in Molly's life or mine with him. I was used to him, I sometimes imagined his responses to things, they'd been part of my life for so long. Once or twice I actually moved towards the telephone with one of these impulses. But then I'd think of Brenda, of her waiting, watching, listening while he talked to me, of how distanced and polite his voice would be. And I would remember how it was when we actually did spend time together on his visits to Molly – awkward, formal. What I wanted from him – and I wanted it often that first year – was comfort, familiarity, and that wasn't possible.

But now another feeling began to quicken in me, and I began to look at men. I watched them sometimes in restaurants or on the street when I went out. I liked to think of putting my hands on their bodies. I didn't think of their hands on me. I wasn't ready to turn my body as someone else's hand requested me to, to be responsive. But I was aware of feelings, of an appetite that I hadn't known in a long time. A divorcée. Yes. I liked that.

My room in the apartment was square and white and totally regular. Its bareness, after the purchased clutter of my life with Brian, pleased me. In it were a roll-away bed – a cast-off from the marriage – a white formica table, a white lamp. Exactly in the middle of the wall opposite the door was a window with a tattered green shade which leaked light weakly in the mornings. The floor was bare wood, cold to my feet in the winter months.

Even the inadvertent decorating I did – setting my purse or my earrings on the table at night – looked out of place in that room. And when I swung my legs out of bed in the mornings, they sometimes seemed immense and curved to me in the austere space, still brown with the faint tan left over from our days at the pond in East Shelton. I began in those mornings to look at my body, to discover it as though I'd never really seen it before. I'd watch my hands, my knees, the bones shifting under the tight skin, the freckles changing position on the skin with the bones' motion. I touched my breasts, noticed, and noticed myself noticing, the contrast between the softly shaped tissue of my body and the boniness of my hand.

Molly had a stacking toy I'd given her for her birthday in November, a complicated arrangement of rods you could slide plastic discs onto to make different color patterns. Early in the morning I could hear the distant clicking of the plastic pieces through the closed door as she worked on a new design, sometimes her voice a murmuring accompaniment to the percussion. I would lie on my narrow bed, feeling the gentle rocking of the trains and watching the pattern of faint light moving across the wall by the door. In those mornings I began to touch myself. I felt what was at first a shapeless yearning in my body, and I learned to bring it to life. I would reach between my legs, separate the folds of my flesh. My own saliva on my fingertips would make me wet; and I came. I came again and again in those mornings, by myself, with my thoughts all my own. Afterwards, in the sudden peace and stillness of the blank room, I'd hear Molly clicking, her faraway high-pitched voice, signs that she hadn't heard my private clamor.

In the early Seventies, before Molly's birth, I'd belonged for a year and a half or so to a women's group. We were organized by a self-proclaimed feminist, a woman with whom I sometimes played chamber music, a cellist named Cecile Clark. When we met in the women's group, in various living rooms around Boston, one of the things we talked about was masturbation. I remembered being surprised when Cecile, who seemed to me one of the most sexually charged women I'd ever met, said she never had. 'I mean, it's not that I haven't tried,' she said. She was tall and dark. She had thick eyebrows that nearly grew together in a line over her nose. When she frowned, as she did when she told us about trying to masturbate, the separation disappeared completely, her brows became a straight line bisecting her lovely face horizontally. 'I really have. I mean, I've wooed myself. Wine, Chopin, candlelight. God. I wish Charlie would take the time.' Cecile was married, for the third time, to a violinist with the Boston Symphony Orchestra. He was obsessed with money, and she claimed he brought the business section of the paper to bed every night – his idea of foreplay. 'But then I lie there and begin to stroke myself, and I can't help it, every time I start to laugh. To laugh! Can you believe it?'

We had all been intimidated by Lee, another group member, who'd talked about whole evenings spent in solitary erotic play; who loved to taste herself on her own fingers, who'd actually bought a vibrator to increase her pleasure. After Cecile's confession, the others of us who didn't or couldn't masturbate for one reason or another found it easier to talk about why not.

It was a shock to me then to realize that I simply didn't have erotic feelings. Brian and I made love only occasionally. When we did, he was enthusiastic and experimental. But to me the positions he tried felt like just that: positions. Later, when I finally had a successful love affair, I thought of those same positions as *feelings*. But with Brian, I felt as absurd as Cecile felt by herself. He would lie next to me, his face buried between my legs, licking and licking; and I would stare at his swollen cock inches from my face, his brownish hairy balls, knowing that simple politeness, if nothing else, required that I take him in my mouth, but feeling no impulse to do it. Occasionally I came with him, a sudden small convulsion that took me by surprise; but for the most part,

I was neutral towards the whole enterprise. And I never even registered an inclination to touch myself, to work towards anything like sexual fulfillment.

When I said this to the group of women, a little silence fell. I realized that they felt sorry for me, that my offering was as beyond the pale in its own way as Lee's had been. And that it would require some tempering remark in order for the discussion to continue. After a moment, Wendy offered one: she too had once felt that way. She'd really had to *work* to get through the asexual trip her mother had laid on her in order to be responsive. Others leapt in, blamed mothers, religious training, inept lovers. But they all had happy endings, I saw, even solitary Lee who sometimes spent Saturday nights alone, buzzing away. I felt as left out as I had in high school when the other girls had all seemed to know how to control boys and so I could never talk about what I was letting them do to me when the lights went out at parties.

Now in my white room, whose dim light and bareness made me think of the inside of an egg, I felt that I was growing into the feelings everyone else had always seemed to know about.

Of course, once I got up, once the day began and closed in on me with all its routines and demands, I'd forget it all, except for the occasional thought of my room, and the rush of pleasurable contentment its image would bring me, like the rush of feeling, later, I'd get at the thought of Leo in the midst of work or making music. It seems strange now to remember that I learned to have those feelings unconnected with anyone in particular. But it didn't strike me that way at the time, perhaps because all my life my most intense feelings had been born of solitary joy or pain. But isn't that true for most of us? Perhaps not, I don't know.

Molly and my work life took up almost all of my waking hours, especially once I got the rat job. I'd started off early in the fall thinking I could make it on the piano lessons alone. I'd had eleven pupils, but lost four when we moved to Cambridge – they lived in Boston and it was an inconvenient trip over the river and up through Harvard Square for them. That left me with seven. Four of them were beginners. They all played the same three- and four-note pieces, some with such lyrics – I, the jolly teacher, always sang along – as '*CDE, CDE, tell me what you think of me.*' Of the other three, one was an adult: Mr Nakagawa. He played every piece very slowly and precisely in a dynamic range stretching from forte to mezzoforte. But every week, on his own terms, he mastered whatever I assigned him and played it soberly, loudly, exactly as he'd played whatever piece I'd assigned him the week before.

The other two, Laura McEachern and David Humez, were both twelve. Laura was fat and nervously cheerful. Silences embarrassed her, so she talked incessantly whenever she wasn't playing, a quick blush rising and falling in her face as her tongue wagged, as though she were ashamed to hear her own foolish chatter but was still unable to stop. Her fingers were like machines, all pudgy and equally strong. Set the metronome wherever you liked, prestissimo even, they'd respond. But rubato, expression, were beyond her.

David cried every time I corrected him, so that I ended up apologizing for doing what his parents were paying me fifteen dollars an hour to do. 'David,' I'd say gently. 'You're making *such* progress, it really is exciting to me. But in this piece' (his face would pucker slightly) 'you have to lift your fingers between each note. See? They're not like slowly accumulating *chords*, David.' By now his eyes would be luminous shimmery gates to his vulnerable soul; I would think of Molly when I spoke sharply to her about playing with her food or wanting me to help her change her clothes over and over. 'They're separate *notes*.' My voice would have become so apologetic that the words could have conveyed no meaning to him. With David there was no room to be a teacher without also being a monster.

But in general I was known for my skill with young students, for my enthusiasm, for my gift of finding metaphors they could understand for ways to move their wrists, to weight the notes. I was optimistic. I sent notices to the parents of all the students I'd had in the last several years, telling them that I was looking for new pupils. I called other teachers, friends. I walked into the little stores in the fancier neighborhood just south of us on Mass. Ave. and asked to post signs advertising myself, signs with the bottom border cut into little teeth, each tooth bearing my phone number. When I checked these, as I did several Saturdays in a row doing errands with Molly, many of the teeth were torn off, but the three new pupils I acquired all came from friends. It wasn't my fault, one of these students told me. (Ursula Hoffman. An adult.) There'd been a drop in the birth rate. The children simply weren't out there.

'It's because men have given up screwing,' she said, her fingers arched over the keyboard. Not knowing how skilled she was, I'd asked her to prepare a piece for our first lesson.

'I didn't realize that,' I said. 'I'm out of the fray temporarily.'

'They absolutely have,' she asserted. Ursula had a round face with full cheeks and a pudgy, ill-defined mouth and nose. It was as if someone had drawn them in charcoal and then smudged them slightly with a thick thumb. 'All my boyfriend ever wants to do is go down on me. Sometimes I even say to him, "Let's just *screw*. Remember screwing? Where the man gets the erection and puts it in the woman?"'

I nodded, as though she were asking me, though my memory of it was dim.

'He says he doesn't.' She shook her head. 'He says it's because he's Jewish.' Her hand had long since abandoned the keyboard. She stirred the air as she talked. Another talker, another Laura McEachern. 'That he was raised eating salty, spicy foods, and so he has this predilection for oral sex. It makes him feel at *home*, like he's being a good boy and cleaning his plate. God.'

Though this was interesting to me, I thought perhaps we ought to be using the hour differently. I shook my head sympathetically, sighed, and then I used the line I often used to shut Laura up. 'Well, maybe it's time to make some music,' I said.

She nodded and turned back to the keyboard. With the first note struck, her foot slammed down on the loud pedal, and there it stayed, taking an occasional ill-timed breather, until the piece was over. The air swam with blurry notes. When she was finished she turned to me, tension like an unwelcome stranger in her moon face. I dealt first with her strong points, and then suggested she try it again, this time with no pedal.

'Oh, that fucking pedal!' she said. 'Did I have it down the whole time?'

'Nearly,' I said.

'I know, I know,' she wailed. 'I drive the same way and someday it's gonna kill me.'

She turned to the keyboard and stared desperately at the music for a moment. It was a sonatina by Haydn, something Mr Nakagawa might have played too, although in a different style. Little beads of perspiration dotted her forehead. I remember being surprised at how seriously she was taking it. She tucked her feet back under the bench and began again. Without the loud pedal, her mistakes were exposed, stunning in their frequency. She made a small animal noise each time she struck a wrong note. Even more than my young students, she reminded me of myself when I was learning, earnest and desperate to be good, to be better than I was or was going to be. Perhaps the truest defeat of my young life occurred when, early in college, I went back to piano lessons after a three-year hiatus, in spite of knowing that I would never be great, that I was probably preparing for the very career I wound up having: piano teacher.

Through October, I had just Ursula and the nine other students. By our agreement, Brian was paying me extra money through the fall, but I knew that it would end after the new year; and sometimes in the middle of some activity – my arms up to the elbows in scummy dishwater, shifting the clothes into the dryer at the laundromat – I'd start to roll numbers around in my brain, adding, subtracting the figures which stood for our lives, Molly's and mine, month by month. I could never make them come out right. I began to look in the help-wanted ads for something part-time crying out for my skills. But basically, as I discovered, I had none.

Then the car broke down. The man at Bernie's Garage told me he thought it would cost a couple of hundred dollars to fix it. I couldn't afford it. Now twice each day I had the long walk back and forth from the day-care center in which to think about what I would do. It was a rainy fall, and by the time Molly and I were returning home, it would be dark. Bumping her insubstantial stroller over the heaved brick of the sidewalks, I could look into the dry, lighted lives in the big Victorian houses just south of our neighborhood. Sometimes I thought I'd made a terrible mistake, that I was doing what my grandfather later accused me of: willfully ruining my life and Molly's.

More than once I thought of calling Brian, of telling him that I'd been foolish to think I could manage on what we'd agreed on, that I needed more money from him. I knew he wouldn't balk – he had essentially let me name the figure I thought was adequate for Molly's support.

But each time I'd talk myself out of it. At the day-care center I knew mothers who managed school and jobs and childcare entirely on their own, women who had far less education, less privilege in their lives than I. It seemed shameful to me that I couldn't do it, and more shameful still to think of leaning for help on Brian, someone I'd been eager to leave behind.

Slowly it became clear that I was going to have to get a full-time job. I spoke to the staff at the day-care center and they were willing to increase Molly's hours whenever I found something. I typed up a résumé and mailed it to all the schools in the area. Some wrote back to thank me, and that was that. In the meantime, I thought it only fair to warn my students that I might be giving up the lessons on rather short notice.

It must have been Ursula's fourth or fifth lesson when I

broke the news to her. 'Oh, you can't do *that*,' she said. She was wearing a loose-fitting dress covered with leopard spots, and leather boots so tall they disappeared under it. I'd given her pieces several grades easier than the one she'd first played for me, and we were trying to use the pedal minimally. 'Just when I'm starting to get good.' In reality, she had gotten only a little better. She never had time to practice, though each week she vowed things would change. But she was writing a book on female infanticide, and had reached what she called 'the good part.' It was hard for her to take time off. 'What kind of job are you looking for?' She was sitting on the bench, a short piece by Clementi open in front of her. In a small glittery heap next to the music sat the six or seven rings she wore, which she ceremonially pulled off at the start of each lesson. The whole pile rocked and clicked delicately when the trains rumbled past.

'The usual dream,' I said. 'Part-time, no real skills, absolute flexibility in terms of hours. One I could bring my daughter to every now and then if I had to.'

'I've got it for you,' she said. 'I have it. I'll tell you about it as soon as we finish this fucking Clementi.' She turned to the keyboard and launched herself, whimpering and groaning.

And so I began running the rats for Dr Fisher. He was a colleague of Ursula's at BU. Mournfully, at my interview, he told me he knew I was overqualified and wouldn't stay long. It was not intellectually challenging work, he said. I was simply to run the rats through T-mazes, recording how many trials it took them to learn in which direction a food reward lay. Ten correct guesses in a row meant they really understood which side the bread was buttered on. I could come in any time, day or night. I could test five rats in a row, or just one. He wanted about thirty hours a week from me, but which thirty hours didn't matter in the least to him.

'Do rats bother you?' he asked. Dr Fisher was himself a little ratlike. A white whiskery mustache bisected by a red-tipped, pointed nose. Small red eyes swimming in stripes of different widths behind thick trifocals. His sweater was worn through at the elbows and had a little food spill on the front. I thought about it. Had a rat ever bothered me?

'No,' I said. 'Not that I'm overly *fond* of them. My daughter had a gerbil once,' I volunteered, 'and I liked him fine.' A lie. I hated him from the start. And what's more I'd had to kill him. He'd escaped from his cage and I'd stepped on him in the kitchen one morning, mortally wounding him. I had to use the frying pan to finish him off.

'Gerbils,' he said, tragically, 'are more endearing than rats.'

This turned out to be true. Especially of the mood the rats were in when they arrived. They were shipped to Dr Fisher's lab in big boxes full of potatoes. Potatoes were their beds, their food, the medium in which they lived. In the lab they were dumped into separate drawerlike cages in what looked like an immense file cabinet along one wall.

'They're disturbed when they arrive,' Dr Fisher had said. 'It's a terrible experience for them, the trip.' He shook his head, and I could feel my own head swing involuntarily in sympathy.

I was to wear heavy leather gloves that pulled up to my elbows when I handled them the first few weeks. The reason for this was apparent to me as soon as I opened a drawer and extended my hand in to pick up my first rat. Even before I saw him he was attached to my wrist, his teeth sunk in the leather as deeply as he could manage. My heart seemed to slam randomly around inside my ribcage, but I remembered my mission.

'What you want to do,' Dr Fisher had said, 'is to get them used to the human touch.' He looked down at his own hands, locked in each other's grip on his desk. 'To accustom them to handling, to . . .' he cleared his throat, '*love*, in a certain sense.'

With my other leather gauntlet, I reached into the cage and gently stroked the rat trying to kill me. I stroked him and stroked him. 'Nice rattie,' I whispered, I crooned, as his jaw's grip seemed to loosen imperceptibly. 'Nice good rattie,' I said. He looked up at me. He blinked and sniffed.

He let go of my wrist and turned his head slightly to get a better view of the giant who was trying to be his friend. I began to understand how what I would accustom him to was indeed, in a certain sense, love. Or at least the misconception that he was loved. Close enough, for a rat.

The truth was, I grew to like the work, though I tried not to think about what happened to the rats after they'd passed my test. (I put an X on the cages of rats I was done with, and the next day, they were gone.) I also tried not to look at the animals in rooms along the tiled corridors I walked through on my way to the rat room, some of whom had had various kinds of experimental surgery performed on them or electrical implants fixed permanently into their brains.

When I turned the lights on in the rat room, my animals would begin to rustle impatiently in their cages, and some would call to me. I patted each of them every day, fed them, refilled their water, dumped out their dropping trays, then tested the ones that seemed calmest to me. At this stage I could handle them without gloves, and sometimes I found myself encouraging them for a correct choice in the same loving tones I used with my students. Occasionally I worried about screwing up the test results with it, but in the end I decided that was grandiose. Love just didn't have that kind of power.

Somewhat less frequently than once a week I'd go in and have a cup of coffee with Dr Fisher, as he'd asked me to. 'Check in every now and then,' he'd said. 'You'll probably need the human contact, and I'd like to hear how you're doing.'

Usually we talked about everything but the rats. He had a long narrow office with windows at one end, which I sat facing. A sycamore tree grew outside, its spiny pendants the only life left on it by late November. Unless the overhead lights were on, which they rarely were (they hummed – Dr Fisher said he felt nagged by the noise), I couldn't see Dr Fisher's face well while we talked. But in his gentle mournful voice he'd probe my life, ask about Molly, my playing, how my holidays had gone, whether I'd seen Ursula lately. And

I was attracted to his voice. It was like a caress. When I thought of him, I didn't think of how he looked, I realized. I thought of his dim office, the sycamore tree, his sad eager questions. He was married, I found out. He had three children, two in college. Ursula told me that his wife was an alcoholic, that she was notorious for disappearing noisily with other men at departmental gatherings.

Once he said to me, 'You young women are so competent, it's hard to see what you need men for at all.' I had a revelation, then, of how I must appear to him, and it shocked me. Young? Competent? I would have used neither of those words to describe myself, but when he said them, I saw how they could be true, and they became part of who I felt I was. But even more important was the sense they gave me that I occupied some space in Dr Fisher's mind, that he thought about me when I wasn't there. I discovered that he'd read a short story in *The New Yorker* that I'd mentioned to him, that he'd gone to hear a pianist I'd praised. He'd saved a bad review of her performance, too, clipped it out of the *Globe* and gave it to me. Had I seen it? What did I think?

To feel you have life in someone else's imagination is to feel a kind of intimacy with them. I grew to rely on my sense of connection with him that fall and winter. His voice always rose with pleasure when I'd open his door. 'Oh, Anna, it's you,' he would say, and he'd hurry to clear the coats and books off the extra chair. 'Come in, please, just a minute here. I was hoping I'd see you soon.' I knew it was the truth, and I knew Dr Fisher cared for me in some vague and dreamy way that would never require any action on his part, any response on mine.

And I would have settled for my life as it was at that stage: sitting in his darkening office talking our inconsequential talk, making music, running the rats, listening to my students, looking at Molly, hearing her stories of life at the center, touching myself in my room in the morning. It all seemed tentative and unimpassioned; but I was tired of passion, of certitude, I thought, not realizing I'd never really felt either. I told myself I could go on like this forever. And I believed I could, I would, until I met Leo and my world ripped apart.

FIVE

I read somewhere that the blind who once were sighted see again in their dreams, and are grateful for the fleeting return of the faces of those they love. I can remember waking from dreams as a child, happy dreams in which I had things I wanted – sometimes forbidden foods or money. Occasionally I would be playing the piano, making impossibly beautiful music. For a moment at the return of consciousness I would believe so powerfully in the dream that I could still feel the sticky coins in my hand, I could still hear the accomplished music, taste the warm rush of saliva that filled my mouth. The sense of loss on awakening those mornings was wrenching, the grief at coming back to my impoverished, hungry self. But what I feel when I dream of Leo, even sometimes just when I experience his waking memory, is compounded in the way I imagine the grief of the waking blind is compounded. They must mourn not just the things which are gone, the faces they won't see again outside those moments of sleeping grace, but also the lost capacity itself to see. The memory, the moment of sight behind closed lids, is a memory too of the disease, the tragedy which took sight away; the beloved face is also a talisman of that disorder, the panic of that loss.

There are certain parts of Cambridge, certain remembered images, a few photographs that I've kept that evoke that doubled sense of loss for me. Not just the loss of Leo, but the loss of the part of myself that believed he was possible for me, a part of myself that feels as elemental in its absence as taste or touch or sight.

In the last several years, Leo's work has become well-known. Not long ago I was in a bookstore in Harvard Square and I saw his face on the cover of an art magazine, staring out from the cluttered rack with characteristic intensity. I left the store and had walked several blocks, weaving through the crowded sidewalks, before I was fully conscious again of where I was.

When I was married to Brian, I often had the sense of having been absorbed by my role or by him. Sometimes I felt that I'd absorbed him. Either way, we both seemed diminished by having come together.

The year before we agreed to divorce, we went to visit friends at their summer house in Vermont. It was late May, still midspring, really, in that northern world. On the drive up we'd seen snow heaped in granular piles in the woods. The floors of Louise and Mark's house grew dusty over the weekend from the mud our boots brought in; it crumbled everywhere as it dried out.

We sat with our friends on a blanket in the pale sunlight in front of their house. Inside the cool house, Molly napped in winter pajamas. Louise poured red wine into our glasses. Our lips were stained. We were talking about the difference between city dreams and country dreams. Louise said that before the snow had all melted she dreamed the tiger lilies were blossoming orange and yellow underneath it.

I told a city dream. Our buzzer rang, and the voice on the intercom said it was Brian. But when I opened the apartment door to let him in, a man I didn't know in an army jacket with a shiny knife smiled at me and moved forward.

Brian told an elaborate dream. He was walking home through a strange neighborhood. He turned down a dark side street. A man was walking ahead of him. As he drew abreast of the man, who was wearing a loud sports shirt and baggy pants, he asked if Brian had something for him. Brian said no and tried to pass the man, but he speeded up and walked with Brian. He said he knew Brian had something for him, something he would sell him. Brian said, no, he didn't have anything, not even any money he could give him. 'C'mon, you asshole, you know you got some,' the man said. He pushed Brian. Brian started to shake his head no, and suddenly the man had a razor in his hand. He reached out quickly to slash at Brian's face. Brian woke up.

I sat watching a struggling insect that had fallen into my wine. I felt anger and pity for Brian. He had forgotten that it was one of my Chicago dreams. I had told it to him years before, when I first knew him. In bed that night, he and I lay far apart, our bodies curved away from each other, two crescent moons, each in a separate universe. We could hear Louise and Mark making love, her greedy cries of 'Yes! yes!' thickened and muted through the walls. I lay still, breathing evenly so Brian would think I was asleep, and wondered when this had happened to us, when we'd stopped noticing or valuing the separateness of the other.

With Leo that didn't happen, couldn't happen, though there were times when I yearned for the unconsciousness, the self-forgetfulness that would have made it possible. From the start, we fought and then made love, both with a passionate intensity that I had thought as lost to me as the possibility of making great music. I felt I'd been traveling all my life to meet him, to be released by him. It was what Babe had promised me, what my Gray grandparents had promised, what music had promised me: another version of myself, another model for being. Once, in a rage, I swept the dining room table clear after a dinner party we'd had together, a party where he'd been rude to two of my friends – and then stood feeling utterly free amid the shards of expensive china that had been wedding presents from Cass and Orrie, Weezie and Hal. It was like the sensation I had the first time I played a Schubert sonata.

Anything seemed possible. After another argument, when we'd been lovers for about two months, Leo picked me up from an evening making music with friends. Still calling good night to Cecile, I opened the car door. The dim interior light showed me his long body, his limbs absolutely shocking in their unexpected white nakedness.

'What are you *doing*?' I cried out, and slammed the door.

'Christ, Anna, I thought you'd be *pleased*,' he said, leaning across the seat to look up at me through the passenger window. 'It's supposed to be an apology.' And then I was pleased. I opened the door again quickly and slid over to him to end the argument.

About a month or so into our affair, at that happy stage when we kept retracing our steps, telling each other, and so discovering – or perhaps inventing – its history, Leo would try to rewrite our beginning. 'You saw me,' he'd say. 'Instantly you knew. The physique. The heavy-lidded, penetrating eyes. The incredible sense of style. You fell in love. You fell madly in love.'

But the truth was, as I told him, that I had barely looked at him.

'Jesus fucking Christ,' a voice behind me said. I turned around, holding a T-shirt of Molly's. It was bright red, and it said on the front, 'My Mom and Dad went to BARBADOS on vacation and all I got out of it was this lousy T-shirt.' Brian and Brenda had brought it back from their honeymoon for her. Whenever she wore it, whenever I even looked at it, I felt a bruised sense of generosity about letting Brenda share my title. Mom. 'My new mom,' Molly sometimes called her, and I would feel a smart of jealousy I couldn't allow myself to examine.

'Oh,' I said. 'I'm sorry. But they'd been sitting in there so long, and it was the only dryer.' A man sitting on a washer near me, holding a paperback copy of *The Hite Report*, watched us with a bored, blank face.

'Yeah, but they're still *wet*,' he said.

'Damp,' I agreed.

'Fuck,' he said.

I picked up a pillowcase and shook it with a loud snap. 'They'd been in there the whole time mine were in the wash,' I said. 'I'm sorry. All the other dryers were going, and I'm in kind of a rush.' This last wasn't true. It was one of my long weekends alone – Brian was staying with Molly and I was in a friend's apartment – and I'd come to the laundromat to have something to do.

He fingered his damp clothes. A student's, I had thought when I'd put them in one of the laundromat's bright plastic baskets. Paint-splattered jeans, grayish underwear, work shirts, frayed socks with holes. I was surprised that he was older, perhaps my age; but beyond that, I didn't think about how he looked.

In the corner of my eye, he shook his head. 'I get so tired of this jazz, *croyez-moi*. Even at the laundromat it's dog eat dog.'

A light tug of guilt compounded my irritation. 'Look,' I said too loudly. 'I'm *sorry*. I said that. And there are' – I looked behind me – 'three empty dryers now. Maybe you can stop licking your wounds long enough to stuff your wet clothes into one.'

He looked at me for a moment. 'Damp,' he said.

'Fine,' I said, and turned back to my heap of clean clothes.

I didn't think of him again until about a month later when I was back in the laundromat. It was Saturday. Another Saturday alone, except that I was staying at Ursula's for the weekend. She and I had become friends since I'd started working at BU. We were planning on having dinner together that evening, but I thought I should get out of her way for a while, and had sought refuge in doing the wash. Besides, I liked the laundromat – the way it smelled, the rhythmic slosh of the machines, the ticking of buttons, zippers, in the dryers, the odd camaraderie among those placed in life by circumstances which meant they had to wash their dirty linen in public.

Peculiarly for a Saturday afternoon, the place was nearly deserted. The long row of gleaming yellow washers sat silent, lids up, open-mouthed. Only my laundry hummed and clicked in two dryers. At the back of the long room, a girl stood folding her wash at a table provided for the purpose, and reading the notices which decorated the wall above it. I looked forward even to my turn at the notices, the ads for empowerment workshops, used furniture, lost dogs. I'd advertised on the same board in the fall when I was trying to get new students. Until my wash was dry, though, I was stretched out on the long bench which spanned the plate-glass storefront, reading and watching passers-by. The door stood open – it was one of the first warm days of spring – and every now and then the same rangy black dog would come in and check the wastebaskets and changing personnel.

A man walked by the window. He was tall, lean, wearing a jeans jacket. As he passed, he looked in and our eyes met. I remember feeling quickly a little pulse of sexual attraction, and then a sense of pride that such a thing was possible for me. Coming alive, I thought. I bent over my book.

A minute later, he said hello. I looked up, then back at the woman folding clothes, then back at him again. I smiled frostily and nodded; then turned to my book.

'You don't remember me,' he said.

It seemed a tired line, straight out of Little Anthony and the Imperials, but at least he wasn't opening with a discussion of some one of my body parts and what he might like to do with it, which had also happened to me at the laundromat.

'No,' I answered.

'We had an argument in this very spot. Or that spot anyway.' He pointed back to the folding table. 'A couple of weeks or so ago. You told me to stuff it.'

'Oh, yes,' I said. 'I do remember.' I looked at him again. He shifted his weight and put his hands in his pants pockets. He had a long narrow face with very white, smooth skin. His eyes were dark, looked nearly black. But it was a strange angle, looking up at him. I felt I couldn't really tell what he looked like, that he had some advantage over me.

'Are you a student?' he asked. He gestured toward the book with an elbow, swinging his body slightly.

'No,' I said. 'I'm just reading.'

'Oh,' he said. He shifted his weight again. 'Look, can I sit down? Do you mind?'

I thought about it. I'd been asked the question perhaps four or five times in that solitary year, and I'd always answered yes, that I did mind. Ever my mother's daughter,

I was still in some reflexive way frightened of talking to strangers; and also just unready for the slightly sexualized banter necessary to bring off such an encounter. But my own minimal history with this man gave me a sense of safety with him; and I found him attractive, but in a way I can perhaps characterize as *vulnerable* enough to make me feel almost comfortable.

'I guess not,' I said. I swung my legs to the floor to make room for him.

He sat, and turned to me. 'I'm Leo Cutter,' he said. He held out his hand.

'Anna Dunlap.' I extended my hand, and we shook firmly.

'Anna Dunlap, Anna Dunlap, Anna Dunlap,' he said, as though to imprint it on his memory.

We sat side by side in a silence that was just beginning to seem awkward when he said abruptly, 'Look, I'm an asshole.'

'Well, I'm certainly glad to know you then,' I said.

Leo laughed, lifting his head slightly in an odd gesture, like a bird drinking water. 'No,' he said, and his face sobered. 'No, I'm apologizing.'

'What for?'

'For being a jerk, whenever it was. I'd had a . . . God!' He shook his head. 'A horrible day. I just wanted some dry underwear to take home and comfort myself with. And instead I got stuck with this *sodden cold mass*.' He shook his head again. 'But I'm sorry. I am.' He looked at me and grinned. 'I should have been more civil.'

'It's all right,' I said.

He looked at me a moment. His eyes were dark brown, I saw, not black. He had dark hair, almost the same color as his eyes, that curled slightly over the collar of his jacket. 'No,' he said. 'I should have been nicer. Even then I was attracted to you.'

Dammit, I thought. Here it comes, as inevitable as a dog at a hydrant. I stood up and walked to my dryers to see if they were still spinning. 'Are you picking me up?' I asked loudly across the space between us.

The woman folding clothes at the back looked up.

He shrugged. 'I'm trying anyway.'

I leaned back against the washing machines and watched my clothes whirl around. He got up and walked towards me. 'You can't blame a guy for trying.'

He stood near me, his eyebrows raised, a half-smile playing on his mouth. He was taller than I was, and he bent slightly towards me. I had a sense of his making some kind of claim on me. I folded my arms across my belly. 'Yes, you can,' I said, not looking at him.

He turned and looked out the window. The dog came and stood in the doorway briefly, and he and Leo seemed to exchange a long look before he left. 'I see,' Leo said, turning back to me. 'You wanted the lawn party with the formal introduction.'

I think I smiled slightly. Certainly I shrugged, feeling foolish. 'It's just that it's so predictable.'

After a minute, a minute of just standing next to me, he said, 'No, it's more predictable, it would have been, for me *not* to try. Just to walk on and fantasize for a few minutes. That happens much more often, I bet. So either way, you can't escape predictability.'

One of the machines slowed. The dancing clothes flopped to limp stillness. I shut the lid of the washer behind me to give me a folding surface, and crossed to the dryer. I opened the door, leaned into the warm, bleach-smelling air, and gathered the hot clothes. He had to step back to let me set the clothes down. Self-consciously, I began folding.

He cleared his throat. I looked at him again, then back to the clothes. 'Look,' he said. 'I know I might be being an asshole again. The more familiar version.' Even though he wasn't so close to me now, I was intensely aware of him physically. The warm pocket of air around us seemed generated as much by his bending towards me as by the heap of towels and sheets in front of me. 'But here goes. I'm going up the street to Christopher's for a beer. You know it?' I nodded. 'I'd like it if you'd join me.' I kept folding clothes, though I could feel a blush rising to my face. He stepped a little closer to me. 'So, if you feel like it when you're done here, that's where I'll be, OK?'

I didn't say anything, but I could feel my head nod, nearly involuntarily. He walked to the door and turned back. 'OK?' he said again.

I looked at him. 'OK,' I said. My heart was thudding heavily in my chest. Then he was gone.

Slowly I folded the laundry, the unraveling towels, all of Molly's superhero underwear, the overalls, my jeans, the stretched-out bras and mismatched socks. The girl at the back of the laundromat pulled a sweater on and trudged out, carrying her laundry in a big straw basket. A young couple came in, then a mother and a small fussy child. As my heart decelerated, I pushed the sorted piles of folded clothes into my laundry bag, stuffing the box of Tide, the jug of bleach into the top. Then I carried the bag out to the Valiant, got in the car myself, and drove slowly back to Ursula's.

Two weeks after that, as I was leafing through the paper one evening, I saw that there was to be an exhibit of Leo Cutter's recent works at a gallery on Newbury Street. With a rush of contempt for myself, I realized that this changed everything in my mind. It was the lawn party, the set of credentials. It meant he wasn't just some guy at the laundromat. He was a Professional. He had a Career. He was safe, appropriate.

Now, even though I knew it was shabby, I began to hope for another chance with him, another encounter. When I passed the laundromat, I'd slow down and stare into its depths. When I was trapped in it myself, I'd sit in the window and stare out. Twice I took Molly to Christopher's for supper. I never saw Leo.

Then one Friday night late in April, Molly woke me in the middle of the night with a fever. In the morning it was still high. Two circles of fiery red sat on her cheeks, small glowing coals fed by the inner fire which made her body hot to touch, which made her tremble with cold, even under a quilt. I called the doctor and arranged to bring her in.

He looked for signs of strep, for a rash, anything he could treat: but there was nothing. I remembered that the teachers at day care had put up a sign about a viral flu making the rounds. He said that was probably it, that he'd seen quite a few other kids with just these symptoms. On the way home, I parked illegally just outside a little neighborhood grocery store, so I could see her through the glass front while I shopped. She sat silent and stunned in her car seat the whole time, her mouth a little open as if in surprise. I got ginger ale, chicken soup, a kind of arrowroot cracker she liked, and baby aspirin. I had to carry her upstairs, and her limpness, the intense dry heat of her body frightened me. She fell asleep almost as soon as I set her in her bed. I woke her long enough to get some aspirin and water into her. Then I called Dr Fisher to let him know that someone else would have to feed the rats that day.

It was a long, still day. The weather was warm – that gentle humid touch of Boston spring air – and on our trip to the doctor's the streets had been crowded with joggers, lovers, groups of teenagers talking and punching each other. But in the apartment I could hear only an occasional voice floating up from the street, mostly adult, but every now and then the bright high cries of children playing together. Otherwise there were just the trains ratcheting by and the uncomfortable heaviness of Molly's breathing, which seemed to fill every room of the apartment.

I woke her from time to time to repeat my efforts to get her to drink liquids. Shortly before dinner she had a period of feeling a little better, and I read to her for a while and brought her some soup. But at the end of the aspirin-induced respite, her fever went up again and she fell heavily once more to sleep.

I planned to set the alarm at four-hour intervals to try to keep her comfortable through the night, but when I woke at two o'clock, I knew I was getting it too. I had the heavy sense of impending discomfort, though no fever yet. I took aspirin and didn't set the alarm again. By Sunday morning, my fever was 102°, and my sole impulse, like Molly's, was to sleep. I called Dr Fisher again, and then went back to bed.

For two more days we lived like that. I'd wake occasionally and shuffle down the hall to feel her, to make sure she was breathing, to wake her and make her drink, make her chew the sweet orange pellets, eat a baby cracker, pee. Then I'd do the same things for myself and go back to bed. Dr Fisher called twice, Ursula once, to see how I was, if I needed anything; and the phone was so loud in our world of breathing, sleeping silence, that it made my heart pound erratically. We got better simultaneously, and on the third day, both began to walk around, to want to eat. But it wasn't until I took her back to day care on Tuesday and went into work myself that I realized how frightened I'd been by our isolation.

I was in Dr Fisher's office, talking about how much time I'd lost with the rats – they'd been nervous that morning after three days with no one handling them. I told him a little about the course of the disease, about how silent the apartment was, about how sometimes when I woke up I couldn't hear Molly breathe and would panic about whether she might have died – how long had I been asleep? had she been without water? aspirin? and then suddenly I burst into tears.

Dr Fisher rose from behind his desk and hurried around to me. Once at my side, though, he didn't know what to do, and so stood awkwardly patting my shoulder. 'You should have called me, Anna,' he said again and again. And I realized then, feeling his tentative touch, his flurry of confused words, turning away from him as I yearned more than I ever had to turn to him, that I wanted someone I could have called; that I didn't want to be as solitary as I was, as I'd grown used to being.

That evening, on the way to pick Molly up at day care, I bought a bottle of expensive white wine to go with dinner. Half way through it, after I'd tucked Molly into bed, I called Leo Cutter.

He picked up the telephone after the third ring and said,

'Just a minute, hold on.' The phone clunked down and for three or four minutes I listened to loud music, jazz, while Leo and someone else, a man, I was glad to hear, shouted to each other over what sounded like an enormous distance.

Then the music was abruptly turned off. There was a pause. Leo said, 'I'm sorry. Hello?'

'Hello,' I said. 'My name is Anna Dunlap.'

'Anna Dunlap,' he answered. 'Give me a second, I'll get it.'

'I met you at the laundromat.'

There was a tiny silence. 'Oh, Anna *Dun*lap,' he said. 'Yeah.' In his voice I heard a smile. 'Well, it's a pleasure to hear from you.'

'I'd like to try meeting you at Christopher's again, one night this weekend,' I said. I had decided that the best approach was to be straightforward. 'If that's possible.'

There was a silence.

'I mean, I'll understand if you'd rather not.'

'No,' he said. 'I'd sure rather. I'm just, I'm really sort of surprised. And ah . . . Saturday's no good for me. Will Friday work? Friday night?'

In terror I agreed. Molly and I were picking Brian up at the airport at six-thirty, so I arranged to meet Leo at eight.

During the intervening days I thought as obsessively as I had in high school about what I would wear, what we would say, whether I would sleep with him if he wanted to. ('Do it,' Ursula said. 'You haven't been laid in five months and you're worrying about whether he'll think you're a nice girl? Do it,' she said. 'Validate your IUD.')

Before I picked Molly up at day care on Friday, I went home, bathed, shaved my legs and changed my clothes. I'd decided on jeans, in order not to seem as though I'd deliberated a long time over what to wear; but I'd bought a new sweater to go with them, and silver hoops for my ears. I fixed a snack for Molly to keep her happy on the way to the airport, packed a weekend bag to take to Ursula's – she was out of town, visiting an old lover in Philadelphia – and left the apartment. It felt like the beginning of a voyage.

At the airport, carrying Molly back to the car, Brian looked over at me. 'You're looking wonderful,' he said.

'Thanks,' I answered. I felt so tense sexually, so aware of myself, that I was surprised that everyone in the crowded terminal wasn't staring at me.

'Doing something special?' he asked after a minute, and I realized he was still looking at me.

I smiled. 'I have a date,' I said. 'I haven't had many, you know.'

He looked away, and we walked along together, as we had so often when we were a family. Then he bent to Molly who sat along his arm, jouncing with every step. 'Doesn't Mommy look pretty?' he asked her.

Molly looked at me critically for a moment. I stared back at her flat, unreadable eyes. Then she turned to Brian. 'She's not pretty,' she said emphatically. 'She's Mom.' I laughed and touched her arm.

I had dropped the bag off at Ursula's on the way to the airport, so I got out of the car at Porter Square. As I bent into the passenger window to kiss Molly good-bye, Brian leaned across from the driver's seat. 'I meant it, you know,' he said. 'You look great.' His face, tilted and thrust forward at the odd angle to see me, looked strained and unfamiliar.

The noise in Christopher's was deafening, a combination of the jukebox and the effects of Friday's prolonged happy hour. I found Leo at a table in the bar, a beer in front of him. He saw me from across the room and waved. As I approached him, I was intensely aware of my body, a kind of sexualized awkwardness in it that I hadn't felt since my breasts were new and I didn't know how to carry them thoughtlessly in front of me.

I don't remember much that we talked about, just that he was animated and curious. I was tense, but relaxed a little once I had a beer, then two and three. He asked me a lot of questions with an energy and enthusiasm that both frightened and charmed me, and I heard my own voice getting louder, my speech speeding up in response to him. Several times I stammered uncontrollably at the beginning of a word, as though my body itself were trying to slow me down, to insist on its own pace. I had trouble chewing and swallowing. When the waitress removed our plates, two-thirds of the meal was still left on mine, though Leo, intent on what I was saying, didn't notice. We had another couple of beers each and then went outside and got into his truck, a Toyota. He drove us to a dim bar in Central Square. There were four or five beer bottles lying on the floor of the truck's cab. They rolled around during the ride and clunked together musically when we turned corners or changed speeds.

The bar was full of blacks, and thick with cigarette smoke. The band was black too, and they were mostly doing the blues, along with a few hits from the Fifties. There was a space in front of the bandstand where the singer stood. From time to time a few couples would get up and dance, edging him into a dark corner.

Leo wanted me to dance. I leaned forward and shouted in his ear that I couldn't. He turned to me, and our lips brushed. We sat grinning stupidly at our accomplishment for a moment.

I was by now quite drunk. We had a few more beers while we listened to the music. We didn't talk – it was impossible, the band was playing so loudly – and I'm not sure how long we actually stayed at the bar, though it was long enough so that my clothes still smelled of nicotine the next morning. When we went outside, it was raining, a cold drizzle. The light from the neon in the bar window and the marquee of the Store 24 next door were reflected in pocked puddles. We ran the block and a half to the truck.

Our breathlessness was loud in the truck. It smelled of cigarettes and beer and the freshness of rain. I told Leo I was staying nearby, at a friend's.

'Oh, no,' he said. 'I thought you'd come to my place. I'm going to teach you to dance.'

'I can't,' I said.

'Can't what?'

'Dance,' I said.

'Bullshit,' he said, and started the engine. I looked over at him. His damp hair curled tightly around his head. Raindrops sat on his white skin like sweat. He smiled at me as we swung out of the parking space, and suddenly I had the same sense that I'd felt with a few other powerful people in my life – that their energy, their passion could transform me. In my drunken state, I think I focused only on the dancing, but the exhilaration I felt, the sense of possibility, had to do with everything else Leo was and I was not.

We drove up Mass. Ave. past Porter Square again, past the parking lot, past the laundromat. The streets were deserted except for an occasional solitary figure walking fast, hunched against the rain. It felt late, one or two o'clock. In Dunkin Donuts, five or six customers sat on the stools, some turned to look out at the steady downpour.

Leo turned onto a dead side street just past the Newtowne Grille and parked. We got out of the truck and I followed him to the back entrance of the big commercial building which faced out on Mass. Ave. I thought I remembered an insurance office, a karate studio in the storefronts.

The hallway we stepped into was dim. There was a broken mailbox on the wall, and then the stairs began. He preceded me up them. His jeans were baggy over his narrow hips. 'This is my studio,' he said above me. 'But I live here too. It's all illegal, but half the artists in this town do the same thing, and all the landlords know. They don't give a fuck.' As we mounted the stairs, we drew close to a single, perhaps 60-watt bulb hanging over the second-floor landing. In its light I could see that the walls were a peculiar ochre color, perhaps painted, but more likely just the ochre of age, of fingermarks, of years of absorbed smells and dust. Leo turned back to me, walking sideways and gesturing around him, a tour guide. 'You know, I can't afford the rent on two places at once, and as long as I'm not conspicuous, he really doesn't care.' He turned left on the landing, unlocked three locks on a scratched, stained door, and swung it inward. '*Voilà*,' he said. He reached in and flicked a light switch. I stepped into an enormous white space – white walls, white floor. It smelled of paint and turpentine, like our apartment, but more strongly. The light illuminated only what seemed to be the living area of the room, so the other corners were in cavernous twilight, but I could see huge canvases leaned against the walls, and a long, littered worktable stretched across the middle of the room. The ceiling was studded with the black rectangles of big skylights.

Leo was moving quickly around his living quarters, singing in falsetto, '*I can't dance, don't ask me, I can't dance . . .*' He pushed a quilt-covered mattress on the floor out of the way. There was an orange crate next to it, a gooseneck lamp sitting on top. He turned the lamp on and squatted in front of the crate, flipping through the records which it housed. I looked around. A toilet, refrigerator, and sink stood against the wall. On a small wooden table next to them were a hot plate and an array of cups, tins, utensils. There was no bath, but hung on the wall next to the sink was an enormous galvanized tin washtub. I went over and touched it. 'Do you bathe in this?' I asked. He looked up, stopped singing. 'Yep,' he said. He turned back to his task, pulled out a record. 'As infrequently as I can get away with, 'cause it's a big hassle. I try to bum baths at friends' when I can.'

He put the record on and suddenly the room was full of Chuck Berry's guitar. Leo turned the volume up. I began to feel the same exhilarated excitement this music had waked in me as an adolescent. Inaudibly in the racket, I began to laugh.

Leo turned off the overhead spots. He swiveled the gooseneck lamp so it shone on the wall. He pulled me into its light and pointed out our shadows on the white wall. Our heads were immense near the ceiling. The shadows tapered to little human-sized legs. He leaned forward and shouted in my ear, his breath warm on my neck, 'Now, all you've got to do is just move your shadow, see?' His shadow danced. 'Like this, see?' I moved a little. 'Good. *Good* for you!'

The music was deafening. We were both drunk, though I drunker, I think, than Leo. We jumped up and down for a while. We made pictures with our fingers. Leo didn't look at me, only at the wall and his own body. I watched him singing, absorbed in the music and the flickering shapes. After a while, his shirt was stained with sweat, and sweat beaded on the white skin of his face. Between songs he froze, his eyes shut, and waited for the guitar to start again. I began to move, to move like him. I stopped looking at myself or Leo and only watched the wall, the monstrous others. He made his shadow merge with mine, and I copied him. The hydrocephalic figures came together, separated, sneaked up on each other, devoured each other. I had never felt so free of myself. Apart, together. Two, then one.

Then, as our shadows touched, Leo was touching me. He pulled me gently to the floor, to the mattress. Underneath us through the floor, I could feel the vibrations of the bass line of the music. We rolled over each other drunkenly, feeling each other's bodies. He rose on his hands above me, looking down at me. I didn't want him to, didn't want him to see me. I shut my eyes and pulled him down to me. We made love quickly and awkwardly, with half of our clothes still on.

I woke with the beginning grayness in the skylights, a terrible headache pounding at me. I needed to pee. I got up and quickly pulled my clothes on. Leo lay on his side of the mattress, uncovered. His hands rested, curled slightly near his face, like a child's, like Molly's. His bare hipbone carved the air, his penis falling limp down the dark hair pocketed in its curve. His jeans were still attached to one leg. His socks didn't match. I was glad that I was the one who had awakened first, who was seeing him like this, and not the other way around.

In spite of the pressure in my bladder, I decided not to use Leo's toilet. I didn't want to wake him, and I especially didn't want his first waking vision to be of me hunkered over his toilet.

The gooseneck lamp was still throwing its white light against the wall. I turned it off, jumping at the sharp click it made. Leo didn't stir. I shut the apartment door quietly behind me and lightheadedly walked back down the ochre hallway, the stairs with their worn rubber treading.

Outside the sky seemed light, nearing dawn. I started walking. The sidewalks were still dark with last night's rain, puddled with still pools. As I passed my street, I looked down it. The big frame houses loomed silent, as ugly as ever; but the linden trees beginning to green looked frilled, hopeful in the pale dawn. I thought of Molly heavy in sleep; of Brian on the couch; and kept walking.

It took me nearly an hour to get to Ursula's. By then the sky was white, and I was no longer drunk. I peed for an absurdly long, ecstatic interval and ran a hot bath. I fell asleep for a while in the tub. When the water got cold, I waked, dried off, and went to bed. It was eleven before I woke again.

I had had two other lovers since leaving Brian, since Brian left me. One of them was someone I'd brought home with me from a Christmas party while Molly was staying with Brian in Washington. It had been a difficult week for me, the first time Molly had been away, my first Christmas as a single person, Brenda and Brian's wedding scheduled for New Year's; but I had turned down an invitation from my parents to come to Chicago, determined to make it alone. The party had seemed full of other desperately gay people. The man I picked up had chatted with me only briefly about his work – he was a reporter for the *Globe* – before he began telling me how much he'd like to spend the night with me. In almost cold-blooded way I decided it would be better than spending another night alone – the lover-as-electric-blanket theory – and some time before midnight, we'd left together. We made love for a long time, and initially he was passionate and excited. But I didn't come, and there seemed, in the end, a kind of hostility and coldness in his climax. In the morning he said he had a squash game to get to and left without breakfast or even coffee.

The other man was a lawyer, a friend of Charlene and John's. I'd gone out with him four or five times, and made love with him twice, before I realized how much he reminded me of Brian.

I hadn't come with him either, in spite of his solicitude. Nor did I come the first night with Leo. It was too quick. I was too drunk. But I had felt a charge, almost like fear, around him that made me think I could, just as I'd felt I could dance if he'd teach me. When we had danced and I lost myself – in him, in the music, in the shapes on the wall – I was also intensely aware of myself physically. I felt as though my pelvic bones got heavier, shifted somehow. And when he had pushed into me on the mattress, I was wet, though I hadn't known I would be. His warm slide in and out felt not like the intrusion it had always been with Brian, but like something that was already part of me. I hadn't had any sense of wanting him to finish: I'd reached and pushed against him to feel more. Leo cried out something when he came, and I wanted to cry out too, so bitterly was I disappointed at being left behind.

When I got home Sunday afternoon, Brian said someone had called the day before. 'A guy. He wanted to know when you'd be home. I told him around seven tonight.' He was sitting at the dining room table playing lotto with Molly. His tone of voice was carefully neutral, but there was a question stamped on his face, and I could feel myself flush.

That evening, a few minutes after seven, a few minutes after Molly and I got back from taking Brian to the airport, the telephone rang. Leo didn't sound particularly friendly or warm. He asked if we were going to see each other again. I said it hadn't occurred to me that we might not. He asked when. I told him I ought to be able to get a sitter for a couple of nights from then, Wednesday maybe. He said fine, and we agreed on seven-thirty. I said I'd rather meet him somewhere than have him pick me up, and he suggested the Newtowne Bar and Grille.

When I arrived on Wednesday evening, he was there ahead of me again, again drinking beer. I slid into the booth opposite him, but I felt almost unable to look at him. He was unsmiling and, I thought, beautiful. When my eyes met his, it felt like the beginning of a slide down a steep hill, like the physical sense of falling that sometimes comes with the onset of sleep.

'I've already eaten,' I said. It was true. I'd known that I'd have trouble swallowing if I tried to have dinner with Leo, that I'd drink too much instead. I'd fixed dinner for Molly at six and she and I had eaten together. Spaghetti. When the sitter came, Molly wanted to know where I was going. I had a date, I told her. She watched me while I found my purse and keys, while I gave the sitter instructions. When I'd kissed her good night, she said, 'I hate it when you have a *date*.'

'I'll be back before you know it,' I said, trying not to pay attention to her fury. 'I'll come and kiss you again when you're sleeping, and then in the morning I'll tell you all about it.'

'Stupid Mom,' she said, uncharmed; and clomped down the hall.

'Do you mind watching me?' Leo asked me.

I said I didn't, and when the waitress came back with wine for me, he ordered. He seemed to know her. They joked together about the food. Then she was gone and he sat back and looked at me. I tried smiling at him, but just felt idiotic.

'Well, Anna,' he said. 'How come you left?'

I sat for a long moment looking at my hands. It seemed to me, suddenly, that I'd spent all week not thinking about this. 'I was scared, I think.'

'Of what?'

I drank some wine and carefully set the glass down. I shrugged. 'Of waking up by you. Of making love again, in the light. Or *not*.'

He was silent a minute, frowning at me. 'Let me get this straight. You thought we might not make love? That *I* might not want to?'

'I don't know,' I said loudly. It came out sounding as desperate as I felt, and I looked around to see if anyone had noticed. 'I don't know,' I said again. 'I was afraid you would want to, too. And I was afraid of how married it all seemed. That we'd wake up together and have breakfast or something. It was just too close for me. Like pretending to be married.'

'But we made love. Isn't that close, too? Closer, really?'

'Not as much to me, I guess.'

He stared at me for a moment.

'That's just sex,' I said, feeling even as I did so that I was digging myself a hole to fall in. 'I mean *everyone* does that.' His eyebrows went up. 'I mean, don't they?'

He shook his head. 'I'm not the expert, Anna. Don't set this up with me as Casanova.'

'They do,' I asserted. 'That's what the whole sexual revolution was about.' Bravura. I'd sat the whole thing out with Brian, practicing the piano and making curtains. 'But to get up with someone.' I took another quick swallow of wine. 'To go through all those intimacies of rising, being your ugliest, most vulnerable, least presentable self . . . it seems as though you really need to care about someone to do that.'

'And you don't care about me?'

'I don't know you,' I said.

He looked hard at me with his raisin-dark eyes. I thought of how he had risen above me on his hands the night we made love, and looked at me as though he were seeing straight through to some part of me I had only guessed at the existence of.

'How will you get to know me?'

I shook my head. I felt I was being accused of something. The waitress came, set down a paper place mat, a napkin, Leo's silverware. Through the flurry of her arms in the air between us, I could feel Leo's eyes steady on me. When she left, he leaned forward slightly and said, 'I want to make love to you again tonight. Is that going to happen?'

My heart seemed to stop for a minute, to change position in my chest. I nodded. 'Yes,' I said, and licked my dry lips. 'I want to.'

He exhaled and his breath touched my face lightly. 'Yes,'

he said. He leaned back in the booth. 'Well, you know, Anna, I discover that that's all I wanted to hear.' He grinned. 'That's it, just an ego problem I guess.'

'Except,' I said, and then raised my hand as if to push away the question that quickly rose in his face. 'No, it's just that I've got a sitter. I have to go back. It's a school night. Kind of early.'

'What time?' he asked.

'Well, maybe eleven-thirty at the latest.'

He looked at his watch. 'What am I eating for?'

I laughed. 'And that's what *I* wanted to hear.'

But we waited for his dinner, and I was glad. It gave me time to have some more wine, and I felt I needed it. By the time we walked back to his apartment, I was nowhere near as drunk as I'd been on Saturday, but I was relaxed.

We had barely got inside when Leo began caressing me, easing me towards the bed. I felt once again the sense of dropping, of heaviness in my lower body and legs, that I'd felt Saturday. We were awkward, unbuttoning, unzipping each other, and our loud breathing was the only noise above the faraway rumble of traffic on Mass. Ave. There was still a faint light diffused through the room, and Leo's body emerged white, nearly incandescent as he removed his clothes. His skin was smooth except for the shock of dark hair around his penis. After he'd pulled my jeans and underpants down, he moved between my legs on his knees, pushing my legs apart, looking down at me. I felt unlovely, awkward. I was suddenly aware of my knee socks, the harsh sound of our breathing, of a comical aspect to all of this. I tightened my legs slightly, pushed them in against him. He looked up at my face. His face was in shadow, but I could see his puzzlement. 'Don't you want me to look at you?' he asked.

I shook my head, and slid my hands up his arms, pulled him towards me. As he moved forward over me, he pushed into me and we lay still a minute. I thought of our merged shadows on the wall the night we danced, and was grateful for that same sense of obliteration.

'I like to look at you,' he said into my ear. I shook my head again. He nodded his up and down, making of those two movements a joke and a caress. His hands began to move on my body, his body to shift slightly up and down over mine. Without moving his head, without looking at me, he began to talk about me, whispering with warm breath against the side of my face and neck.

'I like your colors, Anna. Here, where you're white and pink, and these blue lines.' His fingers traced the veins on my breasts, lightly touched my nipples. 'I like all your freckles, and how different they are. Such dark dots, like periods all by themselves, and here, where they're pale and so many.' His hand moved down to my belly. I closed my eyes and he pulled away from me slightly to touch my pubic hair. His wet penis slid out of me and lay heavy and warm against the inside of my leg. 'And this wonderful gold stuff. And inside.' His fingers touched me, slid a little inside me, then up and down. I felt lost in his whispery voice, as though I were being given shape and color by him. Somewhere I heard my irregular breath click in my throat. He swung his body over me again, his cock pushed into me easily. For a while he kept talking, kept whispering to me about my body, what it looked like, how it felt. His voice deepened when he whispered, and its deepness was like a musical vibration I felt as well as heard. I moved with him, against him, and looked up at him when he rose above me again. When he came he cried out, 'Oh sweet, sweet, sweet. Oh my sweet, sweet.' For a moment I felt lost in his lostness; then abruptly another part of me, the part that insisted on my not giving myself up, took over again. I couldn't help it, holding his limp body next to, on me, I smiled. I thought of the thrush's sweet sweet call, his '*bonsoir* song,' my birdwatching grandfather had called it. My birdlike lover, I thought. And even though I knew that he had made love to me as quickly as he did because he thought I didn't want him to look at me, to pull away from me, I felt a little wash of irritation at his speed, at his limp satisfaction.

After a long interval, during which I thought he might

have fallen asleep, he rose abruptly on his elbow next to me. 'Hi,' he said tenderly. Then, 'Want wine? Beer?'

I stretched. 'Wine would be nice.'

He swung away from me and in one fluid motion jack-knifed up to a standing position. The room was heavily shadowed, nearly dark now, but even so, as he bent away from me to rise, I could see exactly how Leo was put together from his asshole to the swinging weight of his balls before they tucked front again. It startled me, pleased me some-how.

He bent over the kitchen table and turned on a little lamp. Colors leapt back into the room. He got a bottle of wine out of the refrigerator and picked up two glasses from the table. Carefully he sat back down, cross-legged, uncorked the wine and poured. As he handed me my glass he said, 'You're the silent type tonight.'

I sipped the wine, set the circled base on my breast. 'Hmm,' I said. 'And you're the noisy.'

After a moment, he grinned. 'Just 'cause I came.'

'Just 'cause I didn't,' I said.

'We could fix that,' he said.

'Could we?' I asked, and absurdly, I felt again some answering *yes* in me. Yes, I can dance, I can come, you can make me do those things, have those things.

'Sure. Then would you talk to me?'

I nodded, and we kissed gingerly for a little while, carefully balancing our glasses here and there.

I drank a little more. 'Really, I'm just silent because I'm obsessed about what I'm going to do when I need to pee.'

'I see no problem,' he said.

'I do. I'm of the shut-the-door persuasion, and you haven't even *got* a door.'

He lay back and laughed. 'I think you've got the basic differences between us down.'

'More importantly, though, I drank a lot at the Newtowne Grille.'

'I'll shut my eyes.'

Leo set his glass on the floor and began to touch my

breasts, gently circling each nipple. I watched him looking at me. Then I shifted my body away.

'I need to pee,' I said. 'It's no longer hypothetical.'

'Go ahead,' he said. He grinned at me. It was like a dare.

'Am I the only person in the world this is a problem for?' I asked him. 'What do you do when you have a party, for instance?'

'Well, there are some people who actually trek down to the Newtowne Bar and Grille rather than go here. But I set up a screen, that screen.' He pointed to a burlap-covered frame leaned against the wall next to the sink. 'Even so, those of us who get off on it can *listen*, can *imagine*.' He grinned lasciviously.

I wasn't entirely sure he was joking, but I smiled back. 'Set it up for me,' I said.

As I sat down behind the burlap screen, Leo ostentatiously whistling and rattling dishes in the space behind it, it occurred to me that there was a sense in which this might be the most flamboyant thing, physically, I'd ever done. And so, when perhaps an hour later I came, having lost track of whether it was his fingers or his mouth that was touching me, having lost any sense, exactly, of where the touch was registering, opening my eyes in that space that glowed like the inside of a cloud to see his white face rising over me, still glistening from his work between my legs, I had no sense of surprise.

We talked almost ceaselessly the first few weeks we knew each other – all the time, when we weren't making love. I fell behind on the rat work, kept postponing the runs, and only petted them. They grew fatter and more affectionate in my hands, as though responding to events in my life. I spent whole afternoons bought with day-care time in Leo's white studio, eating, making love, watching him work, talking.

The talk was really just searching for a way to claim love for someone I felt absolutely in need of anyway. Just as I'd found a way to telephone him after I'd felt the impulse to, so now I found a way to care for him, to legitimate and

134

broaden the feeling I had for him nearly from the start. He seemed to sense this too – that we were really just filling in gaps in a framework we'd already intuitively set in place. 'Let's tell each other all the good stuff,' he'd say. Or: 'Well, Anna, when you get around to hurting me, how are you going to do it?'

Eventually we told each other the complete histories, with appendices, with revisions. It was the same history each might have told anyone else, with little or no effect, but it charmed each of us absolutely because each had the desire, the will to be charmed by the other.

Leo was everything my family, Brian, I, were not. A little of it was posture – he was also very aware of what he wasn't, and of its currency in my staid world – but most of it was a genuine sort of recklessness of the heart.

He'd grown up in Arizona. His father was a cotton broker, a loser, he said; a man who'd buy a round of drinks for the house with his last thirty dollars and think later how he'd feed his family. Leo had supported himself since he was a teenager, trying whatever seemed interesting at the moment. He'd done construction work, managed a drive-in theater, been a short-order cook, an ambulance driver. It had taken him seven years to finish college at the University of Arizona, and then he'd won a fellowship at Yale.

His real name was Leonard, Len. He'd changed it when he came East. 'Len,' he said. 'A turd of a name. Who wants it? I mean, a name that ends in a nasalization, for Christ's sake. Leo, now. It's like Anna. They go on forever. You can *live* with a name like that.'

Life seemed to reach in and touch Leo in a way it never did me. Maybe because he welcomed that exciting, random touch. The phone would ring at eleven at night, and it would be friends in from Tanzania or Provincetown or Tucson. Could they stay for a week? Did he want to go camping with them? Meet them in New York? Always the answer was yes. People spoke to him on the subway, in bars, waiting in line at the movies, and he always answered. People gave him their advice, invited him to parties, sold him things. Once he even bought a gun, not because he wanted or needed it, but because he'd never owned a gun before. We were in the same bar in Central Square we'd gone to the first night, when a black guy sat down next to him and offered to sell him one. Leo wasn't sure he could take it, thought it might be too big. 'Will it fit in a bureau drawer?' he'd asked the black guy.

'What you talkin about, man?' the black man had said irritably. 'I'm talking about a *gun* here, not no *lingerie*.'

There was a certain tension between us about our differences. He liked my reserve, my coolness; but on the other hand, it was the way I had gotten angry with him in the middle of being what he called 'ladylike' that had piqued his interest. And beyond that, he said, what *really* interested him was that even then I had only suggested, 'in the most hostile tone possible,' that he stuff his *clothes* into a machine. Nothing personal. 'That was truly elegant,' he said.

As for me, it was his wildness, his openness which intrigued me, which I wanted. But it was that very quality which scared me at the start, and the security of his being *like me* in some way – professional, educated – that had let me move over the edge into his world. As for what kept me there, it was, of course, still his wildness, but it was also things like the whiteness of his skin, the way it filmed over during sex and seemed to grow paler from within; the way his hair curled over his neck when he bent once to tie my shoes after helping me get dressed. It was the fact that during sex I lost track of the boundaries between us, thought of his cock as a feeling inside me, thought of my cunt as a part of his body, his mouth. And because I became with him, finally, a passionate person.

We fought a lot about work, about what it meant to each of us. And sometimes in the heat of those fights, I'd feel a claustrophobic sense of the familiarity of the kind of standard he set for himself, for me. I'd feel I'd come full circle, back to the expectations of my childhood. I can remember raising my voice over a screaming train to yell at him that those issues were completely extrinsic to a relationship, were things individuals worked out for themselves. That people loved each other for other reasons than that.

As the train's noise faded from under it, my voice suddenly sounded harsh, strained. We sat staring at each other across the startling silence in the dining room, and he shook his head slowly.

'It ain't like that in my experience, Anna,' he said softly. 'People love each other *for* things, at least in part. Not after you leave your mom's house do you get unconditional love, love without all those things you think are so fucking extrinsic.'

My sudden teariness took me back to the time before I'd left my mother's house, to a yearning for a kind of love I felt I hadn't had even then. But it was even with some sense of release that I felt the wash of self-pity – or more precisely, pity for the little girl who also had been so exacting of herself. In sorrow for her then, I started to cry; and Leo, somehow able to sense that my sorrow reached beyond what was happening between us, held me until I'd stopped.

No fight was worse than the first one, in part because I was still in the euphoria of getting to know him, which denied even the possibility of such a thing. It was one of our earliest weekends alone together – Brian was with Molly – and we'd gone to a restaurant in Harvard Square to celebrate. Leo had given me a pink silk blouse, loose, low-cut and draped across the bosom (he thought I dressed too suburban and had given me a number of presents designed to transform me: rhinestone earrings, suede pants). I was wearing it, and feeling very beautiful. We parked the car on Acacia Street and walked through a fine spring rain to the restaurant.

We'd been making love all day and hadn't eaten anything. The wine with dinner affected us both almost immediately. We were loud and silly through the meal. Over coffee, I was talking about my piano students. I was amused with myself, very conscious of how pretty I looked in the blouse, and was, I thought, amusing him too; but slowly I noticed that he'd fallen silent. I stopped talking and there was a blank moment between us.

'I'm sorry,' I said. 'Was I talking too much?'

He pretended to be startled. 'No,' he said. 'Not at all. I was enjoying it.'

'I thought I'd noticed that you stopped, though. Enjoying it.'

He shrugged. 'I guess.' I looked across at him. In the dim light I couldn't see where his pupils ended and the near-black of his iris began. He looked away. 'I guess I just get tired of kind of the *way* you talk about your work.'

'What do you mean?'

He shrugged again, and turned slightly in his chair, as though trying to end the conversation. 'It just seems so . . . limited. Like it's just background noise in your life.'

I sensed a great danger, an oddly familiar pit I could fall into. I tried to push it away with an attempt at objectivity. 'Well, I suppose there's some sense in which that's true. But I *like* my work.'

'But it's all pretty interchangeable isn't it? I mean, the rats, the piano students, you know.'

I shrugged now. 'Well, maybe almost. Not quite. I think I feel more utilized in the piano lessons.'

Slowly, as though suppressing more violent motion, he leaned back in his chair, tossed his napkin onto the table. 'Jesus,' he said softly. 'Utilized.'

The contempt in his voice stung me into a silence that lasted for perhaps a minute. Then I started to feel angry. 'Are you objecting to my choice of words?' I asked.

He looked across the restaurant for a moment, as though he hadn't heard me. Then abruptly, he turned to face me. Quietly he said, 'It's just that I can't stand the way you think about your work, your life. You don't care about it. I mean, you don't even *have* work in the sense that I'm talking about.'

'What sense is that?' I could hear the polite contempt in my voice too.

He leaned forward and spoke intensely. 'And don't talk

to me in that fucking ladylike tone,' he said. 'I'm talking about passion. About some kind of commitment to something else besides a way to put food on the table. I mean, when I first met you, I thought you were a musician, that you cared about music.'

'I do.'

'But you *don't*. I mean, I look for some kind of parallel to the way I feel about my work and there just isn't one.'

'Why should there be?'

'Because that's what I *want*, dammit. I want a woman who has that powerful a commitment to something outside herself.'

'I have a commitment like that.'

'To music?'

'To Molly. And to doing carefully and well what I do.'

He looked at me for a moment. I thought of how he'd looked when we made love that afternoon in his light-flooded studio. 'We can't even talk about it,' he said. He picked up the bill and began rifling through his wallet.

I leaned forward and put my hands on his. He looked up. 'Listen to me,' I said. I moved my hands but stayed hunched across the table. 'It used to be that men would say, "I want a woman who" and the list would be a little different. "Who cooks, who sews, who can entertain my friends." But it's the same impulse. The same impulse. It's still *your* judgment, *your* list, your game. Just all the rules have changed.' I was suddenly aware of my breasts, pushed together and nearly fully revealed in the low-cut blouse. I leaned back. 'You're still saying I'm just an extension of you, that I'd better look good to the world so I make you look good. That's all it is.'

He shook his head. 'You're missing it, Anna. That's not it.'

'What is it then?'

'It's really that having those parallel interests, those parallel passions, makes life more *interesting*.'

'So I bore you.'

'I just don't get the way you talk about your work.'

'Because it's different from the way you talk about yours.'

'Right.'

'And if I *were* a real musician, a . . . what? A performer? A composer? What would do the trick?'

'Don't make fun of me, Anna.'

'No, I'm wondering. Really. Because I might have been, you know. I've told you that. That was the plan for me. And I just *wasn't* that good. That's all.' I had begun to cry, but strangely, it didn't, at least for the moment, seem connected to me. I could feel tears springing from my eyes and running down my cheeks, but it was as though they were glycerin, movie tears. 'And so I've made another kind of life for myself. But I *hate*, I really *hate* to be told there's no honor in it. Especially by someone as lucky as you are, with the good *luck* to be as good as you are at what you do.'

I pushed my chair back quickly, stood up and crossed the restaurant. A few people looked up at me and then quickly away as I passed their tables. I wiped at my face with my hands.

It was still raining outside, the streetlight's garish aureole making Mt. Auburn Street ugly. I turned off into Hilliard Street, and the sudden absence of that purple softened and darkened the world. Yellowish light seeped mistily from the houses. In one of them, a woman bent over a table to turn off a lamp. For a moment she appeared all grace in the orange glow. Then she was gone, the windows black, glistening with raindrops.

I heard footsteps behind me. Leo caught up with me, put a coat over my shoulders.

'You left your raincoat behind.'

I turned to him, and let him hold me against his chest. I felt a wild grief, a pain in my throat like a deep cut, but no sound came out and my tears had stopped.

'Anna, I'm sorry,' Leo said. His hand ran over my hair again and again.

'Please don't say that,' I said. 'It's what you meant. You're only sorry it hurt me, not that you feel it.'

'I'm not sure what I feel,' he said. After a moment,

we began walking, half-stumbling, half-embracing on the rain-slicked, bumpy bricks.

When we got to the truck, he unlocked my side and let me in, then walked around. I slid across the seat to unlock his door, and when he got in, I clambered over him, sat across his lap, ground against him, kissing him. The rain drummed steadily on the truck, and the sound of our breathing, the wet, light clicking of our mouths sliding over each other's was intensified in our tiny world. The windows began to fog lightly, and Leo reached up to find my underpants, to pull them down.

'It's a body-stocking,' I whispered. 'It's all one piece.'

I lifted my skirt to show him. He arched up, unsnapped his pants. I raised myself slightly, let him unzip himself and pull his stiff penis out. I bent over and reached between my legs, pulled the body stocking to one side. I moved towards him, onto him, and he came in me a little way, guiding himself with his hands. I rose off him, then down again, each time a little deeper, until he was all the way inside me. I let my weight go and felt him almost like pain, deep in me. I touched his face, moved freely on him. The windows silvered with our breathing, and when he came he cried out my name over and over. In the panting silence that followed, we could hear doubled footsteps, voices passing by closely on the street outside. 'Richard,' a man's voice said. We didn't move, didn't speak until they'd gone.

Molly liked him too, though it wasn't until I realized that this was the case that I also realized how much it meant to me that she did. Initially with her he was much less impetuous, much less active. Around her he was even, instinctively it seemed, less active with me. He let her occupy the center of my life, as she always did, and modeled his behavior on mine.

But as he grew to know her, he got more comfortable and seemed more himself. The third time he came over when she was awake, he brought me flowers, and a box of Band-Aids, three hundred of them, for her, because he'd noticed her affection for one on her knee. For days she was covered in them. At the slimmest excuse she'd slap on one, and I didn't interfere. They were hers, I told her. She could make her own rules for when she needed them. She put Band-Aids on her toys, on me, and finally, one night, on Leo. It was a turning point, her first spontaneous gesture towards him. He had a cold, was honking and sneezing into a Kleenex and complaining about his nose being about to fall off his face. She taped it on, soberly, with four or five big ones.

'God, I can't tell you how grateful I am, Moll,' he said. 'If *your* nose is ever about to drop off, I hope you'll tell me, so I can return the favor.'

Slowly she let him touch her, started to be affectionate to him. They began to have routines they'd go through, just as she'd had with Brian. He'd stop her on her way through the kitchen. 'Just a second, Molly,' he'd say, frowning. 'You've got something in your *ear*, here.' And then he'd pull a nickel or a dime out. 'My God, Molly,' he'd say. 'Look at this, that I found in your ear. Can you believe it? It must be . . . magic!' And she would grin at him, charmed, but dubious.

'Now, Moll,' he'd say. 'Who would you say a nickel like that *belonged* to? Does it belong to the person who found it? Like me? Or does it belong to the person whose *ear* it was in? For example, like you?'

And she'd have to claim the nickel, claim the magical ear, which she always did, but with a little edge of honest worry.

Three weeks after I'd slept with Leo for the first time, I bought a queen-size mattress and box spring and folded up the rollaway bed, and he began to sleep with me at our apartment. At first he would leave late at night. Then more and more, he'd set the alarm and leave at dawn. We almost always made love in that clean half-light, and it was then, in the mornings in my room, that I began to come predictably with Leo. Often I'd wake with his caressing me, entering me, and begin to get there before I was even conscious of desire. Perhaps it was the absence of all those layers of conscious judgment; perhaps it was the utter hopelessness of worrying about all the things I'd always worried about with sex – how things looked, smelled, tasted. In those early mornings it all tasted of sex after a few moments. The sheets would get tangled and sweaty. The whole room seemed full of our commingled, complicated smells. And over and over again I'd come, sometimes still nearly asleep.

Then once or twice when we were very rushed, he asked me to bring him off with my hands or mouth. I did, quickly at first, and a little fastidiously. But then I discovered that I wanted him that way too. All my initial passivity, all his energy, I realized, had made our lovemaking seem in a sense like masturbation. He was so like a fantasy, like someone I might have conjured in my solitary mornings of coming alone. I could simply lie back, as though dreaming a sexual dream, and be made happy.

But now I discovered a different kind of appetite, a kind of active hunger for his body. I loved watching him come in my hands, or feeling him, tasting him, in my mouth, the even more intense connection with him sexually that came from understanding exactly how he came the moment that he did, from helping him get there. All of that made my love for his body more intense, more absolute. I felt there was nothing I didn't want to do for him, wouldn't want him to do to me. We got wilder and wilder, even when we were simply doing it straight. It felt like some shift in dimension, not just the addition of new techniques. Once he kissed the back of my neck softly in the kitchen, and with a little gasping upheaval, I came. Sometimes just looking at his hands circling a coffee cup could stir me nearly to moan aloud.

Still we were trying to keep it from Molly. We didn't discuss it much, and by now Leo was spending three or four nights a week in my bed, but he got up faithfully each morning he slept over and was out of the house before she emerged from her room. Once or twice it was the noise of her beginning to putter in her room which woke us, but then Leo would kiss me, rise swiftly from the bed and pull on his clothes, and be gone barefoot down the long hall nearly as quickly as the half-formed memory of my dreams faded from me.

I'm not sure why we didn't tell her. She seemed irrevocably to like Leo, so it wasn't the fear that it would threaten their friendship. Perhaps part of it was simply that I didn't understand what significance it might have to her to know that he and I were sleeping together, and so wasn't sure how to explain it. As for Leo, he was again following my lead. It was a fatal part of his sweetness to follow me, even in my confusion, to assume always that I knew what I was doing with her, around her. I fostered it. I never articulated to him my anxiety, the sudden rush of feeling I sometimes had with her that I was doing everything wrong. He saw my mothering her, her relationship with me, as implacably monolithic, a given, what was meant to be, and took all his cues from that. Even the grace of his uncomplaining rising in the morning – the quick tilt back of his hips to zip his fly, the wings of his half-buttoned shirt flying out as he turned to enter the hallway – seemed emblematic to me of his assumption of rightness in whatever I was doing with Molly.

But the truth also was that I felt less confusion with her then, that I asked myself fewer questions. When I think about the whole period of time I spent with Leo, I try to rewrite it in a sense, to bring Molly more into the foreground. Surely she nibbled at my conscience, my unconscious, as she had before, as she certainly has since. Surely I always thought of her, I never took her growth, her happiness, for granted.

I don't know, really, but I think there is some sense in which during my passion for Leo, I *forgot* Molly. Maybe in no worse a way than mothers of three or four children sometimes forget one of them for a while, or women living in a time which didn't make them concentrate such energy on the issue of their children's emotional life could and perhaps did sometimes forget them. But the sense of blankness about Molly that thinking of Leo conjures for me now is as horrifying, as accusatory as the memory of her scratched and screaming in the back seat of the car at Sammy Brower's house.

At any rate, one cool night in May, long after Leo and I were asleep, something woke Molly and she came and got into bed with us. I was too soundly asleep to realize the implications of this, or perhaps some part of me was glad for the resolution it would offer and pushed consciousness away. I made room for her and fell deeply asleep again, my arm around her, Leo's body warm and smooth against my back.

When she woke in the morning, she seemed to think it was perfectly natural to find him there too. Her excitement was almost entirely transferred to the idea of having him join us for breakfast. He played along with her by insisting that that's what he was there for: to make breakfast for all of us.

And he did. Shirtless, barefoot, in jeans, his hair wild around his head, he made Molly's favorite, French toast. After that it became, as things did under Molly's stern aegis, a ritual. When Leo spent the night, he got up first, leaving me sleepy, love-satisfied, in our bed. Then he woke Molly, and it was only after I heard their voices, smelled coffee and the sweet vanilla odor of French toast cooking, that I'd rise and pull on clothes to join them.

I felt I'd never been so happy, and perhaps I never was. Our lives seemed magically interpenetrated, commingled, even as we each separated into all the day's complicated activities. I had never expected it to seem so graceful and easy, but Molly's seemingly complete comfort with Leo was like a benediction on all aspects of the relationship, even the sexual.

I remember one night her getting up (and that seemed to be the only symptom of possible trouble – that her sleep became sometimes disturbed, she appeared slightly more frequently at my bedside than before Leo came). Leo and I had been making love, and it's possible that the noise disturbed her. He had come into me from behind, and I was up on my hands and knees pushing back against him, when

I heard her shuffle in the hallway. I stilled myself, and that stopped his motion. Together we lowered ourselves, and as the bedroom door swung open, I turned towards the little halting figure. She came and stood by the bed, her face inches from mine, recarved, narrowed to maturity in the dark. She was having a bad dream, she said. Her voice was thin with terror. I held the covers up to welcome her, and she clambered in and lay down next to me. Though Leo wasn't very deep in me, I was wet, and he could easily move gently, slowly, in and out of me. I asked Molly about her dream. I held her in the curve of my upper body and smelled the damp sweetness of her hair and skin. She explained to me how she'd been playing a game when Jerome, another crazy man at day care, came and took all her toys away. She'd started a different game, and he did it again. '*Every time*, he did that, Mumma,' she said, a vibrato shaking her tiny voice.

I started to talk to her about what would happen in her waking life if Jerome did that. We speculated about which teachers would help her; I got her to imitate what they might say to bad Jerome. Her voice got dreamier, the intervals between confidences longer. Leo moved sometimes, and then lay still. I can remember feeling a sense of completion, as though I had everything I wanted held close, held inside me; as though I had finally found a way to have everything. We seemed fused, the three of us, all the boundaries between us dissolved; and I felt the medium for that. In my sleepiness I thought of myself as simply a *way* for Leo and Molly and me to be together, as *clear*, translucent. I drifted off.

Towards dawn I woke and carried Molly to her bed. When I came back, I opened the tattered shade to let the pale light flood the room. The sky was still purplish blue, whitening at its rim, to the east. The first commuter train ratcheted past, its fluorescent windows flickering like the frames of an old movie running too slowly, shots of a few groggy commuters swaying within. Leo stirred. I crossed to the bed, moved over him, kissing his face.

'Let's make love,' I said.

'Too sleepy,' he whispered, but his voice seemed to fill the room.

'I'll do the work.' I swung over him on my hands and knees and lowered my body to brush against him. By the time my face and mouth moved against his cock in the bluish light, he was hard.

In the morning when I awoke, he was gone, clattering happily in the kitchen with Molly. When I came into the room she turned to greet me. She stood on a chair at the table, wearing her seersucker football pajamas, the pants caught in the crease of her butt. With a long wooden spoon she was stirring the orange juice.

'Me and Leo thought you were never getting up, Mom,' she crowed.

I went to her. When I bent to kiss her good morning, my tongue touched the little ridges my teeth had made on the insides of my lips when I sucked Leo off.

SIX

When I was eleven, and the dream of making music still infused my life with a sense of limitless possibility, my Aunt Babe enlisted me to row her around the lake at my grandparents' camp one evening. It must have been late in the summer: the evening was dusky, the sky purplish, pricked with stars as we pushed off; even though the aunts' voices, the chiming clatter of dishes still rang out with after-dinner exuberance.

Babe was going to fish. She alone among the aunts had rod, reel, tackle box. She brought it all along. As soon as we got out far enough, she dropped her line overboard and let it out slowly, listening intently to the ticking of the reel over the water.

I was sensibly dressed against the night's chill: blue jeans, two sweaters. In the stern, Babe's bare legs winked white as she turned this way and that, adjusting the rod, bracing it to troll behind us. A big sweatshirt covered her shorts, and she wore no shoes. Finally she sat still, her knees hugged to her chest, and looked over the stern at the little rippling wake that formed with my every pull of the oars. Lights had begun to come on in the houses across the lake, and from the cove I'd rowed us into, the voices in that faraway world reached us as clearly as the voices of our parents, grandparents, cousins. From some distant radio or phonograph, brassy band music swelled and faded over the thick dark water.

Babe lifted her head and shivered. For a moment she sat staring across the dark lake at the spot the music seemed to come from. Then she bent her head and gently kissed first one, then the other of her bare knees. She shuddered again and pulled her sweatshirt over them. Never, even later in her most overt wildness, did she seem more aberrant to me, more separated from what I understood my family to be, than in that moment of tenderness to her own body.

For somehow the worldly Calvinism that my grandfather brought with him from his background came to me transmuted, feminized into a fear of things of the flesh. And the agent for this, oddly, was music. For while I made music I was innocent, still my mother's daughter. And it was in the terrifying void that music's departure from my life created that my idea of my sexuality grew. It was with the regretful sense of having failed my mother that I initially embraced my sense of myself sexually: if I could not be great, I could be female. In the changes in my body, the dirty blood that stiffened the crotch of my underwear, the uncaring interest of high school boys, I heard the fainter and fainter music of who I might have been, finally as distant and unreachable as the band music over water. My mother, maybe even sensing the strained negative equations in my head, pulled back from this adolescent side of me, now never touched me, never praised me. Her conversations seemed to be a series of admonitions against the flesh: Was I wearing a girdle? A bra? *Must* I sit with my legs crossed like that? Wear such short skirts?

Years later, during the period of the women's movement when solidarity between the generations was stressed, she took to confiding in me briefly. I was still married: her posture was as one sufferer to another. She half-pridefully complained of my father's ardor. She hinted that the reason she'd had only one child was to please him, that he'd not liked her sexually when she was pregnant. It made me remember all the signs of their passion that I'd pushed away from consciousness as a child: the locked bedroom door, his fingers pushing under sleeves, hems, to touch her flesh, his attentiveness to her moods, the odd sounds that had half-waked me one night in a shared motel room.

Too late for me. Mixed with the feeling which equated

149

being sexual with not being serious was the conviction that incarnation, even *having* flesh, was a form of mortification. When we sang in Sunday school, '*Let sense be numb, let flesh retire*,' it had the force of prayer for me, though it was only the flesh's tumult and confusion I wished away, never its pleasure; for I didn't know it could bring pleasure, so caught up was I in its other meanings in my life.

After my mother talked to me though, I thought again about Babe, about my grandparents, about her family. I saw that there were, in fact, the indications of tremendous sexual vitality in all of them, that the only truly aberrant thing about Babe was her flagrance. Nevertheless, because of the timing of the loss of music in my life, because of my confusion about what had happened to Babe in Paris, because of my repugnance for my mother's physicality (which was based itself on jealous passion for my father), I had misread all the signals. But it did me no good to know this.

Brian was the son of a Methodist minister. By the time I met him I'd slept with six or seven men in college, in the same joyless, guilt-ridden way I'd had sex in high school, though sometimes I'd feel a preliminary sensual stirring before we actually began screwing. What he seemed to offer me was a kind of moral safety net. As soon as we'd slept together he began talking about fidelity, loyalty, marriage. In that context I became more responsive to him. I liked him, understood him. He was as stern, as judgmental with himself as I was with myself. I thought that I would slowly, with his solicitousness, his loyalty as a support, become a more and more passionate person. And though from the start, certain similarities between us repulsed me – his fussiness, his prudery, his humorless tendency to make a moral issue of everything – certain others made me like him, feel infinitely tender towards him. I was initially more relaxed with him sexually than I'd ever been before. But then I saw that he couldn't change me, that we were too alike, really, to lift the other out of himself.

I was unprepared for Leo, for my own responsiveness to

him; for the sense I had that while most lost in myself, most trapped in the flesh I had to wear, I moved so absolutely away from myself, so close to someone else. It seemed undeserved, and part of me all along was uneasy with it. So, just as I was eager, relieved, to find ways separate from my satisfaction of satisfying him, I embraced the disaster, the sense of punishment I felt when I discovered I was pregnant. Ah yes, here was the price that needed to be paid for happiness.

I knew it nearly right away, just as I'd known with Molly long before I missed my period. My breasts and belly swelled; I quickly put on nearly eight pounds nibbling away at a delicate nausea which hung over me every morning like a light fog. I didn't tell Leo, though, until I'd had the test done.

It was June, an unexpectedly hot day. He came over about eight, after I'd put Molly to bed. He was working hard, trying to get ready for a show he was having in New York the next month. I was wearing a loose dress, one of the few that fit me anymore. I led him back to the kitchen. I was still washing dishes. He got a beer out of the refrigerator. He stood in the open kitchen doorway for a few minutes, looking out over the porches on the neighboring triple-decker and the young couple from next door working in their vegetable garden. Then he turned and started to tell me about a friend who'd won a fellowship, listing the varieties of ways he wanted to kill him. I moved my hands around in the warm water.

'You talk as if there's only so much room at the top,' I said. I fished a mug out of the water. Molly and Brian had given it to me for Christmas the year before. MOM it said on it.

Leo walked back to the table and sat down. 'Precisely,' he said. 'And that *prick*, that fatuous *asshole* is in my way.'

I was silent. I rinsed the mug, and reached for the utensils under the scummy suds.

After a moment he said, 'What did you do today?'

I was glad my back was to him, that I didn't have to be

responsible for the way my face looked. 'I found out that I was pregnant.'

There was silence behind me. I tried not to imagine what he looked like. Carefully I scrubbed egg off the tines of a fork. His chair scraped. He came behind me, put his hands on my shoulders and turned me to him. I held my hands, dripping, useless, in front of me. His face was gentle and sad. 'I'm sorry,' he said. He looked at me, looked for some response. I think there wasn't one. He pulled me against his chest. I turned my head to the side and looked at the things sitting on the counter. A red coffee can, crackers in wax paper, a tin of Nestlé's Quik. He was stroking my back. 'I'm so sorry,' he said again.

'Why?' I asked.

He stopped rubbing me, pulled back a little to look at me. 'Why?' he asked. He was frowning.

'Yeah. Why are you so sorry?' I could hear the edge in my voice.

He shook his head, shrugged. 'That you're pregnant. That it'll be hard.'

'Having an abortion, you mean.'

'Yes,' he said. He pulled me against him again. Where my hands had rested on it, his work shirt was spotted.

After a minute I said, 'So that's that.'

'What?' he asked.

'I'm getting an abortion.'

He said nothing, but I could feel his body tense slightly.

In a minute, when my body still hadn't responded to his holding me, he stopped rubbing me and stepped back. He wasn't looking at me. 'Is there some option you see?' he asked.

'Well, there's the obvious one.'

'Having it.'

'Yes, having it,' I said. Outside a train rattled. The dishes in the rack tinkled delicately against each other. In fact, I hadn't seen it as an option. All day as I'd gone through my routines, running three rats, three colossally stupid rats; working with Laura and then Mr Nakagawa on their pieces;

stopping at the Xerox place to pick up invitations to my students' upcoming recital; picking up Molly at day care – all day I had thought about an abortion, only that. The baby seemed real, a little Molly – though I knew it was more like a fish, a seahorse now – and I thought of it being removed from my body. And I'd wondered about the practical aspects: what kind of place I'd go to to have it done, whether my insurance would cover it. Still I was irrationally offended at Leo's assumption, at his not even having asked me what I wanted to do. I was picking a fight.

He cleared his throat, stepped to the table and picked up his beer bottle, drank. Then he shook his head. 'No. I don't. I don't see it as an option.'

'Why not?' I said.

He shook his head and stood mute a minute. 'It isn't just you, or me, or us,' he finally said. 'Though I don't think we're ready to take that step. It's more . . .'

'What?'

He shrugged. 'I'm just not anxious to have *any* kid. There's a way in which I see it as a form of self-indulgence, really. I mean, I don't think of life as being all that grand a proposition, I guess.'

I turned back to the sink and dropped my hands into the hot water. My fingers closed over a plate, and I held it, shut my eyes. After a minute I heard him walk around the table and sit down again.

'What about Molly?' I asked quietly.

'What *about* Molly?' I could hear irritation in his voice. Suddenly I purely hated him.

'You think my loving *her*, my taking care of *her*, is a kind of self-indulgence?' I was seized by a convulsion of self-pity, an image of my life as a series of selfless chores undertaken entirely on behalf of others. I could feel tears prick my eyes.

Leo sighed. 'Jesus, Anna. Do we have to do this?'

I whirled around. Droplets of water arced in front of me, were gone. 'Don't you be so fucking contemptuous of me,' I burst out. 'You're the one who started making judgmental remarks.'

'I didn't aim them at *you*.'

'Is there another person in the room who's had a child? Who's been that *self-indulgent*?'

We stared at each other a long moment. I could hear my breath rasp, the wind stirring the trees outside.

'Anna, I was talking in the abstract . . .'

'But you see the connection, I hope. Or maybe now I'm being paranoid!' Though part of me knew my hysteria was self-willed, I also really wanted to ride it beyond some boundary, to let it set me free. And I was close. I was about to be able to sob, to throw things. But Leo bowed his head and didn't answer for a while. When he spoke, his voice was soft, controlled. 'Anna,' he said. 'I love Molly. *I* love her too. And I like the way you're a mother. It's really part of what attracts me to you. But I love Molly because she's *here*.' He looked up at me. 'That's different from the impulse to have a kid, isn't it?'

I picked up the dish towel from the counter and dried my arms. I went and stood in the doorway. Below, the couple was gone, but not finished. A rake, a spade lay angled awkwardly in the black rectangle where green was pushing up in neat rows. 'Yes,' I said. 'I'm sorry.'

Behind me he expelled air. I turned. He tilted his chair back, lifted his bottle. 'Want a beer?' he asked.

'Sure.' I sat down and he brought me a beer. My throat was dry with the impulse to tears, but the cold beer cut at it, cleared away its ache. My eyes stung now with tears from that near-pain. Like Molly with beer. Leo sat down opposite me.

'I know we can't do it,' I said to him. 'I don't even really want to. But then also, I do. And it scares me, I guess, what it might mean about you and me that we know, that we know so *quickly* that we don't want to.'

'Why should it?'

'Because it cuts at all my fantasies.'

He nodded, then frowned. 'But the facts must cut at them too.'

'What facts?'

'The simplest facts about you and me. That we've known each other for all of . . . what? Two months? That we're both broke. That we're both incredibly busy and strung out. That there's nothing clear about where we'll be or what we'll be doing even a year from now.'

'What do you mean?'

He drank from his bottle, then set it on the table in front of him, began to peel the label. 'Well, at some point, I'm going to have to move to New York. That's pretty clear.'

'I hadn't realized that.'

'Anna.' He looked at me with his dark eyes. 'I've talked to you about it a dozen times.' And he had, I realized. But it had seemed a distant dream to me. I hadn't thought it pulled at him in an immediate way. Perhaps he'd even half-deliberately presented it to me with that sense of remoteness in order not to pop the bubble of transparent happiness that floated us. Hadn't he used the words *someday*? *maybe*? Or had I just interpolated them as he was talking?

'Because of your work?'

He nodded. 'Yeah. You know, finally, Boston's kind of an outpost. And after you've done a certain group of galleries or shows, there's no place left to go. I mean, I've been at the MFA, the Rose, DeCordova, the ICA. Now what?' He shrugged and ripped the tinned paper from the dark green bottle. I watched his hands as I liked to watch them while he worked, or when he was touching me.

'When will you go?' I asked.

'I don't know. I want to see what happens with you and me. To give that its time.' He looked up at me. 'Maybe you'll want to come too.'

'That'd be hard,' I said, feeling a reluctance still connected to my anger.

'Why?'

I shrugged. 'Molly. Brian. Our agreement. My life.'

He persisted. 'But maybe we'll want to work that out, Anna. That's one way it might happen.'

Suddenly I wanted to believe in it again. 'Yes. We might,' I said.

155

He looked at me a long time. Then he got up and went to the refrigerator. Standing in its open door he turned to me. 'You want another?'

'I'm fine,' I said.

He came back, twisting the cap off, and sat down again. In unison, we drank. He looked at me. 'I didn't think this could happen with the IUD.'

I grinned. I recognized the impulse to argue with reality. I'd had it too, in this case. 'Well, of course, in theory it *can't*,' I said. 'Nonetheless.'

'Well, thank God for theory,' he said. 'Let's drink to that. To the theoretical impossibility of this event.' We clicked bottles and glugged. Then we sat looking at each other for a long moment, the smiles slowly fading.

He got up again, came and stood by me and pulled me to him. My face rested against his jeans, and I could smell the faint odor of turpentine that permeated everything he owned.

'I'll come with you,' he said. 'When will you do it?'

'I don't know,' I said. 'I haven't talked to the doctor yet. Just the nurse told me the test results. I have to call him in the morning to see what comes next.'

He knelt by my chair. I bent towards him and he reached up and gently pushed the hair back from my face. 'You know I love you,' he said.

'Yes,' I said. Again I wanted the release of tears, but I didn't cry.

I was lucky, Ursula told me. It was legal anyhow. 'God, it's absolutely *mundane*, it's like going to the dental hygienist. It's like having your fucking *car* tuned up.' We'd finished her lesson and were having a glass of wine before I went to pick Molly up. Ursula sat on the couch, the late-afternoon sunlight lying like a slanted grid across her, making all her baubles and rings and earrings sparkle and gleam whenever she moved. She'd already spilled some wine on her turquoise pedal pushers, making a grand gesture. She leaned forward.

'In the *old* days, . . .' she said, and then stopped and laughed.
'Listen to me. Those bad old days.' She shook her head.
Then abruptly, she frowned. With her stubby face she looked
like a child trying to concentrate. 'But I mean it,' she said.
'It was *terrifying*. One time – my first—' I started to ask
of how many, but she raised three bejeweled fingers in
anticipation of my question, twinkled them back and forth
as she went right on. 'I was living in Philly at the time, and
that reminds me of a joke, but I'll tell you later; and God,
I had to get in this *car* on a street corner. That was the
arrangement if we can dignify it with such a term. I had six
hundred dollars in cash in my pocket, and I just drove off
with this asshole I'd never seen before, wearing *white shoes*.
This man who could have been a killer for all I knew. I
mean, I wouldn't have been surprised if my mutilated body
had turned up floating in some river somewhere. And on
the phone when I arranged it, the guy said, "Don't have
nothing to eat or drink the night before."' She raised her
eyebrows. '"Don't have nothing!" Can you imagine the
confidence that inspired, that particular double negative? I
mean I'm not a snob. I can misuse the language with the
best of them, but this particular man was going to be using
some very sharp tools on me.'

It occurred to me that when Ursula talked, she seemed
to make up for the musical discipline I imposed on her by
denying her the loud pedal.

'You almost make me look forward to it,' I told her.
'Although the dental hygienist hasn't ever been my favorite
person.'

'Oh, I know,' she said. 'The idea of those fingers, all the
mouths they've been in.' She shuddered, and another little
wash of wine leapt onto her lap. 'Shit,' she said.

'It isn't that with me. It's how much it hurts.'

She was thoughtful. 'Yes, it does hurt, doesn't it? Scrape
scrape scrape. I guess I'd kind of forgotten that.' She sipped
some wine, simultaneously brushing at the splotches on her
lap. Then she set her glass down. 'God, why are all my
objections always so *frivolous*, so aesthetic? It fucking *hurts*.

I forgot that.' She punched her thigh. 'It makes me think that Leo was right.'

'Right about what?'

'About my insensitivity to pain. About my killer instincts.'

I remembered. Leo had accused her of these things at a party a couple of weeks earlier, although among my friends Ursula was his favorite, for her casual profanity, her benevolent wackiness, her obsession with her work. But she'd been drunk and was talking loudly, persistently, about patterns of female child murder in India. There was a kind of self-satisfaction in it, but I hadn't been paying much attention to her. I was talking to a friend of Leo's (we'd embarked, a bit self-consciously, on a campaign to meet each other's friends), a performance artist who was describing a project involving a live pig.

It was hot outside, but also raining heavily. The black windows in the living room were gaping open, noisy with rain, but the air was thick, brought no relief, and everyone's flesh – there were eight of us in the room – seemed slightly filmed in the candlelight, as though we'd all been coated with a sweet glaze. Leo's and Ursula's voices got louder and louder, and I started to listen to them, though I kept frowning and nodding at the details of Steve's performance, which involved his making a film of the pig's entrance into fancy restaurants.

'Let me know what you want me to do about it, Urs,' Leo was saying. His voice was hard. 'Cut my cock off or what.'

'My God, I didn't mean for you to take it so personally. You're being *perverse*.'

'I don't think so,' he said. 'There's this accusatory note in what you say – can't you hear it yourself? This really vindictive, accusatory note, as though I should be held somehow responsible for all these female deaths, for all these little girls in India.'

I watched Ursula's little-girl face pucker with sincere, drunken intensity over the issue. 'Well, maybe in a really global sense, you are.'

I laughed, but no one noticed except the performance

artist, who turned and began listening too. Leo had twisted back in anger, and then, on the attack, leaned forward again as he spoke. 'Give me a fucking break, Ursula. And if what we're talking about here is purifying ourselves of certain *impulses*, then let me say that no matter how egregiously sexist I am, I think you've got violence problems. I think you *love* this stuff, all these . . . homicidal methodologies.'

She sat back, her button mouth open a little in pain. Then a problem, light as a moth's touch, flickered across her face. Frowning slightly she said, 'Um, do you mean methodologies, or methods?'

'Jesus!' he said. He took an enormous gulp of wine. 'I mean, what I mean, Ursula, is that you've got *killer* instincts. Got it? Or else you've just been around this stuff too long, it's got no meaning for you anymore.'

Ursula had sat nodding and nodding, examining her drunken soul. Now her face had that same self-absorbed blankness.

'I wouldn't worry about it,' I said.

'But I do,' she said. 'I mean here the whole reason I got involved with this project was because it made me weep, the idea of these little babies, just because they're girls, being *refuse*, having absolutely negative worth. And it's true, now I can go on for hours about how they did it in China, and why it's different from how they do it in Iceland, and the logical reasons for the differences fascinate me.' She shook her head, and gently stroked her wine-splattered lap. 'And here I am, telling you what a piece of cake your fucking abortion is going to be. Where are my *values*?' she wailed, and gulped some wine. 'But no kidding,' she said then. 'It'll be a breeze.'

The night before the abortion, to calm me, Leo got a babysitter and we went to the Square for dinner and a movie. We had Chinese food, and drank a lot of beer. In my fortune cookie, the little paper banner proclaimed, 'From now on, everything will go your way,' and we clinked our bottles together in honor of that thought too.

The movie was Lina Wertmuller's *Swept Away*. We had more beers afterwards and agreed we hated it. It seemed just one more version of every woman simply needing a good fuck. On the long walk home, talking about something else entirely, Leo abruptly said, 'There was one part of that movie I liked though. You know where she says she wants him to fuck her ass? She wants him to do something to her no one's ever done? I liked that. That seemed real to me, that impulse. Didn't it to you?' In the purplish light from the street lamp, Leo's white skin looked dead, gray. I looked away, over the whizzing cars on Mass. Ave. at the garish sign for the Holiday Inn. Behind the high blank fence around its pool, I could hear the happy splash of its patrons.

'Yes, sometimes I feel that way. That I'd like you to *claim* me in some special way.' I was thinking of the baby, but I knew he was not. He was high on beer and with that characteristic wound-up intensity that seemed entirely self-generated.

'And the *way* she said it.' He deepened his voice: '"Sodo-*mize* me." Like opera, no?' Now he sang it, over and over, slowly and tenderly at first, then with a Pavarotti-like tenor crescendo. People walking past turned to smile and stare. I smiled at him too; and I can still smile when I think of him, walking along Mass. Ave. on a summer night, the changing colors of storefront lights transforming him and retransform-ing him, singing imaginary Italian opera to dirty words. But even then I felt the pang of distance between us. 'Italian,' he said when he'd finished his solo. He shook his head. 'Imagine being able to speak Italian.' In his voice I could hear the pure yearning to be elsewhere, and I knew that he'd left me far behind.

In fact, the only really hard part of the abortion came just before it. The social worker assigned to me, a graying, elegant woman named Mrs Sack, wanted to talk to me and Leo about our feelings, about what the procedure would be like, about what we were going to use for contraception from now on. Her tone was kind, and I responded; but Leo stirred restlessly in his chair and didn't look at her, even when she held up diagrams and traced, with the eraser end of her pencil, what was going to happen to me. Near the end of the interview, she turned to him. A bright official smile lighted her face. '*So*, I take it this was a completely mutual decision, a decision you both feel comfortable with.' There was a moment of silence. 'Is that right, Mr Cutter?' she asked.

Staring fiercely out the window at the parking lot, Leo waited a moment before he said, 'Yes.'

She frowned at him, and then directed a few more questions at me. I told her about my yearning for the possibility of having the baby, about my worry that our decision reflected something permanent about our relationship; but said that I knew it was basically the right choice. When I was quiet, Mrs Sack sat for a moment, again looking at Leo. Then she said, 'What I find myself wondering, Mr Cutter, is whether you might have something to share with us. I mean, you seem awfully angry to me.'

There was a long silence. Then Leo looked at her for the first time and said, 'No. Nothing to share.'

She bowed her head a second, came up smiling and efficient. 'Well, then, I think we've really covered everything. Do you have any more questions, Anna?'

'No, I'm clear.'

'You feel you understand the procedure.'

'Yes.'

'And I'll be there the whole time if you have any questions then, or just need a hand to hold.'

I thanked her, and we went back to the waiting room until it was my turn. The other couples in the room were all much younger, and Leo and I, as if by some agreement, sat at a distance from them. He took my hand and held it, but he seemed jumpy still.

'What is it with you?' I asked after a minute.

'It didn't bother you?'

'No. I thought she was nice.'

He shook his head. 'A fascist. A fascist of the spirit.'

'How do you mean?'

'You're so fucking *orthodox*, Anna. You're always willing to do things the way they're supposed to be done. But none of that stuff is any of her business.'

'But she was trying to help.'

'And did she? Did she help you?'

'No. Not really. Except to understand what's going to happen. But I can see that it might help someone. Maybe one of these girls.' I nodded to the group of adolescents across the dingy room.

He shook his head again. 'In the old days, some stern old fart would just have lectured you about sin and damnation or something, but at least that's honest. Here, there's all this solicitude, but by God, it's the same thing. It's the same thing prettied up. It's really, "You've done an awful thing, a terrible thing, and now we have the right, we've got the *entrée* here to your personal life, your emotions, your sex."' He paused a moment. 'And *I'm* the asshole for not wanting to fucking *share*.'

I leaned my head on his shoulder. 'A world-famous asshole.'

He put his arm around me. 'Sorry, sorry, sorry,' he whispered and kissed my hair. And we sat like that, like the other couples, until they called me.

The doctor's voice was kind behind his mask, though I'd noticed when he introduced himself that there were black hairs which bristled from his ears and nose, a few even sprouting from the dark pores on top of his nose; and that a delicate arc of dried blood dotted the chest of his green surgical shirt. But he talked gently, kindly during the procedure to me, using the tone I used with Molly while I cleaned a cut or drew a splinter from her foot. And Mrs Sack did let me squeeze her hand as tightly as I wanted while he dilated me and inserted the vacuum. The drug he injected into my cervix before starting had rocketed to my brain by the end of the procedure, and when the nurse gently rolled me over at the hip to attach a pad between my legs, I felt the way a sleepy baby must feel when she's being diapered.

In the recovery room, the thin teenager with bright blue eyeshadow in the bed next to me talked incessantly to her social worker. Her parents were furious with her; her boyfriend had wanted her to drop out of school and have the baby, but she knew she shouldn't, that an equivalency degree would get her nowhere. 'Everyone knows it's just a piece of shit with your name on it.' From far away, I heard my own giggle.

Down the hall somewhere, a woman was having slow, persistent hysterics, and we could hear the murmur of a nurse trying to bring her peace of mind. For a while the two voices would seem almost connected, the patient singing several octaves above the nurse. But then she'd break free and her voice would loop and meander wildly in the upper registers, until the nurse's steady accompaniment brought it down again.

I began to have spasms of pain, though I could feel the blood wetting the bulky pad. One whole wall of the room was leaded windows, and the light which flooded everything seemed benevolent, seemed to consecrate the pain, the blood, the wild whoops down the hall. The nurse brought her face down in front of my unfocused eyes and asked me if I wanted a pain killer. I shook my head. I welcomed the pain, I realized, as I would have welcomed the terror, the illegality of Ursula's kind of abortion. In my drug-fogged, cramped euphoria, I was making some distorted equation, striking a bargain. And what I thought I was buying with my suffering was the right to my happiness with Leo. Every slow convulsion of my womb seemed like part of the purchase price, and I grunted softly, as I had early in labor with Molly, and counted up my treasure.

The piano recital was three days later. Because I was still bleeding heavily, Leo carried the rented chairs up to my dining room. Ursula had called twice the evening before to inquire about whether she shouldn't change her piece to something easier; and David Humez's mother woke me at eight to say that he was feeling sick to his stomach and she wasn't sure he'd make it. By three o'clock, about twenty-five people had gathered, were sitting in the neat rows Molly and I had arranged, talking in muted voices as if a church service were about to start.

David had arrived, white and big-eyed with terror, and Ursula was pacing in the long hallway, wearing her recital best, a Suzy Wong dress slit to the upper thigh. Dr Fisher, invited by Ursula, sat in the back row and smiled at me encouragingly whenever he caught my eye.

When it seemed as though everyone who was coming had arrived, I stepped to the front of the room and welcomed them. Then one by one, the students trooped to the piano and made their versions of music. First the beginners, fumbling and awkward. Then Ursula and David. Last Mr Nakagawa and Laura. The relief in the final applause was palpable, and when we moved into the living room afterwards for drinks and punch, the noise of conversation rapidly became deafening.

I was happy that everyone had done adequately, and some even well; and I had a few drinks really fast. The room, the noise, suddenly seemed to float at some distance from me. I noticed Ursula sitting on the couch as she had the day she told me the abortion would be easy, talking animatedly to Mr Nakagawa's wife. Dr Fisher, in passing, touched my shoulder, said something inaudible. I bent forward to hear something Laura's grandmother was saying, something about the Suzuki method, how awful it was for children; and with my body's motion, a little pulse of blood flowered warm and wet on the pad strapped between my legs. In my mind's eye I saw it there, the bright red of injury on the white pad, not like menstrual blood. I imagined it spreading, gathering force from deep within me, cascading down my legs, staining my shoes, the rug, in front of the polite company, the strange shameful measure of the happiness I'd earned. But no more came. And after a few minutes, I excused myself and went to the bathroom to change the pad.

SEVEN

It had gotten cooler in the night, and when I waked, I was covered with a blanket Leo must have found in the closet. It smelled of camphor, mothballs. I was disoriented by the scent, by the strange light in the room. It seemed to be coming from the wrong place, then wheeled oddly around me into familiar patterns. After a few dizzy seconds, I realized I was home. I was lying in my own bed. But it took me a moment to remember why.

Molly had left a week and a half earlier to stay with Brian in Washington for a month; and Leo and I had been spending most of our nights in his loft, at first out of a sense of adventure and liberation, but then, I realized – for me anyway – it was just as much because I was fleeing the emptiness in my apartment. I didn't like being there without Molly. Everything around me seemed to refer to her absence. And so we slept at Leo's and made love for long hours every night, since we didn't have to get up at any specific time. And often in the hot bright mornings, we'd picnic on muffins and coffee in bed, and then make love again amid the crumbs. Frequently I didn't get into the lab until the early afternoon, and the rats scolded me for food and attention.

We had come back to my apartment the night before, though, because we'd had a party in the studio, a send-off party to celebrate the opening of Leo's show in New York two days hence. We'd all gotten drunk and danced, and someone had spilled beer on Leo's mattress. At around two in the morning, we'd turned the lights out on the beer bottles, the half-empty plastic glasses and overflowing ashtrays, and walked through the still night to my place.

We didn't talk. We hadn't made love, either. I'd been angry at Leo. The party was mostly his friends, mostly artists. As a group, they seemed to me less genuinely crazy than some musicians I knew; but certainly wilder, more flamboyant. I'd felt accountantlike, orderly, moving among the wild costumes, the exaggerated speech patterns; though I'd danced, and drunk maybe six or seven beers. Towards the end of the evening, there were people sprawled all over the mattress and floor, no one speaking lower than a shout, and the open window gasping for a breeze. I had been quiet for a while, sometimes getting more beer out of the refrigerator or changing a record, or listening to one of them. Leo was watching me from time to time, with that by-now familiar mix of impatience and affection in his face. Finally he reached over and picked up a whistle one of the women had worn around her neck because she was walking home alone. He blew it and there was silence.

'And now we will have,' he swung his hand towards me, 'a word from Anna.'

Their faces turned to me, not that they really cared whether I talked or not, but because he did.

I was silent for an eternal minute.

'I think the word is asshole, Anna,' suggested Clarkie, a tall black woman who taught with Leo at the museum school. They laughed and turned away. I had laughed too, but I didn't forgive him. Still, I didn't want to fight – he was leaving for New York the next day – so when we got to my apartment I stayed in the bathroom until I thought he might have fallen into a drunken sleep. When I came to bed he reached for me, but I didn't respond and he fell quickly back to sleep.

Now I heard him padding around barefoot, coming towards the bedroom. I turned to the open doorway and watched him walk through it, carrying two cups of coffee. He was naked and his limp penis swung slightly from side to side as he walked. His skin had the luminous quality of eggshells. I felt the familiar dropping sensation in my body, the trigger for desire.

'You're awake,' he announced.

I sat up and reached for my cup. He carefully handed it to me, then crossed to the window and raised the shade, squinting into the bright light.

'It's actually nippy out today,' he said. 'Move over under there.' He came to the bed and got under the covers with me. His skin felt cool and dry.

'Mmmm. You're warm.' He sipped his coffee and set his cup on the wooden box which sat at his side of the bed. 'God, just warm me up a little here.' He burrowed towards me under the covers. I took one quick swig of coffee, set my cup down and shifted my body towards him.

His cold hands wedged between my legs. 'Oh God, you're so warm.' His hands nestled into my crotch. 'Oh warm, warm, mmmmm.' We were silent. Our bodies made little adjustments to increase our comfort. His hands got busier between my legs, and I opened them wider to make it easier for him, and concentrated fiercely on what he was doing. As I started to come, he leaned back away from me to watch me thrash around. When I had relaxed he said, 'It looked nice.'

'It *was*.' I was still breathing unevenly. 'But nice is not really the word.'

'It looked . . . *swell*. It looked smashing. It looked . . .'

'What we want is a word, a word which characterizes its *way* of being nice.'

He touched my lips with fingers that smelled of me. 'It looked fucking nice.'

I swung my head on the pillow. 'That's just an adverb. A puny modifier.'

He shook his head too. 'It's no adverb.' He moved onto me.

'Fucking is not an adverb?' I asked.

He grinned.

It was past eleven when we got up. Then we had to rush because Leo had a friend, Peter Damigella, coming over at noon to help him load his paintings for the trip to New York. He had to pick up the Ryder truck before then. I drove

167

behind him on the way back from the rental place in the Valiant, through the sunstruck and barren streets of East Cambridge, the thicket of tiny stores and bars in Inman Square, and then back up past the shopping center to his loft. When we pulled up to the side door, Peter was sitting in his car, a '62 Volvo with replacement panels of various colors, listening to a tape of jazz, Coltrane I think it was.

'God, it's yellow,' he called out. 'Fantastic. I've got color film.' And he insisted on posing us in front of the truck.

Peter was a photographer. He let Leo share his darkroom to develop the photographs Leo often used as starting points for his paintings. Peter was wiry and dark, with a mop of curly black hair and a large Zapata mustache. He'd been at the party the night before with a new woman, a model named Maisie. He'd met her doing a brassiere ad. But, he confided in me, she had no breasts. 'Little bitty titties, Anna,' he said. 'Why would they want someone like that, someone with virtually *concave* breasts, to advertise bras?' I had told him, honestly, that I didn't know; and he had gone on to ask the question of many other people at the party, until Maisie, furious, left. Only then did he seem to be able to enjoy himself.

I still have the photograph he took of us that day. The temperature had risen quickly again once the sun came up, and Leo had taken off his shirt after we'd picked up the truck. I was wearing cutoffs and a red T-shirt. We lean against the hot yellow truck and laugh at the joke Peter is telling us. When I look at the picture now what I see is the slight tilt of our bodies away from each other and the inch-wide stripe of yellow that holds us apart. My eyes are shut, my mouth open. I could either be laughing or crying out in pain.

It took us over an hour to load Leo's truck. The gallery, a good one in SoHo, wanted to exhibit all his preliminary work too. Although in every case what Leo ended up with was a large painted canvas on stretchers, part of what was interesting about his work to those in the field were the exacting studies in various media which led up to the finished piece.

His recent paintings consisted of images, figures, which he wanted to appear as existing at different depths on the canvas, as though you were looking at one through another. In some of the studies for these, he experimented with bringing various figures forward, or pushing them back, trying to see at which level the images should live. He often worked on sheets of clear plastic which he set at different depths in wooden frames with grooves built in the sides. But he also looked at the figures purely in terms of shapes, colors. For these flat studies he worked in tempera on plaster, which drank depth he said, or on gridded steel sheets. All these maquettes were heavy, awkward to carry.

Peter and Leo shared a joint before they started. I had a drag or two and then didn't like the way I began to feel. But they sat on the damp mattress and passed the joint back and forth and discussed, laughing, the various techniques they might use to get the plaster studies down the stairs. Peter told Leo about a mutual friend who'd constructed an entire puppet stage in his studio which he discovered was too large to go through the door. He'd had to knock down a part of one wall to get it out. His landlord had sued him, and it cost him about half of an NEA to have the wall rebuilt.

'Our tax money,' Peter said. He kissed his fingertips. '*Arrivederci*.'

'Not mine,' Leo said. He'd gotten up and had hoisted the first of the plaster studies onto a dolly he'd rented with the truck. He started to slide it across the floor. The wheels wailed.

'Well, what I mean is *tax* money,' Peter said. He was still sitting on the mattress, watching Leo. When Leo stopped at the door, he got up and stood by the dolly, poked it with his foot.

'Why do you pay taxes?' Leo asked. 'I don't suppose that's occurred to you.'

'Taxes,' Peter laughed. 'We all pay taxes. You have to

pay taxes. Otherwise there's not enough money for the NEA.'

Leo shook his head. 'Not me,' he said. 'I'm a painter. I *get* the NEA.'

'That's what I mean,' Peter said. 'That's how Stoney rebuilt his studio.'

They disappeared into the hall. I began to carry the canvases out to the top of the stairs. Peter and Leo were struggling on the stairs, laughing and swearing at each other. They'd left the door propped open at the bottom, and reflected light from the hot street filled the hallway, along with the jazz from the tape Peter had left playing. The next time I came out with a painting, they were at the bottom, panting in the little rectangle of light. The horn poured in from outside, as though it were the sound of sunshine; and when I passed with the canvas across the top of the stairs, Leo looked up at his work floating above him with amazement stamped on his face.

When Peter left, Leo locked the truck and came back up the stairs. I was standing in the middle of the studio, near the littered table. I was still faintly stoned. As he crossed the room towards me, I saw us both as images from his paintings: just as sometimes when you've seen a powerful movie, you speak, move for a while in ways touched by the behavior of the characters whose lives you've witnessed. My memory of that moment is strong. The studio seemed barren, our bodies huge and separate. And in the time since then, my other memories of him have become more like that, like the series of images which echo through his work. I reorder them, angle them one way or another. They become fewer, sharper, as I draw them in my mind, working perhaps towards some final version.

He was nervous. He embraced me quickly, then crossed to his bureau and pulled on a T-shirt. On the front it read SAL'S FRUITS AND VEGETABLES.

'Do you have to go right away?' I asked. I wanted to make love again.

'Jesus. I think so.' He jangled keys, coins, in his pocket.

'I feel like that's my *life* down there in the truck, I can barely stand here. I shouldn't have smoked that stuff.'

It was one of the moments when the dislocation between us seemed absolute, when I would have given a great deal not to feel so mired in my body, my needs; because I could understand so clearly his need to go, to act, to be off and away.

'Did you get your bag?' I asked. I knew he hadn't. It sat on the floor by the kitchen table.

'Of course not,' he said. 'Where is my fucking bag?' His eyes found it and he crossed to it. He picked it up and without looking at me again, he walked out of the room. I followed him out the door, locking it behind me with my key. I honestly think he might have forgotten me if I hadn't trailed along after him, blinded by the sudden darkness of the hall, watching his black silhouette bounce ahead of me into the light at the bottom of the stairs.

On the sidewalk he turned to me. Standing next to the yellow truck, he seemed to relax a little. He reached over and rubbed my neck. 'God, I'm excited,' he said. 'Sure you don't want to come?'

I shook my head. I'd decided not to for a number of reasons. The first was simply that I needed to catch up with the rats before I went to Washington the following weekend. Our indolent mornings had put me behind schedule. But also I wasn't entirely comfortable in Leo's world. And I knew if I went along it would be an effort for me to stay up 'to meet and greet the New York freaks,' as Leo put it. And that part of his pleasure would be dissipated by his concern for me, about whether or not I was having a good time.

'I'll miss you,' he said.

I smiled at him.

'A little anyway,' he said, grinning back. 'When the pace slackens, you'll be there, driving me mad.' He nodded. 'True,' he said.

'Well,' I said, 'here's hoping the pace never slackens.'

We stood, facing each other foolishly, smiling. Then he leaned forward and kissed me gently.

171

I looked at him a long moment. This was the first time since we'd met that we were going to be apart. 'Is that it?' I asked. 'You're going to leave me mooning around here alone for three days and that's all I get for good-bye?'

He dropped his bag and grabbed me, bent me backwards at the waist. Flailing, I felt his lips, his tongue all over my face and neck, in my mouth. Someone on Mass. Ave. whistled loudly.

Then we stood panting, grinning at each other again. Moisture cooled like a private breeze over my face. 'That was to grow on,' he said. He turned, walked to the truck's door, unlocked it and swung his bag and himself up. The engine started, and the yellow monster eased slowly away from the curb. He beeped twice, froglike and thick as he rounded the corner out of sight.

By the time I got to the lab, it was two in the afternoon. Even as I turned the key in the lock on the rat-room door, I could hear the animals beginning to stir. When I opened the door, their excitement made a buzzing, a fretful vibration in the air. I turned on the overhead lights, and the low flickering hum of fluorescence provided a steady accompaniment as I began to go through my routines. I fed the rats I wasn't going to run, caressed them. The sound of the cages sliding in and out made the remaining rats more and more frantic. When I pulled their drawers forward, they'd be riding the front edge, their delicate paws on its lip, sniffing at me, turning their heads sharply from side to side to get me in focus. It may have been the faint aftereffect of the dope, but my senses were somehow dilated. I had an acute feeling of pity and tenderness for the rats that afternoon, their short days beginning with the opening of the drawer, their definition of life, I imagined, formed largely around whatever it was they perceived me to be. When they faltered in the maze, as several of them did, when they took seventy or eighty tries to make the requisite ten right-hand turns in a row, I felt none of the irritation and impatience I sometimes had towards them.

Once in the long afternoon I stopped for a break, and

wound my way through the corridors to the food machines in the basement. As I stood there eating bologna and cheese on Wonder Bread, sipping a diet Pepsi, four o'clock came and went, and the students, released from their classes, flooded past me like water around a rock, talking of parties, teachers, sexual attraction. The silence they left behind them astonished me. I walked slowly back to the lab, my sandals slapping loudly down the tiled corridors. Many of the doors were shut now, happy experimenters having gone home early for a long weekend.

Under the fluorescent lights in the windowless room, I lost all sense of time. I ran four or five more rats in a haze of tenderness. I was startled when I stepped into the corridor to check the wall clock and discovered that it was nearly seven. I went back in and fed the few rats I hadn't tested yet, petted them, then washed the animal smell off my hands. I took the charts of the rats I'd done up to Dr Fisher's office. He was away, spending the month on Martha's Vineyard with his family. Before he'd left, he'd picked up in his office; and this evening as I entered it, I was startled again by its uncharacteristic tidiness. His desk was bare, his jackets and sweaters hung in a row on pegs on the wall. The papers on his spare table were stacked, squared off in orderly piles. Even the grains of Cremora and sugar that usually laced the table around the coffee machine had been wiped away.

I felt utterly solitary, alone in a way I couldn't remember feeling in a long time, perhaps not since before Molly was born. I sat in Dr Fisher's chair, looking for a kind of company, I suppose. Through the leaves of the sycamore I could see in the fading light outside the angle of a shoulder of someone walking by underneath, the rhythmic swing forward of his alternating feet. I turned to Dr Fisher's desk. Facing me on it was a photograph of a young woman, her hair and clothes in the style of the Fifties, her lips dark and shining around her smiling mouth. She was coming down the steps of some remote front porch. One foot was missing under the circle of her wide skirt. The other was pointed out, wearing a ballet slipper. Her head was slightly bent under the blow of the sunlight. I picked the picture up and stared at it. His wife. It touched me, the notion of his wanting to remember her like this, to think this kindly of her. I knew from Ursula that she'd spent the month just before this vacation drying out in a clinic. And Dr Fisher himself had told me he was taking more time away from his work this summer than he ought to, but that it was very important to his family that he be around. My notions about the place I occupied in his fantasy life seemed suddenly shabby to me. I set the picture down. I got up from his desk, shoved the new data into a folder in my pile on the spare table and left the office.

At home, too, my state of heightened awareness persisted, like the sense of deep pleasure in ordinary things you have after recovering from a fever. When I came into the front hall, the last slants of pinkish sunlight fell through the living room windows. I stood in the hall for a moment, then sat in the living room until the darkness had thickened outside, unwilling until then to leave the light's last traces.

I walked down the long dark hallway to the dining room without turning on the lights. There, the purplish light from the lamps above the train tracks pulled me towards the piano. The ivories gleamed cold and pure in the light. I sat down and played, from a part of my memory I couldn't have consciously exercised, all of Mozart's Sonata no. 7 in F major, a piece I'd had for a recital in my early teens. My fingers looked like someone else's as they moved across the keys in the strange light.

I moved slowly around the kitchen preparing myself a fancier dinner than I'd planned – cold squash soup, lamb chops, minted zucchini. I set a solitary place for myself in the dining room, lighted a candle against the glare from outside, opened a bottle of red wine and poured myself a full glass. I ate slowly, and when I was finished, sat at the table sipping another glass of wine. I was imagining a solitary life for myself, a life in which I had only my own schedules, my own work and pleasures to consider. I was imagining this life with a sense of yearning strong enough to make me wish Leo away, even Molly, when the telephone rang. I remember that I got up and went to answer it with such eagerness, such gratitude, that I was conscious of feeling a kind of private embarrassment at my capacity for distortion. In this confusion of feelings, it took me a moment to recognize Brian's slow voice. But he didn't greet me, just began talking, began telling me about having tried to reach me all day.

I interrupted. 'What is it? Is something wrong?'

He laughed, an unfamiliar laugh. 'Oh, not now. No, Molly's fine, if that's your concern.'

'What is it then?'

He didn't answer for a moment.

'Brian?'

'I'm just calling to warn you.' His voice was flat, had gained a higher pitch. 'I'm keeping her.'

'What do you mean?'

'She's staying with me. With me and Brenda. She's not coming back to you.'

'What are you *talking* about?'

'You just ask your boyfriend. Ask him what I'm talking about.'

'Leo?'

'*Leo*. Yeah, Leo.' He said it venomously. 'Yeah. Ask this Leo fellow why I'm taking Molly away from you.'

'Brian,' I said. I could hear the fear in my own voice. I felt I was trying to conjure the Brian I knew, that this was some nightmare version I didn't know how to talk to. 'Tell me what you mean. Tell me what you're talking about.'

There was a silence. Then he said, 'Right. You've got no *idea* what I'm talking about. Right?'

'That's right,' I said.

'Well then, Anna, I'm calling out of a sense of fairness. I've filed papers, there'll be a hearing, you'll get a subpoena fairly soon. I'd get a lawyer if I were you. Lots of people wouldn't even have warned you, but I still have some feelings, I still have a sense of what we . . .' his voice caught, and I waited. He didn't go on.

'Brian,' I whispered. 'Tell me what you're *talking* about.'

I had to wait for perhaps thirty seconds. His voice was calm, but thick, nearly unrecognizable to me. 'He's living with you?'

'He has his own place, but he's stayed here a lot, yes.'

'You've left her alone with him?'

'Brian, she's known him for months now. She likes him. They have fun together.'

'*Ask* him about the fun, Anna. Ask him how much fun he had with my little girl.'

'What are you suggesting? That he did something wrong with Molly?'

'He did, Anna.'

'He didn't.'

Brian laughed bitterly. 'That'll be the argument, Anna. In court. In court.' His voice began to tremble. 'And let me tell you. You better get someone good, because I'm going to win this. She's told me, she's told the shrink. He *did* it, Anna. You ask him.' I didn't know what to answer. 'And *you* let him. You're in charge of her. And *you* let him.'

'He didn't do anything to Molly,' I said. 'I know that.'

There was a cold pure hatred, contempt in Brian's voice. 'I'm not going to argue this with you, Anna. I wanted to call you, and even this much was probably a mistake. But I'm telling you because I still . . . because I still have some feeling for you. Some *pity* for you. But I'm not going to argue with you over the phone. Just . . . just get a lawyer. Get a fucking lawyer.' And he hung up.

I stood in the dark kitchen for three or four minutes, listening to the dial tone. When the wail that signaled I should hang up came on, I set the telephone gently in its cradle. Then, after, I think, a few minutes more, I went to find my address book, to look up Brian's number. I remember stopping in the dining room to look at the table. The wineglass sat, still half full, in the candlelight. A crescent of blood beaded with butter congealed on the plate's inner circle. I felt as though the person who had consumed that meal had been someone else, occupying another world. Yet I still didn't accept any of what was going on as real. It wasn't until I'd tried calling Brian six or seven times in the next few hours, sometimes waiting half an hour between calls, sometimes only a few minutes; sometimes letting it ring thirty or forty times, that I began to believe that he was going to do what he had said. And that he believed what he'd said about Leo.

I was sitting in the kitchen. Somehow I hadn't wanted to turn the lights on, so I'd brought the candle in from the dining room. It had burned nearly all the way down. The purplish white glow of the lights over the train tracks seeped into the kitchen too. I had no sense of what time it was. The time I'd existed in since the call had all been framed as the time *until I got through to Brian* – the real Brian, the Brian who would explain everything.

Abruptly, though, in the midst of one of the calls, listening to the ring of what I understood now was probably an unplugged, unringing phone, listening to that sound which wasn't really a sound anywhere in the world, I realized I wasn't going to get through. And that the reason I wasn't going to get through was that Brian didn't want to talk to me. And suddenly I began to think about what Brian had said about Leo. I stood up, hung up the phone, and turned the kitchen lights on. Squinting, feeling as you do when you're abruptly wakened from deep sleep, I moved nearly automatically to pick up my dirty dishes; ran the water and squirted in the thick white soap, viscous as come.

A dozen images of Leo and Molly together swelled and faded in my mind. One evening I had gone into the labs after dinner, and come home to find them both asleep on our bed, Molly hugging close a stained rag doll she had named Veronica, a book fanned open on Leo's belly, its upright pages waving delicately as palm fronds with his slow breaths. Leo, holding Molly in the water at Walden Pond earlier in the summer, his big white hand stretched across her chest and belly, obliterating them, his other hand supporting her invisibly under the water. 'I've got you,' he'd said. 'Pretend you're taking a snooze here, 'cause I won't let you go.' And she'd lain back in absolute trust, looking up at his face while he, the magician, levitated her body horizontal and motionless on the surface of the clear brown water. Leo bathing her, Leo wiping her bottom, Leo gently toweling soap out of her eyes during one of her disastrous biweekly shampoos. Leo dancing her around the living room, her tiny bare feet desperately gripping his sneakers, the two of them twirling and twirling to Johann Strauss. I realize now that I was examining these pictures as though they were maps of Leo's subconscious. At the time, though, all I felt was a terrible tension as they rose in my mind. My hands had clenched tight under the flow of the water. I made them relax. It was impossible. He hadn't done anything. I knew it. I knew it.

But Molly had told Brian he had. So something must have happened. Something she misunderstood, or perhaps something she'd seen go on between us that we hadn't been aware of her knowing, something she'd played out in her imagination. I wanted to call Brian again then, to call him and explain to him about Molly's imagination. About the time her teacher had told her how big, how grown-up she was getting; and Molly had burst into hysterical tears because I'd told her when she was grown up she'd move away from me and have her own house. About the time I'd called the woman on the first floor a witch because she objected to our music; and Molly claimed she'd seen her in the night floating outside her window, with a pointed hat on.

Perhaps Molly had *imagined* some sexual contact with Leo. She did have romantic feelings about him, Oedipal feelings. She'd told him she wanted to marry him when she was big. 'Then you'll be the daddy and I'll be the mommy,' she'd said.

'Great,' he answered. 'And what can *your* mom be? The refrigerator?'

We'd all laughed.

'*Leo*,' she'd said, trying to bring him back to earth, her earth.

We'd had her in bed with us from time to time. And of course, there was the night Leo had stayed inside me after she'd climbed up next to us. But she was asleep then. I had been holding her, had felt her deep relaxation. And always, I thought, there'd been some final clear boundary between Molly and whatever went on with me and Leo. Always.

When I finished the dishes, I stood for a moment looking down at the kitchen floor. It was black linoleum, with speckles of red on it, as though someone had dropped a bucket of paint, or blood. I could see food spills, sticky spots here and there too. I got out the mop and bucket and washed it. It was almost midnight when I was done.

I went into my bedroom and pulled the shade against the train lights and lay down. But sleep didn't come. I kept reviewing what I'd say to Brian, to Leo, how I would make everything all right. Sometime around two, when the lazy rumble of a late-night freight mocked me by gently rocking the bed, I got up. I heated up some milk, poured in a slug of bourbon, and ran myself a hot bath. But even after two trips to the kitchen to refill my mug, I couldn't derail my brain. It kept running around the same track, trying over and over to arrive at the same destination, to establish the inevitability of that destination. I lay in the tub and watched the steam rise and thought that I just needed to get through to Brian, to explain how impossible it was, how wrong he was. I imagined flattering him, cajoling him, suggesting I fly down to Washington and meet him for lunch. At four in the morning, I stood dripping in front of the bathroom mirror, alternately wiping the rising steam off the cool silvered glass and applying makeup. I had taken out an old collection of partly used up lipsticks, pencils, eyeshadow sticks. Somehow I had it in my mind to try to reproduce what had been attractive for Brian when he first loved me. I remember that I was neither ashamed nor embarrassed to be doing this. In the desperation I know now I was pushing away, it seemed the perfect answer. I was using it, I think, to give me direction, motion. And I was moving fast. In a kind of frenzy of purpose, I picked up a peeling bronze tube and opened one end. Inside was a tiny stump of cold metallic blue. I leaned over the sink towards the mirror and stroked the color on my eyelids. I lined my eyes, top and bottom, with black. I smeared on foundation and painted my cheeks with a color called Dusty Rose, my lips with something called Lickety Pink. I took out the electric curlers I hadn't used for months and heated them up. When I extracted them from my hair, it fell into something like the curls I'd worn early in our marriage.

I walked naked into the bedroom. From the back of my closet I pulled out three or four dresses I'd worn when we were married, dresses Brian had liked. Two I rejected as being old-fashioned, outdated. But I tried on the other two, back and forth, over and over. I finally settled on a black silk shirtwaist, the kind of dress I'd sometimes worn to the symphony, or to a dinner given by someone in Brian's law firm. I put on panty hose, heels; then spent some time deciding what jewelry to wear.

When I was ready, I opened the closet door and looked at myself in the full-length mirror. I was nearly unrecognizable, someone pretty and brittle and utterly cold. Somehow, this satisfied me at the moment. I went into the kitchen to get some wine. Abruptly and nearly without consciously deciding to do so, I dialed Brian's number again. It rang and rang. I hung up. I took the wine into the living room. I sat on the sofa, sipping it rapidly. Outside, the sky was whitening fast, the beginning of day. I got another glass of wine and drank it, and then another. I lay back, just to rest a moment on the couch, and almost instantly, gratefully felt the dizzying slide away that I knew would be sleep.

I awoke with complete alertness several hours later, as though startled by a loud noise. The odor of the makeup I was wearing was like the scent of misery. It brought back the feeling before I remembered why I should have it. I got up and turned off the lights I'd left on – nearly every light in the house, except in Molly's room. I thought of how it must have looked in the night to a stranger's eyes – a lone rider on an unheard train, someone walking by himself down the dusty street – blazing brightly, lit for disaster.

In the bathroom I looked a long time at myself in the mirror, trying to remember the impulse that had brought me to this: the rumpled dress, the flattened fake curls, the smeared makeup ringing my eyes, flaking on my dry lips. The foundation I'd put on had formed a delicate white tracery in the tiny creases on my face, like a photographic negative of my own growing old.

I washed it all off with soap and a washcloth. Then I changed into jeans and a shirt. Numb with lack of sleep, but feeling a little restored to myself, I went into the kitchen and called Brian's number again.

Brenda answered.

I asked for Brian.

She said he wouldn't talk to me. Her tone was calm, absolute.

'I need to talk to him, Brenda. He's wrong about this.'

'He really can't talk. I didn't even want him to call you last night. It's just not kosher in this situation.'

'He's wrong about this. I can explain it to him. Let me talk to him.'

'I can understand how you feel, but I can't let you talk to him. We'll all talk in court.' She was not unkind, just secretarial, impersonal.

I tried to keep the same quality in my voice. 'Look, Brenda. What he thinks happened, whatever he thinks happened, it just didn't. I know that. It just didn't happen.'

She didn't answer, and after a moment, the line went dead.

I pushed the button down and dialed again. She answered.

'It's Anna again, Brenda. I'd like to talk to Molly.'

'I'm sorry,' she said crisply.

'What?' I asked. 'Sorry what?'

'I can't,' she said.

'She's my child. I want to talk to her.' I could hear my voice get strident.

'She's not here now,' Brenda said.

'When will she be back?'

'Anna, I can't let you talk to her at all until this is settled. Surely you can understand that.'

'No.'

She paused. I could hear her expel air. Then: 'Look, Anna. I don't want you to call again. If you call again, we'll have to take some action on the calls themselves, do you understand? We're in adversarial positions here. There's no possibility of communication between you and Brian or you and Molly. It's just out of the question. Do you understand?'

I said no and she hung up.

After a minute I dialed again. This time Brenda's very pleasant tape-recorded voice came on saying they couldn't come to the phone right now, but if I wanted to, I could leave my name and number at the sound of the beep.

I hung up.

For a while I stood in the kitchen. I have almost never again had the feeling I had then. I simply didn't know what to do next; and it seemed to generalize, the feeling, so that I didn't know even whether I wanted to go to the stove and fix coffee; or to try to go to work; or to sit for a while, or to raise my hand, or to close my mouth. I'm not sure how long I stood like that, feeling I had to do something but not knowing what. Then I was aware of a sharp pain in my throat. Tears began to slide down my face. In the release of some absolute tension, I sat down on the clean kitchen floor and wept – as much, I think, out of terror at that moment of powerlessness as out of the thought of the seriousness of the situation.

But I only let myself cry for a few minutes. Some other kind of terror seemed to wait in that direction. I wiped my face. Then I got up and made coffee. Once again I reassured myself, was conscious of reassuring myself: it would be all right, because it *was* all right, because nothing had happened, and we could clear it all up. Everything would be fine, everything was fine, really. I think I may actually have been talking out loud. At any rate, suddenly I wanted some other noise, a voice. I turned on the radio, and listened for a few moments to the deep self-satisfaction in Robert J. Lurtsema's voice, caressing every syllable even of the record labels he had to announce, *Deutsche Grammophon* in this case, the conductor also Germanic and delicious to Robert J. The music was Schubert. I sat down at the kitchen table with my coffee and tried to let it seal me off from my world. For a few moments I succeeded; but then I resisted. I remembered that I'd always objected to this answer in my musical friends: hum a few bars and the problems of the world slipped away. I thought of a woman I'd played with in a weekly sight-reading group just after college, Susan Van Dusen – she'd inexplicably held on to her maiden name. In one of the last fights she and her husband had before they split up, a fight during which she actually turned away and started to play Vivaldi, he broke her viola and hit her with one of the pieces. She showed me the marks the strings had made as they whipped across her arm. But even as I looked at the thin red stripes and clucked over his brutality, I felt some compassion for him. Rome could have burned down as she deedled away. I turned the radio off.

My address book was still lying on the kitchen counter by the telephone. I flipped through it, found my lawyer's number. I let it ring as I had Brian's telephone the night before, over and over. Then I realized I was using the hollow noise to feed a feeling of helplessness in myself. In disgust, I hung up. I had his home number. If I really wanted to reach him, I told myself, I could bother him at home. If it was real, if Leo really had done something, I could call him, now, at home. If it wasn't, I could wait until Monday and call him at his office, tell him Brian had gone off the deep end. I found my car keys, put on some lipstick, and left for work.

At BU, the long corridors were deserted, the doors locked, though the animal smell, just to the right of barnlike, leaked out and hung in the antiseptic halls. Today I felt a tremendous distraction as I handled the rats. I made errors. Two of them I simply lost count on, failed to record a couple of trials. I had to discard their data, return them to their cages and put the ominous X on their feeding charts. One animal I dropped; and though he wasn't hurt, it took me a long time to coax him out from under the cages. I knelt on the floor with my head down and we looked at each other. I made gentle noises to him, kissing sounds. Finally I set a little trail of pellets. He came out, nibbling, and I scooped him up. I sat on the floor for a little while, petting him and watching him eat in my hands before I discarded him too. As I slid his drawer back in, I realized I was again near tears. It made me angry at myself.

When I got hungry, I couldn't bear the thought of eating alone at the machines. I decided to go to Kenmore Square to a delicatessen. The Red Sox were playing at Fenway, and the square was thronged with honking cars, with people pushing past each other, buying hats, peanuts, Red Sox banners. I sat in a booth by the window in the delicatessen and drank three or four cups of coffee with lunch, watching the crowd until it thinned to normal levels. Then I went back to the lab. I stayed there until evening again. Whether it was the coffee or not, I found myself able to concentrate now. I pushed everything else out of my mind, and focused on the rats, the choice they had. I was supposed to punish them for a wrong choice by dropping a trap door behind them, shutting them into a tiny dark space with no food, no way out. They were to stay there for one minute as negative reinforcement, then be released, petted, and started again. In the morning, one of the mistakes I'd made more than once was simply to forget the rat in the box for several minutes. A couple were panic-stricken, too upset to go on by the time I got them out. One had tried to bite me.

Now I was machinelike and efficient, my eye on the clock, my hands poised to open the maze. I handled the rats smoothly, reassuringly, even several very stupid rats who took an hour or longer to complete the task.

When I drove back over the BU bridge to Cambridge, the sun was setting over the river in garish hues that would have put Maxfield Parrish to shame. A lone power boat made its way up the river, its wake cutting the glassy pink into a furious roil that stretched into even ripples wide behind it. I descended into the shadowy residential streets below Central Square and passed the large Victorian house which contained Ursula's oddly shaped apartment, full of windows you had to prop open with sticks, floors which tilted towards the corners. She was away now too, visiting her mother who lived in New York. It occurred to me that I hadn't thought of her, hadn't missed her since the call from Brian. I would be ashamed to discuss it, I realized, even with her. For some reason, this frightened me momentarily.

As I got closer and closer to home, I felt a powerful resistance to going there, to being alone in that space. What I saw in my mind when I thought of it was Molly's room, the telephone, the piano. I drove past my street and parked on the side street by Leo's studio. I went up the dark hallway and let myself in. The spotlights overhead burned at my eyes, made me squint. I quickly turned on the little lamp on the kitchen table and switched them off. I stood and surveyed the room. With so much of Leo's work gone, the studio seemed especially vast, the walls dirty and bare. I got some crackers and cheese out of the refrigerator and sat at the table to eat, looking with fresh eyes at the familiar things around me, curiously charmless in the new arrangement and without Leo.

When I'd finished eating, I washed my few dishes. Then I crossed the room and bent over a box of papers by his worktable. I began by telling myself I just wanted to go through his work, the things he hadn't taken with him – his earlier drawings, for instance – to see what they were like, how he'd changed; to comfort myself by being close to the things he had made. But very quickly I stopped pretending. I was asking myself whether I really knew him. How well I knew him. I was looking at his things to see whether he had secrets from me. His apartment, his possessions became a kind of adversary from which I wanted to wrest a kind of answer. Are these the things, the creations, the belongings, of a man who would molest a little girl, my little girl, Molly?

There was no storage space in the studio, but pushed against the walls, under the tables, into corners, were wooden boxes – orange crates, crates that had held olive oil, Chinese food – and they were all jammed with papers, photos, sketches, letters, notes from other people, from Leo to himself. I worked my way up to a secretarial speed rifling through them. What had been an idle flipping through the leaning canvases, the boxes of sketches and papers, became methodical, then frenzied. I opened old mail, bills. I looked through photographs, box after box of early drawings, notes, lists. I opened his drawers and pushed his clothes around. When I slid the top drawer of his tall bureau open, I was startled momentarily to see the gun he'd bought when I first knew him. It was still folded into the white handkerchief it had been wrapped in when he'd gotten it; but its muzzle stuck out, shiny and black in the dim light.

And in one of the boxes there was a folder of pornographic photos and sketches, but I'd known about those too. Leo was fascinated with the inability of painting, print, to convey a sense of the pornographic in the way photography did, and with what that suggested about the visual imagination. He had done a whole series of preparatory works for a painting he was going to call *Olympia*. He was working with images from pornography. I picked up one 8 × 10 glossy – a woman on her hands and knees, her open cunt, ass towards the camera, her head staring upside down at the photographer from under her dangling breasts – that made me remember abruptly the posture Molly had assumed one night, after her bath. We'd been in the living room talking, and she was running in and out naked. I'd asked her four or five times to find her pajamas, but she was clearly enjoying the way the air felt on her flesh. When she bent over and looked at us from between her legs, what she'd said was, 'I see you.'

'Yeah,' Leo said. 'And *I* see *you*.' We'd all laughed at our different jokes. Now I put the picture back in the stack, next to the woman playing with herself, the two women licking each other.

'I think what it is with photography,' Leo had said, 'is that everyone gets off on the idea that the real woman was *there*, was willing to *do* that. Nobody thinks about the photographer. Whereas a drawing, a painting, is always in some sense about the artist, the way he thinks. And that does something else for some folks, but it doesn't turn anyone on. I think.' But he'd tried playing close to that line, to where, he said, the image was pure, impersonal, was lifted nearly without translation from photography. And he had reviews from his shows which indicated that his work struck particularly some feminists as pornographic. But, he argued, they were focused in a knee-jerk way on content, not on effect. 'Take your average group of sleazy *guys*,' he said, 'and they'll tell you loud and clear that's not pornography.'

I couldn't help realizing as I went through Leo's things how they would strike someone else, how they would strike Brian. There was dope in the refrigerator, the gun in the bureau, these photographs and drawings. The room still had beer bottles, glasses with cigarette butts floating in them stashed here and there from the party, though Leo, Peter, and I had all picked up a little as we moved the paintings out. The toilet, permanently stained and scarred, hunkered close to where we fixed meals. I saw all this with clear eyes that night, with the eyes of a social worker, a lawyer; but I still would have defended it, and Leo. Because although Leo was keenly aware of the way he lived as having a seedy romance, though he cultivated his own bohemianism, it was at the same time the honest outgrowth of a balance he had struck in his life having to do with the importance of his work to him. It was familiar to me, dear to me, like the price you paid for music, though most of my friends who'd made it in music had passed earlier out of this stage. But Leo had started later because of where he'd come from, his background; and he'd only slowly taken in what he needed to change. And here he was. The only real alternative to begrudging his work the poverty it cost him was his flamboyance in enjoying it. So, although I could understand that some of the poverty, the weirdness, was self-indulgent, self-willed, I saw even that as connected to his work, and I admired and envied him for all of it.

No, the things I was surprised at, disturbed by, were other. There was a slim sheaf of letters held together by a fat dirty rubber band, letters from Leo's father. I read the top one without taking the band off. In a child's careful script he asked Leo for money, told him about a convention for cotton brokers he'd been to in Dallas. Leo always spoke of his father with such contempt that I was startled that he'd keep letters from him. It suggested a vulnerability he wouldn't have acknowledged to me.

And there was a whole group of photographs of Leo with other people in someone's studio, probably in New Haven, where he'd known so many artists. He'd described his life there as a kind of continuous rotating studio party. In three or four of these pictures, Leo had his arm around the same girl, a pretty girl with burned-out eyes. I recognized her. She was moderately well known in the New York art world now. I knew that Leo had known her in New Haven too, but the pictures argued for a different kind of relationship from the one he'd described. There was no reason for him to have made clear to me whether or not they were lovers. And maybe they hadn't been, after all. Or maybe it had been brief, unimportant, an affair that lasted for a week, or a few months, for a few parties in different studios. But not to know, to be surprised by anything at all about Leo right now made me uneasy. I thought of calling him in New York – I had the number of the friend he was staying with. But then I remembered: today was his opening, his party. Even if he was back at his friend's house by now, he'd be high, he'd be surrounded by people, he wouldn't be able to give me what I needed: reassurance that he was exactly as I thought he was.

When I stopped rifling through things, it was on account of a wave of fatigue as dictatorial in its strength as the relentless energy which had kept me up nearly all night the night before. I crawled into the bed. It still smelled of beer. For the second night in a row, I fell asleep with the lights on.

On Sunday, my first thought on awakening was that Leo would be home that night. As I got up, washed my face, I held that in my mind: he would be home, he would tell me it was a mistake, he would help me get Molly back. I went to my apartment to change my clothes. I moved through it quickly. I avoided looking at her toys, her books, the photographs of her everywhere. I realized how little I'd thought of her, purely her, since Brian had called. I'd imagined scenes with her and Leo, but I'd not let myself miss her, think of her, think of my life with her, for fear that it would bring slamming after it the panic of the possibility of life without her. That was not possible. I didn't even look into her room while I was home; and I went out for breakfast, to a little basement restaurant in the Square. I sat for a long time over the paper, pushing my way slowly through articles I'd find myself reading sections of six and seven times in a row. A woman who worked in the day-care center came in and sat down at a table near me. She nodded at me, but was with a man who talked loudly and steadily to her about the efficacy of co-counseling for as long as I sat there. Others in the restaurant looked hard at him, rustled their papers, turned their bodies away. Oblivious, he rolled on enthusiastically, talking about human potential, about how he'd successfully gotten out of what he called his 'victim space.' Helpless, she listened and nodded politely.

I finally left. I'd begun to yearn for the silent company of the rats. At the door, though, the day-care teacher caught me. She was plain, with long flat hair, and she wore thick glasses. I remembered that they slid down her nose when she bent towards the children. 'I wanted to ask,' she said breathlessly, making a kind of apologetic gesture towards the air behind her, 'about Molly, how she's doing at her father's.'

'Oh, that's nice of you,' I said. 'Fine, I think. I'm supposed to go see her this weekend.'

'Oh, *neat*,' she said with absolute sincerity. 'Please say hi to her. Tell her we miss her.'

'Sure,' I said, and started to turn.

'It's Maggie,' she said. 'My name. In case you forgot.' And she went back to her aggressively empathic friend.

Through the afternoon I carried her image with me. Maggie. Molly had liked her, though she wasn't the head teacher, wasn't there every day. Once in the fall when I was doing parent time at the day-care center, I'd watched her in the bathroom with a group of Molly's friends. She got the two girls settled on the toilets, then helped unsnap and unzip the three little boys. As they stepped together up onto the platform which made the urinals their size, Maggie had paused, poked her thick glasses up her nose, and then said, 'OK, you guys? Ready? Aim . . . fire!' Two of them squirted each other, turning to her to laugh at her joke.

It seemed talismanic, a good omen to have seen her. For the first time that weekend, I let myself think about Molly, about how of course I'd see her the next weekend, about what we'd do. I imagined her compact and smooth body, its belled-out stomach and stubby legs. How she smelled, how her thin straight hair felt on my cheek, like a delicate expensive fabric.

I had fewer rats than I'd thought left to run, and I was finished by about five. I went home and took a bath, put on fresh makeup. When Leo wasn't there by seven, I walked down to Christopher's and ate nachos. There was a rerun of *Psycho* on the big TV over the bar; and when Anthony Perkins approached the shower curtain with his knife, the bartender rang a bell so no one would miss watching Janet Leigh die. I was glad to be absorbed in anything. I watched the black blood disappear down the drain and drank a beer. When I'd finished, I called my apartment, then Leo's studio, on the pay phone. There was no answer in either place. I had another beer.

I went home around nine. I read a story in the magazine

section of the *Globe* about the Museum of Transportation. When I was finished, I read it again. At eleven, the weight of the weekend hit me. I went into Molly's room. The room smelled of her, a kind of delicate sweatiness that made me think of the back of her neck, her sturdy legs. Her things were set out on a low shelf I'd installed along one wall in the first weeks we'd lived in the apartment. Nearly all of them came in little pieces, or had parts. There was coffee can after coffee can of Legos, of Mr Potatohead, of marbles, of shells and rocks. Her dolls, her animals sat among them, with blank eyes, maliciously innocent. I stood by the bed. I could not lose her, I thought. Let me not lose her. I looked at her dolls and thought I was going to cry; I left the room.

I went into the bathroom, stood there. Where was Leo? I needed him. I needed him to tell me it was fine. As I got ready for bed, I began to make equations. If he came home now and said it was fine, it would be fine. Molly would come back, we would be happy again. I washed my face, changed into a nightgown.

Leo didn't come.

I told myself magical thinking was dumb. There were reasons why he wasn't there which had nothing to do with Molly, with whatever Brian thought. I told myself to remember the faith that I'd kept through almost the whole weekend that Brian was just wrong, that we would simply clear this up. I heated up some milk and took an Actifed to make myself sleepy. I looked at myself in the mirror just before I went to bed. Under the bright light in the bathroom, my face looked haggard, old. I saw tears welling in my eyes. I reached up and pulled my cheek, hard. No drama. I went and lay down, rigid, in my room. The bright light from the train track flooded everything with a horrible light. A few tears slid down into my ears, but I held my face hard and concentrated on the ceiling and stopped them.

When Leo came, I was deeply asleep. He smelled of the night, of cool air, of everything but me. He was kissing me, and his breath, his saliva tasted sweet and real. It was all I could think of. I wanted to drink and drink him. His hands were cool on me, lifted the nightgown, nested where I was damp and sweaty and tired of being alone. He was claiming me, clearing everything else away. I felt him slide in me, like a dream I was having of how it could always be like this. We pushed against each other. I reached to touch him past the bundled clothes, our limbs. 'Ahhh,' he said, and held away from me to let me. And then I placed him again, lower this time, by my ass, and pushed a little. His face above me was startled, foolish with unbelieving eagerness, like a high school boy's. He was still. He let me push. It hurt, nearly too much, and I thought I wanted to stop, no matter what. Through the drug and my fatigue, I could feel some deeper consciousness, some other pain, returning. But I eased against it, against him, opened to him, and then slowly, it didn't hurt anymore. It was easier and easy, and Leo pushed too, but gently. He slid the nightgown up and over my head and looked at me, my legs swimming in the air around him. I wanted this, just this. I wanted it lasting forever. Then he tilted back into the purplish light and I couldn't see his face any more. We moved slowly, and when he began to cry out, I felt myself shake from somewhere in my spine, I felt only him, only him, it was a different thing; and then the same; and then he bent gently towards me, he lay on me and kissed my neck.

I felt him slip away into sleep lightly, just as I moved sharply back into the world, just as everything returned.

'Leo,' I said.

'God,' he answered, his voice whispering slowly, dreamily. 'What other wonderful ideas did you have while I was gone?'

'Leo,' I asked. 'Leo, did you ever touch Molly, her body I mean. Did she ever touch you? Wake up,' I said.

His fingers reached towards my face, felt my wet hair, my open mouth. We lay in the garish silence a minute.

'Yes,' he said.

EIGHT

When I called my lawyer on Monday, he was reassuring. This kind of thing happened all the time, he said. Threats about custody, they were like a post-divorce sport. It would probably turn out that Brian was negotiating for something – less money, more time, something like that – and was introducing the issue of custody as a red herring, just to soften me up.

'What I'd do if I were you,' he said, 'is just go on about my business. You planning to go down there on Friday? Go on down there. My guess is no one'll say anything about any of this. The name of the game is intimidation.'

'So you wouldn't worry about it?' I asked. I hadn't told him about Leo, and I was glad it seemed that now I wouldn't have to.

'I sure as hell wouldn't,' he said. 'In these kind of situations, don't worry about a thing till you're holding the papers in your hand. You get some kind of papers, then you call me back and we'll worry together. That's what I'm here for.'

He was a heavyset, avuncular man, balding and oddly graceful in small things. I had met him only once, during the divorce proceedings, when I went downtown to his office to review the agreement with him. He had urged a few changes; had acted frustrated by my unresponsiveness. 'You're not really getting your money's worth out of me,' he'd said, shaking his big head. And I'd felt almost apologetic that I didn't want more from Brian.

He had come with me out to the elevator when I left, and as I watched him walk away, I was struck by his gait, something dainty and controlled in it, as though before he put on all the weight he'd been a dancer, an athlete.

I told Leo that Muth thought it was all right, didn't think we should worry.

'You told him about the thing with Molly,' he said.

'No, but he said that it was most likely just a threat, anyway, that Brian would turn out to be working out something else, like less money or something.'

'But you didn't tell him what happened,' he persisted.

'Do you want to call him back?' I burst out. 'I don't think we need to worry about it.'

He looked at me. I'd been awake and dressed long before he'd gotten up, and had called the lawyer promptly at eight-thirty. We hadn't touched or kissed this morning. We'd moved around the kitchen getting our separate breakfasts, doing our separate chores, like an old married couple sunk deep in habitual solitude, but without that sense of comfort or familiarity.

'No, fine,' he said. He was sitting at the table, wearing the same clothes he'd been wearing when we made love the night before. His white skin was puffy around his eyes. 'Whatever you say.'

'I say let's forget it,' I said angrily.

'I hope we can.'

On Wednesday morning, I was sitting alone in the living room in my nightgown – Leo was still asleep – when the guy came with the papers. As soon as the doorbell rang I knew what it was. I felt as though I'd gone through it already. I stood in the hallway and watched him below me slowly mounting the twisting stairway, as though he were a memory. I felt as distanced from the coming event as one does from a dream; but curious too: whose face would he wear? what words would he say?

He looked up at me from the landing below. 'You Anna Dunlop?' he asked. He was young, wore a maroon jacket that read *Cambridge 1977 Babe Ruth All Stars* on its breast. On the arm that held out the envelope, the same gold script spelled *Bud*.

194

'Dunlap,' I said.

He looked at the envelope as he moved up towards me. 'Oh, right,' he said, and grinned sheepishly. He was homely, with crusts of acne clustered beardlike around his mouth and chin. He held the envelope out. 'This is for you,' he said.

'Many thanks.' I took it.

He shrugged, and immediately started down the stairs, moving backwards for the first few steps. 'It's a job,' he said. 'What can I tell you.' When he'd rounded the second landing and was more or less out of sight, he started taking the stairs two and three at a time, thundering down them like a child released from some social constraint.

I shut the door and walked down the dark hallway to the kitchen, tearing open the envelope as I went. I set it down for a moment to dial the telephone, but even as it began to ring, I was reading. The words on the papers before me also seemed familiar, but shocking. They leapt up: *complaint for modification of agreement . . . motion for temporary custody . . . sexual irregularities with minor child* . . . I didn't want to see more. I folded the papers and put them back into the jagged envelope. The secretary was telling me that Muth hadn't arrived at the office yet. She took my number in a chirping, efficient voice.

I got another cup of coffee when I'd hung up, and took it out onto the back porch. I sat on the wooden chair there. After he had begun to spend his nights with us, Leo brought his galvanized tub over for Molly to use as a pool on the back porch. Now it leaned, empty and rimed with white, against the brown clapboards. Next to it was a milk crate full of plastic bottles and cups, tubes, toy boats, all the things she played with in the water.

Across the yard, my neighbor moved in her window, waved. I lifted my cup in response, as though it were just another day.

The phone shrilled. It was Muth. As I talked to him, I heard Leo groan, could imagine him stretching, in my room.

I told Muth that Brian had sent papers, that I had received them earlier this morning.

'*Aha*,' he said. 'Well, I was wrong. Down to business, huh?'

'I guess so,' I said.

'Well, can you tell me, Mrs Dunlap, I mean, is it clear from what he says, on what grounds he's making the motion? Or do you wanna read it to me, or what?' I heard Leo get up, his bare feet approaching the kitchen. I turned my body away from the open doorway.

'Sexual irregularities, he says.'

'Sexual irregularities?'

'Yes,' I said. Leo's steps had paused at the door.

'With who?' Muth asked.

'My lover,' I said. 'The man I've been seeing.' Leo was motionless behind me.

'*Aha*,' Muth said, and waited. I said nothing. Then: 'Well, you wanna tell me where this is coming from, Mrs Dunlap? I mean is this coming out of left field, or where?'

'Not exactly.' My voice was low, my shoulders hunched away from the doorway.

'So you mean, this guy had some kind of contact, some kind of sexual contact, with, ah, the kid. With Molly?'

'Yes, in a certain sense, yes. Or it could be construed that way, yes.' I heard Leo turn, pad away toward the bathroom.

'*Aha*,' he said. And waited again. But I couldn't answer right away. I heard Leo down the hall, the rush of water, the singing of the pipes. I felt ashamed. *You* let it happen, Brian had said. It seemed as palpable a failure to me as the long swollen scratch on her dirty cheek at Sammy Brower's house.

'I'd like to come in and talk to you,' I said finally.

'Yes,' he said. 'Yes, it's clear that that's what we'd better do. The sooner the better, I'd say. And, ah, can you bring your friend? He's going to have to, most likely, be included in all this. You know, there'll be a hearing, et cetera. You know, as a matter of fact, Mrs Dunlap, maybe you could check these papers and see if there's a date, a date you're supposed to show up. Did you check for that?'

'No,' I said.

'Well, you wanna do that now?' he asked.

'Sure,' I said. I set the phone down, took the papers out again, leafed through them. There it was – August seventeenth. I picked the phone up. 'It's here,' I said.

'What do we get?' he asked. 'A week, ten days?'

'It's Friday,' I said. 'A week from Friday.'

'*Aha*,' he said. 'Well, I'll tell you, then, I'll give you to my secretary, and ask her to set you up pronto. I think I might have a space even today. Tomorrow for sure. We ought to get going on this, you know, figure out what angle we're going to take, that kinda jazz, pretty soon. As soon as possible, actually.'

'Yes,' I said, and he clicked off. After a moment, the secretary's flutey voice came on the line. Mr Muth had time late in the morning tomorrow, she said. Was eleven-thirty all right? I agreed. She told me Mr Muth wanted to be certain *both* of us were coming.

There was no problem, I told her. We'd both be there.

When Leo emerged from his shower, I was dressed, back in the kitchen, washing up. He stood in the doorway again and watched me, gripping a towel around his waist, his drooping curls raining silver drops on his shoulders. I looked at him. 'That was my lawyer on the phone,' I said.

'I wondered.' He pulled the towel to the side, held it tighter at his hip. He would never have worn it before. It was like the sign of our mutual fall from grace; but I was, for the moment, glad not to see him naked.

'I got the papers today,' I told him.

'Oh,' he said. His face asked me how bad it was. 'It's real then.'

'It is,' I said. I tried to keep my voice determined and cheerful.

He shook his head. 'Jesus, Anna. I know you know it, but . . . I'm sorry.' He stepped towards me, into the kitchen, but I raised my hand.

'I don't see this as *your fault*,' I said. 'I don't want you to tell me that.' And I turned back to the counter, making big circles with the pink sponge.

'Muth can see us tomorrow,' I said.

'Did he say anything?'

'About what?'

'Well, about what would happen. About whether this was . . . about getting Molly back.'

'Not really. I didn't really talk to him in much detail.'

'But you told him what happened?'

I looked at him. 'Roughly, yes, but not in any detail.'

He turned, as though he were going to leave the room. His arched footprints left a quickly fading steamy print on the linoleum, like the breath of his feet. At the door he stopped and said, without looking at me, 'I'd like to be able to talk about this stuff, Anna. It's like you keep wishing it will go away if we don't discuss it. That's hard for me. It doesn't help me. Or *anything*.'

I shook my head. 'And I don't want to talk about it,' I said. 'I don't see how that would help. It's done. I don't *blame* you. That's not what it's about. But it's just that I feel like I'm holding on by a thread here, plus I've still got stuff I have to do at work. To keep going. These fucking rats.' I shrugged. 'I just need to do this my way, I think. But I am sorry, I really am sorry, if it makes it worse for you.'

'That's not it. It's not that I'm feeling sorry for myself. I . . . Jesus. That would be pretty self-indulgent. I just . . .' He looked at me. 'I don't want to lose you.'

'That's not the issue, is it?' I asked. 'Your losing *me*?' And I turned away. In a moment I sensed, rather than heard, that he'd left the room. When I went to find him a few minutes later, to say I was sorry, he was gone. I imagined him swinging down the hall barefoot, partly dressed, as quickly and silently as he had in the spring when he'd wanted to get out before Molly heard him.

Leo wore a jacket and tie to Muth's office the next day. He'd had to borrow them from a friend, since he didn't own either. The jacket was a little tight, and Leo's cuffs, his big hands, stuck out. He looked like a farmboy visiting in town.

'That's very sweet of you,' I said. 'Wearing that.' We were driving down Storrow Drive in light midmorning traffic. Summer school students lay reading, sunbathing on the green banks of the river. He looked at me quickly to be sure I was sincere. When he saw that I was, he thanked me. It struck me suddenly that much of our conversation for the last several days had been just this polite – apologies, thanks, careful backing away from demands or questions. Each of us was behaving as though the other was fragile, easily damaged. Nothing was natural between us. We hadn't made love since Sunday night, the night Leo returned; and as I remembered all that, it seemed to me that I had known, even as we did it, that it marked the end of something. Now we lay in the same bed together each night, sometimes touching each other lightly, without passion, before we turned away and sought sleep. But sex seemed unthinkable.

So did sleeping alone though. It was as though neither of us wanted to face himself. Even the night before, when I'd gone to his house just to apologize after I'd finished up at the lab, when I was sure each of us would want to be alone, we were unable to find a way to separate.

'I don't need to stay,' I'd said, standing in his doorway. 'I just came to say I was sorry for being so sharp this morning.'

'No, no, that's OK,' he said. 'I understand. Come on in. I mean, I'd *like* you to stay.' He stood back to make room for my entrance, then hesitated. 'Unless you want to be alone or something.' We looked at each other a moment. The thought of being alone terrified me.

'I'll stay,' I said, and instantly felt how much I didn't want to, how much I *had* wanted to be alone. But I was already crossing his threshold, I would hurt his feelings if I left, it was too late. And so we slept together another night with our backs curved towards each other, just as Brian and I had done in the last stages of our marriage.

In the morning, I'd gone home to change my clothes, then driven back over to Leo's to pick him up. He was waiting for me on the corner by his building, and I almost drove past him, he looked so unfamiliar in his costume. In the car, I kept looking over at him as I drove, but he seemed unconscious of me, lost in his own nervousness. His hands drummed on his knees. Once or twice he popped his knuckles.

We parked in an expensive lot downtown, and then, because we were early for the appointment with Muth, we stopped for coffee. The cafeteria was dim, functional, with small formica tables. The people around us were a curious combination of bums and businessmen. They seemed completely at home in one another's company. It was we who were out of place in this world – both wearing uniforms that seemed uncomfortable on us. My dress was a little too fancy, not secretarial enough. And when I saw the businessmen, dark and tailored, I realized that Leo looked worse in his attempt at respectability than he would have if he'd just worn a T-shirt and jeans. There was something that appeared nearly psychopathic to me abruptly, in the ill-fitting disguise. I sat across from him, sipping the burnt-tasting coffee and talking about what Muth was like, and I wanted to reach over and loosen the tie, wanted to ask him to take the jacket off. But I couldn't. He'd done it for me, to help me get Molly back.

Upstairs, when Muth approached us across the carpeted expanse of the firm's outer offices, I watched his face carefully for signs of his response to Leo; but it was unreadable, pleasant as ever. He was in shirtsleeves, rolled up, and a tie. He shook Leo's hand and mine as though we were perfectly respectable people.

In his office, he arranged the chairs for us, making small talk in his rambling way about the Red Sox. Once he'd got us settled, he sat down behind his desk, and asked me for the papers. I handed the torn envelope across to him. Leo and I sat in silence for three or four minutes while he read through them, neither of us looking at the other. I was intensely conscious of Leo though, of his restless shifting in his chair. I hoped he wouldn't be rude if Muth probed too deep.

Muth's face, bent over his desk, fell into a somber frowning pouchiness. Once or twice he ran his hand over his balding head. But when he looked up, he was neutral, boyishly middle-aged again.

'Well,' he said. 'The news is not good, I guess.'

I found myself smiling politely, making some agreeable answer. Leo stared at me.

'I think what would help me right now,' Muth said, extracting a pencil from a jar of them on his desk, 'is to find out exactly what you think it is that's got Mr Dunlap so fired up here. I think the phrase he uses is *sexual irregularities*, and I think *you* said on the phone, Mrs Dunlap, that there *had* been some kind of contact between Mr Cutter and . . . ah, Molly. That right?'

'Yes,' I said. I nodded.

'Well, that's what I need to get straight then. Just what it was, when it happened, how often, that kind of thing.' He looked up, expectantly, pleasantly.

'Once,' Leo said.

'Once,' he repeated, and wrote something down. He smiled at Leo. 'Can you, ah, can you fill me in on it a bit, Mr Cutter?'

I looked at Leo. He shifted forward in his chair, and without looking over at me, he started talking. As he began, I thought, *Why, he's practiced this.*

'It was sometime in June when it happened. Anna had left Molly and me alone for the evening. She was at the lab or something, I don't remember what, but she was supposed to get back in time to tuck Molly in. Molly and I had gone out to get ice cream. I'd given her a bath' – Muth's pencil whispered quickly on the page – 'gotten her into her pj's, all that stuff. It was hot. I'd been working all day. Molly was in her room, playing, and she sounded happy, so I figured I'd take a shower. I told her I was going to, so she'd know where to find me, if she needed me.' Leo's hands had been folded in his lap at first. Now, as he relaxed a little, they came to life, helped him tell the story.

'I, you know, got in the shower, and after a while, she came into the bathroom, started talking to me. It was like she just wanted company. She was just talking about this and that, the stories she'd picked out for her mother to read to her, some stuff that happened to her at day care. She was just sitting on the toilet seat, talking, the way she sometimes did.'

'She'd come in before when you were in the shower?' Muth asked. He didn't look up.

'Me, or her mother, yeah. She liked the company.'

Muth nodded.

'When I pushed the curtain back and started drying off, I noticed Molly was staring at me, at my' – there was the slightest hesitation as Leo chose the word – 'penis. But she'd seen me naked before, I didn't think much of it. I was fooling around, you know, dancing.'

'Dancing,' Muth repeated.

'Yeah. I was dancing and singing actually.' Leo's voice had begun to sound angry. I leaned forward. He looked up at me, then moved uncomfortably in his chair. When he spoke again, his voice was calm. 'Singing "Singin' in the Rain." She liked that.' He shrugged. 'And then I finished, and I was just drying off, and she said, out of the blue, "That's your penis?"' He cleared his throat. 'You know, she was learning that stuff, those words. She had a book that talked about it, and they did the body parts at day care. Her mother – Anna – had talked about it some too, telling her the names of stuff.' He shrugged again. 'So I said yeah. She was, she was standing up, she'd gotten closer to the tub. I was, actually, a little uncomfortable about it. But I'd seen how relaxed Anna was about it all, and I didn't want to screw that up or anything. So I tried to seem natural, not cover up or anything.

'But then she said, "Can I touch it?"'

Muth looked up sharply at Leo, his pencil still on the yellow pad. 'I honestly didn't think about it for more than

202

a second. I just said sure. And, um, she did. She . . . held it for a second. And just the contact, I guess. The contact, and I think, the kind of . . . weirdness of the situation made me . . . that is, I started to get an erection. And I said, "That's enough, Molly," and I turned away. I put the towel on. She made some other comment, some question about my . . . about it getting big. And I told her that sometimes happened with men. And I went and got dressed.' He looked at Muth, as if awaiting judgment.

'And that was that?' Muth asked.

'Yes. Pretty much.' He paused. Then: 'She did talk about it some more that night. She seemed a little anxious about it actually. She talked about the facts of life. Of sex. You know, she knew the purpose of an erection in a vague sense. She knew, sort of, what it was for, and I think it confused her. That I had one. So I tried to explain. I'm not sure how well I did.'

'Aha,' Muth said. 'And did you discuss this with Mrs Dunlap?'

'No.' He shifted in his chair.

'Why not?'

'I was . . . To tell the truth, I was embarrassed. And I thought I'd handled it OK. Or as well as anyone could've. So I didn't see that it was a problem.'

'Aha,' Muth said. Then he looked at Leo. 'Can I just ask you, Mr, ah, Cutter, why you didn't just say no to the child. You said it made you uncomfortable. Why didn't you just tell her she couldn't touch you?'

'I didn't think that's what Anna – Mrs Dunlap – would have wanted me to do.'

'You didn't think Mrs Dunlap would have wanted you to?' Suddenly Muth seemed lawyerlike to me, in a way he never had before. I could imagine him being mean in a courtroom.

'No,' Leo said. 'I thought she'd want me to be as relaxed, as natural with Molly, as she was. About her body and that kind of thing.'

Muth made a note, then looked up again.

'So you might say you misunderstood the rules.'

Leo shrugged. 'I thought I understood them.'

There was a long pause. Then Muth said, 'I think when the time comes, Mr Cutter, it'd be better for Mrs Dunlap in the situation we've got here, if you just said you *mis*understood them.'

After a moment Leo inclined his head slightly, stiffly.

Muth began to talk to me. He asked me what the rules were; how much Leo and I were naked around Molly; whether she'd been in bed with us; how much she knew about the facts of life. He asked me to describe the book I'd read to her, to describe the pictures in it. (They were cartoon figures, cheerful, dumpy, humorous.) He said he'd like me to bring the book in next time I came, that it might be helpful, depending on what Molly had said to Brian. He asked me how long Leo and I had been involved, how long he'd been spending nights at our house, how much Molly understood of our relationship, how often Leo had been alone with Molly. He took notes throughout, and sometimes as he wrote, his face took on the same frowning cast it had had when he bent over the papers from Brian; but whenever he lifted it to me and Leo, it was bland and open as a curious baby's.

Mostly I talked, though occasionally Leo offered an observation. Muth asked about how things had been when I'd been married to Brian, what his attitudes about sex had been, whether the patterns in the house had changed a lot since then, whether Molly had seemed at all disturbed by those changes. When finally he seemed to be running out of questions, I asked him what he thought would happen, what he thought Brian's chances were.

He shook his head. 'This kind of thing is tough to call, Mrs Dunlap. A lot depends on what Molly said, on how bothered she seems to be about it. But these judges, you know, they're by and large conservative. They don't like to hear anything about sexual stuff with kids.' I sensed Leo moving slightly in his chair. 'You know,' Muth gestured with his slender fingers open, 'they hear terrible stuff all the time. After a while, they lump everything like that together in their minds.'

'What if . . .' I cleared my throat. 'What if I said I wouldn't see Leo anymore. Would that make a difference?'

I could feel Leo snap to alertness, his eyes on me. My mouth parched. But Muth knew only strategy, seemed unconscious of anything that passed between us. He was already shaking his head.

'They hear it *all* the time. You can try it, for sure, but they don't believe it anyway. A promise, to them, is what someone is willing to say to get a kid back. Period.'

The silence in the room was now explosive. Muth, unperturbed, looked from Leo to me. 'OK, then,' he said. 'If it's all right with you, Mr Cutter, I'd like to talk to Mrs Dunlap alone for a few minutes.' He stood, Leo stood. 'If you could just wait outside . . .' He crossed to the door and opened it for Leo. 'It was good to talk with you,' Muth said, extending his hand. Leo reached out and shook it. 'I appreciate your honesty.'

Leo made a murmuring noise. Then without looking back at me, he left.

Even watching his stiff back out of the room, I was so focused on what all this meant for Molly, for Molly and me, that I didn't realize I could have managed not to ask my question in front of Leo by waiting only a few minutes longer. At the time, hurting him, alienating him, seemed inevitable, part of the price I had to pay.

Muth sat down. His tone was confidential. He invited me to share any doubts, any observations about aberrant behavior in Leo. I told him I had no doubts about him, that Leo had, except in this instance, behaved with Molly as I would have wanted him to.

'So it was just in this case that he misunderstood you?'

I waited a moment before I answered. 'Yes,' I said, feeling that I was betraying Leo as much by my agreement with Muth now, as I had by my question in front of him earlier.

Muth went on to talk about my work schedule, about how much Molly had seen Brian since the divorce, about how much she'd seen of him when we were still married, about who was taking care of Molly in Washington while Brian and Brenda worked. Three or four times he circled back around to Leo again, what I knew of his background, his sexual history before me. I tried to sound firm and confident, determined to try not to betray him any more than I felt I already had.

Finally he leaned back and tossed his pencil onto the pad.

'Okay,' he said. 'Now I think the approach here is gonna be to downpedal all this stuff about permissiveness. *You* know and *I* know that it's probably healthier for a kid to be pretty much open about this sexual stuff, right?'

I nodded.

'But what we're not gonna do here is, we're not gonna try to educate the judge about it, OK? Because that's not gonna work, right?'

I nodded.

'What we're gonna focus on is how happy she was, how much time you spent with her, how responsible you were. How Mr Dunlap's a bit of a workaholic, how his wife has the same kind of job, how the choice is really between a loving mother and a paid babysitter. OK? Let them ask the stuff about this sexual thing with Cutter. It's gotta come out. But we're not gonna defend it or tie it in with the idea of sexual openness or anything. It's just gonna be a mistake *he* made. Got it?'

I nodded, ashamed. *You*, Brian's voice said, *you* let it happen.

'Now, let me tell you what I think we oughta do,' Muth said. 'See if you agree with me.'

'OK,' I said.

'I think that with what we've got here, our best chance is gonna be an expert, a shrink. See, you and Mr Cutter both are clearly, you know, you come off, well – articulate, concerned with her, with Molly. With a guardian, a psychiatrist appointed by the court, you could talk, you know, the way you have with me here, and I think that would be our best shot. With their training, they look beyond just the

206

bare facts. They're there to pick up, you know' – his hand circled in the air – 'attitudes, feelings. My sense is, if we go with that, if I make a motion that we get a shrink to make a recommendation, that within a very short time he'd see what I've seen here: it was a mistake, it was, basically, Cutter's mistake, it's not about to happen again, right?'

'Right,' I said.

'So, then he recommends she stays with you; and the judge, they give a lot of credence to that. I think . . . well, that's what I'd suggest anyway.'

'That sounds reasonable to me,' I said. And then, not to seem too passive, 'Are there alternative strategies?'

He shook his head. 'Not that readily come to mind. You have anything on the father?'

'What do you mean?'

'Well, like this.' He gestured at the papers. 'You know, like what he's got on you. Has he done anything you can point to where it's clearly bad judgment, incompetence?'

'Not really. He's very *busy*, as I've said. He always had trouble finding time for her.'

'Sure, yeah, we'll *use* that, but in itself that's not enough.'

'No, I really don't have anything.'

'*So*,' he said, and lifted his big shoulders. 'Let's go with the shrink?'

'Yes,' I said.

'Even with him though, I'd downpedal the specifics. But you could tell him, I mean he might be very interested that Mr Dunlap was what you might say, *uptight* about sexual stuff. And it wouldn't hurt if you could remember, like, a scene where, if he might have frightened Molly a little with that strictness or something. But it will just be a more relaxed context, if you know what I mean. Less concerned with exactly *what* happened and more concerned with why, and that's to our advantage. You understand?'

I nodded. He came forward in his chair, leaned towards me.

''Cause what happened, on the face of it, isn't good.' He shook his head. 'I mean, *I* can understand how it happened,

207

you can understand how it happened, but I can also tell you how their attorney's going to present it, and it's not going to sound good.' He shifted back again. 'You know, there's a certain way of looking at this stuff – and I hate to tell you, but it's how a lot of the world sees it – and what we've got here is a guy, a guy kind of down and out, no regular job' – he raised his hand as I stirred, letting me know he knew it wasn't so. I was again struck by his hand's delicacy, the fingers that curved in slightly like a dancer's – 'left alone with a kid, cavorting around in front of her, encouraging contact, aroused by her touch. They may suggest a lot worse, too, and he'll be the only one to deny it. You see what I mean. And depending on the judge, on how much he's able to imagine another context for that behavior, that'll be how it goes. That and the recommendation of the family service officer. So that's one thing potentially in your favor. That and Mr Dunlap's pattern of fathering.'

'And how soon will all this happen? When?'

He shrugged. 'First there's this hearing, right?'

I nodded.

'OK. The procedure there is we all make these motions, and then probably we get sent to the FSO.'

'The FSO?'

'Yeah, the family service officer. It'll be like an interview. It's usually a woman, a social worker, you know, young, bright. She'll sort of assess things, make sure this guardian deal with the shrink seems appropriate, work out the details. So, we oughta find out then, by Friday, a lot of stuff: approximately when you'll all see the shrink – and the kid will too, Molly, and the father – and maybe even, I think I'll push for it, a court date set.'

'And that's when it'll get decided? The court date?'

'Right, the trial. Depending on how long it takes to see the shrink, that could be a couple of months. Maybe less. And that will take a couple of days, the trial. You know, you'll testify, your ex-husband will, the shrink, the whole thing.'

'And is it true that I can't see Molly until then?'

'No way,' he shook his head. 'No. It's not true. Chances are your ex-husband will get *temporary* custody – he's moving for that, till the trial, you know, and that's pretty typical. But we'll fix you up with visitation, don't you worry. No,' he said, and grinned, 'he's just making points telling you that, showing everybody how seriously he takes all this. We'll have no trouble getting you visitation once he's done proving that.'

We sat for a moment. He cleared his throat. 'Now, about money,' he said.

For a moment I didn't understand him, thought he was referring to some part of the financial arrangement between me and Brian. Brian had paid him for the divorce, so I'd never thought of a fee as part of this transaction.

'Oh,' I said, and I couldn't keep the surprise out of my voice. 'Of course.'

'The retainer'll be twenty-five hundred. And it might be, I suppose, another thousand or so in the end.'

I hoped my face wasn't registering the shock that I felt, the sharp sense of my idiocy. 'I'm sorry, I don't know this, but *when* do I pay you?' I tried to keep my voice smooth, the question academic.

'Yesterday,' he said, and grinned.

I looked quickly down at my hands. When I thought I had control of my face, I looked up at him and tried smiling back. 'I'll have to make it tomorrow or the next day.'

He nodded. 'I understand,' he said. 'I won't say "I told you so" about your divorce agreement, but I understand.' He rose, and I did too. 'But I will need it before the court date,' he said, and he crossed to the door.

'You'll have it,' I said, my mind already racing through my possibilities, turning down one dead-end corridor after another.

He walked me back to the reception area. Leo sat in one of the boxy upholstered chairs, and I was startled again at how the ill-fitting jacket robbed him of all his grace and poise. He seemed a liability, sitting there, and I felt a pulse of rage at him. I stood a little distant as Muth shook hands with him again.

We rode in silence in opposite corners of the carpeted elevator. Two women stood in front of us by the doors. One of them was talking about what sounded like her divorce. 'My lawyer keeps saying "Now, we're not out to punish anyone here, we just want what's right," but I don't think he understands. I don't *care* what's right, I want to fucking *punish* the guy.'

Her friend shook her head. 'Sure you do. After what he's put you through?'

The doors opened. We crossed the marble lobby, stepped outside.

Muth's office, the reception room, the elevator, had all been windowless, lit by overhead spots. I was startled to see the sunshine, feel the light summer air push my dress against me. We walked the short block to the parking lot, and I paid the attendant. I was aware of the rigidity of Leo's presence, of his anger; but I was, in a serious way, preoccupied. And so I was startled, when I got into the car next to him and shut my door, that after a moment of inert silence, he violently struggled out of the jacket and threw it against the dashboard. Then he tore at the tie and pulled it off. He caught his collar, yanking at it, and the button at the neck of the shirt pulled off, ripping the cloth, and ricocheting with a sharp snap off the windshield. We sat locked together among all the empty cars, the sound of Leo's panting rage filling the space between us, and I wondered how we'd get through the next ten days, two weeks, without damaging each other. In my several seconds of terror, when I thought he might be going to hurt me, what I had felt for Leo was a cold, welling hate.

NINE

I couldn't remember where the road had once ended, but at some point I crossed the line and was driving in new territory. Though it looked the same – the brown clayey dirt deeply rutted; ferns, skunk cabbage, wild blueberries clustering close to its sides as it dipped and curved – I was aware that I could no longer anticipate the curves, the sudden blind rises where, earlier, I'd known reflexively to tap my horn for an oncoming car. Through the trees on my right, I still caught occasional glimpses of the lake. Far out on its surface the power boats looped around a few still sails.

I circled close to a swampy inlet, thick with water lilies, that I remembered once or twice trying to row through. The long stems of the lilies had tentacled around the oars, and the lily pads made a hissing sound against the wooden boat bottom at my lurching glide through them. Then I was back in woods again, the cleared road a stripe of sunlight across them.

I'd been on this part of the road only once or twice as an adult – it had been cut through the woods during the early years of my marriage to Brian, and we had come up together a few times. But I didn't remember it, and it seemed to me I'd been on the new part much too long. I was actually thinking that perhaps I ought to turn and start back, when I saw the sign that said *McCord* by the parked cars. Then I recognized my grandfather's car, a new model Volvo sedan. There were two other cars parked in the turnaround near it – one with Connecticut plates too, one from Rhode Island. I couldn't remember who else was here, though I knew my mother had kept me informed. The family had a regular rotation to ensure that my grandparents weren't alone for longer than a day or two.

I pulled in next to the Rhode Island car. It was a Volkswagen. In the back seat were a tennis racket, a fat laundry bag.

When Muth had told me that I'd need twenty-five hundred dollars, my grandfather was the third or fourth possibility that ran through my head. None of my friends could have afforded to loan me such an amount, presuming any of them even had it. And though I knew my parents would have it, I rejected the idea of borrowing from them – the emotional interest rates would simply be too high. Leo had offered, awkwardly and angrily, to try to raise it, but I didn't want to do that.

It seemed to me that there was a sense in which I had least to lose by asking my grandfather. He had the money, and he liked to loan and give it to his children and grandchildren because that tightened his grip on them. I had already heard his judgment on the way I was conducting my life. There would be no surprises. He might be hostile when I asked, openly contemptuous, but all that would be clear, clean. Beyond that, I think I may even have imagined taking a kind of perverse pleasure in the idea of involving him in a situation which he'd find distasteful.

I hadn't called ahead of time. I knew that I'd find them at home. It was summer, after all.

It had been a hazy day in Boston. An inversion made the air feel thick. It stung at the eyes and tasted metallic. But on the highway coming north the sun had shimmered lighter and lighter behind the white haze, until the blue seemed all at once to burn through around it. The shadows on the ground suddenly sharpened and I felt a responsive sense of hope lighten my heart.

There was a big green metal wheelbarrow set by the turnaround to carry luggage or groceries in, just as there had been when we parked on the other side of the lake and rowed over. I ignored it and followed the cleared path into the woods. Rusty pine needles lay across the earth, and raised roots striped the path. The sun flickered through the high cover here and there, and the smell of the lake and pine tar drew me forward.

Before I really saw them, the buildings were around me, partially hidden by the trees. For a moment I couldn't make sense of them because I wasn't sure at what angle this path cut into camp. But then, suddenly, they took position in my head. At a distance down to the right was my grandparents' cabin, barely visible, except in front where the trees had been cleared to give a view of the lake. In front of me were the two guest cabins. The path led uphill and slightly left, to the icehouse, since early in my youth empty of ice, full of bunk beds where the boy cousins slept. I could only dimly remember the ice itself, cut from the lake in winter, gray and solid with glacial mystery all summer long under its bed of sawdust. When you leaned your head into the dark room, your breath whited, the cold pinched your nostrils. Even after the ice was gone and the bunks hung by chains from the walls, the sawdust persisted, pushing up again and again from between the cracks in the floorboards. The boys were required to sweep it out before breakfast each day.

As I came round the corner of the icehouse, the big house loomed into view. In spite of myself, I felt the sense of safety and peace that the camp had meant for me as a child. The place was utterly still except for the call of birds and the distant mosquito whine of motorboats. But I judged it to be sometime in the early afternoon – I'd left right after breakfast, I'd been waking with the first gray light these days – and I remembered that everyone lay down, by an unspoken dictum, for more than an hour after lunch. I crossed the packed dirt of the dooryard, thinking I'd sit on the screened porch until my grandfather got up.

I gently opened the screen door to the kitchen and passed forward through the house. The ticking clock over the mantel in the main room seemed to pulse with my heart; and everything was as familiar as the detail of a recurrent dream. I stepped onto the porch, and looked out over the lake. The sun danced white on it out in the center, but its deep green was revealed in the shadows of the trees lying across our inlet. I looked around the porch. The same pale green tables ringed with odd chairs, the overflow from the sisters' city houses; the trunks holding bedding, children's games, lining the porch's inner walls; the striped curtains strung across the winged sides of the porch to separate those sleeping areas from the public area in front. And then I saw my grandmother.

She lay arranged and frozen on a daybed at one end of the porch. Her hands were folded across her midriff; her skirt was neatly pulled down to cover her knees. Her eyes were shut, her jaw slack. Her glasses sat on the little white table next to the bed. For a moment I was frightened; I had the fleeting notion that she was dead. But as I crossed the porch to look more closely at her, she stirred slightly, her lips shut once or twice with a light smacking sound.

There was a wicker chair near the foot of the daybed. I put my purse down on the floor and sat in it and looked at her. I sat there for what seemed like a long time, perhaps a half hour or more. I listened intently to the noises around me. I could hear just the lap of water, the distant boats buzzing, the birds, the trees softly groaning in the sibilant wind, my grandmother's breathing, and once or twice, the mutter of her flesh as she passed wind. It seemed that no one else was here except my grandmother and me. I decided that my grandfather and whatever cousins were staying must be in the cabins. And there probably were very few cousins anyway. In recent years, I knew from my mother, most of them tended to vacation in other, more comfortable and interesting places – places where they could play tennis and golf, go to the theater. Even she and her sisters now made only token visits – a weekend, five days. There were elaborate arrangements for the younger, still poor cousins to babysit the grandparents; but the sisters didn't go and stay anymore, as they had when their children were young. My grandmother stirred, shifted slightly to the side. Her pale, white-lashed eyes opened, looked blankly at me.

'Who's that?' she said harshly, reaching for her glasses.

'It's Anna,' I said. I got up.

She hooked her glasses over her ears and swung her legs off the bed. Still looking confused, disoriented, she allowed me to kiss her cheek.

I went back to the chair and let her look at me. After a moment, she said, 'I was napping.'

'I know,' I said. 'I hope I didn't wake you.'

She thought for a moment, then raised her wrist close to her glasses and tilted her head up to see through the lower lens of her bifocals. 'No, it's time,' she said. She reached around her waist and patted her blouse into her skirt. Then she looked at me again, frowning.

'I must have forgotten you were coming,' she said.

'No,' I said. 'I didn't tell you. It's a surprise.' I smiled. 'And really I'm just here for the afternoon. A quick visit. I can't stay.'

'Just visiting?' She gave the word two syllables. Her eyes were sharp on me through the watery distance of her glasses.

'Yes. And I need to talk to Grandfather about something.'

'Money?' she asked.

I nodded.

'That's the way of it,' she said.

'I'm afraid so.'

'It's nothing to be ashamed of,' she said. 'He'll be back in a while. I sent them all off for a picnic. Thought I'd make pie for dessert tonight. They're getting the berries.'

'Who's here?' I asked.

'You know Celia?' she asked. 'Weezie's girl?'

I thought of Celia, disgusting in her plumpness to me and Babe. Babe had once said we weren't going to be able to tell when Celia got real breasts, because she'd had little fat boobies since she was about two. That was our nickname for her after that. *Fat boobies*, FB for short. It covered her shape, and what we regarded as her colossal stupidity – though what we were really objecting to was that she, years younger even than I, followed us around, wanted to know what we were doing all the time. I nodded.

'She's here. She's pregnant, you know. Her husband's coming too, but I can't quite remember when. And Garrett's up, just for the weekend, doing chores for your grandfather.'

'Not many people by the old standards,' I offered.

'No,' she said. 'Though we see a lot of the younger grandchildren from time to time.' She looked at me. 'Where's your baby?' she said.

'Molly,' I said.

'Molly, yes,' she said irritably. 'Now I knew that.'

'She's visiting her father for the month,' I said.

'Oh!' she nodded her head, as if remembering suddenly all the circumstances of my life. 'Well, that's hard. You must miss her.'

'I do,' I said. 'I can't wait to see her again.'

My grandmother sat in silence for several minutes. Then she got up laboriously and excused herself to go to the bathroom – a chemical toilet off the kitchen now, installed so my grandparents wouldn't have to make the arduous trip out to the outhouse anymore. When she'd gone, I lifted the curtain by the wing of the porch Babe and I had occupied for all those summers. The sagging hospital beds were shoved against the wall, out of the weather. The stiff horse-hair mattresses were bare and stained. I went in and sat on my bed.

After a few minutes my grandmother called from the kitchen and I went back to her. She was just going to get a few things going for supper, she said. They didn't want her working in the kitchen alone anymore, but since I was here, she thought she'd take the opportunity. I could help, if I liked. They were going to have potato salad, and she showed me the bowl of boiled new potatoes in the refrigerator, the hardboiled eggs, the onions. She was going to start the pies. She had the apples for one of them.

We set to work in opposite corners of the primitive kitchen, working silently as we had years before when I, the oldest granddaughter, was expected to help, and to learn from helping about the responsibility of being wife, mother, of serving others. The silence between us then had always

216

seemed complicated and rich to me, unlike the blankness of the silence I remembered from my visit to my other grandmother in Colorado.

This time it was full also, but now of Molly. Of Babe, too, and my recollections of what it had been like to be a girl here; but I came back to Molly again and again. Oddly, in this place where I'd never brought her, I missed her more keenly than I had at any moment since Brian's call.

'That man,' my grandmother said, abruptly. I looked at her. She was bent over the oilcloth table. 'Brian was his name?'

'That's right,' I said.

'He's in Washington?'

I said he was, and explained what he was doing there. I tried to keep my answers expansive, relaxed, but in between them, I realized, I was listening for the sound of the returning motor which would signal my grandfather's arrival.

My grandmother was cutting fat into flour with two knives. They clicked sharply against the blue ceramic bowl. In spite of the slowness with which she got around, her arms and hands moved with efficient grace.

'Divorced,' she said out loud. I had the sense she didn't realize she'd said it. Her upper body rocked quickly with each flick of the blades. Her face was intent on what she was doing.

I turned back to the potatoes. I began to peel another one, but after a moment I stopped. My grandmother had never said anything to me about my divorce, and I realized I had no idea what her attitude might be. Somehow now I wanted her to understand it. I spoke to her moving back.

'I know it may be hard for you to understand, Gram, but we simply didn't – couldn't – make each other happy.'

She turned around to look at me.

'What makes you say that?'

'What?'

Her body swung back to the table. '*I* understand,' she said. 'That's easy enough to understand. Happy!' She began the knives' alternating motion again. After a minute she spoke. Her tone was slower, less sharp, but her arms kept that quick rhythm.

'There was a period of my life where I used to wake up each morning and wish I'd died. Just wished I'd passed away in the night. I never would have *done* anything, you know, but each day I'd open my eyes sorry that I had to.'

Clickety, clickety, clickety went the knives. My thumb pressed a sliver of purple skin against my knife and pulled it away from the white flesh of the potato. My grandmother had never said anything more intimate to me, and I didn't know how to answer, or even whether I should. Finally I asked, 'How long did you feel that way?'

After a moment she said, 'Oh, perhaps ten or fifteen years, I suppose.'

I tried to look at her, but she wouldn't interrupt her work for that. 'I never knew that, Gram,' I said.

'Why should you? No one did.'

'What ended it?'

'When I had Edith. Your grandfather didn't take too much of an interest. Hadn't wanted her in the first place. He'd got his son by then, you know. She was mine, I felt. The only one that was.' Then more slowly: 'The only one that was.' Again, I wasn't sure she knew she was speaking aloud.

We worked for a few minutes quietly. My grandmother was pushing the fatted flour into a flour paste she'd mixed in another bowl, shoving her arm down into the blue dish with a twisting motion. Her lips were pursed with effort. I was sitting in the darkest corner of the room, by the soapstone sink with its arching cast-iron pump. There was a small screened window next to me, but pines hung over it, scratching gently against the screen, and shadowing the house.

My grandmother stood across the room in the light from the one full-sized window. With her white hair, her white blouse, she seemed nearly incandescent to me. I watched her. I thought again of the deep moat of silence around my

Gray grandmother, and of how I'd always felt closer to Grandmother McCord, always found her silence restful, inviting, like the stillness in the middle of one of the small islands that sprinkled the lake – the noise of lapping water, boats all around, but the sense of secret peace really all you noticed. How wrong that had all been, apparently.

She set a breadboard on the oilcloth that covered the table, and reached into the flour firkin for a handful of the white powder. She sprinkled the board, and set the grayish ball of dough on it. From a hook on the wall, she lifted down the rolling pin. She floured it too and began to roll out the dough.

I'd finished peeling the potatoes. Now I crossed to the refrigerator and got out the hardboiled eggs. I took them to the sink, and one by one I rolled them against its stone surface, watching their perfect surfaces crackle into intricate patterns. I had started to peel them when I heard the boat, its noise separating out from the general distant buzz of boats further out on the lake, growing steadily in volume, then abruptly stopping as the engine was cut. Voices floated up, the oars splashed.

My grandmother looked at me a long moment, as if to assess my need for support. She paused, seemed nearly to shrug, then offered: 'You wouldn't have believed how handsome your grandfather was when we first met. I imagined I'd die if I didn't get him. I just thought I'd die. I didn't know anything about it.'

She turned and banged the pin down again on the ragged circle of dough. I wanted to touch her. I knew that she'd meant her statement as a kind of apology for how difficult it was going to be to borrow money from my grandfather. What she couldn't have known was the kind of forgiveness it seemed to offer me for my blinding, disastrous passion for Leo.

Through the window behind my grandmother, I could see my cousins and grandfather plodding up the stairway cut with logs into the steep hillside above the lake. Celia's voice floated high and gay, and it occurred to me again how much more relaxed the younger cousins were around my grandparents. It seemed that to them the sternness was just a part the grandparents played, something they could all joke about. The few years that separated me from them had altered completely the meaning of the long family history of forbidding expectation.

'Celia,' my grandmother said, watching her approach the window. 'She's a talker.' There was fondness in her tone.

And Celia was in midsentence when she yanked open the screen door and stepped into the shadowy kitchen. Tilted backwards, bow-legged from the downpulling weight of her pregnancy, she carried also a big wicker basket. 'Yoicks!' she said, interrupting herself. 'It's Anna.'

She stepped up to me and bent forward over her own girth. Her belly brushed insensate against me. She leaned back away, the words tumbling from her mouth. How long would I stay, why was Gram working, she'd said *she* would do the pies this time, did I know her husband was coming day after tomorrow, and couldn't she persuade me to call wherever it was in Boston I needed to get back to? No? Oh well, dinner anyway. She couldn't imagine going up and back in one day. As she spoke she began to unpack the basket, throwing away the salty, crumpled wax paper, putting the sticky tin cups into the sink.

Pregnant, her face had puffed up, coarsened, and she looked suddenly like Aunt Weezie. Garrett came in, greeted me over Celia's running stream; and then finally my grandfather arrived at the back door. He stood in the doorway for a minute, the outside light still falling on his white hair, his sturdy frame. 'Ah, Anna,' he said. Then, knowing I would not, as the others did, just visit, he asked, 'To what do we owe the pleasure?' and stepped forward towards me into the crowded room. I embraced him formally; then he went to kiss my grandmother, as he frequently did after even just a short absence. She didn't turn fully towards him, but let him place his lips on her cheek. 'Where's my blueberries?' she said, as though they were a tribute he owed her; and Celia, gifted like Weezie with hearing through her own steady chatter, said she needed to wash and pick through them – Gram would have them in a minute.

I offered to do it. Celia was effusively grateful. She turned to Garrett, who was drinking milk from a carton in front of the opened refrigerator, and said, 'Hear, male piggie? How come it's always *women* who help?' He lowered the carton and snorted at her. Across the room, I heard my grandmother say to my grandfather, 'Anna needs to borrow money.' He bent his head to her for a moment, then lifted it and looked across at me. Our eyes locked momentarily. Then I took the colander down from its hook on the wall and began to work the pump.

When Celia had finished unpacking the hamper and putting things away, she sighed dramatically. She was going to go out to her cabin to 'rest a little minute,' she said.

'Yes, yes,' said Gram. 'May as well go get it over with.'

'See you at dinner,' she said to me as she went out. I could see her crossing the needle carpeting of the yard. Then her screen door lightly tapped shut. Garrett had gone out before she did, and from somewhere down near my grandparents' cabin I could hear him hammering rhythmically.

I bent over the colander and picked out the tiny stems, the hard green berries. 'When you're done,' my grandmother said, 'your grandfather's waiting in the other room.' I looked up at her, but she was hunched over the table, working.

After a few minutes I crossed to her. I set the bowl of dark berries next to the floured breadboard. I wiped my hands and stepped into the living room. My grandfather was on the front porch in a rocker. I could see him through the old crazed windows, moving jerkily in their prismatic panes. I crossed to the opened doorway, stepped outside into the soft light, the sound of water. He turned from the lake to me, motioned acknowledgment with his head. His real rocking seemed dreamlike in its smoothness. I sat down in a straight chair by one of the tables.

'Well, Anna,' he said. His hands were folded across his slight paunch. He looked tired. It occurred to me that he probably hadn't had his nap.

'I need money,' I said.

He smiled at me. 'Not to put too fine a point on it,' he said.

'I'm sorry,' I said. 'I don't mean to be rude. I just do. Need it.' I tried not to look at his face, fallen into hard lines, the curling brows frowning now.

He rocked a moment, his feet lifting slightly off the floor on the backswing. 'You'll forgive my curiosity,' he said. 'I'm wondering why the urgency.'

I picked up the glass salt shaker, dusted the grains off its bulbous nickel head.

'You haven't rushed up here because you've suddenly decided to hire someone to care for your daughter, surely?' I looked quickly at him. He'd resurrected his smile, deepened it when our eyes met.

'No,' I acknowledged.

He rocked, the gentle creaking joining all the familiar noises, an ominous minor theme. In the kitchen I could hear my grandmother's slow step, crossing the room, the clatter of pans.

I shrugged. 'Brian's started a custody suit, he wants Molly. I need money for a lawyer.'

The steady rocking continued. Then: 'What makes him think he can win such a suit? The whole weight of the law is in your favor, isn't it?'

I shrugged. 'He believes he has some grounds.'

'I see,' he said. A boat swung noisily around the point into our inlet. He looked out over the water, watched it jealously until it buzzed back out towards the islands. Then he turned to me again. 'I was under the impression – correct me if I'm wrong – that the mother would have to demonstrate some kind of incompetence to lose such a case.'

'I think that is correct,' I answered.

'What?' He frowned, leaning forward.

'I said, I think that's right.' My voice was loud, slightly defiant.

He rocked back again. 'Well, then?'

How like a hundred scenes from childhood this was! The gentle mocking voice, the weighty sense of guilt, a foot-dragging silence the only resistance possible, mere temporizing with fate.

Finally I answered. 'Brian has grounds.'

'He has grounds, based on your incompetence.' My grandfather was asking, but it was flat as a declaration.

I looked at him. My words came fast in sudden anger. 'I've had a lover, Grandfather. Not an unusual event for a woman in my situation. Someone living with me, essentially. Molly's been aware of that. She's *seen* some of it, not to put too fine a point on it. She must have talked to Brian about it, and he's angry. He's taking legal steps to get her back. That's the scenario.'

He rocked. 'Not pleasant,' he said mildly.

'No,' I agreed.

'And you've talked to a lawyer?'

'Yes.'

He raised his eyebrows to ask me. 'And?'

'And he'd like twenty-five hundred dollars to start with.'

There wasn't a pause in the rocking, but after a moment he said, 'I meant, *And* what does he think your chances are for keeping custody?'

I met his eyes, steady and intelligent on me. 'Ah,' I said, genuinely surprised. It seemed to me there was a kind of acknowledgment of the justice of my misunderstanding in the smile that lifted his mouth. 'Well,' I said. 'He doesn't talk about it in that way exactly. But it seems to me he's suggesting that Brian has a reasonable chance.'

'Brian has a good chance of getting her?'

'I believe he was suggesting that to me, yes.'

After a moment's silence, from the kitchen came the slow dry squeal of the pump two or three times, then splashing water.

'You're satisfied that this lawyer is competent?'

'Yes. I had him for the divorce, actually. He comes highly recommended. He's in one of the big law firms.'

My grandfather nodded.

'And who is this . . . lover of yours, this man Molly has seen too much of?'

'Does it matter, Grandfather?'

'To me it does, yes.'

'Why?'

He smiled, 'Why not?'

I had, without thinking about it, at some point in this conversation, taken the cap off the salt shaker and poured a small amount of it onto the pale green table. Now I drew a line with my finger through the white crystals. 'Because,' I said flatly, 'it seems prurient to me.'

His face seemed to enliven. 'But you *would* like my money.'

'Yes.'

He spread his hands in the air. 'It seems to me I have the right to ask a few questions then.'

I said nothing for a minute. Then, 'I simply don't see the relevance of my personal life beyond what I've told you. And I don't think you *do* have the right, the entrée to it.' His rocking continued. 'If you're not going to give me the money, just say so, so I can figure out what to do next.' Having said this, I was reminded that there was some sense in which he was my last resort. I thought fleetingly of my parents again, but then imagined my mother asking these same questions, but tearfully, anxiously.

After a moment he said, 'Are you still seeing this man?'

I said nothing. My finger traced circular patterns in the salt.

'You drive a hard bargain, Anna.' I looked up sharply at him. He smiled.

After a moment, I shook my head. 'Not in the sense you mean, no.' Suddenly, like a chasm opening below my feet, I understood the utter impossibility of going on with Leo, with our life together. It was over. I had to turn my head away from my grandfather. As I did so, I saw my grandmother through the window, standing in the center of the living room, her head held tilted up like a blind woman's at a busy intersection, listening for danger.

'In what sense, then?' my grandfather asked in his mocking voice.

I wasn't sure I could speak, so I didn't answer.

'In what sense?' he persisted after a moment, the smoothness stripped from his voice. I swallowed, struggled to get my voice in control.

My grandmother moved in my peripheral vision, disappeared from the window, appeared suddenly in the doorway. I looked up at her.

She looked from one of us to the other, then spoke quickly to my grandfather. 'Here now,' she said, as though he were a naughty boy. And then her mouth worked a moment. Then, 'Stop this,' she said.

'You do not need to concern yourself with this, my dear.' His voice had changed. It still had the same self-important sternness, but the edge, the mockery were gone.

'I'm talking to you, Frank,' she said as though he'd said nothing. 'Do you hear me?' Her bony hands were at my eye level. They gripped the door frame, and I watched the thickened nails whiten around their edges as they squeezed. I had never heard my grandparents so much as disagree. I felt a child's terror, a wish to disappear.

'This is between Anna and me, my dear,' he said.

She waited a moment, pushed her lips together, then had nothing to say. After a long silence she whispered, 'No.'

'Yes,' he said, gently. 'Anna has asked *me* for help.' He too spoke as if to a child; and it struck me that neither of them had a tone, a vocabulary, for conflict with the other, and so each borrowed from his relations with children, those with whom you could be assertive, or condescending, to disagree.

'Then hadn't you better help her?' she said, shrilly.

'That's for us to arrange.' His tone was final, dismissive.

He rocked again, and waited. She had no choice but to withdraw, and we all knew it. Her moment of defiance in memory of . . . what? her ten years of misery? Babe's misspent life? her other children's constricted, obedient ones? was over. I almost couldn't bear to look at her, but I wanted to find a way to release her, to let her go with some dignity.

My hands, gritty with salt, gripped each other tightly in

my lap. I turned to her. She stood framed by the open doorway, her look faraway over the lake.

'Thank you, Gram,' I said.

It was as though I'd waked her. Her head swung towards me. She brought me into focus with her sharp eyes. Then she said, 'You could ask *me*.'

I looked at her blankly for a minute.

'I have money, too. My own money,' she said. 'You could ask *me* for money.'

'Eleanor,' my grandfather began.

'It's my money,' she said to him, over my head. Then, again, to me: 'You could ask me.'

'That's not what your money is for, Eleanor,' he said.

'It's my money,' she said.

'You're not to spend your money on the family, Eleanor. That's not the way we do it.' His voice had a nervous quality I'd never heard in it.

'It's my money,' she said. She kept her eyes on me. 'You could ask me,' she said.

My grandfather's voice was suddenly stern. 'Now, Anna's not going to do that,' he said. 'Anna's asked me and that's that.'

'She could ask me, too,' my grandmother said. She looked at me again, her eyes pleading. 'You could ask me, Anna.'

My grandfather stood up, stepped towards her. As he spoke to her, his hand reached up to touch her shoulder in some final assertion or claim. She was, after all, his wife. 'Anna has asked me, Eleanor,' he said, and his strong male hand, the back of it furred lightly with white hair, gripped the frail bones under her blouse.

She yanked herself back from him. 'But you're not *giving* it to her!' she shrieked. Her voice echoed, *to her, to her, to her,* and we all listened to it until it had faded. Then there was just Garrett whistling somewhere, the boats, the hissing trees. I looked from one of my grandparents to the other. She was braced in the doorway as though he were going to attack her.

He stood openmouthed, frightened, at a loss. I remembered, suddenly, that he was in his eighties.

When he spoke, his voice was hoarse. 'Yes, I am,' he said.

'You are?' she asked.

'Yes, I will give Anna the money,' he said, as though he were making a kind of vow to her.

'Let me see,' she said.

He waited a moment, then stepped towards her. As though to avoid his touch, she swung back. He stepped into the living room, and I watched him cross the crazed panes of the two windows to the left of the door. I heard one desk drawer after another slide open and shut, the smooth whisper of wood. He bent over the desk for a few minutes. She stood near the door, watching his back. Under her gaze, he returned, stepped down, handed me a check. I looked at it. He'd made it out for five thousand dollars.

'That's that, then?' she asked.

'Yes,' he answered.

She waited, looking at me.

'Yes,' I said, looking only at the check. 'Thank you.'

There was a pause. I imagined I could feel each of them straining towards the other, though I don't think either of them was looking at the other.

'Well,' she said softly. '*Good* for you, Frank.'

'I think I'll nap now,' he said, turning to her. 'I skipped that today, getting the berries and so forth; I'm tired.'

'I think you should,' she said. She turned and went back through the living room to the kitchen. Without a word to me, he followed her. I didn't hear them speak to each other, and after a moment I heard the gentle smack shut of the kitchen screen door. As I looked off to the right through the woods, I saw my grandfather's figure move slowly down the path to his cottage, every few seconds his white hair blazing with the brilliant strobe of the sun through an opening above. In the kitchen the pump squealed again, and the pans clattered under the rushing water in the old sink. I looked at the check, at my grandfather's enormous black signature coiled assertively above both their printed names.

TEN

The fat woman leaned forward and showed the judge where her husband had knocked her tooth out. He frowned at her, then looked away. 'Fine, fine,' he said. 'You can shut your mouth now.'

'Your honor, my client no more knocked that tooth out than – well, I don't know. But that tooth has been missing since I don't know when.'

The judge shook his head at the elderly lawyer – a gent, with pomaded white locks carefully trained over his bald spot. 'Well, but your client didn't come to court to tell us that, did he now?' The judge wore half-glasses, and when he looked over them at the lawyer and the woman, he was stern, fussy, a spinster schoolteacher.

I couldn't hear the lawyer's answer. Next to me, Muth had taken his pen out, was making a note on his legal pad. The room was stifling and dark in spite of the two big open windows on the wall behind the judge. The shades on the other windows were pulled down, but these two opened nakedly out on Cambridge Street. I suppose someone was trying to cool the room, but more noise than breeze wafted in. Trucks, buses roared by, portable music swelled and faded occasionally. Across the street I could see a sign for *The Barrister Dining Room* in plastic gothic letters.

The wooden bench was uncomfortable. I recrossed my legs and looked around again. Brian was sitting with his lawyer, Fine, behind us in the corner to the right. Scattered here and there in these few back pews were real people, clients, but for the most part the room was full of lawyers. You could tell the difference easily. The clients were nearly

228

all frumpy, attentive, silent. The lawyers were natty, even those who wore cheap suits; and they sat differently. They crossed their legs expansively. They were relaxed.

Though the room was hushed and even the lawyers presenting their cases spoke in muted voices, there was a steady level of noise: the traffic going by outside, phones ringing distantly in the vast old courthouse, the double doors into the hall whumping and squeaking with the flow of people in and out. There was a large fan set on the floor under the windows which swung its face back and forth, exhaling loudly across the room, ruffling everyone's papers.

The judge had granted the order for the woman's husband to be evicted from the house; now he was trying to arrange a time for the man to get his clothes, his belongings. It was hard for the woman to imagine how this would work. Someone needed to be there to be sure he didn't hit her again.

'But you've lived alone with him up till now, haven't you?' the judge asked.

'Yes, but I didn't have no order kicking him out of the house up till now.' Out from under the shoulders of her cotton housedress, the straps of her slip looped over her shapeless upper arms.

The judge was patient. 'Well, who could you get to come and stay with you? Could your daughter come over?'

The woman thought for a moment, offered some objection. Back and forth they went, the judge resourceful, energetic. Finally, as though he'd worn her down, she consented to one of his arrangements. The judge talked to the lawyers for a moment, handed them some papers, and then the fat woman waddled slowly after her lawyer and her husband's lawyer out of the room. 'Whump whump, whump-whump-whump,' went the doors behind them.

The clerk picked up another folder from the pile on the edge of the judge's desk – some were in colors as bright as children's lunchboxes: green, orange, blue – and called out, 'The Carney matter.' Muth leaned to me. 'I think we're next, after this guy,' he whispered.

Carney approached the bench. He was young, bearded, wearing workclothes. He had stood directly in front of Fine when the lawyers lined up to hand their papers to the clerk. Carney bent forward, towards the judge, spoke inaudibly for a minute or two.

The judge looked down at the papers on his desk, then up over his glasses at the nervous-looking young man. 'OK, so you're Edward Carney?' he asked in his ringing voice. Carney assented.

'You're the father of this ... John Edward Carney?' Again a murmur.

'And this woman, Dolores Carney Diglio, she's the mother?' Carney's head moved. 'And she's remarried?' A nod.

'You understand what you're doing here?' Carney's voice, hesitant, too soft to carry, buzzed for a moment under the other noises in the room.

The judge listened. 'OK, now,' he said when Carney had finished. 'But I've got to officially explain this to you. That's my job.' He scanned the papers, looked up again. 'You understand that once you sign this, you give the child up to the mother and her new husband?' Carney turned so that no one in the courtroom could see his face. His head bobbed.

'You no longer have any rights or obligations to the child?' Carney seemed to make no response. 'You understand that you can't see the child?'

The clerk stood off to one side, talking to a lawyer. The lawyers seated by themselves in the front rows looked at their own papers, checked notes, crossed and recrossed their legs, paid no attention to Carney's shame as he gave up his child. Now Carney signed something on the judge's desk and started to walk away. I couldn't help it. I stared at him, at his blankened, neutral face.

'Ah, ah, ah, ah, Mr Carney,' the judge called out, scolding. Carney spun around and approached the desk again.

'No, *now*,' the judge said. 'We gotta do it all over again for the mother's lawyer and the State of Michigan.' And he began his litany, the awful booming questions, the silent answers, again. Carney gripped the edge of the judge's desk, and always kept his head bent away from us.

When they'd finished, the judge talked for a moment to the clerk. Carney listened attentively. The clerk and the judge agreed that Janie'd better Xerox this stuff. Carney was sent to the second floor, carrying all his papers with him. He looked at no one as he walked to the door.

'OK, next case,' the judge said as the doors whumped behind me. 'Come on, let's go, the next one!'

The clerk pulled another folder from the stack, handed it to the judge. For a few minutes he stood talking to the judge with his back to the courtroom. They laughed about something. Then the clerk turned around. 'The Dunlap matter,' he said and looked up expectantly.

'Sit here,' Muth said. He got up.

Fine too went up without Brian. The two lawyers – slender Fine, bulky Muth – huddled in front of the clerk. The judge watched them over his glasses. I couldn't hear them over the room's breathing sounds. My own blood seemed to slam noisily in my ears. The judge suddenly spoke up. 'You agree on the guardian?' he asked the lawyers loudly.

They seemed to be saying yes.

'Yeah, well, let's get a stipulation.' He nodded over and over at what they were saying. 'Yeah. The family service folks.' He listened a minute more. 'All right then, off you go. Let me see it when it's done.' Muth and Fine turned and headed in opposite directions out of the maze of desks and pews in front of the bench. As Muth approached me, I could hear the door swing shut behind Brian and Fine.

'Let's go,' he said.

'We're all set?'

'We're all set in here for the moment.' I stood up and followed his broad puckering back out of the room. He was wearing an expensive linen suit, but it looked, as all his clothes did, slightly rumpled.

Outside he caught my elbow, bent over me in his courtly way. 'We're headed for the family service officer here. Now remember I told you about her visit? So just relax. Every-

231

thing's going great from our perspective.' We walked down the long corridor, the high ceilings echoing our footsteps and, beyond them, a kind of universal din. The corridor fed into a large waiting area with a high dome over it. Most of the noise was generated here. A crowd as ragtag as what you'd find in any bus terminal: children jitterbugging around, yelling to each other, a large brown woman trying to nurse a wailing baby. There were even a few people with suitcases and the patient hopeless air of having taken up residence. Muth and I skirted them, turned left down another dark, echoing hallway.

Halfway down it, Brian sat on a bench against the wall. The glass door next to him was open. Muth stopped outside it, turned to me. 'OK, the deal is, the lawyers go in first and talk to her about what we're asking for. Then she'll want to see you, and Mr Dunlap.' He nodded towards Brian. 'Then we'll all confer together, in that order. OK?' He was talking softly, as though to exclude Brian. I nodded and sat down, and he stepped behind the glass door and closed it.

Brian and I sat at opposite ends of the long wooden bench. I was closer to the door, could hear behind the frosted glass the murmur of our lawyers' voices; but the activity in the echoing hallway made it impossible to pick out anything that was being said. Brian got up from the bench, paced down the hall, stood for a while by the waiting area. I watched him from a distance. When he started back down the broad hallway towards me, I stared straight ahead. He sat again, and the bench rocked slightly with his weight. I thought of all the times I'd wanted to call him, to speak to him in the last few weeks; of how sure I'd been that all it would take was my physical presence, my voice, for him to realize he was wrong about me. But now that he was here I felt in his implacable silence the distance he'd traveled from me. It was as though there were a thick substance in the air between us. I felt charmless now, not female, not sexual, not anything to Brian. Some process had begun which had seized me and already transformed me, in his eyes and my own.

I looked over at him. He too was transformed – calm, impervious. I looked down again quickly when he shifted weight. My hands were knotted tight in my lap, the white bone showing under the skin, the freckles dark. The difference between us was that Brian knew all about these peculiar legal steps. He knew what to expect, how to ride events. He was at home with Fine, even with Muth, my Muth, in a way I would never be. I looked at him again, the expensive suit, the relaxed posture. I thought of Leo in his borrowed jacket and felt suddenly helpless.

After a while, the lawyers came out, carried on a friendly burst of conversation. The family service officer was behind them. She leaned out and beckoned beyond me, to Brian. As he went in and shut the door, Muth sat down next to me.

'You OK?' he asked.

I nodded.

'You look scared,' he said.

'I am,' I whispered.

'No need to be,' he said. 'You just relax, be yourself. She'll just want to know sort of *how* it happened. You just downpedal the whole thing, like I told you. Right?'

I nodded.

'But *don't* pretend like it's not important. She wants to know you're sorry. That's very important here, and with the GAL.'

'GAL?'

'The guardian, the shrink.' He lifted his delicate hand, used it to weight his words. 'You're *sorry*, Leo *misunderstood* you, maybe you both used bad *judgment*, you know. But basically you're involved, you're concerned, et cetera. You get it?' He bent towards me, and I had the momentary impulse to rest my head on his shoulder, to ask him to hold me. Beyond him, down the hall, I could see Brian's lawyer leaning against the wall, smoking a cigarette, watching us. He was small, dark, feral, as unlike Muth as I could imagine someone being. I nodded at Muth, sat straighter.

'I've told her our concerns, you know, that you need to

233

see Molly, all that stuff. I think that's all set. Everyone's real happy with the guardian arrangement, so I think we're in a good position here. Real good. Now,' he gestured with his head down the hall, 'I've gotta make a few calls back to the office about some stuff, so I'll head out. I'll be back by the time you're done. I'll see you then, OK?'

I said it was, and he walked gracefully off down the hall. As he passed, Brian's lawyer said something, smiled slightly at him, then took another drag on his cigarette.

Brian's voice rose and fell inside the room. The family service officer had a light voice, too soft for me to hear. When she asked him something it was like a musical absence, a rest. Every now and then I could hear a word or two Brian said – *absolutely, criminal*. I watched my hands. Fine sat on a bench further down the hall, lighted another cigarette. I sat there for fifteen minutes or so. When Brian finally came out, he looked down at me, a clean contempt in his face. I saw that it had been feeding his rage just to talk about me, and I was frightened.

'Mrs Dunlap?' the light voice said.

I stood and she held the door open for me. She was a big faded blond woman who had once been very pretty. She still had that carriage, that confidence. Her skin was flawless, though now lined, slightly pouched at the jawline; and her makeup was very careful, very restrained. She wore a pink dress. She seemed impeccable, innocent, and she reminded me of my mother. I wondered what horrors she had dealt with today, every day, whether the ugliness my life had become was of any consequence to her.

'I'm Mrs Harkessian,' she said, when the door was shut. She held her hand out and I shook it. 'Anna Dunlap,' I answered. Her grip was firm.

'Sit down,' she said.

The room was tiny, but had the same high ceilings as the hall, so the space above our heads was ample, mocked the box we sat in. There were a table, four chairs, a window, then the high walls, painted a worn, pale blue. The room had been partitioned at one time, and the blank sheet rock cut brutally into the elaborate molding at the baseboard and the ceiling. I sat by the window. Outside, below me, three workmen watched a fourth slowly stirring cement in a wheelbarrow.

Mrs Harkessian sat too, and explained to me that she just needed to ask a few questions. Her tone was apologetic, as though I were doing her an enormous favor by granting her this interview. She began. The questions were at first harmless – What did I do? Could I describe the arrangements I'd had for childcare? Had I had other relationships since the divorce? How serious was my relationship with Leo? Then she focused on him. How long had I known him? Could I tell her a little about his background? When did I start bringing him to the house? Had I noticed anything unusual in his relationship to Molly? Did I know about the specific episode which had triggered Mr Dunlap's complaint? Was I present? So I just had Mr Cutter's description of it to go by? Had Molly seemed upset around this time? What was my attitude about what had happened?

At first I was nervous. I could hear the fear in my own voice, in my breathlessness. But somewhere midstream I found a persona in which to answer the questions and I began to feel more comfortable. I frowned. I took each one very seriously, and I carefully disposed of it, as Muth had instructed me. It was as though her polite professionalism, her sincerity, suggested an answering image for me. Mr Cutter, I said, had misunderstood my attitude about issues relating to sex. Though it was clear to me how the episode could have happened, I didn't condone it. As I talked, I kept thinking of my mother, of how I'd lied to her in high school, the long elaborate stories entirely fabricated about what had gone on at parties. Yet this was all the truth, everything I was saying to Mrs Harkessian. What made it feel the same way?

She mentioned that Mr Dunlap thought there had also been times when Mr Cutter and I had Molly in bed with us. Could I explain to her my thinking about that?

I looked down at my hands for a moment; remembered

235

Muth's advice. I shook my head. 'It was a mistake, I know that,' I said. 'I was very caught up in my feelings about Leo, and I just didn't give enough thought to Molly, to what might be confusing or difficult for her in all of it. She was doing so well, she seemed to like him so much. It was as though we were a family.' I paused. 'In my defense, I guess, the one time we were . . . having intercourse, she was asleep.'

Her face firmed, suddenly looked younger, tougher. 'But you *did* actually have intercourse at least once while the child was in bed with you?' My heart stopped.

I should have lied, I realized. This was something they couldn't have known except from me or Leo, and I'd given it to them. Then, unbidden, tears rose to my eyes. I felt a nearly vindictive joy at their arrival. I stared through them at Mrs Harkessian's pretty, unmoved face. 'Yes,' I said softly, as though feeling deep shame. One tear spilled over, and I wiped it away with the back of my hand. 'But she was asleep. She'd had a bad dream and I'd comforted her about it.'

'I see,' she said, and bent her head to make a note.

Then she looked up and smiled coolly at me. 'One last question,' she said. 'If the court makes it a condition of custody that you keep Mr Cutter away from Molly – which would certainly alter your relationship with him – would you be willing to do that?' She tilted her head slightly.

'Yes,' I said.

She made another note, smiled again, folded her hands. Now, she said, Mr Muth had told her my main concern was getting to see Molly soon, and she could certainly understand that. Was there anything else I wanted to ask about, wanted to add? No? Well then, she'd get Mr Dunlap again, and the lawyers.

They all trooped in behind her from the hall. Brian sat down, but Muth and Fine remained standing, behind Brian and me. Mrs Harkessian sat down again too, and looked around at the lawyers. 'Now, let me explain my role to the Dunlaps for a second if you will, gentlemen,' she said.

She looked at me and Brian. 'Since there's a guardian

appointed here,' she said, 'what I'm really responsible for is just laying out the ground rules temporarily for both of you. Mr Dunlap's concern is simply not to put the child at risk during this period. Mrs Dunlap's concern is to be able to see her regularly until the question of custody is settled. And the court is concerned with both these issues too. I think what I'm going to recommend to the attorneys and ask them to work out is that Mother be able to see the child at the intervals agreed on.' She looked sternly at Brian. 'But that Mr Cutter must be out of the house, nowhere around during those visits.' Now she looked at me. I nodded. 'And I'm going to recommend that the child be kept where she is, basically in Father's custody, except for visits, until the trial, to avoid shifting her back and forth unnecessarily.' Brian leaned back suddenly and I looked at him. He was faintly smiling. He glanced back at Fine. Fine's eyes, under the heavy lids, flickered to him and quickly away. I understood this was a victory for them. 'But I'm going to stipulate that the trial be speedy, ask to get back within six weeks or so. OK?' Muth and Fine made agreeable noises. She looked again at me and Brian. 'Do either of you have any questions?' she asked. Brian shook his head.

'When will I be able to see Molly?' I asked.

'You're overdue for a visit now, aren't you?' she asked.

I nodded.

'You guys work that out for as soon as possible, then,' she said, looking up at the lawyers. 'Now, who's got the good handwriting here?' she asked. No one answered. 'Come on, you guys, let's get this going. I'm going to start dictating this thing.'

'I'll do it,' Fine said. He stepped forward. Brian shifted closer to me to make room for him, and Fine sat down at the table. He smelled strongly of some gingery aftershave.

Mrs Harkessian dictated in her firm light voice. That the parties agreed upon a psychiatrist to be appointed by the court to examine the child and make a recommendation as to custody. That we would come back to court within six weeks. That during the interim, Brian would have physical custody, but that I would see her regularly. Muth and Fine haggled a little over the language, but mostly we sat in long silences listening to Fine's pen scratch on the yellow paper. When we were through, Mrs Harkessian looked it over quickly. Then she said, 'Great!' She looked up at Muth. 'You want to check it, counsel?'

She handed it over Brian's head, and Muth read it, moving his big head slowly up and down.

'OK, looks like we're all set then,' she said. She passed it first to Brian, then to me, for our signatures. Then she stood up. We all rose. As the lawyers sidestepped past her to the door, Brian had to move back towards me to make room. He stumbled over my foot and caught himself by grabbing my arm. I felt his weight momentarily on me and reflexively held out my other hand to steady him. As though I carried infection in my touch, he recoiled from me. The lawyers were in motion, on their way out, but Mrs Harkessian watched us steadily and smiled her pretty smile.

I didn't get home until after five, because I waited until Muth and Fine had gone back before the judge again. The telephone was ringing when I walked in. It was Leo. I told him everything had gone fairly well, that the court date was set for October. He wanted to come over, but I asked him not to, said I wanted to be alone. As soon as I hung up, though, I couldn't bear the idea. I called Ursula. She said she'd stop for pizza and be over in about an hour.

'I hope you like anchovies,' she shouted up from deep in the stairwell.

'A little goes a long way,' I said.

'Oh, shit, you don't like them?' She sounded genuinely stricken. She leaned into the open space, her hand to her bosom. Her face was a white circle below me. I couldn't see her expression.

'I love them,' I said. 'I'm ecstatic to have about two. The rest I'll just pick off and give to you.'

'Thank God. Then it all works out for the best. I like dozens,' she said, disappearing. She panted up the last flight of stairs. She was wearing high-heeled sandals and very short shorts. Delicate silver stretch marks gleamed on her outer thighs. She bent her face, with its smudgy innocence, into the air next to me and made a kissing sound.

'Was it terrible?' she asked, pulling back, frowning.

'Not really,' I said. 'I find I'm very good at discussing my guilt.'

'Fuck guilt,' she said. 'It's all relative. Can you imagine if I ever had to expose my sex life? It'd make Moll Flanders look like she needed hormone therapy.'

'You don't have a kid.'

She was trailing me, clomping loudly down the long dark hallway. I'd set the table for us in the dining room.

'Do you want wine or beer?' I asked.

'Beer. And the reason I don't have a kid is 'cause I'm too irresponsible. And you're not. So I don't want to hear about guilt.' She set the pizza down, moved to the piano and began to play the piece she'd been working on when we'd stopped her lessons for the summer, a sonatina by Beethoven. I went into the kitchen. I was standing at the counter, looking in the messy utensil drawer for a churchkey, when she stopped in midmeasure and called out, '*Everyone* knows you're a good mother, Anna.' And then a minute later, 'My God, smell these anchovies.'

My eyes had clouded quickly with tears. No one except Ursula had said anything positive to me about being a mother since Brian had set this whole machine in motion. She'd gotten back from her visit to New York about a week earlier, and since then she'd been in touch with me daily. She was aggressively, assertively in my corner. It was to get this, I realized abruptly, that I had called her tonight, that I wanted her more than I wanted Leo, whose presence only made me doubt myself.

'Did I tell you my anchovy theory of sex?' she yelled.

I thought of my open windows, imagined neighbors called in to testify about my social life, my friends.

I wiped my eyes and called back. 'Just a second.' I found the churchkey, brought it and two beers back to the table. She was pulling the pizza apart, setting a piece on my plate.

239

The big box flapped open, and the smell brought saliva to my mouth. I realized I hadn't eaten all day. All I'd had were three or four cups of machine coffee as I sat, a stray among strays, in the waiting area of the courthouse.

'What's your theory?' I asked, sitting down.

'Well, you remember that guy I was going out with last fall? Mike Levine? Who mostly liked oral sex?' She said this as someone else would say, 'Who had brown eyes,' or 'Who was a doctor.'

I opened the beers. 'I remember your talking about him.'

'Remember that he said it was 'cause he was Jewish, was raised on salty, spicy foods?' She rested her chin in her jeweled hands. Her eyes were big, innocent.

'Mmmhuh,' I said. I'd begun to pick the anchovies off.

'Well, right after that I started going out with this *other* guy, very straight, very WASPy, no insult intended. I mean, he wore like lime-green trousers, if you can believe it. I was really trying to prove to myself that I shouldn't be so judgmental. I mean, why should I go around judging someone by the *pants* he wears. Can you imagine if people judged *me* by how I look?' She raised her eyebrows. 'Anyway, he was an all-right lover, but he wouldn't go down on me. And I was thinking, you know, it's either feast or famine here, what *is* this? I mean, I'd even ask him to, and he'd still sort of avoid it, or do it for two *very* unsensuous seconds, you know what I mean?'

I told her that I thought I did, yes.

'So, one time we're sitting in this restaurant – oh, thanks!' she said, as I heaped extra anchovies on her triangle of pizza. 'And I ordered Caesar salad. And he ordered Caesar salad too, but he said to the waitress "Only skip the anchovies"; and I said, "What is a Caesar salad without the anchovies?" And he said he hated anchovies, that if an anchovy had even been on his Caesar salad and was subsequently removed he wouldn't be able to eat it.

'So I'm sitting here opposite this guy, listening to this, looking at his green pants, at the crocodile on his shirt, and I'm *fondly* remembering Levine, and I realize I probably have in front of me a fairly accurate test for women who'd like to know *before* they get into bed with a guy what the routine is going to be. And I've checked it out since then and it's pretty reliable. Isn't that fabulous?'

'A nifty theory,' I agreed.

'Better than that.' She took a big bite and pulled back, grabbing the strands of cheese with her fingers.

'The old anchovy test for oral sex.'

'I'm going to patent it,' she said with her mouth full. 'But till then, I'm just sharing it with close friends whose best interests I have at heart.'

'I appreciate it,' I said. 'But I don't think I'll use it any time soon.'

'Well, *you've* got Leo,' she said.

'I guess so,' I said.

She stopped chewing and raised her eyebrows. One cheek was full, and she looked, for a moment, like one of the rats with a food reward. She chewed a moment more, swallowed, and then said, 'Explain?'

'There's not much to explain. Just that this is hard for both of us. We try not to blame each other, but we do. I do anyway. And then I'm angry at myself for that. And sexually, it seems.' I shrugged. 'It's just not possible for the moment.'

'But you *love* Leo.'

'That doesn't make everything all right, Ursula.'

'But you yourself told me it wasn't his fault.' She popped an anchovy into her round mouth.

'It wasn't. And I don't really blame him. It's just that its having happened . . . changes things, changes everything.'

'That's ridiculous,' she said. 'You're the same people.'

'But I thought something was possible with Leo . . . It's that I blame *myself* too, for thinking something *was* possible with him that's not. Some kind of . . . life without limits or something. And it's not. It's just not. It's as though I was dreaming, and now I'm awake. *This* is real. Brian's real. He's really Molly's father. And having to cope with this stuff.'

'It is *not*. This stuff is crazy,' she said. 'All these weirdos messing around in your life. Who else do you know that it's happened to? What you and Leo had, *have* is what's real.'

Suddenly what I most wanted was to stop talking about this. 'You just want someone to have true love, Ursula, so you can believe in its being out there somewhere.' I sounded irritable even to myself.

She looked at me levelly a moment, then shrugged, capitulating. 'Oh, I know,' she said. 'You're right. *You* bear the burden of all my cheap and shallow dreams, which I probably have in the first place so I can go on being a slut. Let other people have love, just let me fuck around.'

'By the way,' I said. 'I told Leo I wanted to be alone tonight, so I'd appreciate it if you can avoid talking about seeing me.'

'Any *special* reason for not wanting to see him?' she asked.

'I don't know.' I said. Then, 'Yes I do. They've made it a condition of my seeing Molly that he not be around. And I just couldn't face telling him tonight.'

She opened her mouth a little. 'Jesus,' she said. 'Can they do that?'

'Apparently so.'

'But for good?'

'I don't think so, for good. I talked to Muth for a little while afterwards, and he said it was unlikely they'd set any conditions permanently, that if I got custody it'd be because they agree nothing so bad happened. Except maybe therapy, something like that.'

'Don't say *if*. You're going to. Nothing so bad did happen.'

I looked away, out the window over the tracks. She reached over and patted my hand. 'Take it from a slut like me, honey,' she said. 'I know *bad*. This is all gonna work out.'

I looked down at her hand. Painted down the middle of each fuchsia fingernail was a jagged lightning bolt of black.

Ursula stayed until about ten. She had started down the stairs, carrying her heels so the clumping wouldn't wake my neighbors, who were sunk in deep silence below us, when she remembered the drugs. She came running back up, rushed past me. In the hall she fumbled in her purse. She pulled out a baggie and dumped its contents on the table. Whimsically colored, like the pieces of one of Molly's plastic toys, the pills bounced and rolled across its surface. Ursula bent over them, started drunkenly to sort them by color.

'Some are Librium, these black and greenies, and there's about a dozen Valium,' she said. 'And then these beauties' – she indicated the bright blue and red ones – 'Tranxene. They're absolutely the best, and guaranteed nonaddictive. I take one every night.'

'They're gorgeous,' I said. 'It's like getting a bouquet of flowers. Only I really don't think I'll use them.'

'Oh don't be such a *Protestant*,' she said. 'It's a chemical age. And you might as well do this as sit up drinking all night.'

'I'm just an old-fashioned girl, I guess,' I said.

She scooped them back into the bag. 'Tell you what,' she said. 'I'll put them in the medicine chest for a rainy day.' She ignored the half-dozen or so rolling silently to the distant reaches of the dark hall, and disappeared into the bathroom. I heard the medicine cabinet slam. Then she trooped silently back on her bare flat feet.

'You make me feel like a pusher, Anna,' she complained. She picked up her shoes and hugged them to her chest, then grinned at me. 'But someday you'll thank me for turning you on,' and she started down the stairs again.

After she left, I somehow had the buoyant sense that everything would work out. I hummed as I brushed my teeth. I slept well. And in the morning before I left for work Muth called to say he and Brian's lawyer had spoken earlier. Brenda was coming to Boston the following Monday for a couple of days' work. She'd accompany Molly on the plane, and I could pick her up at the airport in the morning, and return her there late Tuesday afternoon, if that was agreeable. I said it was and he gave me the flight times.

'Now remember,' he said. 'Cutter's got to be completely out of the picture. That could really foul us up here.'

243

'I know. There's no problem.'

'You don't want me to talk to him about it or anything?'

'No, it's clear to both of us,' I lied.

'OK,' he said. 'Enjoy. And I'll be in touch about the arrangements for the guardian stuff. Might be a couple of weeks. Your ex-husband wants to arrange a kind of marathon, you know, so he can just come up once with Molly and get it all done in a few days. So it might be quicker than we thought.'

'Is that good?'

'Not good, not bad. You just need to convince the guardian whenever that you're a responsible mother. You know, *concerned, involved.* Pull out all the stops: the children's museum, music lessons, the aquarium. You get the picture.'

'Yes,' I said.

'But I'll talk to you anyway before you go in, a day or two before, you know. And you call me if you get worried about anything.'

'I will,' I said.

'But don't let Cutter near her next week.'

'No,' I said.

'Great,' he said, and hung up.

I called Leo before I left for work and invited him for dinner.

When I answered the door that evening, I was dressed as Leo liked to see me. I was wearing the blouse he had given me and a soft white skirt that swung against my legs when I moved. I'd put on my eye makeup carefully. There were three bottles of white wine in the refrigerator, the chicken was marinating in oil and wine and rosemary and garlic in the kitchen. I'd washed the lettuce, made a salad dressing. I'd set the hibachi on top of Leo's inverted tub on the back porch, and started the coals.

Leo followed me to the kitchen and I poured us both white wine. We walked single-file back down the hall to the rickety porch off the living room, where I'd set a table with crackers and cheese.

It was with the best of motives and the worst of motives

that I'd done all this – I did want to cushion the blow I had to deliver: that the court had ruled he couldn't see Molly; that I'd accepted that. But I also wanted to signal that perhaps now he and I could find a way to be kind to one another again, even to be ourselves with one another. I had missed him, I realized when he stood in the evening air on the porch and looked down at me.

There was no roof over the porch. It opened out to the pale evening sky, yellow with gases over Boston, bluing as the eye lifted. Children yelled distantly in the street far below us. 'You're looking very beautiful tonight,' he said. The light in the sky was behind him, his face slightly shadowed.

'Thanks,' I said. 'I worked at it.'

He swung his head away, then looked back sharply. 'I meant it, Anna.'

'I'm sorry,' I said. 'I'm not trying to be flip. It's just that I was conscious, when I got dressed and everything, of wanting you to think that. That I was beautiful.' I shrugged. 'I was confessing.'

He was silent a moment, placated. 'All you had to do was accept it. You *are*,' he said. 'But I'm glad you wanted me to think so.'

'Tell me what you've been doing the last couple of days,' I said after a moment.

'Not working,' he said.

'I'm sorry.'

'No, it's been fine actually. I spent one day with John and Susan in Newburyport, and then I've been trying to assemble this grant-application stuff for the Mass. Council. Slides and stuff. Besides, I feel like I need to lie fallow a while after that big push last month.' He sat down and we sipped our wine. 'I've sold three so far. Mady called today.'

'That's wonderful,' I said.

'And there was another good review.'

'Fantastic.'

He made a muscle, flexed it. 'Stick with me, baby.'

I smiled.

His face sobered. 'I'll have some bucks, Anna. I could help a little with this stuff.'

I was already shaking my head. 'No, no.'

He turned in his chair, set his glass down, hunched towards me. 'No, look,' he said. 'I know we said no before, but I've been thinking about it, and Anna, it would help *me*. It would make me feel better.' He held his hands out, palms up, in front of him. 'For God's sake, I feel like shit watching you go through this and being so powerless to help you. No, listen to me,' he said as I tried to interrupt him. 'Maybe it's crass, and maybe it's self-serving, but I feel as if, if I can do something, even if it is just money – and it seems like that's about it – I want to. You've got to let me Anna. I don't see how we can rescue anything between us if you don't, if you won't let me.' He was sitting on the edge of his chair, leaning towards me.

I looked out over the variegated asphalt rooftops of North Cambridge, the listing brick chimneys. 'There's an awful lot you're going to have to do anyway,' I said.

He shifted back. 'I don't care about the testimony. Or the shrink.'

'Muth thinks it might get pretty ugly,' I told him.

He shrugged. 'I can imagine,' he said. 'But frankly, I think they'll believe me. I don't know why. I just think they will.' He made a face. 'My eminently trustworthy mug or whatever. *And* I'm going to get a haircut.'

'Don't,' I said. 'Don't cut your hair for that.'

'Why not? It can't hurt.'

I shook my head.

'Don't get a haircut, don't give me money, don't borrow a jacket and tie, don't do any of it!'

He stared at me. 'What's wrong, Anna?' he said at last.

I set my glass down. 'I get Molly for two days on Monday,' I said. I held up my hand to stop the happiness that started to lift his face. 'But one of the conditions is your absence. You can't come anywhere near here, or us, or her.'

After a moment's silence, he asked, 'And who worked out this deal?'

'Leo,' I said.

He didn't respond. I looked away, then, after a moment, back to him.

'It's the recommendation of someone called the family service officer. It's a compromise she worked out, on her own.' I couldn't see his face, turned away from me in the night air. 'Leo, I didn't do anything yesterday. I didn't even testify. It was all this big machine working, and this is what popped out.' I waited for him to respond.

'How is this a compromise?' he asked finally.

'That I get to see her at all,' I answered. Then, in what was a nearly unconscious manipulation, a demonstration to him that I was suffering too, suffering more than he was: 'Brian keeps her till it's all settled, till the court date, early October.' He looked up at me, as I'd known he would. 'He gets *that*, and he gets the *protection* from you. And I get to see her on a regular schedule, to be arranged.'

'Jesus, that's no compromise.'

I shrugged. 'She's *at risk*. And I'm the one who put her there, by their lights.'

We sat together. The street lamp had come on with a hard nasal hum, and it was already darkening in the street below us, but the sky overhead was still light.

'By loving me,' he said at last.

It took me a moment to answer. 'Yes,' I said. I swallowed the last of my wine.

'Anna,' he said suddenly, then stopped. 'Now don't get pissed off, but isn't there another way to do this?'

'To do what?'

'Well, what I mean is, do you have to just, let this *happen*, all of this stuff? Isn't there a way to, *some* way, to fight it?'

'I don't think so.'

'But this way, Jesus.' He stood up, held the peeling railing, looked down to where the children were still playing. He shook his head and turned to me. 'I can't believe you have to allow it, just let it roll over you like this.'

I waited a moment, feeling my anger. 'It depends on what

you want, I think. I just want Molly. I don't care about *dignity*, or *pride*, or any of that stuff.' My voice was trembling audibly, was sharp with adrenaline. 'I just want Molly.' I stopped. 'I've got to put the chicken on,' I said. 'Or we'll never eat. Will you pick some music?'

We ate in the living room with just two candles burning and the music around us, as though we were at the beginning of something. And if someone could have ignored the loud despondent silences that fell between us, we might have seemed like people at the brink of love, so kind, so interested were we in each other. And I really did feel that way. I was grateful for Leo's easy acquiescence to the conditions Mrs Harkessian had imposed; for his not arguing with the lie we were all perpetrating about him – that he was dangerous, that his presence was pernicious, and therefore that mine was perhaps less so. I wanted to make it a pleasant time. And after a while, I think we both began to enjoy ourselves. At some point late in the evening I went into Molly's room to get some cards – we'd decided to play gin rummy – and looking around, I felt for the first time since she'd left a sense of happiness. She'd be here soon, sleeping in the bed, lifting the toys off the shelf, spreading the pieces all over the floor. I'd be able to hear her from the kitchen, the living room, humming, talking to herself, calling out to me: Mumma, where are you? Mumma, I need you to show me this. Mumma, when will you be done in the kitchen? Mumma, I fixed this all by myself.

I found the cards, went back to the kitchen for another bottle of wine. When I returned to the living room, Leo was lying stretched out on the couch. The wine and our friendliness had relaxed him, and he looked the way he'd looked to me earlier in the spring and summer. In the candlelight his eyes seemed entirely black, his white skin delicate, thin, all of a piece, like some fine fabric stretched taut over the long nose, the sculpted cheekbones. My hands were full, but on an impulse I bent and kissed him.

His lips, then his body, responded. His arms circled me, pulled me down. I could feel in his quickened breathing, his corded arms how much he wanted this, how much he read in it of forgiveness, of reconciliation. I set the wine and the cards on the floor by the couch, and we made love, fueled by his energy. I felt as distant from it, from him, as I had with Brian near the end. Yet I responded, I arched against him, helped him, moaned aloud. When he began to come, I recognized the pure relief in my gladness. I saw that what I was doing was binding him to me, ensuring his cooperation. I felt somewhere in me still the deep hateful anger, the fear of his anger at me, at what he could do to me and Molly with that anger. I watched myself lift and move my hips as he cried my name in loving abandon. I was glad his eyes were shut, and I turned my face away when he slid forward onto my shoulder.

Over the weekend, I worked four or five hours each day, but we spent the rest of the time together, as though everything were all right between us again. Each afternoon, he stopped by in the truck to pick me up, and we drove out to Walden Pond. We hiked around away from the bathhouses, the crowded concrete piers, to the illegal beaches on the far shore. Even there, the beaches were full until four or five in the afternoon. But then the teenagers, laden with squalling boxes, would leave to get ready for the night; the families would pack up their squabbling children and cooler chests and foldout chairs; the solitary bronze sun-worshippers would put their tubes of coconut lotion into their leather bags, their Guatemalan baskets, and slip away, silent as Thoreau down the eroding paths, and there would be left only a reader or two still engrossed in a book, a few couples.

Both days, Leo packed a picnic – wine, sandwiches, fruit, cheese. We would eat and swim, and lie next to each other again, the occasional train roaring past in the clearing far across the lake the only reminder of home.

The water was nearly perfect. You could float on your back motionless on its tepid surface, hearing nothing, seeing only the high blue sky circled by the pointing dark fingers of the pines. Occasionally a stately cloud would ride across it slowly, nearly without changing shape from horizon to horizon.

Leo and I didn't talk much; but each day as dusk fell and the silent wardens circled the paths on horses big as nightmares; each day as we slowly packed the tinfoil and plastic cups and utensils into the basket; each day as we shook out and folded the blanket, backing away and coming towards each other as though we were performing some ancient dance; each day I felt a mingled sense of relief and dread. Relief that another marker was gone by, Molly's arrival was that much nearer. Dread at the idea of another long evening to pass through with Leo, the false intimacy, the touching, the lovemaking bitter reminders of what it had all been like when I felt it, wanted it. He had tried the first night to go down on me, touch me, to do the things which had always brought me sure pleasure. I had stopped him, told him I was too distracted to come, and he seemed to accept that. Still, he was full of tenderness which I didn't feel. It seemed to request an imitative response in me, and the need for that brought with it rage at both myself and him for my dishonesty.

When he left late Sunday night, I felt such relief that I could not go back and lie down in the bed where we'd just finished making love. I stood in the doorway and looked at the sheets – rumpled, falling to the floor at the foot of the bed; at the pillow pulled into the bed's center to raise my hips; at the wet stain near it. I turned and went back to the living room. For a while I rested on the couch. Then I went into Molly's room. I pulled back the clean sheets I'd put on her bed and slid between them. Watched by the solemn unwinking glass eyes of her dolls and animals, I waited for sleep.

ELEVEN

The piano students started again right after Labor Day, but I canceled them during the week we were scheduled to see the *guardian ad litem*. I had only three appointments myself, but Molly needed to get back and forth to his office an additional three times; and she was staying with me while all of us – Brian and Brenda and even Leo – took our turns talking with Dr Payne.

Muth had told me about the arrangements as soon as everything was 'finalized' – Muth: my lawyer, my ally, my conduit. I'd come to rely on nearly daily calls from him, even if there was no news, or the news was just that he hadn't gotten through yet to Brian's lawyer. His voice on the telephone was gruff but gentle. In response to him, I became quieter, more dependent. I'd ask questions I already knew or guessed the answers to in order to feel the comforting expansion of his personality. That would, in turn, make me feel more genuinely as though I couldn't possibly make it through all this without him. It was like the phenomenon that had occurred with Mrs Harkessian. At some point I couldn't tell the difference myself between the feelings I was having because they worked well in the situation, and the feelings I fully owned.

With Leo too, I had this sense of artificiality, but it was perhaps more intense for being only slightly off from what seemed real. And he was the only one with whom I was aware of the impulse to say what I truly felt. Often I wanted to tell him how angry I was, how unresponsive sexually. Especially at those moments when I was washed by the old love, I'd have the sense that I could tell him, and sometimes

I nearly would. But then there'd be the nagging *what if*: what if he got angry, what if he refused to testify, or testified in ways that would be damaging to me. What if he talked about our long days of lovemaking while Molly was in day care, or those moments – in the bathroom or the kitchen – when we'd come together quickly, listening to her playing down the hall.

During all of this I felt sometimes as I had in the period of my adolescence when I'd stopped making music and started letting boys touch me: there was that same nauseous sense of falseness in myself as I woke next to Leo, felt his waking arms reach for me, or as I dialed Muth's number and prepared myself for the comfort I felt at the sound of his voice. But then I'd think *Molly*, and put those hesitations aside. If this worked, it was worth anything. It would make my need for what I thought was truthfulness seem self-indulgent.

I'd gone downtown to Muth's office to prepare for the talks with Dr Payne – *the shrink*, as Muth kept calling him. We went over the strategy together, and Muth coached me again in his possessive, comforting way: 'Now what we wanna do here,' 'Now, what we're *not* interested in . . .' I set out for the sessions feeling high, feeling I would manage it all, whatever question Dr Payne asked me.

After the psychiatrist had poured me a cup of coffee and set it on the table near me, he sat in his swivel chair, tilted back, and smiled at me. He was a short, ugly man – beetle-browed, dark, with oily skin and the shadow of a beard making his face look unwashed. When he smiled, he revealed big gaps between his teeth. I looked away, picked up my cup. I wondered whether Molly would be afraid of him. He looked like a Maurice Sendak monster in one of her books. Then, as I swallowed the overperked coffee, the powdered milk, I realized that *I* was afraid of him, of the patience with which he sat waiting opposite me. He was giving me no cues. I didn't know what to say, what to do. I looked over at him and smiled back.

'People probably say it all the time,' I said, 'but *Payne* seems an unfortunate name for a psychiatrist.'

His smile broadened. 'They do say it all the time. And then I always say that it's a kind of truth in advertising, after all.'

There was a little silence.

'And it gives people a way to begin talking,' he said. 'That's a help.' His gaze was steady on me from under his thick brows. Like a little ape, I thought. Though the smile had faded slightly, he still had the attitude of expectancy. Behind him, on shelves along the walls, a collection of dolls, puppets – toys he'd use to find out from Molly what had happened to her – seemed to wait, too.

'I don't know how I'm supposed to begin,' I said.

He put his arms up behind his head. 'Why not just tell me about the events that brought you here?'

'That could take a long time, depending on where you want me to start. My whole life got me here, in a certain sense.'

He laughed. 'It was a pretty dumb question. OK. Well then, let's start with your little girl. Molly?'

'Yes, Molly.'

'Tell me about Molly. What kind of kid is she?'

'She's bright, imaginative. But kind of private.' I shrugged. 'That's pretty general, I know.'

'Uh-huh. Well, tell me, for instance,' he swung his chair around, 'which of these toys do you think she'll pick out when she comes in here?' He gestured at the shelves crammed with bright objects.

I looked. 'It'll be a toss-up, I'd guess, between the bear – she has one like him – and the tea set. She likes little things, lots of parts. Arranging them.'

His head bobbed. 'And what would she do with the bear?'

'Well, in some sense the same kind of thing she'd do with the tea set. She'd be the boss, and then also the bossee. If you put them all together, for instance, I can imagine her bossing the bear around about the *right* way to drink coffee, or juice or tea. And then being the bear, refusing and being bad. That kind of thing.'

'*Yes*,' he said, and nodded, as though this were a keen observation on my part. Then after a minute, 'She was in day care while you worked?'

I nodded. 'Yes,' I said.

'Did she like that?' he asked.

I stiffened. 'She seemed to, very much.'

'She get along with other kids? Have special friends?'

'Yes,' I said. 'Everything was normal.'

'Normal?' he said, and frowned. 'I'm not sure what you mean by that.'

'Well, nothing unusual,' I said. 'She liked the other kids, they liked her. She played at their houses some, and they sometimes came over to our house.' I shrugged, but my mouth was dry. Muth had told me Payne was the key to keeping Molly. Now I sat opposite him in his windowless basement office and felt I was failing some test. What did he want from me?

He was frowning again. 'I guess what I'm really asking here, what I'm wondering, is how she was – how she *is* – special. What you see as particular, or characteristic of her, that might be different from other kids.'

I looked at him. He seemed only curious after all. Maybe he really just wanted to help me begin.

I started talking about Molly, giving him examples of her intense involvement in her play, of what I thought of as her unusual compassion for other kids. Through it, he sat and listened intently, always with a slight smile. Sometimes he'd repeat a word I'd used, interrogatively, to get me to expand on an idea; or he'd ask what I meant by something; but mostly he listened. Once or twice he redirected me: 'Tell me whether you noticed changes in her play around the time of the divorce.' 'I'm wondering whether you're the kind of mother who really likes to play with Molly, or who'd rather watch, let her run her own games.'

I had just finished a long description of the way Molly had played with a particular friend from day care, a Korean girl who had no English when she started, but who'd liked what Molly called *acting silly*. He sat smiling, looking at me. I actually felt relaxed, I'd taken such pleasure in the memory of the two little girls laughing together. In the same posture and without dropping his gentle, gap-toothed smile, he said, 'Tell me about Leo – his background, his life.' And he leaned back, as though expecting I would be as expansive on this topic.

I drank a little of the cold, terrible coffee. After a moment I asked, cautious again, 'What would you like to know about Leo?'

He shrugged, generous. Anything, his smile said.

'I don't know what you're aiming at,' I said. 'His work? His relationship with me? Or Molly?'

He didn't respond.

'His credit rating?'

'Not his credit rating,' he said.

'OK,' I said. I sat up straighter. 'His relationship with Molly. It was good. It was wonderful. It was a source of infinite gratification to me. He loved her. She loved him.'

He looked at me, tilted his head quizzically. 'And his relationship with you?'

'Much the same,' I said quickly.

'Much the same?'

I felt he'd tricked me. 'With the obvious differences. We were lovers,' I said. 'But it was a good relationship.' We sat in silence again. I remembered Muth's assurance: He's gonna like you. You just talk clear and articulate, and he's gonna hear that you're more concerned than anyone about her welfare, that the thing with Cutter was strictly his mistake.

'I don't know what you're aiming at,' I said again. 'I want to help. And obviously, I want Molly back, but I don't know . . . You have to help me more.' My voice was trembling.

'Well, that's fair,' he said. 'You didn't ask to come here. Or to have your life probed this way.' His voice was steady, gentle. 'But let me say I'm not *aiming* at anything.' He smiled at me. 'That has a hostile ring to it, and it sounds as though I'd already formed a judgment on the whole thing that I'm just trying to get you to confirm.' He shook his head. 'Not so. I'll meet Leo, and I'll meet Molly and Brian, and I'll get to know them. All of them. So you don't need to feel entirely responsible for what I think of them. Or responsible at all. What I'm interested in today is knowing *you*, and part of that is knowing how you see them.' He shrugged. 'Pretty simple.'

'It's simple, yes,' I said. 'But high risk for me. Everything is right now.'

He nodded. 'I understand your feeling that way. But I hope you don't think there's any process like *one false move and you're dead*. That's just not how it works,' he said. He waited.

'I know that,' I said reluctantly.

After a long pause, in which I was shaping my answer about Leo, he said, 'Tell me why you think Mr Dunlap's doing this. Trying to get custody.'

I felt nearly dizzy. How had we gotten here? 'I'm sure he thinks it's right,' I blurted. 'He's a very careful man, a *caring* man in lots of ways. I mean, I can imagine him hearing whatever it was Molly said and just freaking out.'

'Did he call you after she'd talked to him? Ask about it? About what you knew about it?'

'No. He *moved*.' He looked blank, shook his head. 'I mean, he saw a lawyer. But that's who he is, after all.' Then, suddenly, it occurred to me that I might appear to be acting, to be pretending to be understanding about Brian's response, that Payne might think this was all a posture, a lie. 'Not that I'm not enraged at him about it all,' I said. 'It's just . . .' I felt dizzy again, and put my hand along my face. 'It's just I can so perfectly imagine him, even imagine him zipping around his apartment or whatever, deciding *which* lawyer, getting the phone number, being terribly efficient.'

'I see,' he said, and nodded. Then he frowned. 'But, why do you think he wouldn't have called you? I understand from your lawyer that you had a very amicable divorce, and good relations around custody and visitation up till now. Why didn't he call and say, "Gee, Anna, Molly's saying some strange things to me about this guy you're dating. What do you know about it?" Wouldn't that have been in character in some sense too?' He waited. 'Or not?' he said, after a minute.

I hadn't asked myself this before. As I thought about it, I had two simultaneous responses. One was an honest consideration, an open asking: why hadn't he? The other had to do entirely with whether the answer could somehow turn to my advantage.

'Well, maybe things weren't so entirely amicable,' I said. 'They seemed amicable, but I suppose there was a lot going on underneath the surface.'

He watched me. I felt for the first time that we were collaborating, as Muth and I had. I felt a kind of rising excitement, a sense of discovery. 'I mean, we both wanted the divorce, but he wanted it more, right at the time, because he'd met his present wife.'

'She was the reason for his wanting the divorce?'

No, I explained. No. And I tried to describe the year Brian and I had spent agonizing over our marriage, working towards leaving each other, and how Brian had resolved everything, all his feelings about me, by getting involved with Brenda. 'But it seemed to me,' I said – and even in saying it I was seeing how it might be true – 'that in spite of that, or maybe because he moved so fast into that relationship with Brenda, that he still had some . . . unresolved feeling about me. And he wasn't comfortable about my dating. I mean, he took an interest in it that didn't have any connection with Molly, with the question of how it might be affecting her, a kind of, maybe, possessive interest.'

'Does that seem unnatural to you? Did you have no interest in his affair with Brenda?'

'No. I *was* interested. We actually talked some about that. But we were still married then.'

'You mean, you felt you had more right to be interested?'

'Well, more right to *talk* about being interested anyway. By the time *I* was dating, he'd remarried and moved away. He was supposed to be attached to someone else.'

'But you never actually talked to Brian about your dating.'

'No. And not about Leo. But if I was going out, he'd notice how I was dressed, and sometimes comment. And once or twice he asked me in a vague way, but – I can't describe it. *Anxiously*, I guess. "Seeing anyone these days?" That kind of thing.'

'And how do you connect that with his response now?'

A long silence. I didn't want to be responsible for offering the interpretation. Finally I said, 'Is it possible that he's jealous in some way? He's getting back at me?'

'Is that what you think?'

'Well, I hadn't thought about it before, but it seems as though it might be . . . feeding his response now, anyway.' I looked at him for the friendly yes, but he was blank, though very interested. I panicked. *Show remorse*, Muth had said. 'Not that he didn't have good reason to be wild. I'm not saying that. Just that there might have been other steps he could have taken. Even if he got to this one eventually. He might have called, as you suggested.'

'Did I?'

'Didn't you?' I asked.

He looked at me a moment, then smiled gently. 'I did ask why he hadn't, I think. Yes. I did.'

I looked away quickly, over at the toys.

'I'm curious,' he said. He leaned back in the chair and tented his hands together, his stubby fingers arched against each other. 'If he *had* called, if he'd asked about all this, if he'd said, "She says she's been in bed with you and Leo while you were naked, while you were having intercourse: she says she's touched his genitals" – if he'd asked you about that openly and directly—' He paused, frowning, concerned. 'What *would* you have said to him? How would you have defended, explained, what happened to Molly?'

I was stung. I sat for a long while in confusion, feeling attacked in spite of his politeness, and the interest which

258

creased his ugly face, feeling completely at a loss for what to say.

'Well, it's an interesting question, isn't it?' He smiled. 'Perhaps you'll remind me to start with it next time.'

I still said nothing.

He leaned forward, put his hands on his knees, elbows up. 'I'll look forward to meeting with you again on Wednesday then.' He smiled again. 'This has been a good talk, a good discussion.' He stood up, and more slowly, I rose. I noticed as I shook his hand and moved awkwardly ahead of him to the door that I was taller than he was. That he was, really, quite a tiny man.

But driving home past the wide lawns, the stately colonial houses of his neighborhood, I had the sense of him as large, as dangerous, more dangerous for me than anyone else I'd had to answer to. I began to plan what I'd say on Wednesday. A woman in shorts by a stop sign looked up from her baby carriage to stare at me, and I realized I was talking loudly, gesturing, to myself.

I was at home, standing stupidly in the kitchen, before I thought of the shopping list I'd made earlier. I had to get back into the car and make another trip to the store for crackers, mozzarella cheese, popcorn, apples. Molly was arriving the next day, Tuesday. Brian would drop her off after her first visit with Dr Payne in the morning. Three weeks earlier she'd stayed with me for the two long-awaited days the family service officer had stipulated, and it seemed then that there were already certain rituals that she wanted to be part of our new relationship. Food was important. She'd insisted on what she called 'stretchy cheese sandwiches,' 'Friday night supper' – popcorn, cocoa, and fruit. I filled the pushcart thinking of her; but thinking too, over and over, of Dr Payne's smiling ugly face.

'Mumma! Mumma! Mumma!' Molly hollered, running up the long walk. I was startled, as I had been on the earlier visit, by how big she was. Her baby shape seemed to be dissolving. Her legs looked long and white and nearly skinny as she ran. Behind her, at the curb, Brian was fussing with a bag, something else. I squatted to take her in my arms, and she slammed into me. When I picked her up, I could feel the wiry grip of her knees at my waist. I twirled her around and around, and she leaned away from me, laughing. As we whirled, Brian came up the walk. He was watching us closely, I could tell. When I stopped and looked at him, he had set the suitcase down, and on top of it placed Molly's old bear, Sleazy, and a new one I hadn't seen before. He nodded to me. Molly's body swung out to look at him too, her weight settled on my hip.

'We'll pick her up on Friday morning, about eight-thirty or so?' he asked.

'Fine,' I said. Our voices were cool, impersonal, but polite. I could feel Molly's taut attention as she watched us.

'There's a list in the bag of everything, so her clothes don't get mixed up,' he said.

'Thank you,' I said.

His eyes moved to her. 'Can I get a kiss good-bye from you?' he asked. Even with her, in this situation, his tone was stiff. I set her down and, seemingly sobered, she walked over to him, raised her face and arms to his descending head.

'See you Friday, lambie,' he whispered to her. 'I love you.'

'I *know* that,' she said, pulling hard on his neck. Then she released him.

He straightened and walked down the path. Halfway down it he turned to wave, but she was already picking up her bears and talking to me. It was I who returned his wave. Reflexively he swung his hand out again; then caught himself and turned away, continued down the path. Molly and I gathered her things up and went inside.

As she had on her first visit, she went straight to her room. I trailed her with the bag and her baby quilt.

'My room,' she said.

'Indeed,' I answered. I set the bag down on her bed. 'Do you want to get changed out of that fancy dress?'

She shook her head. Her hair was long enough so that it

260

swung slightly. When had it gotten so long? 'No, this is my *best*,' she said. She held the skirt out and looked at it. 'I want to wear this the whole day.'

'It's awfully pretty,' I said. It was new, expensive, a smocked pinafore of a light blue cotton, the same color as her eyes.

'Brenda bought it for me. She buys me *everything*.'

'She knows what you like,' I said. 'You clotheshorse.'

'Silly,' she said. '*I'm* not a horse.' And she turned away.

I stood, hovering in the door for a minute as she began to take her toys off the shelf, talking to me about each of them. I had to force myself to go to the kitchen to fix us some lunch. But even out there, I found myself listening for her, wanting her to call me. On her earlier visit too, I'd had to make myself back off. Otherwise I was unable to leave her alone, to behave as though our life together would go on and on.

Then, she had seemed completely relaxed about me. But now, after only a few minutes, I turned to see her in the kitchen doorway, dragging her quilt behind her. Three or four animals were heaped on it.

'*Here* I am,' she said.

'How delightful,' I answered. I was slicing the mozzarella cheese, arranging it on bread for sandwiches.

'I'm bringing these animals here because this is their house – I mean, I mean, my *quiltie* is their house. And they're moving.'

'There's lots of room in here,' I said. 'They could have their house by the back door.'

'But I have to go back and get the rest,' she said. At the door she turned. 'You stay here. I'll be *right* back.'

And in a few minutes she returned, her arms laden with furry creatures which she unceremoniously dumped on the quilt. 'I forgot about these guys, Mom,' she said. 'I didn't even remember I *had* them.' And she sat on the quilt and started to arrange the animals around her, talking to them, then stopping sometimes to watch me as I heated the sandwiches, poured out the milk. I brought her lunch over to her and she sat on the floor and ate it. The back door was open, a train flashed past. Her eyes rounded, then she smiled. 'That dummy train,' she said, and wrinkled her long nose. 'It's *too* noisy.'

I talked with her over lunch about her toys, about her clothes, about the woman, Mrs Reinhardt, who took care of her at Brian and Brenda's. We planned our afternoon. After her rest, we'd go to the Raymond Street playground for a while, then get some ice cream and go throw rocks into the Charles. Before we came home, we'd stop in the Square and buy a new book for bedtime.

'Do you still sometimes fall asleep at rest?' I asked. I was washing our dishes, setting them in the rack to dry.

She shook her head. 'I never do. All's I do is lie there waiting and waiting and waiting for it to be time.'

'Not me,' I said. 'I curl up and pretty soon I'm out like a light, I'm snoring away, I'm sawing the big ones. Rest is the best.'

'*Mom*,' she protested. And then after a moment she asked, 'Do you really fall asleep, Mom?' The animals were fanned out in a circle around her, like the rays of the sun in a child's drawing.

'Sometimes I really do,' I said.

'I hate rest,' she said vehemently. Then: 'Where are you lying for rest, Mom?' Her voice had tightened.

'I thought I'd lie in my bed,' I answered.

'I don't like that,' she said. 'It's too far.' I looked over at her. She was frowning.

'I could lie down in the living room,' I offered. 'Would that be better?'

'Yah, that would.'

'Why don't you go and fix up your bed with your animals, and I'll be down in about two minutes to kiss you and read you a little story. You could pick out a story, too, a small one, maybe one of those tiny books. You know the ones I mean?'

'No, I want to wait for you,' she said.

'I'll just be a second, baby. Why don't you go ahead?'

'*No*,' she said, and looked away. I didn't say anything more.

When I finished putting the food away, we each took an end of her quilt and carefully carried all the stuffed animals back to her room. She went into the bathroom to pee, then I took off her pinafore – 'But I can wear that again *after* nap, right Mom?' – and sat with her on her bed. I read her the story of Dorothy and the imaginary friend who did naughty things. Molly asked after each episode, as she always did, 'But it was really Dorothy, wasn't it? She *really* did it, right?'

When I pulled the sheet up and bent to kiss her, she asked, 'Am I staying with you all the day tomorrow?' Her face was solemn.

'All day tomorrow and the next day, honey.'

'Two days more? Tomorrow and *then* the next day?'

'Right, and then you go back to Washington.'

'The next day after that?'

'Yes. After two tomorrows.'

'Am I going to that doctor with the toys again?'

'Yes, but just for a little while each day. I'll take you. Dr Payne is his name. And then Debby' – her favorite sitter – 'will have you for a little while each day when I talk to him. She can take you to the Common, where that big slide is.'

'He has all those toys 'cause he likes kids.'

'Yeah, I saw the toys. They were neat.'

'Were you there when my dad was there?'

'No, I was there another day. The day before. But I thought he had great toys.'

'He does have great toys.' Then she frowned. 'But I don't like all those' – she patted her cheek gingerly, while her features wrinkled in disgust – 'all those little black *dots* he has.'

'They're just his beard, honey.'

'No, *not* a beard, Mom. Just all those little,' she patted again, 'yukky black *dots*.'

'The dots are called a beard too. They're all the little hairs that are too short, too tiny. But if he grew them longer, they'd be a beard.'

'I *hate* that,' she said.

'All men have that. Dad has it too, but his aren't so dark.' I didn't mention Leo. Neither of us had mentioned Leo. 'That's why he shaves in the morning.'

'I *hate* that men have that,' she said violently. 'Dr Payne should shave and shave and shave in the morning.'

'Why don't you tell him so, next time you see him?' I said. I stroked her hair back from her forehead. When I turned at the door to blow her a kiss, her eyes were sober on me. 'Stay in the living room, Mom,' she said.

'I'll be right here, honey,' I said.

I checked her in twenty minutes or so. She was asleep, breathing quietly and evenly. I lay down on the living room couch and looked out at the cloudless sky for a while, wondering whether she had been this clingy, this tense, with Brian when he was the visiting parent. It saddened me to feel how changed with me she already was.

At some point I fell asleep too. I was wakened by her crying. It was nearly three-thirty. She'd been asleep for two hours, a long nap for her, and she'd wet her bed. I peeled back the damp sheets and held her. She smelled of sweat and urine, and she was inconsolable. By the time I'd finally calmed her down and bathed her, it was after four, and we decided what we needed most of all was ice cream.

'How's your visit going?' Dr Payne asked, as he poured me more coffee. We'd been talking for the first twenty minutes or half an hour about my life, my background, my feelings about achievement, how I integrated Molly and work. I felt I was doing well.

'Wonderful, of course,' I said.

'No problems?'

'That's not quite what I said.'

'I know. I'm asking though.'

He straightened and brought the cup over to me. A light scum of the powdered milk floated on its grayish surface.

'Thank you,' I said, setting the cup on the table next to my couch.

'It sounds like you had a nice day yesterday,' he said. He sat in his chair and leaned back. 'Molly enjoyed it.'

'She did. I did too. It's just that . . . she's very tense, I think. Nervous about letting me out of her sight. She wet the bed at naptime, and woke two or three times in the night. I think she was confused about where she was, and worried that she'd do it again. Wet the bed.'

'So you're both tired today.'

'Do we seem so?'

He nodded. 'She seemed much less resourceful here today than yesterday. In a way though, that's good. It helps me see her more clearly. Her defenses are down, as it were.'

'And what did you see?'

'I think I got to see a lot of her worries.'

'Did she talk about Leo?' I asked.

'A little,' he said. 'She likes Leo, as you said.'

I felt relief.

'And maybe we can talk for a minute now about that hypothetical question I raised the other day, about what you might have said to Brian if he'd called to talk about Leo.'

I had thought about this, had had time to construct my answer. I took a few moments, inhaled, exhaled slowly, trying to remember what I'd decided I would say. 'Well, of course,' I began, 'I didn't know that Molly *had* touched Leo at the time she told Brian about it.' *It was a mistake Leo made*, Muth had told me over and over. 'So I would have had to check with Leo about it.'

I thought a pinch of annoyance squeezed his eyebrows slightly closer together. He folded his arms across his chest. 'Well, let's just forget that part then,' he said.

'Forget it?'

'Yes, let's just focus on your allowing her in bed with you while you were having intercourse.'

Once again I felt the dizzied sense I'd had before with Dr Payne, of his unpredictability, of being surprised and therefore attacked by him. And as usual, I looked up to find him smiling at me.

'You seem to be attacking me,' I said after a pause.

'In what way?'

'I don't know. But I hear you. Blaming me.'

He shook his head. 'I'm not. I just want to hear what you have to say.'

'But you're suggesting . . .'

He tilted his head to one side as he studied me. 'You may have heard blame, accusation, in what I said. But I can assure you, Anna, that all I expressed was curiosity, was my concern to know.'

'Well, I felt . . . I honestly didn't feel, with Leo, that there was the need for all the rules, the lines. We were all – Molly too – we were all happy. We *had* been naked around her, it's true. We had her in bed with us when we were naked. And to me, it was part of this whole world that Leo had opened up to me where . . .' My throat burned. Payne watched me, saying nothing. 'Where I was beautiful, and our sex together was beautiful, and Molly was part of our love, our life. You have to understand,' I said, leaning towards him. 'Brian and I stopped having sex a long time before we split up. I was frigid with him. I'd always been frigid.'

He nodded, as though he'd known this.

'And with Leo, that changed. My life changed. I changed. I became, in every way, more expressive. And it was *good* for Molly. I know that. I *was* . . . I *was* busier. Less focused on her, but we were like a family. We had *fun*. I didn't fuss as much about her every little . . . You know.'

'You relaxed your vigilance about her life.'

'Yes. I just didn't spend as much time as I had right after the divorce imagining her every feeling, worrying about her. And so. Well, that night, when she came in, Leo was just gently still inside me, lying behind me from her. And I held her, and she fell asleep. And he *was* in me. But I'm sure, I'm convinced, she didn't know. And so, yes, we had her in bed with us, but it's not this. It's not the picture that's somehow been painted, of her lying there watching us banging away. That's not what happened.'

266

'I see,' he said.

'And it was in that context, that same kind of context, that Leo let her touch him. Because he . . . *misunderstood*. What the boundaries were. She asked, she was curious, and he said yes. And *both* of us, in retrospect, *both* of us should have been clearer. And Leo shouldn't have let her. It was a mistake. We both made mistakes.'

After a moment Payne said, 'It's interesting to me that you say that at this time you were less *focused* on her. Because Molly mentioned to me a time, some incident, when, as she described it, *you* got lost. I was struck by that way, her way, of perceiving it. By her sense of your absence, as it were. She said, I think, that she had to wait in the car a long time, until you found her. She told me that – these are her words – she cried so hard her mouth almost broke.'

I raised my hands to my face.

'Can you tell me what incident she might be referring to?'

I nodded, but had to sit a few moments to gather enough self-control to talk. Then I described our summer holiday just before the divorce went through, and the morning I'd left her asleep in the car. I told him how she'd looked, the raised stripe, the eyes swollen nearly shut.

'You sound very upset with yourself,' he said after a minute.

'I can't forgive myself,' I said.

'It's something it'd be hard to forgive yourself for.'

I nodded.

'You blame yourself,' he said gently.

I was weeping.

'It's terrible, I know, to have hurt a child, your child, someone you're responsible for.' He held out a box of tissues to me. I grabbed one and blew my nose. He leaned back and didn't talk for a while. Then he cleared his throat. 'What seems most on Molly's mind, to me, is that very theme, of absence, of your not being there for her. There *is* some anxiety about sexuality. But my feeling is on that score, she's most anxious that something she said about Leo upset her father as much as it did. *And*,' he bounced his head back and forth as though weighing one side of it against the other, 'maybe a little interested in how much attention it got her. We all enjoy that, and she's not above being a little manipulative.'

'You mean she's making things up?'

'No no no,' he said. '*Not* what I said. Just that she's keenly aware of all the attention focused on her right now, especially from her father, whom she usually doesn't get to see an awful lot of. No, what I'm really suggesting is that for Molly the resonant emotional issue is feeling that you were pulling away from her. But,' he shook his head, 'we all have our adult lives to live too. And sometimes that means having less energy for a child. And what's hard for kids isn't necessarily, in the long run, bad for them, either. I think you *were* distracted, withdrawn in a way she could feel.' He paused, and wrinkled his brow. 'But I see you also as very hard on yourself. You say I blame you, but I don't feel I have to say very much before you supply the blame, the guilt.'

He waited for a response. 'You know, this legal stuff, it says if this one's right, this one's wrong. If this one wins, this one loses.' He shook his head, and smiled ruefully at me. 'Don't buy into that. That's not life. OK?'

After a moment, I nodded.

'And now,' he said, 'we've got to go. We've run over.'

'By the way,' he said. I turned at the door. 'You were right. She chose the bear.'

'Thanks,' I said. I smiled at him. 'Thank you.'

I drove down to the Cambridge Common, where I'd taken Debby and Molly after her appointment with Dr Payne earlier in the morning. I could see Debby, a sunny, plump college student who'd worked sometimes at the day-care center, reading on a bench within the circular fence of the tot-lot. The lot seemed oddly empty to me as I approached it, just a few very small children, toddlers, staggering around, their mothers arched over them. Then I remembered: nursery schools, grade schools, they'd all started up again. For everyone else, life had resumed a fall order, the annual pattern.

Debby looked up as I got near the bench, and seemed to be embarrassed to be caught reading. She pointed Molly out to me in a wooden playhouse across the lot. I could see two or three other, smaller children moving in the windows of the playhouse with her. I paid Debby, who left to meet a friend in Harvard Square, and took her place on the bench.

When Molly leaned out of the house and saw me sitting there, I heard her squeal. She jumped down into the sandy dirt and ran over.

'I didn't know when you came here,' she said. She was wearing overalls and a T-shirt, what I thought of as her real clothes.

'I wanted to surprise you,' I said, and kissed her.

She climbed up next to me on the bench. Despite my encouraging her, she didn't want to go back and play. 'I want to stay *right* by you,' she said, and she wiggled over so she was, indeed, pressed against my side.

'I've got that yummy lunch I packed,' I said, and held up the box I'd given to Debby in case they got hungry. 'Remember what's in it?'

'Yogurt, and honey, and apples, and bread, and bananas, and raisins,' she said.

'Want some?' I asked her, and she said yes. We opened the box, and ate, sitting on the bench, watching the other children slowly disappear home to lunch and naps and diaper changes.

When we were done, we packed up our trash and headed home for our rest too. On the way, though, I swung into the Porter Square shopping center. I needed to pick up a few groceries for our dinner.

I didn't need much. I could have fit everything into one of the brightly colored plastic baskets. But Molly was sleepy and a little fussy. I took out a big cart and she climbed in onto the rack underneath it, where other shoppers had big boxes of detergent and dog food.

I began weaving my way up and down the long aisles,

269

picking out coffee, spaghetti noodles, English muffins. I'd just loaded a bottle of apple juice into the cart and was nearing the end of the aisle when I lifted my head and saw Leo turn the corner towards us. His face opened with gladness as he saw me, and he kept stepping towards us – he was wearing a T-shirt I'd given him that read MEN DO THE STUPIDEST THINGS FOR LOVE in gleaming silver letters – but my head had already begun swinging, no, no, no. I yanked the cart sharply to turn it, and he saw Molly, I saw his eyes seeing her. He spun around and vanished from the aisle.

Ambling back down our aisle to give him time to leave the store, I began chattering to her. 'What do you think, Moll? Do we have enough food? Is there something else you're dreaming of?' What I was thinking was, *Did she see him?* Did she? I could imagine how she might tell it: 'Leo was in the store with us.' 'Leo and us were getting groceries.' And I could imagine Brian's quick response.

'I want to go *home*,' she whined.

'OK. Just a second more. About two more things,' I told her. 'Things you love.' I headed for the fruit section, at the opposite end of the floor from the checkout lanes.

I took three or four minutes picking out blueberries, bananas, apples. Molly grew fussier. 'I know how long is a *second*,' her offended voice rose from under the food. Between the berries, the muffins, I could see the striped legs of her overalls. 'This is *much* longer than a second. You said just a second till we go.'

'Don't be such a pill,' I told her. 'We're on our way right now.' There was no sign of Leo at the front of the store. I fed blueberries down to Molly as we waited in line, and then we were out in the sunbaked parking lot, no Leo, and in the car, turning down our street.

When I finally tucked Molly into bed, she seemed stunned with sleepiness. I sat for a moment on her bed. Then I couldn't help myself. 'It's too bad you can't see Leo while you're visiting,' I said.

There was a long silence. Then she said, 'Leo is bad.'

'What makes you say that?'

'My dad told me. Leo is bad, and I hate him.'

'Sometimes you didn't feel that way. Sometimes you liked him.'

'No,' she said, hoarse with sleep. Her eyes swung up a little in her head. Her lids lowered.

'Did you see Leo?' I asked her.

She didn't answer.

'Molly,' I whispered. 'Did you see Leo?'

Her lids lowered all the way, her breathing deepened. But just at that moment, just as she drifted off, I had, for a second, the sense that she was feigning sleep, pretending, as she sometimes did, so she wouldn't have to answer the question. I felt a quick anger, and then a kind of internal shock: I saw her, too, as the enemy. Molly, the very impediment to getting Molly back. And I saw that part of my behavior with her – the part that made me keep silent about Leo – was as false as my dependent femininity around Muth, my easy remorse with Mrs Harkessian. If I'd thought about it earlier, if anyone had asked me, I would have said that not mentioning Leo to Molly was a way of trying not to influence what she had to say about him. But in that moment of hatred for my own sleeping child I realized that she had real power over me, the power to use whatever I said or did, whatever happened, against me, against us. I watched her sleep, locked in her secret world, her own meaning, and I wanted to shake her, to hurt her. 'Molly,' I whispered. 'You didn't see Leo.'

On Thursday, towards the end of our last session, Dr Payne told me he'd reached his conclusions about our situation. He said on the basis of his inquiries – by then he'd talked to Brian and Brenda, to Leo and me, to both our lawyers, to the family service officer, to several teachers at Molly's day care, to Molly's pediatrician, and of course, to Molly herself – he'd found that the incidents that Brian described, though they indicated very bad judgment on my part, worse on Leo's, were not part of a pattern of abuse, nor had they been traumatic for Molly. They had raised questions which continued to disturb her, and he talked about Molly's pain over the divorce and losing Brian, about her intense attachment to me, about the anxiety she was already showing about having been separated from me for so long. Then he said he thought it would be a mistake, cruel, to ask her to endure a permanent separation. He was going to recommend to the court that custody be restored to me.

TWELVE

Brian went first. He sat comfortably in the witness chair as Fine led him through all the historical material about how we'd met and married, about Molly's birth, the divorce, the move to Washington, his remarriage. He had turned into a handsome man, I realized as I watched him. When we'd met, he was too thin, too young. Acne still peppered his shoulders and back, and his short hair was savagely trimmed around his ears, making them look bigger than they were. Now he had weight and authority, the kind of attractiveness that money brings to some men as they enter middle age. He looked like one of my uncles.

With a magnanimous air he spoke of having relinquished custody to me at the time of the divorce because I had more time for Molly then, and because I had seemed to him to be responsible, a concerned mother. He often turned as he spoke to the judge, who sat listening attentively and sometimes drinking from a red coffee mug with a large white numeral one on its side. Though it was a different judge, a different courtroom – the luck of the draw, Muth had said – it all felt familiar. The only real change was that it was quieter now with the windows shut. The heat came on occasionally, though, and the clunk and hiss of the pipes still made it difficult to hear the lawyers when they turned to face the witnesses. I had to strain to understand Fine until he turned sideways, as he now did. 'Tell me, Mr Dunlap,' he said. 'What were the arrangements for visitation between you and Mrs Dunlap at this time?'

'Well,' Brian said, and he too shifted his posture slightly, seemed to grow increasingly alert. 'Either Molly would come down to Washington accompanied by someone – a friend in the firm going back and forth, or me, or my current, my present wife – because she's too young, Molly, they don't let her fly alone – or I'd come up and stay with her in my ex-wife's apartment. The latter, the last is what mostly happened. I think she only came down to Washington two or three times. Two, I guess.'

'So for the most part, your ex-wife would relinquish her apartment to you for the weekend?'

'That's right. Because of how young Molly was, we thought that would be less confusing.'

'Now, Mr Dunlap, can you tell the court about any changes you noticed in Molly or in her environment during these visits?'

'Yes.' Brian looked at the judge quickly. 'Yes. The first indicator was that she, my ex-wife, would sometimes get calls from different men.'

Muth stood up swiftly. 'Objection, your honor. The witness doesn't know who called, whether they were different.'

The judge didn't seem to have to think about it. He smiled at Muth. He was thin, in his mid-forties, with dark hair slicked straight back. 'I'll sustain,' he said.

'She got calls,' Brian said. 'Calls from some male person or persons. While I was there. And then, by the next visit, there was evidence that a man was living at the—'

Muth stood again. He looked fierce, bearlike. '*Objection,*' he announced.

The judge, coffee cup to his mouth, nodded.

Fine turned back to Brian. 'Let's back up a step or two, Mr Dunlap. When was all this?'

'This was in May, when she got the calls. And in June.'

'And you found some articles in the house at that time which belonged to a man?'

'Right,' Brian said. He looked angry.

'What were they?'

'In the bathroom: a razor, a can of shaving foam. In the closet: a man's hiking boots, a blue jeans jacket. That kind of thing. And toys – a gyroscope, a box of Band-aids, things my daughter said he'd given—'

Muth jackknifed up again. 'That's hearsay, your honor.'

'It absolutely is,' the judge said, smiling. 'I'll sustain.'

Fine asked Brian what his response to all this was. Brian said that he wasn't really concerned in any way, though he had wondered how serious I was about the mysterious man. 'I had assumed that my wife – my ex-wife – would start dating at some point. On account of Molly I might have felt a little jealous.' Brian grinned suddenly and shrugged, looked over at the judge. 'You know, "She's *my* little girl, will this guy take my place?" that stuff.' He was a little sheepish, charming.

Fine leaned on the rail which encircled Brian. 'Any other changes, changes in behavior?'

Brian looked at him, suddenly serious again. 'Yes. Well, I noticed when I stayed with Molly those last times that she'd started to have real problems sleeping at night. A couple of times on those visits she got up and came in to me where I was sleeping – I slept on the couch – and once I found her down in her mother's room, crying. Looking for her mother. And that was unusual. She was, she'd always been, a very heavy sleeper. Anna – my ex-wife – is a musician. She played in the evenings, or had records on a lot. And Molly just slept right through that racket.' There was a little murmur of laughter from the policemen in the room. The judge smiled, and Brian looked up. 'Excuse me. *Noise.*' He turned back to Fine. 'And when she came down to visit me this summer, that continued, that sleep problem. It got worse, actually. Every night Brenda or I had to get up with her, and carry her back to her room and stay with her till she fell asleep. At first I thought all this was just, you know, the newness of it, of having me at her house, of being with us in Washington; but it didn't get better.

'And then she had other things. She was very curious about my, about our bodies. In a way that was new. It seemed inappropriate to me. When she came in in the morning, she'd look under the cover to see if we had pajamas on. She'd *ask* about our bodies, you know, "You have breasts?" "You have a penis?" It was . . .' he shook his head, 'excessive. We've never. We were always quite, *careful*, I guess is the word, not to scare or distress her by having her see us naked.'

'When you say *we*, you mean?'

'Well, actually, in both marriages. It wasn't, it isn't that we'd hide. Just that we're careful. And it seemed to me that Molly had . . . *changed* around this issue, that there was something preoccupying her, frightening her. It was like a constant thing. Once we were sitting around the table for dinner, and somehow we were talking about, you know, the head of the table, the foot of the table, and we were fooling around, asking her if she was sitting at the arm or the leg of the table, because she was at the side; and she said, "Dad, you're at the head, and I'm the arm, and Brenda is the penis."' There was again the ripple of laughter. 'Well, it's funny,' he said, grinning a little. Then he frowned. 'But I can't tell you how . . . obsessed she seemed. And knocking on the door all the time when I was in the bathroom. And then one time she asked me, just asked me straight out – I was shaving – if she could see it. And so I said no, that was my business. And she said, "Leo lets me see his penis, he lets me touch it, and it got big when I touched" . . .'

Muth was on his feet even as Brian began quoting, and his voice was loud over Brian's: 'Objection, objection, objection.'

'Sustained,' the judge said, quieting them both. 'You know better, counsel,' he said to Fine after a moment. Brian, who'd been leaning forward when he talked about Molly, relaxed back again.

Fine stood silent for a few seconds, began again. 'Tell us what you did, Mr Dunlap, when you noticed this . . . altered behavior on the part of your daughter.'

'I got a referral to a child psychiatrist and had Molly seen. And then I saw a lawyer, filed the complaint, and here we are.'

'Yes,' Fine said. Then he asked Brian to describe his life with Brenda in Washington: their apartment, Molly's room, Mrs Reinhardt, the woman who took care of Molly during the day. I saw the picture emerging: Brian and Brenda, who'd done things the right way, who kept their pajamas on, whose life was ordered, productive. All this would be weighed against my life, my failures, my relationship with Leo, who sat in the pew at the rear of the room in a different jacket, one he'd bought for the occasion; he'd had his hair cut, and it made him look long-necked and vulnerable.

Mr Fine thanked Brian.

Now Muth stood up, walked over. He spoke softly to Brian, in the same gentle tones he used with me. I could barely hear him.

'Now, isn't it a fact, Mr Dunlap, that the person mainly responsible for the care of your daughter at your house has been a hired nursemaid, this Mrs Reinhardt?'

Brian's face firmed. 'No, it isn't.'

'It's not a fact?' Muth sounded genuinely surprised.

'No, it isn't.'

'Well, what time do you leave for work in the morning?'

'At seven-forty-five or so,' Brian said.

'And what time do you get home, generally speaking?'

'Oh, six-thirty or seven.'

'Or sometimes seven-thirty?'

'Occasionally as late as that, yes.'

'And Mrs Dunlap? The present Mrs Dunlap? What's her schedule like?'

'About the same.'

'It *is* Mrs Reinhardt who makes the child's breakfast, is it not?'

'She makes all our breakfasts.'

'And lunch.'

'Of course.'

'And dinner,' Muth said softly.

'Sometimes. Sometimes *we* make dinner. And on weekends, of course we do it.'

'Of course,' Muth said, and then frowned. 'But Mrs Reinhardt *is* the only adult with the child for often nearly twelve hours a day, isn't that correct?'

'I wouldn't say often.'

'Well, often between *ten* and twelve hours,' Muth offered, generous.

'Yes, I guess so.'

'Of the child's waking time.'

'Yes.'

'Tell me, Mr Dunlap, what time does Molly go to bed?'

'It varies. It depends on her nap. Sometimes eight, sometimes closer to nine.'

'So, during the work week, it sounds like you're with her for, gee, like half an hour to an hour each day.'

'Sometimes an hour and a half. Two hours.'

'Sometimes?'

'Yes.'

Muth stood for a moment, looking worried, concerned. Then he turned around, so we could all see him better. His tone changed. 'Now, Mr Dunlap, you met the present Mrs Dunlap sometime before your marriage to my client ended, did you not?'

'Yes, but we had . . .'

'A simple yes is good enough for me, Mr Dunlap. And you had begun your relationship with her before that time, had you not?'

Fine stood, silently and quickly. 'Your honor, I object to this line of questioning. It's not relevant to the issues involved in this case, to any of the issues around custody.'

Muth held his graceful hands out, palms up, to the judge. 'Your honor, Mr Fine and his client are trying to demonstrate a moral weakness in my client. Surely I can . . .'

'I'm going to sustain the objection, counselor.'

Muth lifted his shoulders, perplexed. After a moment he looked at Brian again. 'Mr Dunlap,' he asked, 'have you ever heard of Oedipal feelings in children?'

'Yes.'

278

'Can you tell us what those feelings are?'

'They're feelings of attraction in the child to the parent, to the parent of the opposite sex.'

'That's right,' said Muth, in his friendly, agreeable way. 'And did you know that your little girl, Molly, is at an age when those feelings are strongest for her?'

A pause. 'No. I don't know that to be true.'

'That's what the books tell us, the experts,' Muth said and lifted his shoulders again, as though helpless before this horde of experts. 'Now, doesn't it seem to you, then, that a good deal of your daughter's interest in your body and in what might be your sex life, et cetera, is natural?'

'It is not natural, no.'

'That it springs from this very natural attraction she has to you, a wish, even, to be, in some sense she doesn't understand, *married* to you?'

'No, I don't believe that.'

'You don't believe Molly has Oedipal feelings?'

'I don't believe that's what, they're what made Molly do what she did or say what she did.'

'So you believe in Oedipal feelings, but you don't believe Molly has them, is that correct?'

'I . . .' Brian's mouth tightened. 'I know Molly has Oedipal feelings. I think her behavior stems from something else.'

'I see,' said Muth. His head bobbed slowly. 'OK, well, let's ask about some other behavior that distressed you, Mr Dunlap. Let's ask about these sleep disturbances.'

'OK by me.'

'Now, Mr Dunlap, you describe Molly as having problems sleeping now.'

'That's right.'

'And you trace this to the beginning of my client's relationship with Mr Cutter.'

'Whatever his name is.'

'His name is Mr Cutter.'

'Whatever.'

'That this was *the* major disruption in her life.'

'Yes, being exposed to their sex life, yes.'

'Now, Mr Dunlap, it is the case that Mrs Dunlap has been the major psychological parent of your daughter, Molly, since her birth, is it not?'

'I don't know what you mean by "psychological parent."'

'Well, really,' Muth's hand looped around in the air, 'the parent who did the most for her, to whom she was most attached.'

'I did a great deal with my daughter.'

'But your working hours were approximately what they are now, were they not?' Muth seemed genuinely perplexed, confused.

'Yes.'

'And she went to bed somewhat earlier as a younger child, did she not?'

'Yes.'

'So you saw her, perhaps, less than you're seeing her during this present period?'

'Yes. I suppose so.'

'And far less than Mrs Dunlap did at that time.'

'Yes. Except on weekends.'

'Mr Dunlap, will you describe your pattern of visitation with Molly since the divorce?'

'I have rights to see her one night a week and every other weekend, and for eight weeks vacation time during the year.'

'I don't mean as they're *written*, Mr Dunlap. I mean as you've exercised them since you moved to Washington.'

'I've seen her about once every three weeks for the weekend, and we had her for a week at Christmas.'

'Except you missed a couple of those weekends, didn't you? Of those *every third weekends*.' Muth was suddenly sharp, sarcastic.

'I might have.'

'So it might be more like once a month on the average that you actually saw her?'

'I . . . yes.'

'So Molly has actually moved to an even more absolute

280

dependency on her mother in the year since the divorce, hasn't she?'

'I wouldn't say so, no.'

'*Oh*,' Muth protested, as though Brian wasn't playing fair. 'But wouldn't you say that my client was the really available parent figure during all this time?'

'No, because I have a strong relationship with Molly, and I saw her consistently throughout this period.'

'About once a month.'

'Yes.'

'So that as this pattern became clear to Molly, what *she* must slowly have been facing and realizing is that your arrival meant that her mother, on whom she depended for everything, would go away, is that right?'

'Is what right?' Brian's voice was flat with irritation.

'Isn't it correct that it was, in fact, your not seeing the child very often, and then the loss of her mother when you *did* come, that upset Molly?'

'No.' Brian shook his head vigorously.

'The effect, in other words, the *delayed* effect of the divorce itself?'

'No.'

'And isn't it a fact, Mr Dunlap, that having wanted *out* of this marriage so you could marry your *present* wife, you are now blaming your ex-wife for the effect of the very divorce *you* initiated, in order to try to take her child away from her?'

'No.'

'And that the reason Molly has so much trouble sleeping at your house in Washington is that she misses her true psychological parent, her mother?'

'No.' Brian swung his head. 'No.'

'OK. Well. OK, Mr Dunlap. Let's take another tack here.' Muth stroked his hair back. 'Were you aware that Molly had a book which explained sex to her?'

'No.'

'You were *not* aware of that?' Muth sounded surprised, nearly hurt.

'No.'

'Were you aware that the day-care center had done a project on anatomy, body parts, with the kids, which included sexual parts?'

'No.'

'You were *not* aware of these events in your daughter's life?'

'No.'

'So you were not aware that the book she had read frequently at home, a book highly recommended by child psychiatrists and pediatricians as being nonthreatening, easy to understand, actually had drawings of the sexual parts, and of a male erection? That Molly had known about this from her reading, from this book?'

'No.'

'Well, now that you have been *made* aware of this, Mr Dunlap, doesn't it seem clear that Molly's preoccupation with sexuality, with your body and her stepmother's, might have had a great deal to do with these learning experiences, rather than anything else?'

'No.'

'No what?'

'No, that's not clear to me.'

'I see,' Muth said, gently shaking his head. 'Well, that's all.'

Fine got up again, seemed even smaller, darker, tighter than he had before. He asked Brian to describe my apartment, which he did, accurately; to talk about my work, my childcare arrangements. Brian said that even before the divorce I'd had Molly in day care part time, while I was teaching, and that now she was there every day from eight-thirty to five-thirty.

Fine said that was all.

The judge took a break after this. The clerk and the policemen talked loudly across the room to each other. 'How many with milk?' one of the cops asked, walking towards the door.

'Three,' the clerk answered. The double door swung,

thumped behind me just as the doors in the other room had.

'How do you think it's going?' I asked Muth. He was flipping through his notes.

'OK. OK,' he said thoughtfully. 'He's good, your husband. But we got our points, I think.'

'What comes next?' I asked.

'Their shrink,' he said. 'Dr Herzog.' Muth had told me that Brian had hired someone else to see Molly after she'd seen Payne. A doctor in Washington. 'Standard operating procedure,' he'd said. 'I'd do it too. No one's gonna go in there with empty hands, with the guardian's report against them.'

After the break, Fine put the psychiatrist on the stand. He was a far more impressive figure than Dr Payne. He had silver-white hair, a thick drooping mustache, a long pink nose like a crooked, beckoning finger in the middle of his face. He wore a tweed suit. Twisting my sweaty hands in the overheated room, I wondered how he stood it.

Fine led him through a presentation of credentials that seemed endless. Muth stood up once and said he was prepared to grant that Dr Herzog was well-qualified; but Fine said he'd like to enter the doctor's credentials anyway, and the judge let him.

Then Fine established that Herzog had seen Molly twice, talked once to Brian and Brenda. He asked the doctor to describe Molly. Herzog said she seemed immature for her age, though she was bright, clearly above average in intelligence. He thought she was an unusually flirtatious little girl, both with himself and her father. He described his process of getting to know her, said that not until the second hour had he given her anatomical dolls to play with, said she was consistent in reporting and in acting out with the dolls the way she'd told Herzog that she'd touched Leo. He said she'd exhibited extreme anxiety when asked to talk specifically about the event, anxiety which was typical of a child her age to whom such an event had, in fact, occurred. Fine asked how she displayed that anxiety. Herzog described her as being silly, changing the subject, prattling baby words.

Twice she had gone to the door, he said, to be sure her father was still in the waiting room.

In his opinion, the doctor said, she'd been exposed to a level of sexual activity not customary or healthy for a child her age, and she was manifesting symptoms of that overexposure.

'And what about the issue of Oedipal attraction to her father?' Fine asked. 'Could that account for some of her behavior?'

'Well, as for the Oedipal stuff, yes, it's her age,' the doctor said. 'But *because* of that, she more than ever needs ... I mean, this is a crucial time, when the child comes to grips with these impulses, and *has* to learn. It's part of the struggle to develop her identity, this understanding of her separateness from her parents, that she can't have or be in that adult world. All that inner turmoil is only confused by the message she's been getting from that adult world. She needs those limits set.' He shook his head, and narrowed his eyes. 'I see a little girl very much at risk here, very much confused about her own power, her own seductiveness. I see some very inappropriate behavior.'

Had the doctor observed her with her father and stepmother?

He had. And at Fine's request he described his impressions of their relationship, of Molly's dependence on them, of their stability. Based on all this, could he form any opinion as to what award of custody would be in the best interests of the child?

'I feel I can form such an opinion.' Herzog spoke with a strong sense of theater. His voice rang out.

'And what is that opinion?'

'That taking into consideration the child's fragile emotional state, the clear indicators that she has been exposed to an inappropriate level of sexual activity on the mother's part, my recommendation is that she continue to live with her father as she has for the last two months. The stability, the clear and appropriate limits the father is able to set with the child, the order and discipline in the house-

284

hold are obviously important, and *will* be very important, to the child's development.'

'And would visitation with the mother be important as part of this custody arrangement?'

'Oh, yes, very important,' the doctor said generously. 'It's crucial that she not feel abandoned. But also, and more importantly, it's essential that she live with a parent who gives her back her childhood. Who says, "Here's the line."' Dr Herzog opened one hand and sliced across it with the other. '"I am the adult, and my sex life is over here, with me. You are the child, and it's not your concern." The other is,' he shook his head, 'not good.'

'That's all,' Fine said. 'Thank you, Doctor.'

Muth took over. He shambled up to the doctor, seemed almost apologetic about having to ask questions. He inquired whether Herzog had read the report of the *guardian ad litem*. Herzog had. He asked whether Herzog was aware that the guardian had recommended I get custody.

He was, Herzog said.

Muth asked whether Herzog hadn't felt a little handicapped in making his judgment, by not being able to see me. Herzog said he felt, on the basis of what he observed in the child, that he could fairly recommend custody go to Brian and Brenda, that it was clear to him that in my home she had been exposed to an unacceptable level of sexual activity.

'Your opinion, based on . . . ?'

'Based on my observations, on what the little girl said to me.'

'But not on having seen or talked to Mrs Dunlap?'

'No.'

'Would you have been in an even better position to justify such an opinion, Doctor, if you *had* seen Mrs Dunlap?' Muth was ingenuous.

'I suppose so, but I have no . . .'

'So that the guardian, who in this case *did* see Mrs Dunlap, really was in a better position to come to that type of conclusion?'

Herzog frowned at Muth a moment. 'He might be.'

'Thank you. Ah, have you read the book, Doctor, *Beyond the Best Interests of the Child*?

'By Goldstein, Freud, and Solnit?'

'Yes, that's the one,' said Muth, as though delighted to have something in common.

'Yes, of course.'

'Are you aware, Doctor, of the importance they give in that book to the idea of continuity of caregiver?'

'Yes, but in my opinion, the risk here is great enough to offset that advantage.'

'But, Doctor,' Muth frowned, confused, 'wasn't it their point that we should *stop* thinking of risks as offsetting that advantage? That this *is*, in fact, what's most important, no matter what?'

'I believe that is a crude summary of their argument, yes. But I disagree with them in this case.'

'In this case,' Muth said sadly.

'Yes.'

'Doctor, who's paying your expenses for coming here and testifying. *In this case?*'

After a moment, Herzog answered. 'My arrangements are with Mr Fine.'

'Yes. What are they, though?'

'Well.' The doctor lowered his voice. 'Expenses, transportation. And a fee for testifying.'

'How much is that fee?'

'Just the testimony?'

'Yes. What's your professional fee? What has Mr Fine agreed that his client will pay you?'

'Fifteen hundred dollars.'

'Fifteen hundred dollars . . . a day?'

'Yes.'

'And does that include your travel time here and back?'

'Yes.'

'When did you come, Doctor?'

'Yesterday. I arrived last night at eleven.'

'Last night at eleven. And you'll go home tomorrow, so that's two days?'

286

'No, I'm leaving tonight. My reservation is this evening.'

'So that will be fifteen hundred. For the trip. For testifying.'

'And compensatory fees for patients I've cancelled.'

'Plus, I suppose,' Muth looked at the judge wide-eyed, 'the office fees for Molly and the Dunlaps. And, consulting to Mr Fine? That too?'

Herzog nodded.

'How much total?' Muth asked.

'Five thousand dollars, sir.'

'Five thousand exactly?' Muth asked.

'Around five thousand,' Herzog said.

'Well, thank you,' said Muth. 'Thanks so much.'

We broke for lunch. Leo and Muth disappeared together, to talk about Leo's testimony, scheduled to come up next. I went over to the Barrister by myself and had coffee and pie, and watched the clock on the wall. It was the kind that clicked over after each minute had passed, so you were always catching up, always being reminded by the little sharp noise, the twitch of the hand, that you were slightly behind. When I got back to the courtroom, just the policemen were in it. Someone had opened one of the windows to cool the room off a little, and the shade billowed out, then tapped against the glass again. Dr Payne came in and sat in back. Brenda arrived, sat in the pew in front of him. The policemen wandered in and out, carrying sheaves of paper, laughing with each other.

Leo looked terrible to me when he took his place. His neck seemed long and white and skinny. His eyes flickered quickly from Fine to the judge. A whooping crane, I thought; and then suddenly remembered his bird cry the first time we'd really made love.

Fine asked him to describe his relationship to me.

'We've been going out since early May.'

'Going out? What does that mean?'

'We've been lovers,' Leo said, looking scared.

The radiator started to hiss. Fine turned to the judge and said something I couldn't hear.

287

'OK, yes, I've noted that,' the judge said.

'What?' I whispered to Muth, 'What's happening?'

'He made him a hostile witness. Watch.' Muth gestured at Fine. 'It's like cross-examination.'

'It's a sexual relationship you have, isn't it, Mr Cutter?' Fine said. He was smiling. It seemed to me it was the first time I'd seen him smile.

'Yes. And emotional.'

'Please just answer the question. How long had you known Mrs Dunlap before your relationship became sexual?'

'Several months.'

'You'd gone out with her several months?'

'No. I'd met her several months before.'

'How long had you gone out with her before you slept together?'

'Once,' Leo said softly.

'Once,' Fine echoed, his voice sharp, cheerful. 'I see. Now Mr Cutter, you are currently unemployed, are you not?'

'I'm self-employed.'

'You have no job, is that not the case?'

'I'm a painter. An artist. I paint. I sell paintings.'

'But you are not currently working at a job, are you?'

'Not in that sense, no.'

'Just no is sufficient, Mr Cutter. And when *is* the last time you had a job, *in that sense?*'

'I taught a course last spring, at the museum school.'

'And before that?'

'The year before, I was an artist-in-residence at a high school north of Boston.'

'So, Mr Cutter, it's fair to say that you live a fairly unstable life, economically.'

'Yes, that is fair.'

'So that moving in with Mrs Dunlap represented a *good deal* for you, didn't it.'

'I never moved in.'

'But you slept there every night, isn't that a fact?'

'Yes.'

'Had your meals there?'

'Usually.'

'But you *didn't* move in.'

'No.'

Fine looked up at the judge and smiled. 'We won't quibble over this one, your honor.' He turned back to Leo again, walked slowly past him, talking. 'Now, tell me, Mr Cutter, you took care of Molly, my client's daughter, from time to time, didn't you?'

'Yes.'

'Mrs Dunlap left you alone with her?'

'Yes.'

'Let you bathe the child and put her to bed?'

'Yes.'

Fine turned, faced Leo. 'And it was on one of those occasions that you were naked in front of the child, was it not?'

'Yes.'

'When there was no one else around?'

'That's right.' Leo's voice was neutral.

'You told the child to touch your genitals, did you not?'

'No, I didn't.'

'You did *not* tell the child to touch you?' Fine leaned towards Leo.

'No, she asked if she could.'

'The child *asked* if she could touch you sexually?'

'Yes. No! Not sexually.' Leo's hands came up, gripped the railing.

'She *asked* if she could touch your genitals,' Fine said slowly. 'Yes.'

'A four-year-old child spontaneously requests to fondle a grown—'

'She was curious!' Leo burst out. I could tell he was near the edge. *Don't*, I thought. Just a little more. Just a little worse.

'So you – of course, who wouldn't?' Fine shrugged cavalierly – 'you said "yes."'

'That's right.' Leo had quieted.

'*Sure, great*, go ahead!'

'I said *yes*,' Leo said dully.

'And when she touched you, Mr Cutter, is it not the case that you responded sexually to her touch?'

'Yes.' Leo looked down.

'That you were aroused by her?'

'No.'

'You responded, but you were *not* aroused?'

'Yes.'

Fine smiled at the judge. 'Another nice distinction, your honor.'

Muth stood up. 'Objection,' he said. 'The witness has answered. Counsel doesn't need to comment on the answer.'

'Sustained,' the judge said, but he smiled at Fine.

Fine turned back to Leo. 'You got an erection when my client's little girl touched you.'

Muth stood again. '*Objection*, your honor. He's already answered this.'

The judge nodded. 'Sustained,' he said again.

Fine turned and smiled slightly at Muth. Then back to Leo. 'OK, let's talk about something else, Mr Cutter. On multiple occasions, you and Mrs Dunlap had the child in bed with you, didn't you?'

'Yes.'

'You would both be naked, and the child would be in bed with you?'

'Neither of us wore pajamas.' Leo spoke quickly, angrily. 'If the ch . . . if Molly got into bed with us, that was the situation, yes, but we never *took* her to bed with us naked.'

'Thank you, Mr Cutter, thank you for the explanation. And when you *happened* to end up, two naked adults and a four-year-old child, in the same bed – on any of those occasions, Mr Cutter, were you and Mrs Dunlap actually having intercourse?'

'Yes. Once.' Leo's voice was nearly lost.

Brian spun sideways in his chair. The judge looked over at him, then quickly, back to Leo.

'So you were making love while Molly was in the bed with you?'

'She was asleep.'

Fine turned his back to Leo and the judge, spoke contemptuously over his shoulder. 'I have no further questions, your honor.'

There was a long silence in the room. The shade ticked against the window. A distant phone rang. 'Mr Muth?' the judge said finally.

Muth stood up. 'No,' he said. 'I have no questions, your honor.' And sat down. Leo looked at him, at me. I touched Muth's arm lightly, but he looked down at his papers, made no response.

'You may step down,' the judge said to Leo. Leo looked at him for several seconds before he understood what had happened. Slowly he got up.

Leo didn't show up in court the next day.

I wasn't surprised. I'd called him after I'd gotten home the night before, and then, because he sounded so upset, I'd gone over to his studio.

He was drinking. He was enraged at Muth for 'cutting him loose,' as he called it. 'I mean, Jesus, Anna, if he was going to do that, he could have *told* me. That's all I mind. He implied I'd get a chance to tell the story my way, so I was a good little boy for the cross-examination, and then he pretended not to fucking *know* me.'

'He was just trying to help me, Leo.'

'Anna, I'll do *anything* to help you, to help him help you. I told you that. If he doesn't want to talk to me in court, *great*. But he should have told me. That's all. He should have fucking told me.'

'He probably thought you'd perform better, if . . .'

'I *know* what he thought! He was wrong to do it the way he did.' We sat in silence at his table, not looking at each other. Leo got up and started pacing around the room.

'Maybe I should go,' I said.

'Whatever,' he agreed. He was standing at his worktable, his back to me.

But I just sat at the table.

After a while, Peter came over.

Leo told him what had happened, repeated his objections to the way Muth had dealt with him. Peter agreed. He told Leo that Muth sounded like a colossal asshole, a mind-boggling asshole. For a while, Peter really enjoyed talking about it. But then we started to bring him down, he said. 'Jeez, I wanted some company tonight,' he complained. 'I can live without this.' He gestured at Leo and me.

'Go fuck yourself, Pete,' Leo said. He was sitting on the mattress now, the drink in his hand.

'After you,' said Peter.

'I mean it,' Leo said. No one spoke for a while.

'Well,' Peter said. 'I got to admit it. I just can't keep up with a pace like this for very long.' He pushed himself up from the room's only comfortable chair. 'Thanks for the stimulation, guys. I gotta go.'

'Me too,' I said.

Leo looked up at me.

'I've got to do it again tomorrow, Leo,' I said. 'I'm going to have to talk. And I *trust* Muth. I've *got* to trust him.' I shook my head. 'I really can't stay with you when you're feeling this way.'

He looked back down, nodded.

I squatted by him. 'We can't talk tonight anyway.' I touched his face. 'Can we?'

He shook his head.

'I'm sorry,' I said.

'I'm sorry too,' he answered. We squeezed hands.

I left with Peter, and didn't look back. I didn't want to see him there alone.

Outside, Peter tried to persuade me to go dancing. I eased away from him, got into my car. 'You'll be sorry, Anna,' he shouted to my closed window. 'Dancing. It's the very thing for what ails you.' As I drove away, he was tapping across the sidewalk to his patchwork Volvo.

When I stepped behind the paling the next day, I was already trembling. Like Leo, I'd worn a costume – the old dress I'd put on the night I imagined I could still talk to Brian.

Muth grinned across the railing at me, then led me at a leisurely pace through the opening questions, the story he wanted to establish. He particularly dwelt on the amount of responsibility I'd always had for Molly's care: that I had had contact with doctors, teachers, parents of friends. That I had made the arrangements, accompanied her on trips to the aquarium, the children's museum. That I had selected babysitters, chosen the day-care center. That I had purchased Molly's clothes, planned her meals. That when she was disturbed in the night, I was the one to go to her. As we slowly talked about these details of my life with Molly, I began to relax. I sat back, as Brian had done, and tried to look as comfortable as he had.

Muth had been facing me and the judge all this time. Now he turned out to the courtroom. 'Now, Mrs Dunlap,' he said. 'Tell me the history of your relationship with Leonard Cutter. When did you first meet?'

'We met sometime in April.'

'And you began going out in . . . ?'

'We started dating, we became lovers, in May. And Mr Cutter would often spend the night, starting in June, really.'

'And on some of those nights, did Molly sleep with you?'

'Yes, she did. She sometimes had nightmares, or bad dreams – I think lots of kids really start to at her age – and when she'd wake up with them, she'd often come down the hall to my bedroom and climb into bed with me. With us.'

'So she'd sleep in the bed with you, as any child does under those circumstances?'

'Well, if I were alert enough, I'd carry her back to her bed. But occasionally, I let her stay and she'd fall asleep next to me, yes.'

'Describe that arrangement to us.'

'The sleeping arrangement?'

'Yes.'

'Well, Molly would be on the edge, the side closest to

293

the door, where she'd come in, and I'd be in the middle, and then Leo – Mr Cutter – would be on his side of the bed.'

'Now, Mrs Dunlap, tell us how Molly related to Leo.'

'Oh, she adored him. He'd worked very hard to gain her affection. He was very reassuring, very steady with her. She enjoyed being with him.' Below me, Brian shook his head slowly in disgust. I tried not to look at him.

'And from time to time, did you leave her alone with him?'

'Yes. Sometimes just to dash out and get groceries, but occasionally for longer. Once or twice so I could catch up on my work in the evenings. And sometimes they *chose* to spend time together – she'd ask him to take her somewhere, to the beach or something.'

'Now, Mrs Dunlap, what was your response when you heard of this incident that's been referred to, where there was contact between Mr Cutter and your daughter?'

'I was shocked really. I was appalled.' This was the answer we'd agreed on. I was glad Leo wasn't in the courtroom. I said it softly.

'And did you express that opinion to Mr Cutter?'

'Well, I didn't find out about it until afterwards, but at the time I learned of it, yes, I expressed my dismay.'

'You let Mr Cutter know that you didn't condone such behavior?'

'Yes.'

'Do you recall the words you used?'

I remembered lying silently a long time next to Leo in the half-dark after he'd explained it to me. The light's purple glow made everything ugly. I didn't remember saying anything. I had been crying.

'No. Just that it was bad, that I didn't understand how he could have thought it was all right.'

Muth nodded soberly, approvingly. 'Now, Mrs Dunlap,' he said, 'I know that at various points in investigating this situation, various people have asked you about whether you'd be willing to give Mr Cutter up if that were a condition of custody. The family service officer and Dr Payne, the guardian, have asked you. What has your response been to that?'

'That I would be willing. I'd be willing not to see Mr Cutter again.'

'OK,' Muth said. He smiled gently at me, looked at the judge. 'That's all.'

Mr Fine paced in front of me slowly for a moment before he began. I avoided his dark, bright eyes. He paused, spoke directly to me. 'Now, Mrs Dunlap, is it true that on at least one of the occasions when Molly came down the hall and got into bed with you, you had intercourse with Mr Cutter while she was in that bed?'

'We were having intercourse when she came in, yes.'

'And you continued to do so, isn't that the case?'

'Mr Cutter stayed inside me.'

'Which is what we define, I think, as intercourse. It will do for me anyway.' There was muted laughter here and there in the room, and Mr Fine's lips curled slightly, as though to acknowledge it. Then his face sobered, he frowned at me. 'So that you, who so properly object to Mr Cutter's having *allowed* your little girl to touch him, you yourself *allowed* her to be in bed with you while you were having intercourse, isn't that so?'

'Yes.' I tried to keep my voice firm, steady.

'Do you feel there's some qualitative difference between these two, *modes of behavior*, shall we say?'

Muth stood up behind him. 'Objection your honor. That calls for a judgment.'

The judge looked over at him. 'I think I'd like to hear the witness answer,' he said, frowning.

'I don't know,' I said, after a moment.

'What?' said Fine sharply.

'I don't know if there's a difference.'

'But you do disapprove of what Mr Cutter did?'

'Yes.'

'Do you disapprove of what *you* did in letting the child watch you have intercourse?'

'She *didn't* watch.'

'*Do* you disapprove of your own action?' he repeated, as though I were slow-witted.

'Yes, I do,' I said softly.

'You would not do it again.'

'No, I wouldn't.'

He watched me a moment with his bright eyes. 'Tell me, Mrs Dunlap, at what point did you change your mind?'

'Excuse me?'

'You changed your mind about your behavior, isn't that the case?'

'No.'

'No? But once you felt it was fine and dandy. Now, apparently, you don't.'

'I never felt it was fine and dandy.'

'But you *did* it.'

'Yes.'

'Without feeling it was all right?'

'Yes. I didn't think. I didn't think about it.'

'I see,' he said. He walked away, over to his table, looked down at some papers, then walked quickly back. '*Now*, Mrs Dunlap,' he said. 'Would you describe the number of hours you worked prior to your divorce?'

'Somewhere between ten and fifteen hours a week.'

'Because *Mr* Dunlap worked hard, made enough money so that you didn't *have* to work all the time, did you?'

'No. Yes, that's right.'

'And Molly went part-time to this day-care center you'd found.'

'Yes. My piano students were all after school, in the afternoon, and she went to the afternoon program there.'

'And this year you upped her time to full-time.'

'That's right.'

'Because you're working more.'

'Yes.'

'Which is how much?'

'Well, over the summer it was thirty hours.'

'And now?'

'And now. Now I have piano students back, it's forty or so.'

'So when you had custody of Molly, she was at day care forty hours a week.'

'Approximately, yes.'

'And that would be the schedule if she were to return to your custody?'

'Yes.'

'And do you have anyone to help you in your home, Mrs Dunlap?'

'No.'

'So you work forty hours a week away from your daughter, and then still have all the work and maintenance involved in the home to do also.'

'Yes.'

'As well as your *social* life, isn't that the case?' He smiled slightly again.

'Yes.'

'That's all, your honor.'

Muth got up slowly when the judge called on him, as though there were no urgency, nothing to worry about. His tone was relaxed. 'Now Mrs Dunlap, both the jobs you work at have rather flexible hours, don't they?' He grinned at me, my friend.

'Yes.'

'And could you tell the court,' he swung his hand out towards Fine and Brian, 'what you'd do, what you *have* done, when Molly is ill, and needs her mother?'

'Well, if she were sick, when she's been sick, I just cancel everything. Or even occasionally if we just felt like, well, not going to day care that day, having a picnic or something. Not that I could afford to do it often. But I stay with her when she's ill. Occasionally I still have the piano students come, because I'm right there, down the hall if she needs me. But I can always have someone else take care of the animals at the lab where I work, and just make up the work time later. And that's part of why I have that job, so I can respond to her, so we can have those times together.'

297

'Thank you,' he said, and nodded to the judge. 'That's all.'

Doctor Payne looked tiny, bobbing to the witness stand. When he sat back after he'd been sworn in, his face was partially obscured from me by the railing around him. Muth had him recite his credentials too, at great length. He asked him for an account of how many cases he'd testified in, of how many times he'd recommended custody for the mother and how many for the father. He got from him a tedious description of the number of hours he'd spent with each of us and in writing up his report. Then Muth asked him to talk about Molly, about how she'd behaved in her sessions.

Payne smiled. 'Well, Molly was, in some ways, a tough cookie.' Then he shook his head, sobered. 'But I think all the changes in her life, and her confusion about what's going to happen now, have made her wary of opening up. And I think she sensed that what she said to me was going to make a difference in terms of where she ended up. But by the second session she'd relaxed some, and I was able to do some play therapy with her, to use dolls and toys to get at what her feelings were. And she became more open. And she's really quite articulate about what she thinks, once she's comfortable.'

'And did she show signs, Doctor, of having been traumatized by the events described here?'

Payne's head moved quickly. 'No, I think not. In part because, as Anna has suggested, it occurred in a context where there *was* a fair amount of nudity, a fair amount of physical contact going on; and she had gotten comfortable with that. That was all familiar to her.' He frowned. 'I did find her *preoccupied* with those issues, to a degree. But it was hard for me to sort out the reasons for that. And it seemed to me just as likely that she'd picked up on Brian's response to her telling him about it, about what happened.'

'Could you explain that?' Muth seemed not to understand.

'Yes. Molly misses her father, cares for him very deeply, but doesn't see him often enough. And when she does see

298

him, he's frequently got his mind on other things – work, or his new marriage. In that situation, she brought up this episode with Leo Cutter, and suddenly found her father intensely interested in her, in what she had to say. In a purely unconscious way, without being aware of doing it, she may have responded to that increased interest.'

'And *this* would account for her preoccupation?' It was a revelation to Muth.

'It might at least in *part* account for it. Children,' Payne smiled ruefully, 'use what power they have.' Then he sat forward and grew serious again. 'But another real source of preoccupation, I think, is that the rules are so clearly different from household to household. And where you have that, when a child has to manage that, often she spends a lot of time exploring the boundaries, testing the difference in limits. It's a difficult transition for a small child to make, between different standards of behavior, and it's not unusual for them to spend a lot of time right on the *edge* of that difference.' He made a gesture oddly like Dr Herzog's the day before, a slice across his palm with his other hand.

'I think in all likelihood what we're seeing in Molly is some of a little of each of these kinds of behavior.'

Muth frowned, the slow student. 'But you don't find her damaged by the episode we've heard about?'

'Not damaged.' Payne shook his head and sat back. 'I don't think she perceived it as frightening or threatening in any way.'

Muth nodded slowly, taking it in. Then he said, 'Doctor, you've heard testimony from Dr Herzog, who also saw Molly.'

'Yes.'

'Do you know Dr Herzog's work?'

'I don't. But the psychiatric world is large, and we're from different regions.'

'Well, Dr Herzog concluded, from watching Molly play with these' – his hand made its dainty circle – 'anatomically *correct* dolls, that she *had* been traumatized, that she was suffering from the effects of the experience. Can you respond to that?'

'With all due respect to Dr Herzog, I can't agree with him. And I'd suggest that these dolls' – he turned to the judge – 'I don't know if you've seen these dolls, your honor.' The judge nodded ambiguously, and Payne turned back to Muth. 'Well, these dolls are themselves, I think, terrifying.' Payne's thick brows had lowered. 'Preoccupying *themselves* . . . for a child. The male genitals are . . . deformed, at best. The female genitals look like a wound, an injury. Maybe, at best, some strange animal. And there's all this *hair*. It's the child's nightmare of what sexuality might be.

'So if a child was unable to stop focusing on those genitals, well, I'd say that was all too predictable a response. A fascination with that. I really must say,' he shook his head sternly, 'I disapprove of the use of a prop so distracting, so insistent on one meaning. If a child can't bear to look at them, we say he's traumatized. If he can look at nothing but them, we also say he's traumatized. Yet either response, given the bizarre, disturbing nature of what he's looking at – *she's* looking at, in this case – seems perfectly understandable to me.'

'So you do not agree with Dr Herzog's findings?' Muth frowned.

'No. And the most relevant observation I had had about Molly had nothing to do with these sexual issues at all.'

'And what was that observation, Doctor?'

'Well, that Molly's real concern, the driving force for her right now, is a fear of being left, of abandonment. When she played with – what I'll call more *nonthreatening* toys, just dolls, animals, puppets – what got acted out again and again was her sense of being left alone, her anger at *both* her parents. If she's at risk in any sense, it's around that issue.'

'Aha,' Muth said. 'And what do you see, as the source of that fear?'

'The divorce, of course, is the main source, and connected with that, her father's departure. She has internalized that, blames herself for it to some degree, in spite of what she's been told by both parents.'

'Which is?'

'That it's not her *fault*, that Daddy and Mommy couldn't get *along*, and so on. She *knows* those things. If you ask her why her parents got divorced, she'll tell you that in a quite reasonable, quasi-grownup voice. And then she'll play out for you a little girl who's so naughty that she's put in a room all alone.'

'I see. And—'

'But she also fears her mother's abandonment,' Payne interrupted. 'It's in *that* sense that her mother's relationship with Leo has been difficult for her, though there's also the shift to full-time day care to take into account. But here you've got a little girl who's lost her father, been very close to Mother. And now she begins to lose Mother in some sense too. And so we see the immaturity, the acting out, the need for attention.'

Muth nodded, silent for a moment. 'I see. And can you talk for a minute about the child's relationship to the mother?'

'Yes. It's very close, very intense. Not inappropriately so for a child her age. But the mother has been the main source of affection, though she's also deeply attached to Father.'

'But he's more remote.'

Fine stood. 'Objection your honor. He's leading the witness.'

The judge nodded. 'I'll sustain that. Rephrase your question, Counselor.'

'Ah,' Muth said. 'OK. So you'd say . . . so, who, in your opinion, is the psychological parent in this case?'

Payne smiled. 'Well, I don't draw the line in quite that way, Mr Muth. I do know what you're talking about, but the child here is attached to both parents.' He turned to the judge, frowning. 'That's part of the difficulty in this case, your honor. And both parents are very attached to the child, too. It seems to me that neither is using custody in any way to punish the other. They both feel that the child would genuinely be better off with them. Each feels he can offer the better environment. But I would say that your client,

301

Mr Muth,' he turned back to Muth, 'your client, Anna, is more important to Molly's psychological health at this point. That Molly is at some risk around the issue of feeling abandoned. And that to lose her mother now would be yet another, even more painful wrench – the most painful wrench possible, given their closeness – and that would be the most damaging thing I could think of for this little girl right now.'

'And it's on this basis that you offer your opinion?'

'Well, and feeling that there's not a risk in the home, Mother's home, if she stays there.'

'And on what do you base that? *That* opinion?'

'Well, first of all that everyone realizes that what happened shouldn't have. That Anna's ready to have counseling if that's the court's recommendation. And she's also ready to stop seeing Mr Cutter, if we wish to make that a condition.' He looked up at the judge again. 'I look on the episode as just that, an episode. An episode of bad judgment. But *not* worth changing custody over, particularly when the child is so attached to her mother, and the mother is perfectly capable of caring for her.'

Muth's head bobbed slowly, soberly. 'Thank you,' he said.

Fine walked directly up to Payne when he was called, talking even as he approached.

'Now, Doctor, you call this an episode of bad judgment.'

'Yes.' Payne nodded.

'You mean the incident where Molly touched Mr Cutter's genital organs?'

'Yes.'

'But the fact of the matter is, isn't it, that for the entire duration of her mother's relationship with Mr Cutter, the child was exposed to a high degree of sexual activity?'

'That's not my understanding.' Payne's mouth tightened.

'That's not your understanding?'

'No. For the first month or so, Molly was exposed to nothing.'

'*Oh*,' Fine said sarcastically. 'So it was only for the last

302

several months of the relationship that the child was exposed to their sexual activity.'

'No. I don't consider nudity sexual activity.'

'Do you consider intercourse sexual activity, Doctor?'

'Certainly.'

'And on at least one occasion they had intercourse in front of the child, did they not?'

'The child seems to have been asleep, Mr Fine.' Payne's voice was soft, controlled.

'I see.' Fine turned and faced the courtroom. 'And is this something you recommend, Doctor, having intercourse in bed with a child who may or may not be asleep?'

'No, it isn't.'

'So that would be *another* episode of *bad judgment*.'

Payne paused. 'Yes,' he said.

Fine turned. 'And the amount of nudity, Doctor. That the child was apparently quite used to seeing her mother and Mr Cutter naked in bed and in the bathroom. Is that bad judgment?'

'I don't think it was a good idea, no.'

'And that they waltzed around – excuse me – walked around, the apartment naked? That she watched Mr Cutter take showers? Is that another example of *bad judgment?*'

'Well, in the best of circumstances, I think it wouldn't happen.'

'So time and time again, Mrs Dunlap showed *bad judgment* around these sexual issues with her daughter.'

'In this relationship, yes.'

'But you would recommend the child go *back* with this mother?' Fine's tone was incredulous.

'Nobody is a perfect parent. The child is deeply attached—'

'Yes or no, Doctor.'

'Yes. I do recommend that.' Payne set his mouth in a tight line.

Fine's tone changed. 'Now, Mrs Dunlap works at two jobs, doesn't she?'

'Two part-time jobs, yes.'

'And this has meant she's had to put her child into day care full-time, hasn't it?'

'Yes.'

'And you mention in your report that Mrs Dunlap has been psychologically more absent, I think you said, since the beginning of her relationship with Mr Cutter?'

'Yes, that's true.'

'So there's some sense in which the abandonment you speak of as having traumatized the child has been caused by the mother's withdrawal, and by her having to work more.'

'I've said that already, yes. But that's no reason to abandon her *more* . . .'

'All right, Doctor, fine. Let me ask you this, Doctor. Isn't it the case that Mrs Dunlap is consenting to give up Mr Cutter just to improve her chances of getting her daughter back?'

'Well, not *just*. There are other complicated aspects . . .'

'In part, then, to improve her chances?'

'Well, I suppose so. Otherwise, I assume she might not.'

'So, if the court had *not* intervened, *at the instigation of my client*, it would not have *occurred* to her to give up Mr Cutter, is that correct?'

'It might not have.'

'*Or* to change her sexual behavior in her home?'

'I can't know that.'

'Yet you say the child is not *at risk* in this home.'

'That's right.'

Mr Fine stared for a moment at Payne. Then he looked up at the judge. 'That's all,' he said, after a pause.

Muth got up again and asked Payne to speculate on the damage to Molly if Brian got custody. Payne grew expansive again as he talked about her need for stability, for the continuation of her close tie with me, her most important tie.

'So in this sense, Mrs Dunlap has been a reliable figure in the child's life?'

'Absolutely. And in some sense Molly's sense of herself is

304

premised on Mrs Dunlap's continuing presence in her life.'
He leaned forward. 'Now I'm not saying that she couldn't
survive. But it'd be like deliberately, say, breaking her arm,
knowing it would heal, but that some treatment would be
necessary, some long or short period of recovery, certainly
some excruciating pain. What I'm saying is that to move
her to her father's care now would be to wound her, scar
her again. I'm saying you have to take this into account.'

Muth nodded. 'And you're saying this, in spite of Mrs
Dunlap's present busier schedule, and the increased hours
of childcare?'

'Yes,' Payne said firmly. 'I realize that no parent can
spend every minute with a child, and it would be harmful
to a child if a parent did. Now it may be, and I think it *is*
the case, in this case, that neither parent really has an ideal
amount of time to spend with this child. For different reasons
each of them has to spend more hours away from the child
than I'd recommend. But there *is* no ideal home. And the
fact is that Molly's relationship with her mother, with Anna,
is a strong one, that she has Anna as an internal parent,
that Anna has done that . . . *homework* with her, as it were.'
He smiled. 'And that's why she's been able to withstand as
much separation as she has, because her mother *is* part of
her, she has enough experience of her mother *coming back*,
over and over, even when she goes to day care. Having her
mother is like an inner strength she carries with her, that
enables her to step towards independence, that independence we all want for our kids. But it's because Anna's like
a piece of her. What I'm suggesting is we not compromise
that now, not say to her: "Here, you've stood all this so well,
we're going to test you even further – by taking the person
who's *given* you that strength away." *That's* putting her at
risk, in my book.'

Muth, nodding steadily, slowly through this, waited a
moment to let it all sink in before he said, 'Well, thank you.
Thank you, Doctor.'

The last person Muth called was one of Molly's day-care
teachers. Not Maggie, the one I'd seen in the restaurant.

This was a woman named Pat. Molly had been in her group the year before Brian and I split up, and Pat knew the teachers who'd had Molly last year. She testified that while she'd been Molly's teacher, I was the one who'd brought Molly to school, picked her up, came to parent conferences, helped at the center. That when Molly cried during the day, mine was the name she called. That Molly was a happy child who'd had a few adjustment problems since the divorce, but seemed normal to her, seemed very attached to me.

Fine declined to cross-examine, 'In view of the hour,' he said.

Then each lawyer stood and presented his case once again, using their elaborate language of blame and justification. While they talked I had the sense, suddenly, that what they were saying had nothing to do with me. Muth was ingenuous, shocked at the preposterous nature of the motion; Fine was sarcastic, appalled at our attempt to excuse my behavior. Watching them, I remembered their muted, somehow conspiratorial greeting in the echoing courthouse hall, their laughter coming out of Mrs Harkessian's office together. They were *acting* now, I realized; as I had acted, in my fancy dress and my repudiation of Leo; as Brian had acted, in his indignation; as Leo had acted in his haircut, his new jacket. Only Payne had been himself, had escaped playing some part. The rest was all a kind of elaborate charade, it had nothing to do with who we really were or what really ought to happen.

But when I looked at Brian, he was alert, interested. He nodded his agreement with Fine's points as though that were my life up there, and his, and Molly's. I felt an impulse to stand up and shout out some truth, to begin this again from the start, to change the vocabulary.

But the pipes hissed. The judge listened carefully. The lawyers made their pitches. And then it was over.

'All over but the waiting,' Muth said to me, smiling, as he bent to shut the car door after me. I smiled back at him through the thick glass, and started the car.

THIRTEEN

It was an oddly warm day for October. The sun was shining brightly, though the shadows were long. The streets were full of people. I drove Leo home in silence. On the sidewalk in front of the Cambridge Street projects, three women lay on cheap webbed chairs, wearing shorts, smoking and talking. Donna Summer blared from a box on the concrete next to them. I was amazed at this, amazed that everything was the same. A man I accidentally cut off at an intersection gave me the finger, and I stared at him, unsure of how this connected with me. Leo turned to me at the stoplight in front of Sears. 'What are you going to do now?' he asked. His voice was hoarse, as though he hadn't spoken in a long time. He cleared his throat.

I looked back at him. I didn't understand what he meant.

He waited, looking at me. Then he said, 'I mean, do you want me to come home with you? Or to come to my place?'

The car behind me honked. I looked up. The light was green. My foot pushed the accelerator. 'Or do you want to be alone?'

I nodded. 'Alone,' I said.

After a moment he said, 'I'll walk from your house then. You don't have to go out of your way.'

'OK,' I answered.

He'd come down to Muth's office with me and waited in the car while I went up. The secretary had called at about ten that morning, said that Mr Muth wondered if I could get in today, was there a possibility? One of the piano students I had had to cancel was Ursula, and she had called Leo. I hadn't wanted his company, but he was ardent, determined to help, to comfort me if it was bad, to be the one celebrating with me if it was good. He pointed out that his coming along would mean I wouldn't have to worry about parking, I could just run in quickly and find out. I had picked him up at his corner at two-thirty.

'What will you do?' he asked now.

I shrugged. 'Sit. Try to take it in. Think about what comes next.' He nodded, as though that seemed reasonable. I was turning down my street. The Vietnamese family near the corner was gathered on their porch, squeezed into a diminishing patch of yellow sunlight. Solemnly they watched us drive past. Every time I saw them they seemed to have one or two more babies, sober, uncrying.

'If you want anything, if you need to talk or anything, you'll call me?'

I nodded. I couldn't wait to get away from him. If he asked another question I thought I'd scream. Just let me get alone, I prayed. I could hardly bear to look at him for more than a few seconds.

'Shall I lock it?' he said, as we got out of the car.

'No, don't bother,' I said.

We stood for a moment at the end of the walk back to my house.

'I've got to go in,' I said. I'm sure he could hear the desperation in my voice.

He nodded and reached out to touch my arm. His fingers were sweaty, and when he let go, it felt cold where they'd held me. 'I'll call,' he said, and I bent my head as though to agree and turned down the walk. When I looked back from the front door, he was still standing there. I lifted my hand and went inside.

Upstairs, I walked immediately down the long hall back to my room, not even looking at the closed door to Molly's room. I shut my door behind me and lay down on the bed. Nearly instantly I was weeping.

The decision was final, Muth had said. Later, if there were changes . . . He had jumped up and come around the desk when I started to cry. He had supplied tissues and bent over me, rubbing my shoulder. It was just the luck of the draw, he told me. Judge Sullivan was strict about sexual issues. He'd known it when we went in, Payne had known it. He'd said nothing to me because he didn't want me to worry, perhaps unnecessarily; but he and Payne had talked about strategy. They'd talked, they'd done their damnedest. It was his considered opinion that if they'd had any of the other judges, the decision would have gone the other way. I'd been great, Payne had been great, Cutter had done as well as he could. Now we were just stuck with it, we had to focus on the positive. He'd talked to Fine, they were being easy about visitation, he was going to get me lots of time. Things would be all right, we were going to make the best of a crummy, crummy deal. His hand rubbed my shoulder over and over. I checked my tears quickly and asked him sensible questions, got his reassuring answers. When he walked out to the elevator with me and said again how sorry he was, I felt my throat tighten, but I didn't let go.

Now I curled under the covers and wailed, shouted, like a lost child. I thought of Molly, imagined her more clearly than I had this whole time, imagined having her back, living with her, touching her. After a while, my sorrow seemed to run out of violence. I just cried, let the tears slide from my eyes. Sometime as it was getting dusky, I fell asleep.

The phone trilled distantly in the purple dark. I could feel the thickness of my eyelids as they opened and I remembered everything. I lay and listened to the muffled noise. When it had stopped, I got up and started towards the bathroom. I had no idea what time it was. I made my way down the dark hall. As I fumbled at the doorway for the light switch, a sudden dizzying pain clutched at my head, and I had to bend over and let the blood gather behind my eyes in order not to fall. The pain swelled, faded. I stood up and turned the light on.

In the blazing white of the bathroom I sat on the toilet and peed. That my body could still function seemed a kind of betrayal to me, and the act felt as unfamiliar, as beyond my control, as it had the first time I'd been able to urinate after Molly's birth, nearly a full day afterwards. I sat hunched in the white-tiled world for a long time after I was done.

My face in the mirror was puffy, as swollen everywhere as pregnant Celia's. I washed it in cold water. As I was drying myself, the telephone began again. On the tenth or eleventh ring, I started back towards the kitchen. The ringing continued, regular as breathing. I turned the light on, watched the telephone for a few minutes, then picked up the receiver.

It wasn't Leo. Ursula's baby voice began talking: she was so upset, Leo had told her, did I need someone to be with me? She'd just come and sleep on the couch, she wouldn't say a word if I didn't want to talk.

Alone in my kitchen, I almost smiled at the impossibility of the suggestion. I told her that I really needed to be by myself.

'Are you sure?' she said. 'I couldn't stand it, if I were you.'

'Yes,' I said. 'I want to think through my options.'

'Yeah, but what *are* they?' she asked. 'Leo told me you can't appeal or anything. What choices do you have?'

'Well, I need to figure out what I should do to see more of Molly.' I hadn't consciously thought of this before, but now a logic unfolded in my brain. 'I think it might make sense to move down there.'

'To *Washington*?'

'Yes.'

'Yeah,' she said thoughtfully. I could imagine her puckering brow, her open mouth.

'Yeah, but what about Leo? What about your job?'

'My job isn't much,' I said. 'I can get another job, I suspect.'

'Hey, *I* got you that job,' she said. When I didn't respond, she turned thoughtful again. 'Yeah, I guess you're right.' There was a little pause. 'You know what,' she said abruptly, 'I bet old Fisher could get you something, some research thing or other. He's got connections up the wazoo. Then

310

you could be right near her and really see her almost as much, I bet.'

'Almost,' I said.

'You gotta stay as up as you can, honey,' she said softly, after a minute.

I didn't answer.

'Don't you think I should come over?' she asked.

'No, I'm going to sleep now,' I said. 'I'll take a Tranxene or something. I'll call you tomorrow.'

'I'm counting on it,' she said.

I hung up.

I did take a Tranxene, but I still slept only intermittently. I waked every couple of hours and made myself hot milk and tried to think about whether it made sense to move to Washington. When I finally got up for good, at around six, there was no longer any question of deciding. It was clear. And that nearly passively made decision kept me going for the next three or four days. Muth was arranging visitation rights with Brian's lawyer. I called him once a day. And I made lists. With obsessive precision calculated to keep my panic at bay, I thought up and broke down into minute steps the process of quitting my job here, subletting the apartment, selling my furniture, and moving to a new life.

Leo called me several times a day, checking on how I was, wanting to see me when I was ready. I was always cool and evasive. I told him nothing about what I was doing. I wasn't conscious of misleading him. I imagined I'd tell him when everything became clear, as if only when all the elements of the plan were in place would it really be a plan. Until then, what I said was that I needed time to think. I was doing OK, but I wasn't ready to be with anyone.

I'm not sure why I didn't want to tell him. In part, maybe to avoid the fight that we ended up having when he finally did find out. But I think I felt, too, that he would try to dissuade me; and that if I had all my plans carefully set, he would be less likely to be able to.

Because I had a sense that I might be dissuadable. Some part of me was busy trying not to think of how painful it was going to be to stay involved with Molly. I felt that I could never have back what I'd had with her, and that that would always make whatever we did have seem too little, something lopped off. That feeling, which I was barely conscious of, which I kept pushing away, made me want to do what would be easy: to give up, to see her only occasionally and make what I could out of what was left with Leo. The work of those three or four days alone was pushing that temptation away. And to do that I needed to stay away from Leo.

During the time between Brian's warning call and my final visit to Muth – all through the psychiatric sessions, the legal discussion, the trial – my feelings for Leo had swung from something like the old loving warmth occasionally, to hateful anger. We had stayed lovers, and I pretended that things were the same because I knew my anger was unfair; and because I hoped that if I got Molly back, the sense of exposure and shame, and the spurts of hatred that came with them would vanish or change, that there would be something to recover with him, something different we could have together.

Now that seemed impossible to me. I knew that as long as I was trying for a real life of some sort with Molly, I'd feel some irrational hatred for Leo in my heart for having smashed everything apart.

When I had told Leo that I didn't blame him, didn't hold him responsible for what happened, I meant it. There was no one I blamed as much as myself. I understood that what he had done was exactly what he would have thought I wanted. I could remember clearly the vision I'd had of the three of us in a kind of boundariless Eden, all part of each other. And I could see how that vision and my behavior had led directly, irrevocably, to Leo's letting Molly touch him, even to his getting hard when she did. It was a chain of events set in motion by me, by my euphoric forgetfulness of all the rules. But even so, talking to him on the phone now, thinking about him, filled me with rage, with hatred. I knew rationally that it was wrong, that it was just the measure of the anger I felt for myself, but I couldn't get near that anger. I knew it would be as crippling as self-pity to let myself feel it. So I made my lists, did my errands, and avoided Leo.

I put a sign up in the day-care center about the apartment, and the same evening, three people called to arrange to look at it. By nine o'clock I had rented it to two women. They were both newly separated from their husbands and they were living together to help meet their expenses. They brought their children with them when they came over, two boys, one of whom Molly had known at the day-care center. I showed them around and explained the peculiarities of the apartment, as I had to Brian the first time he stayed with Molly.

The little boys liked the place immediately. They ran up and down the long hallway and thumped on the piano. Then they disappeared into Molly's room. After they'd left – the women gave me a check, postdated until they'd have the money – I looked in where the boys had been playing. They had gotten Molly's Legos down, dumped them all over the floor, and built a few tiny cars. Steeling myself against any response, I crouched in her room as I had hundreds of times before, and picked up all the little pieces.

I had put up notices about the furniture, too, both at the day-care center and the laundromat, but the women wanted it; they were willing to pay me five hundred dollars for everything I wasn't taking. The piano could stay, they said, until I had a place to move it to.

My lists got longer: Call U-Haul, check car for towing, pick up liquor boxes. And always, call Muth, call Muth, call Muth. I was still running the rats each day, but now, when I finished, I'd do errands; and when I didn't do errands, I'd fill the empty liquor boxes with dishes, with books, with Molly's toys. If I couldn't sleep, I'd take one of Ursula's pills and pack some more, till the chemical began to sing softly in my blood.

On Thursday, Leo came over without calling. I was in Molly's room and I heard his key in the lock. I stood in her doorway and watched the front door swing open, watched him walk in. He was wearing jeans and a big navy sweater. His skin had whitened to translucence since summer's passing, and my heart ached with loss to see him.

He saw me and stopped, then shut the door behind him. For a long moment we stood just down the hall from each other, each framed by a doorway. Then he spoke.

'Ursula tells me you're leaving town.'

'She shouldn't have. And I'm not going for a few weeks anyway . . .'

'When did you plan on telling me?'

I shrugged. 'When it all seemed really final, I guess.'

He looked around. Along one wall of the hallway were lined up the taped, labelled liquor boxes.

'This looks final to me.'

I turned away, looked back into Molly's room where I'd been packing her toys away, tucking the few fragile things in among the boxes of soft animals, putting all the parts into coffee cans. 'I guess I was waiting to hear from Muth about the visitation arrangements.'

'And then you were going to tell me.'

I was silent. I didn't want to lie to him again. 'I don't know. I don't know when I was going to tell you.'

He raised his fist level with his waist, then slammed it back down against the door. My hands flew up involuntarily at the noise. 'Ah, what the fuck does it matter anyway?' he said.

After a minute, I said softly, 'I don't suppose it really does.'

'No, I don't suppose,' he answered. He sounded utterly defeated.

'Would you like a beer?' I asked, after a long silence.

'Sure,' he said, as though giving something up.

I started down the hall. He began to follow, and I stopped and turned. 'Why don't we sit in the living room?' I said, and gestured beyond him in that direction. 'The kitchen's kind of a mess.' I didn't want him to see the yawning drawers, the emptied-out shelves.

'Sure,' he said, and lifted his shoulders.

He backed down the hall for a few steps, then turned and disappeared into the living room.

In the kitchen, I got two beers, found some glasses I hadn't packed in the rack. When I returned, Leo was sitting on the couch. I looked around quickly with his eyes. I hadn't done too much in here yet. The two women were going to keep most of the furniture anyway. But the bookshelves next to the fireplace were empty; the pictures had been taken down and the exposed hooks were black and winged on the walls like tiny insects landed among the repeated figures in the wallpaper.

I sat at the other end of the couch from him. I poured the beers. He was looking out the dark windows to the ugly streetlamp. Abruptly he turned. He picked up his glass. His voice was forced, cheery. 'So, when are you leaving?'

I tried smiling, but he only stared back. His white skin looked pinched around his nose and mouth. I noticed that his hand holding the beerglass was shaking.

'I guess what I thought is that when a visit is cleared, I'd go down and see Molly and find an apartment. So it's all a little iffy. I just keep calling Muth, and he says any day now.'

There was a silence. He reached forward and set his glass on the table again, placed his hands on his knees and rubbed them back and forth.

'The women who are taking the apartment don't need to get in until November first.'

'The women who are taking the apartment,' he echoed.

'Yes,' I said, and looked down at my beer quickly.

'Now that sounds kinda, what I call, *final*, Anna banana,' he said slowly. I could feel him staring at me, the heat from his eyes.

Suddenly I was afraid of his anger, and of my own, which I'd pushed so far away. I felt a little of it kick in, a shot of adrenalized pulse, quickened breath. I didn't want it now. I was on another course. I looked away, breathed in and out slowly. 'If you want to fight,' I said, 'I'm not interested.'

'But I don't want to fight,' he said. 'I just want to know what the *fuck* is going on.' His hand punched his leg with *fuck*.

I set my beer down on the table and closed my eyes. 'What's going on,' I said – I could hear the tremor in my voice and tried to control it – 'is that my life is wrecked and I'm trying to find a way to put it back together. It seems that simple to me.'

'And that means I'm out,' he said.

'It means whatever it has to mean about you,' I burst out. 'I'll do what I have to do.'

We stared at each other down the length of the couch. I was breathing hard. It was all I could hear in my head.

His head swung back and forth slowly, the curls moving with their own life. 'A lie,' he said. 'A lie. There's nothing about me you *have* or *have not* to do. It's all *your choice*.'

I didn't say anything.

'Isn't that true?' he persisted. 'No one's making me part of any *condition* at this point. It's all up to you.' He was waiting, tense, poised.

My eyes stung suddenly. 'Can't you leave me alone?' I said. 'What good is this doing? Are you trying to *argue* me into loving you again? Do you think *this* will make it all go away?'

'Tell me my choices, Anna.'

I said nothing.

'OK. *I'll* tell you my choices. I can do nothing, because I feel guilty, because I feel responsible, because I respect your grief. I can do nothing and lose you for sure. Or I can struggle, and impose on you when I have no right to, and fight with you, and maybe *not* lose you. Either way I'm in the wrong in some way, but at least this way I'm trying.'

I said nothing, didn't look at him. We sat for a long time in absolute silence. All I can remember is wanting him to go away, wanting to get busy again. Some curtain had fallen in my mind, and behind it all was all my feeling for Leo, all the power he had for me, over me.

'I wish you wouldn't,' I finally said. I could barely remember what I was referring to. My mind was working hard to stay away from all this.

'In other words, drop dead,' he said.

'*You* said that.'

'Sorry,' he said. 'Let's try this one, then. Roll over, *play* dead. Is that more like it?'

I looked at him, feeling hate.

'Well, I already did that number, Anna. I played dead for you and that asshole lawyer of yours. I agreed: *I'm* the pervert, *I'm* the criminal. I took the rap, while you sat up there and pretended I was just some . . . *accident* that had happened to you . . .'

'Do you think that made up for everything?' I asked shrilly. My hands were clenched in my lap, and the nails, untrimmed because I hadn't played in weeks, bit into my palms.

'No, I do not,' he nearly shouted. 'But I didn't *do* everything.' He looked away for a moment, lowered his voice, made it calm. 'We pretended I did, Anna, and that was fine with me. All I ever wanted was to make it right if I could. But you and I know the truth. Some little soupçon of responsibility falls on you. I'll take the fucking rap everywhere else but here, but with you. I want the truth with you.'

'You keep talking about *taking the rap*, as though what you had to do were so terrible. Doesn't it seem to you that I'm taking the rap too, on and on for the rest of my life?'

'Anna, I did everything I could to make that not happen.'

'Thank you,' I said bitterly. 'Thank you for all you did.'

He made a noise and grabbed my elbow, yanked me toward him. Pain radiated from my shoulder and I cried out. He let go and stared at me. 'Stop it,' he whispered. His eyes were wide, entirely black within, frightened. 'Please, please, stop it.'

'Get out,' I said. And then I shrieked, 'Get out! Get out of here!' and I leaned forward and swung my arm and body across the table. Distantly I heard the glasses hit somewhere, the beer splatter, but I was moving, yelling. I stood against the wall farthest from Leo, hunched against his coming near me, and yelled in a voice I didn't know I had, yelled at him to stay away from me, to get away, get away.

He was across the room and he seemed to be talking for a moment – his mouth moved, he pleaded with his hands; but my voice stayed loud and steady and didn't stop yelling, it was all I could hear, and after a few moments he was gone away.

I stood still after he'd left, tensed against the wall, listening to his footsteps going fast down the stairs, hearing the door far below shutting. Then I crossed to the hall door and closed it. I looked around the living room. Beer had splattered against the wall at knee level and left a wide, drizzling stain; and the curved fragments and bits of our glasses lay everywhere on the floor. I was crying quietly now. I squatted in the mess and began to pick up the glass, to lay the glittering curls in my hand. I moved around slowly. I had collected a handful of glass when I slipped a little in the wet spill. I put my hands out quickly to catch myself, and felt the clean pain slice across my palm and fingers. When I stood up and looked, my hand was already covered in blood. I couldn't tell where the cuts were.

The next morning I woke early. My left hand was stiff in bandages, but I packed awkwardly, favoring my right, until eight-thirty. Then I called Muth. He wasn't in yet. At nine-fifteen I called again and we talked briefly. He hadn't been able to reach Brian's lawyer the day before, knew no more than he already knew, felt nearly positive everything was in place. He'd get back to me as soon as they'd spoken. I told him I needed to do some work at the lab, he wouldn't be able to reach me, that I'd call him in the afternoon.

Then, after hesitating several times, I called Leo to say I was sorry. There was no answer. The thought of his empty studio was a quick temptation. I could leave a note, apologizing, and then I could be done with him, I could move away, I'd never have to see him again. Infected with sudden haste, imagining him returning at any moment, I found my purse and my keys in the mess of boxes, and left.

His truck was gone, nowhere on the little side street near the entrance to the stairs. I parked and went in the dark hallway, up the ochre stairway. I knocked and waited a moment, then let myself into the bright, familiar space.

I'd brought no paper, no pen with me. I fumbled around on Leo's table in a panic, seeing him mounting the stairs in my mind. There were lists, quick sketches, clippings, all heaped together, but I finally found a blank sheet and a pencil. I sat at the little kitchen table and wrote, quickly, and in a hand I could barely recognize as my own: *Leo, I'm sorry. I'm not in good control right now. Maybe in a while we'll be able to talk about all this. Anna.*

I sat for a moment looking at what I'd written. It seemed not at all what I wanted to say to him. It seemed to me that I couldn't even begin to know what I wanted to say until I'd seen Molly and understood a little bit of what our life together, apart, was going to be like. I tore the note up into smaller and smaller pieces and threw them into Leo's trash amid the coffee grounds, the orange peel, the bright red and blue milk carton. For a moment I stood above the big can, feeling an impulse to scoop my hands into the mess, to throw it, to smear myself. But Leo's phone sat on the table. I picked it up and quickly dialed Muth's number again, then hung up, realizing it had only been half an hour or so since I last spoke to him.

I dialed Brian's number. My breath lifted my chest fast; my heart shook in my throat. He would listen to me. I couldn't wait any more for Muth. Now Brian would have to listen to me. The ringing began, stopped. There was a little muffled clunking, then Molly's voice saying slowly, 'Hellooo?'

'Molly?' I whispered.

There was silence.

'Hello,' I said.

'Hello,' she said back. 'My mommy and daddy aren't home.'

'Molly, it's Mom,' I said. 'It's your Mommy. In Cambridge.'

I had to wait a long time for her to answer. 'When are you *coming* here?' she said. Her voice was pinched, shy.

'I'm coming soon, honey. I'm bringing you a big hug. I miss you so much.'

Another long wait, then a clunk. 'Molly?' I said. 'Molly?' I was crying.

An older woman's voice came on the line, not Brenda. 'Hello,' she said. She had a slight accent, British or Scotch. 'Who's there please?'

Gently I sat the phone back in its cradle. I stood struggling to get control of myself, not to give way, looking frantically around Leo's studio, as though to find in it something to hold onto, to give me strength.

And then I saw the bureau drawer, pulled open. I crossed quickly to it, reached behind the grayish worn underwear. I was holding the gun, cold and heavy.

It wasn't until I was in the car, on my way to the airport, that I really thought about what I was doing. I would not *use* the gun, I thought. I would talk to the housekeeper, or Brian, or Brenda – whoever was there – and explain that I had to see Molly. They would understand. They would let Molly come with me. It was only if they did something, if they were ugly, that I would say I had a gun, I meant it. And if Molly and I had to run, had to hide, fine. It would just be the two of us. I still had some money from my grandfather. I could get a job.

But there would be no problem. They would see that it was right, that I needed just to see her. Someone would understand.

Though I felt a kind of deadly calm, tears kept sliding down my face as I drove. I wiped them away carelessly from time to time. I felt no connection with that frightened, grieving part of myself. When I think about it now, it was as though I'd finally pushed the parts of myself into a state where they couldn't communicate with each other anymore. For days I'd kept my grief, my anger, all of my emotion,

320

deeply buried, so I could keep acting. Now the acting was governed by emotion, but not in any way I could perceive. The acting part of me felt it was as rational, as cool, as when I was wrapping glasses in newspapers and tucking them into boxes. The trip to Washington, taking Leo's gun, made exactly that kind of sense to me at the moment, in spite of the strangers in other cars staring over at my disheveled weeping face, my talking mouth. After this experience I forever understood the expression *beside yourself*.

I was driving carefully, slowly, because the rational part of me understood that I mustn't be stopped, I mustn't get caught with the gun in my purse. Courteously, while I wept and talked to myself about what a sensible thing I was doing, I yielded the right of way coming on to Route 93, I let other cars slip ahead of me as we merged from eight lanes down to two at the Callahan Tunnel. In the tunnel, I kept my distance from the car ahead of me. I emerged into the light; and it was only as I pulled into the tollbooth and had to fumble for change through my purse, hunched over it to hide the gun, that I remembered – and nearly wailed aloud at the memory – that other, smaller tunnel I'd have to pass through in the airport, the checkpoint, like the one in the courthouse, where the gun, either in my bag or in my pocket, would show up, and they'd stop me.

The car behind me honked. I stopped looking for change and pulled a bill from my wallet, held my bandaged hand out for the coins and bills due back to me. The teller stared at my tear-streaked face as he filled my hand, then looked away.

In the airport, I drove around the circuit of airlines twice, trying to think what to do. I pulled into the parking lot at Eastern and turned the engine off. I couldn't believe there wasn't some solution, some answer. The planes' roaring takeoff and descent seemed to mock my immobility. In frustration, I banged my head on the steering wheel, once, twice, as hard as I could. The second time I struck the metal inner circle with the bridge of my nose, and the horn sounded, making my heart pound uncontrollably. I started the car again, circled the airport once more, and then drove north, away from Boston.

My head ached from the blows. The next time I wiped at my face, my hand reached back for the steering wheel brilliantly streaked with blood, I looked at myself quickly in the rearview mirror. There was a cut on my nose. I'd smeared the blood across one cheek wiping my face. But somehow this sight of myself calmed me. I licked my fingers and rubbed my face over and over. On my nose I could still feel the slow steady trickle of blood.

I was driving fast, too fast. The idea of motion was the only one in my mind. The prospect of returning uselessly to my life in Cambridge seemed unbearable, though I had no alternative plans.

Then the sign for New Hampshire and Maine loomed green above the highway; and images of my grandparents' camp began to pull at me. It would be closed up, the heavy wooden shutters hung on the windows, the boat stored under the big house, the pump disconnected. But I could break in, hide out there, no one would know where I was. It seemed clear that I should do this.

At Newburyport, though, without even thinking about it, I turned off the highway. I drove slowly through the town, past the mansions perched above High Street, past the common, the cemetery. My nose had stopped bleeding now, though the cut was thick with red when I looked at myself. The bruise had begun to rise on my forehead too.

I took the turnoff to Plum Island, past the tiny airport where you walked across a scrubby field and climbed into the planes unchecked, but flew only in wide looping circles in the sky; across the bridge, past the park warden's booth. There were twenty or thirty cars in the main lot, but I drove down the rutted dusty road with the marshy stream to my right, the hillocks and dunes on my left.

Brian and I had come here often when Molly was a baby. We lugged a pack full of equipment and a red beach umbrella which we rotated like a huge flower in the sun to keep her from burning while she napped. I remembered once taking her down to the water's edge to play. While she stood with one tiny hand resting on my shoulder, I had squatted in front of her and removed her diapers. For a long time I sat beside her, the water lapping at our legs. Over and over I filled the bucket and poured it onto her distended belly. Each time she would tense in excited readiness. Each time her eyes would widen with the anticipated shock of the cold water, and each time she would laugh with relief and joy when it was done, abandon herself to a laughter that shook her whole body. She tired of the game before I did.

I parked the car in one of the tiny empty lots along the road. Through the scrubby growth, the twisted small trees and green grasses, a path led up the dunes towards the sea. I took it, my weighted purse slung on my shoulder. My shoes made walking difficult. 'Sure, there's sand in them,' I remembered Leo saying to Molly as she whined. 'What do you think they call them *sand*als for?' I stopped and took the shoes off. I put them in my purse, on top of the gun.

From the third dune I crested, I could see the bright dark blue of the morning ocean. And then I spotted a kite, orange and yellow, jerking wildly against its string. There would be people by the water, I realized, picnickers even now when it was cool, fishermen in wool shirts and waders, their long lines disappearing out over the water; lovers lying huddled together against the last wall of the dunes.

I turned and started walking to the right, parallel to the sea. I dug my heels into the steep hill as I descended. I hiked east up and down two or three wide dunes, and then came down into a sandy bowl, a crater. I sat down next to a scrubby tree. Small birds were in motion all around me, and the breeze hissed through the stiff dune grass. The sun shone down and my head, where I'd smashed it on the steering wheel, throbbed with my blood. I put my arms across my knees, and laid my head on them. I began to weep again, because I'd given up, I realized. I'd come to the end. I would go nowhere. I had nowhere to go. There was no way to retrieve my life with Molly. Whatever it was

323

we were to have, it would be utterly different from what we'd had before; and I didn't know if I had the strength to shape it. It seemed too full of what would not be: I would not be the name she called in the night or when she was hurt. I would not know the names of school friends, baby sitters. I would miss the odd, funny turns of phrase, the wonderful misunderstandings of the world, I would never have the rocklike comfort of daily life with her. I would be the one she yearned for, as I yearned for her. There was nothing I wanted less.

I wept until my swollen face ached, not caring what noise I made. Finally, exhausted, I reached into my bag, beyond the shoes, for a napkin, a Kleenex, a scarf, anything to blow my nose on. My fingers touched the cold barrel of the gun. I pulled it out and set it on the sand in front of me. I looked down at its metallic black, gleaming dully between my legs. I picked it up – it wasn't a large gun, it felt almost comfortable in my hand – and pointed its barrel down towards the center of the bowl I sat in. I pulled my finger on the trigger. There was no give. I looked and saw the safety. I slid it off, pointed again, squeezed. The noise lifted my hand and was lost in the still air, the sand jumped in a plume. My voice trailed off in my throat, and I realized I'd screamed. The bird noise had stopped. I pulled again, and this time heard my yowl with the crack that was fading even as it sounded. I pulled again, wanting really just the release of screaming, then again. But this last time there was no lifting through my arm, no noise but my own and the empty barrel making a workmanlike click. Three, four, five times more the barrel turned with the empty clicking, and then I sat, silent, in the world I'd silenced, the gun dangling uselessly off my arm.

I don't know how long I sat there. But suddenly I knew I should leave, leave quickly. Someone would have heard the noise, someone would find me. Perhaps they were looking now. I set the gun down and turned to face the hillside on my knees. I made scoops of my hands and pulled the falling sand out as fast as I could, creating a shallow, shifting hole.

I set the gun in it and pushed the cool sand back, smoothed it down. Then, running, stumbling, in my bare feet in the spiky grass, I headed back towards the path.

When I emerged into the lot, a rusty and bruised-looking Jeep was parked a few feet from my car. A man with binoculars around his neck was climbing out of it. From behind the Jeep padded a slow-moving golden retriever. He barked once at me, then shuffled forward, his tail swinging low from side to side, and pressed his nose to my crotch.

'Hi,' I said to the man.

'Stop that!' the man said to his dog. 'Sparky! Get over here.'

I was fumbling with my keys, trying to smile politely and to hide my injured, swollen face at the same time. The man grabbed the dog by the collar and shoved him in the direction of the path. 'So sorry,' he mumbled, turning away sheepishly in a posture almost identical to mine. I watched him follow the dog, up the path towards the ocean.

The car was stifling, the seats burned at my legs. I opened the windows and started driving back. The Jeep's dust thickened the air for the first half-mile, but then settled. The colors seemed oddly intense to me.

I drove back to Boston on small roads, back roads, wanting to avoid the speed of the highway and any sense of retracing my steps. By three o'clock or so, I was in the lab at BU, holding the rats, changing their water, their food. I was intensely conscious simply of *what was*: of the restless cages, the ticking lights, my hands, which seemed enormous, moving so competently in front of me. I had a sense of having returned from a great distance to myself. I tried to think of how my hand had looked, holding the gun, its spontaneous kick up with the noise, the spray of sand arcing beyond it, my scream. It seemed to me that that had been someone else's hand; or that I had been imitating someone else – some more passionate, wild person. I held one of the rats who only ten days or two weeks ago had been so terrified of me he would have killed me if he could, and let him move around in my open palm, sniffing at the Band-aids across

325

my cuts. Gently I touched the hair between his ears, stroked his back. These were my arms, my hands. I looked at them. I needed to clip my nails. I wasn't used to seeing them this long. I imagined my hands at the keyboard, and had a yearning, suddenly, to play, a yearning for the comfort that would bring – watching my own disciplined hands execute the movements, which, two steps away, made music happen. 'Why do we make music?' my childhood piano teacher had asked. She wore tiny gold-rimmed glasses, and she often reached from behind me to correct my hands, her soft bosom pressed like affection against my body.

'I don't know,' I'd said. My mother made me make music.

'We make music to bring beauty into our world, to make it bearable. When you are older, you will see.'

When I went down the hall to the bathroom, I was startled by my wounded face in the mirror, so distant did the events of the morning seem. My forehead was lumped and purplish, my nose had a raised, red, horizontal nick across the bridge. In the lab again, it seemed to me that some of the rats were ready to run, so I began to do them. I finished five before I got tired and went to check the time. It was eight o'clock. I took the data up to Dr Fisher's office. His window was black, the sycamore was only a shadow, and that startled me. It seemed only a week or two earlier that Molly had had trouble falling asleep at her usual bedtime because the light still leaked in around the edges of her shades at seven-thirty or eight.

I drove home and washed my face, dabbed my nose with an antiseptic which stung wildly and brought tears to my eyes. I went out on the back porch in the chill night air, and clipped my nails, watching the crescents drop in the light from the kitchen to the worn porch boards.

I came in and was looking through a stack of music when the doorbell rang. The buzzer system was broken, so I went down the hall and stood outside my door at the top of the stairs.

Leo looked up from the well at the first floor landing.

'*No*,' I said, and started back in.

326

He stood still. 'I've got the key anyway, Anna. But I want you to let me in. No fighting, I swear, nothing bad.'

I was silent. His face lifted up to me, white, vulnerable.

'I know you were at my place today,' he said softly. 'I know you took the gun.'

'Come up,' I said after a minute. I turned and went into the living room. I turned on a light. I sat down on the couch. He came in and shut the door behind him. He stood in the middle of the room, wearing a jeans jacket, paint-spotted Levis. His voice came rapidly. 'Anna, what are you doing? I've been trying to call all day.' Then his tone changed. 'Look, give me the gun, first.' He held his hand out, as though I must have it on my person.

'I'm OK,' I said. 'I don't have it.'

'Where is it? What did you do with it?'

'I didn't do anything. I ended up throwing it away. It's gone.'

'It's gone. You threw it away,' he said. I nodded. He sat down in the chair nearest him and put his head in his hands. 'Anna, if you knew what I've been thinking . . .' He looked up at me. 'What's the matter with your face? What did you do?' He started to get up, but I waved my hand at him, I made him sit down.

'I bumped myself, is all.'

'Jesus, you better talk to me. I pull these bits of some note in your writing out of the trash, my gun is gone and no one has seen you, no one *sees* you all day. I nearly called your ex-husband, I want you to know, I thought . . .'

'I know what you thought,' I said. 'I'm sorry.'

He stared at me, evaluating my reliability, my sanity. 'You want to talk to me?' he said.

'I almost can't,' I said after a minute. 'I'm sorry. I just had had it, I guess. I'd been very contained and doing everything all right and looking on the *up* side, as everyone kept telling me to do. And then our fight; and I *still* don't know about seeing Molly – I just went crazy. I came over to your place to leave you a note, and then I remembered the gun. But in the meantime I'd called Molly. Or I called

Brian – this was from your place – and she answered. And it was just too much, to hear her. So . . .' I lifted my shoulders, as though I'd explained everything.

'So you took the gun, to do . . . what?'

'It's hard to explain.'

'Try.'

I sat with my mouth open.

'Try harder,' he said. 'Anna,' his voice was nearly a whisper. 'I thought you were going to kill yourself.' He looked at me, asking for something. 'I thought you were going to kill me, to kill Brian. I came so close to calling him, to warn him. I called *here*, I came here two or three times. I called Fisher, Ursula, John and Charlene. I mean, I've been going crazy.'

I still couldn't answer.

'I mean, can you imagine if I'd done that?' he asked. 'Called Brian?'

I couldn't think of what to say. It was like some wild disjuncture between us. I felt as though I'd waked from a long complicated dream, one it seemed as though he was still in. *Oh, yes*, I wanted to say. I remembered those things, but they weren't what counted now, they weren't real.

Where had I put the gun, he wanted to know.

'I buried it at Plum Island.'

'Of course,' he said. 'What else would you do with it?' Then: 'Why?'

'I thought I ought to get rid of it. I thought having it could get me in trouble.'

He stared at me. 'OK, let me get this straight. You came to my apartment, you wrote a note, you tore it up. Then took the gun.'

'In between I called and talked to Molly. That's why I took the gun.'

He just looked at me.

'Her voice was so dear. I was going to get her. I can't explain it. It was irrational. But I was going to fly down and the gun was . . . a backup, sort of.'

'And then you drove to Plum Island instead?'

328

'Yes. I'd started for the airport, but then I realized I couldn't get the gun onto a plane, and I just drove north. Going to Plum Island was a whim.'

'As distinct from everything else you did.'

I laughed, and Leo looked startled. Then he smiled back at me.

'Anna, I was so fucking worried,' he said.

'I know. I'm sorry.'

We sat across the living room from each other, silent.

'So tell me how you banged up your face,' he said. 'You look like you've gone fifteen with Marvin Hagler.'

'That part's silly,' I said. 'I don't want to talk about it. I just got frustrated and hit myself.'

'Self-inflicted wounds,' he said.

'Yes.'

'They'll be even prettier tomorrow, I suspect.'

'I know,' I said.

'Can I stay tonight and watch them changing colors?' he asked.

'Yes,' I said.

I put a nightgown on before I came to bed, and when I slid under the covers next to him, he looked at it, but didn't say anything. We talked for a while, about when I might move, about what kind of job I wanted to get in Washington. Then he began caressing me, stroking my body gently through the gown. He lifted it, he pushed it up over my breasts and touched them, making slow circles. He kissed my mouth, my shoulders. I turned to him and held him. His hips were thrust forwards against me, and I could feel the gentle pouch of his genitals against my leg. But he didn't get hard, and after a while we fell asleep, holding each other for comfort like two worn-out children.

FOURTEEN

Ursula helped me move to Washington. It took us two long days to make the drive because we were afraid of straining the Valiant. There was a large-sized U-Haul trailer hooked on behind us, and it swung and bucked at every bump in the road. It was November, and it wasn't so much raining, as that the air was made of a cold dampness that penetrated everything. The Valiant's heater roared inaudibly as we drove slowly along, parching our nasal passages. But as soon as we stopped the car, the cold and the moisture seemed to rise again from somewhere nearly within us.

On the first day Ursula drove. We hardly talked at all, and I slept most of the way. I'd been up until late the night before packing what I had thought would be just a few last small things. I was grateful to Ursula for her energy, but even more for her silence, her discretion. It was hard for her, I knew. She had slipped once after I'd found out I'd lost custody, exploded with anger about Muth, Brian; told me she thought I'd mismanaged things. 'You were just so passive, Anna. You never fought back or *anything*. You should have told them all off from the start.' She'd come over to help me pack, and was wearing an unusually conservative outfit for her: jeans, a gray sweatshirt.

'I thought I could get Molly this way.'

'Yeah, but you didn't, did you? It didn't help. You played along with everyone and it didn't help.'

'What was I supposed to do, Ursula?' I was folding clothes, all the dresses I never wore.

'Tell them off. Get witnesses. Me. *I* would have testified for you. I'm a psychologist. In some cultures, kids watch their parents screw all the time. Even in *our* culture, artists, creative people, have always been deviant. Those fucking rules they were talking about apply to a tiny percentage of the world's population. They were dealing with an incredibly narrow definition of right and wrong.'

'But I knew that. I knew those were the terms.' I tried not to think of Ursula on the stand on my behalf.

'Yeah, but why should they have been? Why shouldn't you have insisted on *other* terms?'

'Because the judge wouldn't have listened to a discussion on other terms.'

'But you never even *tried*, Anna.' And then she heard herself. Her mouth made a little O of remorse. She came across the room, grabbed my hand, and said she was sorry. 'Oh, God. Some friend. Here I am blaming you, and *you're* the one who's hurting.'

Now, in the motel, she chattered about everything else. About other long drives she'd taken across the country – as far north as the roads went into Canada, through all the pueblo villages in New Mexico. She told me about a fight she'd had with a lover on that trip, a fight about how to set their tent up. They were camping next to a stream, and it started to rain. They got out of their sleeping bags naked, and began to argue about where the tent poles should go. She said she got so angry at him that she punched him as hard as she could, right in the face. He hit her back reflexively, and they both started to swing wildly, ineffectually, at each other. 'There we were,' she said. 'It was pitch dark, we couldn't see a fucking thing, and we were soaked, we had nothing on, and we were both crying, and just hitting each other and hitting each other. I don't think either of us ever understood it. When we stopped, we just put our clothes on, got back into the car and he drove me to the bus station in Santa Fe. It was the middle of the fucking night. I never saw him again.'

The motel was a Howard Johnson's, in northern New Jersey. Ursula had bought some wine before we checked in, and she was drinking it and polishing her toenails. She had on a T-shirt that said I GOT SCHROD AT LEGAL SEAFOOD LAST NIGHT, and under it, flashing brightly every now and then, pink underpants. Her long, heartbreaking legs were expressive as hands as she sat on her bed and talked to me. She had inserted little cotton balls between her toes. She was working on her left foot.

As I watched her from my large bed, I suddenly realized who Ursula reminded me of: Babe. That same vibrant energy dissipating itself over the smallest things, energy I'd always wanted for myself. She made me feel – as I had with Babe as a child – parsimonious, careful. It was people like Ursula, like Babe, like Leo I admired.

'Oh, God,' she said, looking up over her knee at the television. I looked too. Leslie Howard had appeared on the screen. 'Oh, what a lovely man he was. God, he's so impeccable. Why doesn't God make men like that now? I mean who are we kidding with fucking Burt Reynolds?' She reached to the nightstand for another shot of wine.

I told her I didn't know, and slid a little further under the covers.

'You gonna try to sleep?' she asked. I looked at her. Her moon face rested on her knee. Washed clean of makeup, she looked like a little boy.

'I'm awfully tired,' I said. 'I don't know how you're still doing it.'

She waved her miniature brush. ''Cause I'm dumb,' she said cheerfully. 'I'll hate myself in the morning.' She sprang up, limped to the TV, holding her left toes off the ground. 'I'll turn down the volume anyway.'

But she was awake in the morning before I was, and drove more than her share even the second day. She said it made her feel macho.

The apartment I'd rented was in Georgetown, the third floor of a townhouse. The couple who owned it lived below, and had just bought it. They'd renovated the attic hastily, cheaply, so they could rent it and pay their mortgage. The windows were tiny casements; the only stairway up wound in a lazy, narrow spiral off the kitchen. There was no way to get the piano in; I'd left it with the women in Cambridge indefinitely.

Molly was to have the bedroom. I would sleep in the living room on a foldout couch. The kitchen was a little prefab unit in a corner of the living room; the bathroom had been installed in a deep closet. There was no tub, just a shower stall. Even so, I was paying more for it than I'd paid in Cambridge. But it was near Molly's neighborhood. I could get her to and from her nursery school, her friends' houses, her life, easily. I thought I was lucky to have found it.

Ursula was noisy in her enthusiasm. On every trip up with a box or a piece of furniture, she found something else to admire: the way the windows swung out, the hand-held nozzle in the shower. 'Can you imagine the sexual pleasure possible?' she called out.

She helped me assemble Molly's bed, and then we drove off with the empty trailer bouncing behind us, to pick up the convertible couch I'd bought the same weekend I'd found the apartment. Everett, the young husband from downstairs, had to help us get it in, finally. It was nearly too big. We lifted it slowly, from stair to stair, perched as vertically as it would go. Ursula was in good form, talking to the couch, encouraging it upwards by calling it *a mother-fucker, a cheap cocksucker, a ripoff piece of dogshit*; and Everett didn't stay for the glass of wine I offered him when we finally got it safely in.

I drove her to the airport the next day, a Sunday. I'd bought her ticket back, over her protests, and insisted on giving her money for drinks. She pressed most of it back into my hands – 'One is all there's time for on this flight, Anna,' she said woefully. I stood watching her plane until it disappeared into the cloud cover. When I came back and let myself into the tiny apartment, still crammed everywhere with boxes of books, piles of clothing, I felt a sense of loneliness so overwhelming that without bothering to move the boxes that would have made it possible for me to open out the bed in the living room, I went in and lay on Molly's bed, where Ursula had slept the night before. Through the walls of the old house, I could hear Everett's and Renata's voices as a dim alternating vibration. The attic light was gray, leaden and heavy, the air smelled of heat from the new electric units. Slowly, hugging myself, I fell asleep. When I awoke, it was black, quiet. I got up, had some yogurt and leftover Chinese food from my tiny refrigerator, and started unpacking. By the time of Molly's first official visit with me the following Tuesday, the apartment looked settled, cheerful.

'Watch her,' Muth had said to me about Molly in our last discussion before I moved to Washington. 'You notice signs of real change, real upset with this situation, we can take another shot at it, if you want. As long as we got grounds.' Grounds, he told me, would be radically altered behavior. If she lost her toilet training, for instance. If she suddenly became aggressive at school, or withdrawn. If she became excessively fearful, had extreme sleep disturbances. And a few times I did think momentarily of what was happening to Molly as *grounds*. Because she was distressed.

I tried to fit myself smoothly into the life Brian and Brenda had structured for Molly. I'd talked to Dr Payne once after the decision had been reached, and he'd told me that the more our life together seemed an extension of Brian and Brenda's the easier it would be for her. But even though I made all kinds of small shifts towards their orderliness, even though everything in my life centered around hers, she still showed the signs that Muth had talked about. More than once I had to carry her, sobbing, limp, or else kicking in rage, into school on Monday because she wouldn't get out of the car, refused to walk. Sullen, furious, she hunched in the front seat. I would squat in the open door on her side, trying to persuade her to get out, to leave me. Around us, other mothers greeted each other, the children shouted and ran around and walked in on their own. Sometimes one of them would stop to try to talk to Molly, or to watch us. A mother would descend, whisk the child away: 'This isn't a good time for Molly to talk'; 'Silly, Molly's *mommy*'s trying to talk to her now.'

And I was. But to everything I'd say, Molly would say, 'No'; or worse, say nothing.

'Molly, it's time now,' I'd say. 'All the other kids are going in. Please, honey, you're going to have fun.'

'No.'

'I've got to go to work now, Moll. And I'll see you in two days' (or five days, or three days).

'No.'

'I want you to be thinking hard of two good things that we can do together on Saturday.

'Molly, I'm going to wait for one minute, so you can get ready to say good-bye to me, and then we're going to walk in together. I'm going to start to count now, so you get ready.'

'No.'

The teachers got used to her desperation on those mornings. When I'd push open the door, the head teacher, Mrs Malone, would cross to me, her arms open, and take flailing Molly from me; and I'd leave, hearing her wails, her shrieks, as I walked back out to the car, hearing them over the next interval apart from her as I went through the motions of my days.

Sometimes she talked openly about it. She'd try to negotiate the terms of her life. Why *couldn't* she live with me, she'd ask.

I told her I wished she could but that a judge had helped us all decide together that it was best if she lived with her father.

'Why?' she'd ask. Her hair was in thin braids, but wisps pulled out, and now, by the end of the day, she looked as frazzled as she had when it was first growing in.

'Because he can take care of you better. He has Brenda to help, and Mrs Reinhardt.'

Molly was sitting up in bed. She folded her arms across her tummy. 'Brenda is a dummy and Mrs Reinhardt is a dummy.'

335

'I don't think you really think that, Molly. Sometimes you love them.' She wouldn't look at me, but she said, 'I can't love them when I miss you.'

'But Molly,' I said softly, 'I have to go to work every day.'

'I can come with you,' she said. She turned to me.

'Honey. That would be silly. There's nothing for you to do there. It's boring. You'd get tired of it in about one second.'

'I wouldn't, Mom. I'd be good.' She was eager now. She had genuine hope. She imagined a toehold here. 'I can be so quiet. I can just draw, or bring my dolls.'

'Molly,' I pleaded. 'We already *decided*, honey. This is the best way.'

'It's *not*, it's not the best. It's not the best for me.'

Sometimes she'd cry. Sometimes she wrecked her room, clearing the shelves of all the toys I'd carefully set across them. I'd sit in the living room, listening to the destruction and steeling myself for the further tantrum that would result when I went in to stop her. Sometimes she hit me. Often she wet her bed, woke screaming in the night, needed help going into a friend's house to play. When I tried to talk about it to Brian and Brenda, they'd say no, it never happened at home. She was easy there, sunny, a good little girl. She loved school, loved visiting friends. And so occasionally I thought of Muth, thought of calling him, thought of starting up all the questions, the pretending again.

But slowly Molly began to seem better, more used to the different rhythm of what we could have together. Though she was never at ease when we parted and still occasionally had nightmares, the extreme behavior diminished; and I was glad I hadn't done anything about it. Because what I had wanted most during those months of her misery, I realized, was not to make some use of it, but to banish it.

And I also realized that what my experience, our experience, with the lawyers, the social workers, the psychiatrist, had left me with more than anything else was the desire never to have to turn my life out to anyone again. Now, as

Molly began to seem more and more *all right*, it sometimes seemed to me that the most terrible part of the experience we'd been through had been that forced intimacy – oh, legal, I knew! legal – with Muth, with Payne, with Fine, with Judge Sullivan, even with the guards who had wandered in and out of the room carrying papers and coffee and watching us all impassively. By summer Molly was, with me too, usually a good little girl, and I was glad to have to take no action.

But sometimes it filled me with shame and a kind of grief that we had asked from her, and she had achieved, at her age, such mastery over her sorrow. Once, early in the summer, we were in a drugstore together and we saw a display of pacifiers, ranging from tiny stubby ones for a baby's mouth to the elongated nipples Molly had used before she finally gave them up. The plastic discs connected to them were bright, cheerful colors: pink, blue, yellow. Molly stopped in front of them.

'Pacifiers, Mom,' she said.

'Yes,' I answered. I was buying toothpaste and aspirin. 'Funny, aren't they?'

'Can I get one?' she asked, after a moment.

I went to her. She looked up at me. 'You want a pacifier, Molly?' I asked softly.

She nodded.

'Why?'

'It would just help me, Mom.' She frowned, making a little line in her forehead. She jiggled her hands vaguely in front of her, as though trying to get at something unnameable. 'It makes me not so *nervous*.'

I looked at her, then squatted in front of her. 'If you're nervous, maybe it would be better to talk about it.'

She looked down, away from me. 'I can't *talk* about it, Mom. I just want to suck on a pacifier.'

'I don't think so, honey. I don't think that's a good idea for someone as big as you. They're really for much littler kids.'

She turned away from me and walked into another aisle

337

of the store. In her posture – the weighted shoulders, the lowered head – was a tired acceptance that made her look, momentarily, nearly middle-aged, that made me ache for all she couldn't say.

The job I had gotten was full-time at Georgetown University, but I could do a little of the work at home, and I played around with that to take off early to be with Molly on Tuesday and Thursday afternoons. I worked in the special scholarship office. There were hundreds of these scholarships, endowed by cultural organizations, churches, individuals. They were in honor of musicians, sanitation engineers, beloved dead sons who had played the trumpet, wives who had kept beautiful gardens, who had always wanted to write poetry. They were established to promote Polish identity, Jewish solidarity, interracial understanding, the study of reproduction in certain one-celled animals, clog dancing, macramé. Some of them were for amounts as low as five hundred dollars a year, some as high as full tuition plus room and board. My job was to investigate people applying to be sure they were, indeed, qualified; to do publicity for those awards no one ever applied for; to rank applicants; and to write letters to the endowers and donors explaining to them who the students were who'd won, and why they were so particularly well-suited to have gotten the awards, how their lives were going to be changed because of them. I had to do this without ever meeting the students, just by looking at their folders. This had been, in fact, the test for the job. It was my skill at doing this, at inventing lives to write about on the basis of some statistics and the student's application, that got me the job.

My supervisor was a massive black woman named Mrs Dellabovey, whose lips were as curved and full, and painted as pink, as the sugared roses on a wedding cake. She called me darling at the first interview, and she loved my letters. She always read them, even though she didn't have to. 'You wouldn't know it was the same boy,' she'd say wonderingly, leaning over my desk. Or: 'Lord, I wish I could send this to her mama. Give her something to be proud of at long last.'

After I'd been on the job for a few months, Mrs Dellabovey suggested I'd advance myself faster if I could type better. And I wanted to advance myself, I discovered. I wanted more money. My life was different now, with Molly, and I wanted to be able to do things with her, take her on outings, buy her things, that I'd never been interested in before. And my expenses in Washington were high. I'd had to buy new clothes to work in, the rent was nearly twice what I'd paid in Cambridge, I ate out more, went out more, because I didn't like being at home alone. I enrolled in night typing classes at an adult education center.

I was a quick learner. It seemed a bit like playing the piano in some ways. In fact, during this period and occasionally afterwards, when I didn't have my piano with me, and I was doing more and more typing at work, I often had dreams which confused the two. So that in my dreams I'd be tapping the typewriter, thinking of words, and music would come out. Or I'd be playing the piano, but the keys would be slightly indented, there'd be a letter printed on each one.

I dated occasionally: a sixtyish retired businessman from my typing class; a graduate student who'd won the Emily Brattsdorf scholarship for the study of early instruments. But I didn't want to get involved, didn't want to have sex, so after a while they didn't call anymore.

Every now and then Leo telephoned, or I telephoned him. Sometimes it was late at night and one or the other of us had had too much to drink; but it was just as likely to be a crisp wintry Saturday morning, with only coffee firing the impulse and the air outside my windows clear and white. His voice always lifted my heart, and for the first few minutes of each call we talked eagerly: what was happening? how was work? Molly? teaching? news of fellowships? grants? Ursula?

But then we'd bump up against the yearning, the impossibility. 'I miss you,' one of us would say.

'I miss you too.'

339

And then there'd be a long silence. Sometimes one of us would ask, 'Are you seeing anyone?' One would ask, 'Are you sleeping with anyone?'

Leo occasionally wondered if I'd come up for a weekend, a couple of days. I told him no every time. Then slowly, politely, we'd extract ourselves from the conversation.

After he moved to New York, in the summer, I agreed to go up there, to 'do the town,' he said. 'It'll be different not to be ghostridden,' he told me. 'I miss you.'

And I thought it might work. But then, lying in bed the night before, I imagined how it would be to touch him, to make love. I knew I wouldn't be able to, and that in spite of everything he said, that was what he really wanted. The morning I was to have flown up, I called and told him I couldn't.

'I don't suppose you can tell me why.'

'I just can't make it work between us.'

'You know that without trying.'

'Yes.'

'Tell me how you know that, Anna.'

I tried to compose my answer. He waited. Somewhere, on some distant other line, I could hear a faint conversation between two women. 'Because when I think of you, I think . . . my thoughts are full of, all the old feelings. But then when I imagine, touching you, lying in bed . . . I can't.'

'I see,' he said.

'Are you seeing someone else?' he asked, after a minute.

'That's not it,' I said.

'But are you?'

'Aren't you?' I asked.

Silence. Then, 'Sure.'

'And does that make a difference to you?' I asked. 'Didn't you still want to see me?'

'I can see that eventually it *might* make a difference. Couldn't it for you?'

'Not anyone I'm seeing now,' I said. 'And I can't imagine it really. But it's possible, I suppose. But that's not *it*, for me.'

'Look, Anna,' he said after a minute. 'Why don't we just do each other a favor? Why don't we not talk anymore, not call. This is just . . . This is really messing me up. I can't be your friend on the phone.'

'I'm sorry,' I said.

'Me too,' he said, and hung up.

After that, I only called him once more, drunk, after the first time I'd slept with someone else. It was a friend of Everett and Renata's. They had invited me down to dinner to meet him, and when the meal and the evening were over, he wound his way up the twisting back staircase with me. I was above him on the stairs, and his hands cupped my buttocks from underneath as we went up. We were too drunk and in too much of a hurry even to pull out the couch. When I woke at three, he was gone. What I remembered about it was crying, and how much I'd wanted it before then. I had seen him only as a shape moving over me in the light from the hall. Now the door still stood open, the yellow light fell on me alone. I got up, wrapping the afghan from the couch around me, went to the phone and dialed Leo's number, then shut the door. I was still sticky and wet between my legs. I smelled the soapy odor of sperm as I slid to the floor, my back against the wall, my bare legs sticking out in front of me. In the dark in my apartment, Leo answered. When I heard his voice, I began to cry again. Afterwards I couldn't remember what he had said, but his voice was gentle and he stayed on the telephone with me until I'd stopped, until I told him I could sleep now.

About four days later, I got a short letter from him, asking me to try not to do that again; telling me that he needed to hold onto his ultimatum – either it was possible for us to see each other again, or he didn't want to be in touch at all; though of course he wished for me 'everything good, everything you want to have.'

Now I read about him sometimes, in little articles in New York papers, or in art magazines. Or Ursula, who stays in touch with him, will tell me some bit of news: he's had a new show, he's gone to Europe for six months, he's bought a loft. These are always offered in an offhand way, usually while she's cooking, or doing some chore which keeps her back turned to me. I comment politely, I am happy for him, as though he were some distant relative, one of my accomplished cousins.

After I'd lived in Washington for about a year and a half, Brian called me one night to say that he and Brenda were moving back to Boston. Brenda was pregnant, he said, four months pregnant; and she wanted to work part-time after the baby was born. The Boston office would be willing to make that possible. The Washington office could not.

How soon were they moving? I asked him.

They were looking for a house now, he said, and would probably move up within three or four months.

I thanked him for giving me notice, hung up, and called Ursula. I couldn't reach her for several days. When I finally did, she told me she'd been at a feminist conference presenting her work. She'd been jeered off the platform, she said, as a male-identified woman; but this had resulted in enormous press attention – she'd appeared on two talk shows – and lots of publicity both for her and her book on female infanticide, due out in a few months. I didn't ask what she'd been wearing when the feminists threw her out.

She was excited that I was moving back, and within a few weeks, she'd found me an apartment near hers which would be available in June. It was the first floor of an old Victorian house, and though the two bedrooms were jerry-rigged out of a little study and a glassed-in sunporch, there was ample space in the large living room and dining room for the piano.

'That's your priority, not mine,' I said.

'It ought to be yours. Ever since you stopped playing, you've been depressed.'

I was about to point out that I'd stopped playing when I'd lost Molly and Leo, but then it occurred to me that there might be other, more complicated connections between those events that Ursula would point out to me that I didn't want to hear.

And so I moved up to Cambridge again in June and music came back into my life. The piano had been treated with a certain lack of reverence by the little boys; the tuner found a Steiff mouse under the wires, and pennies and gum wedged between the keys. But I did find it a comfort to be able to play again. In the fall, I called one of the amateur groups I'd made music with before Molly was born, and time and sitters became a problem, and now I meet with them several times a month. I don't give lessons anymore – I have a full-time job in the admissions office at Wellesley – but I love the shared pleasure of making music.

And, as my Grandmother Gray promised me, it's a gift to my child. When Molly walked into the Cambridge apartment for the first time, she looked around and said, '*Here's* that old piano!' as though she'd been missing something the whole time about me, about our life together, something she hadn't been able, until this moment, to identify. When I played for her that evening, she got out all her 'costumes' – old clothes of mine – and danced and twirled until long past her bedtime, insisting, each time I stopped, on just one more.

The long absence of music from my life, and my pleasure in its return, have made me think a good deal about what it's meant to me, how it's shaped me to play as I do: adequately, but not really well.

When I was young and went to the music camp, I remember envying the other musicians their passionate connection to their instruments, instruments that seemed part of their bodies, that responded to their breath, their weight. I hated my note-by-note connection with the massive machinery of the piano, and knew, even as I touched the keys, that I was failing, that this new, harder teacher was finding my playing empty, mechanical.

'How do you hear this phrase, Anna? In your head, I mean. Sing it to me,' she would say. Beyond her, among the dark trees out the window, the other young musicians walked, carrying their instruments with them.

'I don't hear it till I play it,' I answered.

'Wrong, wrong!' she declared passionately. 'You *must* hear it. *First* there is the music, *then* the playing.' She had a thick Eastern European accent. She seemed to come from a life, a way of feeling, utterly foreign to me.

'I can't,' I would say, as I said over and over that summer. 'I can't.'

But, I would think, *if only* I played a different instrument, maybe I *could* hear it in my head first.

When it was decided that I needn't push myself anymore, that I could get on with growing up to be normal – a wife, a mother, an unaccomplished person – I sometimes blamed my mother for picking the wrong instrument for me, an instrument which was like an obstacle between me and the music. I remembered struggling and struggling that summer for a true legato. 'Think of the violin,' my teacher would say. And I thought of the violin, and hated her, hated myself, hated my music, hated my mother.

It was only later that I understood that no instrument could have made me able to be what I couldn't be, could have transformed me into a truly musical person. And now it seems to me that I am suited to the disciplined distance of the piano as I would have been to no other instrument. That other instruments require a kind of connection and exposure I'm incapable of.

Do these things have meaning in what's become of my life?

I don't know. Molly is seven now, a different child from who she might have been if she'd stayed with me. Muth, my old lawyer, has told me that when she reaches adolescence, she can choose for herself where she wants to go, that she could come to me then if she wanted. But I try not to think about that. Brenda is pregnant again, and Molly is part of a family there. She loves being a big sister, she loves them – Brian and Brenda and Elizabeth, the baby. And sometimes when I imagine how it must be – the order, the deep pleasure in what happens predictably, each day, the healing beauty of everything that is commonplace – I yearn again myself to be in a family.

For a while in the confusion of the move back to Cambridge, I had out an old photograph album from my childhood. Most of the pictures were of the summers in Maine. Molly wanted to look at it with me one night, and so we sat on the couch together and I pointed out my cousins and aunts and me as a little girl over and over. The uncles, whom I could remember standing always in a clustered group taking these pictures, were rarely themselves captured on film. Instead the aunts and cousins squatted, picking blueberries. The cousins stood, skinny and ungainly in their dripping bathing suits on one of the flat rocks that studded our inlet. We bent together holding brushes and cans, painting the bottom of an overturned boat. We paraded across the clearing in the middle of the cabins, performing a play written by one of us, practiced behind the canvas curtains at one end of the porch on rainy days.

'Why don't you ever take me to this place?' Molly asked. 'I like this.'

'It's not there anymore,' I told her.

And though for me this had been the case for a long time, now it was also true for the rest of the family. My grandfather had died the winter before, my second winter in Washington; and the sisters had decided that my grandmother, lost in grief and old age, didn't need to make the long trip up to camp anymore. Orrie had sold the place, and they were using the money to pay for nursing care in the Connecticut house.

I had seen my grandmother only twice since that day in Maine when she made my grandfather give me the money, once at his funeral, and once when my mother came east to take charge of what remained of her life. I drove to Connecticut then, and spent a week helping to rearrange the house so Gram could get around more easily. My relations with my mother were strained – it was clear that she blamed me for having lost custody of Molly. My grandmother recognized Mother only occasionally, and mistook me for Babe or one of my cousins most of the time. It seemed astonishing and sad to me that all the affectionate and

345

difficult hierarchy, the complexity of my mother's family, should have been reduced, finally, to these diminished and fragile connections. Except, of course, for the claim of personality it would exert in different ways on each of us forever.

Now I often think of those long summers in Maine, the safe circle of family that closed the world out, just as surely as the lake kept strangers away. No matter what the price, I think there was value in all that.

But that isn't what I have, nor what I can offer Molly. I've made do with a different set of circumstances – with our distance, our brief times together, with all that's truncated, too little, too small in what we have. And I take a certain pride in how well I've done this, in thinking that perhaps I'm suited to it in some way, as other, more passionate people might not be.

I think often of the first time I saw Molly after the court decision. I was in Washington and I'd just found the apartment in Everett and Renata's house. After I'd paid the deposit and they'd given me the key, I went to a poster shop and bought three prints for Molly's room. One of them was the Degas dancer that I'd had in my room in Schenectady as a young girl. I carefully hung them, pressing the thumbtacks into the outermost edge of each poster. I planned to bring her here, to show her where we'd be together. I tried not to think of how empty it all looked as I shut the door and headed to Brian and Brenda's.

I had instructions to their apartment house, mailed to me by Brenda. Even so I got lost several times. By the time I parked in the lot reserved for visitors, I was twenty minutes late. I rang their buzzer and the British voice I'd heard once before asked who was there.

'Anna Dunlap,' I said. After several seconds the inner door buzzed loudly. I went in, crossed the lobby. There were four or five children playing in it – otherwise it was deserted. They were welldressed boys, perhaps nine or ten years old. They stood behind the square pillars and shot each other with silver pistols, black plastic machine guns. Their voices made the right noises: '*Ack-ack-ack-ack-ack-ack,*' or '*Pkiu! pkiu!*' and the glamorous marble lobby echoed them in what I imagined must be a gratifying way. As I pushed the elevator button, I heard one boy call out angrily, 'You're *dead*, Joshua! You're dead!' A quieter voice answered, 'No, I'm not. I'm not even *in* this game.'

There were four wings, with arrows pointing to them, as I got off the elevator. I turned right, towards wing C, and began walking, nearly running really. The halls were long and dark. There was dull red carpeting on the floor, and beige wallpaper. Every six feet or so, I passed under the burning glare of a recessed spotlight in the ceiling. At the end of the hall there was a T-intersection, another little sign. I turned left as my instructions from Brenda told me to do. Behind every fourth or fifth door I could hear music or a muffled voice, but mostly there was just the rustle of my clothing as I moved, my own breathing in my ears. At the next T, I turned right. The numbers were closer. Suddenly, down near the end of the corridor, the wall opened, light fell in onto the carpet.

A small figure stepped into the hall. Her hand reached behind her, still holding the doorframe. She watched me cautiously until I'd passed under several of the lights. Then, the noise of her footsteps muted in the padded corridor, she ran to me. I kneeled, braced myself for her. She ran into my embrace as she had those weeks ago in Cambridge, and I picked her up, held her tight. Her hands rose to my face, stroked it, patted it, as though this were part of her way of seeing me, as though she were blind. I swallowed hard not to cry, and said her name over and over. Then her hands, smelling of sweat, of soap, covered my eyes. 'Hey, I can't see you. Let me out!' I said. 'Let me out, let me out, let me out.' She laughed and brought her face up to mine. In the secret dark circle of her hands, her breath was warm and sweet on me. She kissed me, carefully, daintily, lips pursed – four, five, six times – exactly on my mouth.

I held her tight for a long moment in our unseeing embrace. It seemed the same, her smell, her touch, the wiry density of her limbs. Then I set her down, let her go. And she turned away ahead of me to lead me to her new life, to show me everything. Her dress was rucked up in back, her hair wispy and wild from our embrace. Everything was familiar, and also unknown.

'*Ah yes*,' I remember thinking, as though hearing a kind of music in my head. '*This is how it begins.*'

Gail Godwin
The Finishing School £2.95

'It is at once her most artful and accomplished novel and an old-fashioned, irresistible page turner. The plot, like that of *A Mother and Two Daughters*, is set in motion by the death of a father and the adjustments demanded of the women he protected. But this time Godwin has made it harder on the survivors, particularly the young daughter who must endure a brief but harrowing rite of passage toward maturity' TIME

'A finely nuanced, compassionate psychological novel'
THE NEW YORK TIMES BOOK REVIEW

A Mother and Two Daughters £2.95

'A novel about the richest of all subjects, families . . . funny, sad, provocative, ironic, compassionate, knowing, *true* . . . everything that a novel should be' WASHINGTON POST

'A major novel from a talented writer really hitting her stride'
KIRKUS REVIEWS

'A novel to live with and live in' NEWSDAY

Daphne du Maurier
The Scapegoat £2.95

Two men stared into the mirror of the station buffet at Le Mans. It was as though one man looked back. The chance meeting gave Jean the opportunity to escape from a way of life he was daily finding more intolerable. It involved John with a mysterious chateau and three beautiful women – Jean's wife, mistress and sister-in-law. For the former professor of history was now the selfish and arrogant Comte de Gué!

I'll Never Be Young Again £2.50

Hesta was so much in Richard's blood that he lost all liberty of thought and action. His former life faded into insignificance as he found happiness in Montparnasse, shedding his youthful illusions in an obsessive love. But could Hesta replace Richard's need to write, or his ambition to reach out from under the shadow of a famous father and find his own success . . .?

'Daphne du Maurier's descriptions of riding in Norwegian mountains, of life before the mast and in foreign capitals ring as true as her transcription of a young man's thoughts and talk' PUNCH

Fiction

☐	**The Chains of Fate**	Pamela Belle	£2.95p
☐	**Options**	Freda Bright	£1.50p
☐	**The Thirty-nine Steps**	John Buchan	£1.50p
☐	**Secret of Blackoaks**	Ashley Carter	£1.50p
☐	**Lovers and Gamblers**	Jackie Collins	£2.50p
☐	**My Cousin Rachel**	Daphne du Maurier	£2.50p
☐	**Flashman and the Redskins**	George Macdonald Fraser	£1.95p
☐	**The Moneychangers**	Arthur Hailey	£2.95p
☐	**Secrets**	Unity Hall	£2.50p
☐	**The Eagle Has Landed**	Jack Higgins	£1.95p
☐	**Sins of the Fathers**	Susan Howatch	£3.50p
☐	**Smiley's People**	John le Carré	£2.50p
☐	**To Kill a Mockingbird**	Harper Lee	£1.95p
☐	**Ghosts**	Ed McBain	£1.75p
☐	**The Silent People**	Walter Macken	£2.50p
☐	**Gone with the Wind**	Margaret Mitchell	£3.95p
☐	**Wilt**	Tom Sharpe	£1.95p
☐	**Rage of Angels**	Sidney Sheldon	£2.50p
☐	**The Unborn**	David Shobin	£1.50p
☐	**A Town Like Alice**	Nevile Shute	£2.50p
☐	**Gorky Park**	Martin Cruz Smith	£2.50p
☐	**A Falcon Flies**	Wilbur Smith	£2.50p
☐	**The Grapes of Wrath**	John Steinbeck	£2.50p
☐	**The Deep Well at Noon**	Jessica Stirling	£2.95p
☐	**The Ironmaster**	Jean Stubbs	£1.75p
☐	**The Music Makers**	E. V. Thompson	£2.50p

Non-fiction

☐	**The First Christian**	Karen Armstrong	£2.50p
☐	**Pregnancy**	Gordon Bourne	£3.95p
☐	**The Law is an Ass**	Gyles Brandreth	£1.75p
☐	**The 35mm Photographer's Handbook**	Julian Calder and John Garrett	£6.50p
☐	**London at its Best**	Hunter Davies	£2.90p
☐	**Back from the Brink**	Michael Edwardes	£2.95p

☐	**Travellers' Britain**	} Arthur Eperon	£2.95p
☐	**Travellers' Italy**		£2.95p
☐	**The Complete Calorie Counter**	Eileen Fowler	90p
☐	**The Diary of Anne Frank**	Anne Frank	£1.75p
☐	**And the Walls Came Tumbling Down**	Jack Fishman	£1.95p
☐	**Linda Goodman's Sun Signs**	Linda Goodman	£2.95p
☐	**The Last Place on Earth**	Roland Huntford	£3.95p
☐	**Victoria RI**	Elizabeth Longford	£4.95p
☐	**Book of Worries**	Robert Morley	£1.50p
☐	**Airport International**	Brian Moynahan	£1.95p
☐	**Pan Book of Card Games**	Hubert Phillips	£1.95p
☐	**Keep Taking the Tabloids**	Fritz Spiegl	£1.75p
☐	**An Unfinished History of the World**	Hugh Thomas	£3.95p
☐	**The Baby and Child Book**	Penny and Andrew Stanway	£4.95p
☐	**The Third Wave**	Alvin Toffler	£2.95p
☐	**Pauper's Paris**	Miles Turner	£2.50p
☐	**The Psychic Detectives**	Colin Wilson	£2.50p

All these books are available at your local bookshop or newsagent, or can be ordered direct from the publisher. Indicate the number of copies required and fill in the form below

12

....

Name_____
(Block letters please)

Address_____

_____

Send to CS Department, Pan Books Ltd, PO Box 40, Basingstoke, Hants
Please enclose remittance to the value of the cover price plus:
35p for the first book plus 15p per copy for each additional book ordered
to a maximum charge of £1.25 to cover postage and packing
Applicable only in the UK

While every effort is made to keep prices low, it is sometimes
necessary to increase prices at short notice. Pan Books reserve
the right to show on covers and charge new retail prices which
may differ from those advertised in the text or elsewhere